ARKLIGHT
REVELATIONS

ARKLIGHT

REVELATIONS

An Ancient Alien Adventure

G. B. HOLLEY

Arklight Revelations
An Ancient Alien Adventure

Spirit Owl Books, LLC
P.O. Box 3547
Seminole, Fl 33772

First Edition: April 2018
Library of Congress Control Number: 2018934758

ISBN: 978-1-7320128-0-6 (e-book)
ISBN: 978-1-7320128-1-3 (paperback)
ISBN: 978-1-7320128-2-0 (hardback)

Printed in the United States of America

Book Cover, Interior Design, and Formatting by: Jera Publishing, Roswell, Ga.

For Terry, my wife and best friend who holds my heart.

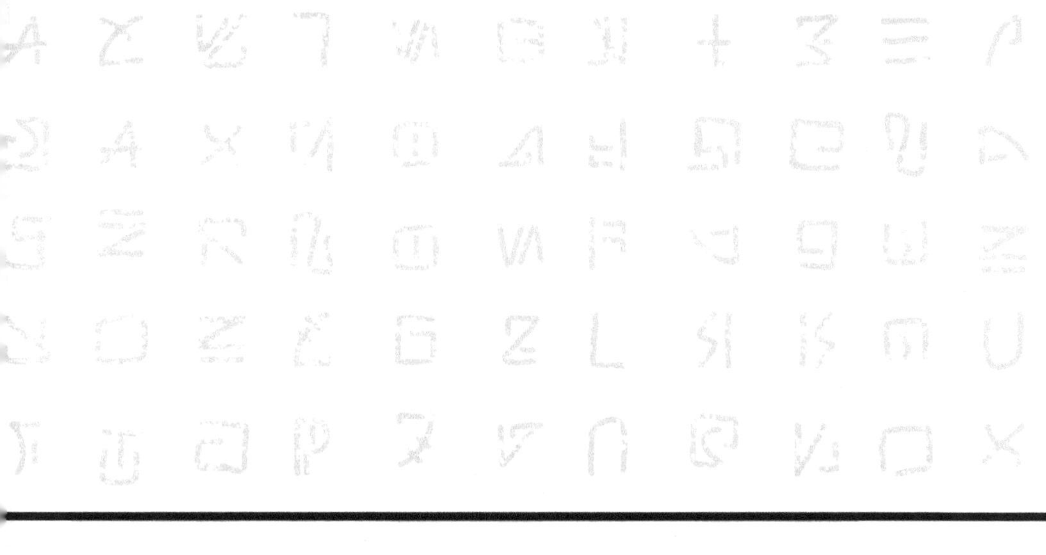

"The most beautiful thing we can experience is the mysterious."

ALBERT EINSTEIN

Kawich Mountain Range, Nevada — June 26, 1947

Unrelenting thunder rumbled across the desert. In the small mining town of Tonopah, Nevada, windows, doors, and even the ground shook. For the people living there, it felt as if a thousand stampeding horses were running through the city streets. Bolts of energy arced across the darkened sky like forked rivers of white gold, lighting up the desolate landscape so frequently that the mountains east of town appeared ablaze. Lightning pierced the towering black cumulonimbus clouds, leaving an unearthly afterglow of electrified ozone.

Hidden from the townspeople was the explosive flash of several supercharged bolts discharging against the hull of a large alien craft. A moment later, the craft lost its battle with gravity and plummeted toward Kawich Peak.

Dennis Hayes and Peter Norris were conducting geological surveys for the Department of the Interior near the peak when the unexpected storm struck. Finding themselves unable to return to their truck before the storm unleashed its fury, the two men took shelter beneath a small rocky overhang. Accustomed to being at the mercy of nature's unusual events, they watched as the electrical light show exploded around them.

The damaged spacecraft plunged soundlessly over their place of refuge. The men could hardly believe what they were seeing. The craft was enormous and was as black as a starless night. They watched in horror as the delta-winged craft continued east for another mile, then exploded in a ravine on the other side of a knoll. As they prepared to run to the crashed aircraft to look for survivors, a blinding white light enveloped the mountain. Seconds later, the once ominous clouds vanished. It was as if God had reached down from heaven and made it so. Before they could comprehend what they were seeing, the shock wave from a second explosion struck their shelter, bringing with it a storm of debris carried by a hurricane-force wind. The outcrop deflected the blast material, saving them from certain death. Boulders, rocks, and pieces of the ship rained down on the overhang above them.

"Was that a nuclear explosion?" Norris asked.

"I don't know, but we need to get out of here, now!" Hayes replied.

Both men understood the danger of radiation exposure. They bolted for their truck parked two miles away. Their thirty-minute trek back was made arduous by the desert sand, which had turned to mud. When they found the truck, they stood panting as they looked at the vehicle. Its paint had been blasted away, exposing bare metal. Still out of breath, they jumped in, started the engine, and drove toward Tonopah as fast as they dared.

When they arrived in town, Hayes pulled into the muddy parking lot in front of the Gold Rush Café. They sat for a while in silence, each reliving the terrible event. Hayes's face was ashen, his knuckles white from clasping the steering wheel in a death grip.

"Dennis, we need to call the Army Air Corps. Come on, let's go," Norris said as he got out of the truck.

Hayes didn't move.

Norris thought Hayes appeared catatonic. Knowing he had to summon help, he ran to the café. When he entered, he saw the place was nearly deserted. An older man with a scraggly, grayish beard sat on a barstool at the counter. The man looked at him while cradling his coffee mug, then shook his head in obvious disgust and turned back toward the counter.

Covered in mud, Norris realized he must look like someone who had been walking through the desert for days.

An overweight waitress walked out from behind the counter. The left sleeve of her uniform bore a dark stain.

"Is there a telephone I can use?" Norris asked.

The waitress frowned at him, then simply pointed toward the back of the café and walked away without saying a word.

"Thanks." He staggered toward the phone hanging on the wall, hoping his uneven gait was the result of shock and not the first sign of radiation exposure. Picking up the telephone handset, he placed a call few people would ever know was made.

PART ONE

"All the past is but the beginning of a beginning;
all that the human mind has accomplished
is but the dream before the awakening."

H. G. WELLS

ONE

The soon-to-be first Secretary of Defense, James Forrestal, and U.S. Attorney General Tom C. Clark sat in silence as they listened to the drone of the twin engines of the Douglas C-47 transport plane. They were the only two passengers aboard. The plane wasn't one of the VIP models the military normally used for people of their political stature. This particular airplane's seats reeked from use by the many troops it had transported over the years.

"Tom, do you have any idea what's going on?" Forrestal asked.

"I have no idea why I'm here or where we're going. Armed soldiers met me and escorted me to a waiting car. All I've been told is it's a national security issue," Clark answered.

"I received the same treatment with the same explanation, but with the caveat that it was by order of the president."

"That's not good," Clark said.

"Usually not," Forrestal replied.

Alamogordo Army Air Field, New Mexico — July 24

Atomic Energy Commission Chairman David E. Lilienthal had just finished his evening reading and was preparing to go to bed. There was a knock at the front door.

"Yes?" he asked, opening the door. He was surprised to see Captain Katzer, his military liaison, standing there.

"I have orders to get you on a plane immediately," Katzer said.

"What? At this hour?"

"Yes, sir."

"Where am I going, and who ordered me there?"

"All I know is the base commander told me to put you on a plane immediately."

"Very well. Give me a moment to get dressed."

Fifteen minutes later, Lilienthal found himself inside Hangar 301 staring at a small, two-seat military training aircraft. The pilot was grinning down at him from the cockpit. Lilienthal climbed the ladder and sat down behind the pilot. Katzer followed him up, buckled him in by tightening the restraining straps until they dug into his shoulders, and put a headset on him.

"Must they be so tight?" Lilienthal asked.

"They need to be as tight as you can stand them," the pilot said over the headset, then started the single-engine aircraft.

They taxied out of the hangar and took off, headed south.

El Paso, Texas — July 25 — 0100 hours

Deep beneath the El Paso desert, President Harry S. Truman found himself in a hardened concrete-and-steel bunker, code named "Phoenix Five." It was 248 feet beneath a nondescript aircraft hangar on Biggs Army Airfield. The bunker was the latest addition to the American defensive network, stocked with enough food and water to sustain twenty men for a month below ground. Truman did not intend to be there that long.

Phoenix Five was one of fifteen similar bunkers constructed and strategically placed around the United States. All of them were buried deep underground and equipped with the latest electronic and communications technology. Designed to withstand a direct strike from a nuclear bomb, the bunkers would serve as command-and-control stations in the event of a nuclear strike. They would ensure that the United States military command would survive and respond to such an attack. Truman knew it wouldn't be long before the Soviet Union became the world's second nuclear power. He had ordered the network of bunkers built to stay ahead of the curve. However, on this night he contemplated a much different type of attack.

President Truman adjusted his wire-rimmed glasses and straightened his red bow tie out of habit. His tired, bloodshot, hazel eyes looked as if he had been crying like a schoolchild. Little Man, as his friends knew him, had not been crying. He was just exhausted from lack of sleep.

Truman looked around at the drab surroundings, rubbed his temples, and smoothed down his steel-gray hair. It had been a very intense and demanding month, and he saw no respite in sight. He was the president, and it was his job to lead the nation through conflict.

He had ascended to the presidency following FDR's unexpected death. Truman desperately wanted another term in the White House, one he earned himself, not a hand-me-down. To be elected he must garner the respect and trust of the American public. Now, he believed the nation faced a new unfathomable threat, and he knew scaring them to death wouldn't help his chances. How could he tell the world that alien beings from outer space had crashed on Earth? How many more of their ships were out there? He didn't have an answer, but he had a plan. The president had lived through the radio broadcast of *War of the Worlds*, and he knew what havoc the Orson Welles broadcast had wrought. That was fiction. This was not.

His first briefing on the crash in Kawich, Nevada, was a month ago. The Army Air Corps quickly secured the crash site and kept it from the public. Since then, there had been additional unidentified sightings and another crash in Corona, New Mexico. Unlike Kawich, the 509th Bomb Group had created a media frenzy by announcing the Corona event.

Truman hoped peace would follow the war, and he wanted to turn his attention to the American domestic agenda, putting the country back on a solid, peaceful economic footing. With this new development and all of its global implications, he now believed that national security would remain center stage for the remainder of his term. Stalin's machinations in Europe only added to his belief. Truman had decided to keep the public in the dark about the aliens, as well as almost everyone else in his inner circle. He needed to be able to reassure the public that their government could deal with the alien threat before he disclosed their existence.

He'd summoned the three men sitting at the conference table opposite his desk for that very reason. When he had met them in the hangar, Forrestal had a smirk on his face, while Clark paled when he saw him. Lilienthal looked as if he had just come off a carnival ride. These men were going to lay the foundation for how best to deal with the new threat, and they had little time to accomplish the task.

The three men seated in the bunker had learned from the intelligence reports that the Kawich and Corona crashes were the most significant events to happen to America since Pearl Harbor, but they were not the only reason for concern. The radar tracking reports detailed the extraordinary speed these spacecraft could achieve. Their ability to hover, accelerate, and decelerate rapidly and to change altitude far more quickly than any aircraft the United States had in its inventory was more than troubling. The reports also revealed the airships could make abrupt ninety-degree turns at incredibly high speeds, producing g-forces no human could survive.

President Truman had read, and reread, the classified reports so many times he could recite them verbatim. The debris collected from the two crash sites had been sent to Wright Field in Ohio for examination. The aeronautical engineers assigned there were the best in the country, and he was counting on them to determine how the alien craft functioned. So far, the analysis of the debris recovered in Nevada revealed it wasn't anything like the remains found in New Mexico. The debris found in Nevada was scattered over a twenty-square-mile area. Many of the pieces weighed over a ton. The New Mexico debris consisted of mere fragments that were scattered over only a few acres. The reports indicated the two ships were not only different in size and shape, but the metal alloys from each craft were different in composition, with only one exception. A small metal plaque found in the Nevada wreckage had the same molecular composition as the debris found in New Mexico.

The metal found at both crash sites was composed of unidentified alloys not found on Earth. The fragments were flexible and heat-resistant and couldn't be cut, even with a diamond-tipped saw. A footnote in one report said any craft entering the atmosphere would be exposed to extreme heat, and the scientists had determined the metal found at both sites could withstand such temperatures.

The engineers speculated that the largest melted mass of metal from the Kawich site was part of an engine. They believed that an engine overload was the most probable reason for the explosion that had destroyed the craft. The heat generated had to have reached temperatures as hot as the surface of the sun.

The most startling revelation, discovered yesterday, and the reason President Truman was deep underground, was the unidentifiable biological specimen found in a piece of debris from the Kawich crash. The specimen was only six inches long and two inches wide, and a photograph of it was included in the intelligence briefs. Because the specimen had been found wrapped in a flexible metallic fabric sandwiched between two larger pieces of metal, it had survived the intense heat of the explosion.

The medical examination of the specimen revealed that the epidermis appeared ash gray and was rigid to the touch. The pinkish muscle tissue beneath the epidermis was attached to a paper-thin piece of fractured bone. The bone resembled the hollow bones of a bird's wing. The reports on the blood and tissue samples revealed it was of unknown origin. It was not human. The recovered specimen, along with the photograph of the symbols found on the metal plaque, prompted Truman to take action.

The president stood and walked to the conference table. He rubbed the back of his neck as he looked around. He noted the only picture hanging in the room was one of him, taken when being sworn in as president. *Probably a last-minute addition after the base commander learned I was going to be utilizing the bunker,* he thought.

The other three men in the room whispered words of disbelief as they continued to read the intelligence briefs. Truman looked at his watch and decided the men had reviewed the material long enough. It was time to get on with the meeting. He needed to be airborne and on his way to Canada before sunrise.

"Gentlemen, I want to thank you again for being here on such short notice and meeting in this rather unusual setting at this early hour. I apologize for the secrecy, but I think you all now understand why it was necessary. As you have read, we are not alone in this wondrous universe." Truman paused as he read the expressions on their faces. "What's not included in the intelligence briefings is that these two crashes are not the only incidents reported over the last two months. Let me give you the highlights, then I'll answer your questions."

The three men shifted uncomfortably. Truman said, "Most of the sightings have occurred in the Pacific Northwest and Alaska. A glowing saucer-shaped craft over Maury Island in Washington State dropped slag onto a boat as it hovered over the bay. The only casualty was a dog that was aboard. The boat captain threw the slag and the animal overboard, so no physical evidence was collected at the scene.

"I'm sure you all know about the twenty-four June sighting near Mount Rainier, where a pilot saw nine saucer-shaped aircraft flying in formation. The Signal Corps tracked them traveling at an estimated speed of fifteen hundred miles per hour. The targets disappeared off Southern California." Truman rubbed his neck again.

"There have been numerous reports over the last year of unidentified flying objects over western Alaska. The Eskimo National Guardsmen who witnessed these sightings described the objects as orbs of light. The most recent sighting was reported last week by a fisherman. He claims he saw a black triangular-shaped aircraft hovering near Kodiak, Alaska, and it disappeared beneath the sea as his vessel approached. Military intelligence speculated Stalin must be testing a new type of aircraft, but we now know differently. I'm not even sure our pilots were imagining the foo fighters during the war."

Truman sat down at the conference table and picked up a photograph. He stared at the picture of the metal plaque. The image in the metal was recognizable, and it appeared to have been stamped into the metal when it was forged. The Egyptian ankh, the "breath of life," appeared on one side of a pyramid, and a representation of a crescent moon was above and to the right of the pyramid. The images were in the right proportion and size if its creator stood on the ground near the pyramid, looking up at the night sky.

Truman sighed, then continued, "We don't know the reason these ships are here, nor do we know their intentions, but we know they are not Soviet or terrestrial. These ships are far superior to anything we can put in the air. They've shown no hostile intentions yet, and based on the biological remains, they appear to be mortal."

Truman adjusted his bow tie. "What is important to me is that the public be kept in the dark about what's happened, at least until we can determine the true nature of what we're dealing with here. To that end, I will be signing into law the National Security Act, creating a National Security Council, which I will chair. With the Atomic Energy Act having become law almost a year ago, I've asked Chairman Lilienthal to this meeting for a very specific reason."

All three men remained silent. Clark and Forrestal looked at Lilienthal. Truman continued, "I believe it is in the best interest of our country to investigate this phenomenon to determine the level of threat we are facing and to do it covertly. If these creatures have hostile intentions, we need to know that, and fast. If they are just exploring our world, we need to know why. If they are here because of our leap into the nuclear age, we need to know why they care. The metal plaque found in the Kawich crash is composed of a metal different from the rest of that debris. I want to know why."

Truman tossed the photograph back onto the table. "We must maintain a balance between the scientific and military options as we investigate, and this must be kept absolutely secret until we know more. I can't overemphasize this point. I don't want panic in the streets or a collapse of our financial markets. I don't want religious upheaval to cause a schism between neighbors. If information becomes public that alien creatures have crashed here, our position would be untenable, and that Soviet lunatic would think we are up to something."

All three men nodded their understanding.

"According to Mr. Lilienthal, the Soviets will have their own atomic bomb in less than two years. Isn't that right, David?"

"Yes, it is."

"I don't need Stalin thinking these creatures, or their ships, are under our direction. The fact that these damn things crashed on American soil is both a nuisance and a blessing. I haven't decided which yet." Truman was known for his fiery temper, and it didn't help that he was stressed, tired, and frustrated.

Truman paused for a moment to gather his thoughts. He was about to entrust them with the future of humanity, and he needed them to get it right the first time. There may not be a second chance.

"This may shock you, but I don't believe this should be a military operation. I can't afford anyone seeing a threat under every rock and attacking these creatures, at least not until we determine if they are a threat. Our first contact needs to be from a peaceful, but firm, position. If they should prove to be hostile, then we will commit to a military engagement."

"Mr. President, I have to interrupt," Forrestal said. "I wholeheartedly disagree."

Truman stared at him for a moment, then said, "The National Security Act, which I will sign into law on my way to Canada today, will create the Central Intelligence Agency. I don't feel it's appropriate to include them in this matter either, at least not for now. I want the investigation of these incidents and anything associated with them buried." Forrestal began to interrupt again, but Truman raised his hand and cut him off. "Mr. Forrestal, before you interrupt me again, I want you to clearly understand that I don't want military oversight. Please, hear me out."

Forrestal managed a weak smile.

"I have decided to create an alien research command to investigate. It will operate independently of any existing federal agency or branch of the military. Those selected for service must be patriots first and not interested in brokering or leveraging information for personal advancement. Preferably, the members of the unit should be unmarried and without family. The people selected need to be the very best we have to offer our country." Truman stopped to catch his breath.

"The new command needs to be small enough to be hidden in the budget, but still have access to unlimited funding and the authority to work with other government agencies and the military. A leader devoted to putting mission first should command it. I will explain my reason for that requirement in a moment. The people selected for this assignment need to be focused on discovering the truth and have the balls to kill these creatures if they have hostile intentions. Am I clear?"

"Yes, sir," they answered in unison.

"Good. Mr. Lilienthal, I believe the Manhattan Project was under S-1 within the AEC, correct?" Truman asked.

"Yes, Mr. President, that is correct," Lilienthal replied.

Truman adjusted his glasses. "Mr. Lilienthal, where do you think we can best hide this command from prying eyes?"

"Do you mean organizationally or physically, sir?"

"Organizationally, the group is going to be yours, Mr. Lilienthal. I believe that if we bury the group within the AEC, it will be under less scrutiny from appropriations review. Most everyone knows the AEC is responsible for our secret atomic research, and the locations and activities within those secret facilities falls outside of public scrutiny. When it comes to nuclear research, even the press doesn't go snooping. The only fly in the ointment I can see with housing it within AEC is keeping the other four members of the commission in the dark."

Lilienthal glanced at Forrestal, and Clark and took a deep breath.

Truman could see he was trying to hide his uneasiness.

"Mr. President, if I had been given some advance notice, I could have provided you with a recommendation for a site," Lilienthal said. "As to the other members on the commission, I can keep them in the dark for as long as you need." After a moment, he leaned forward. "I recommend attaching the new command to S-3. It already exists, the other members of the commission are aware of it, and they would be none the wiser if we simply snuck the project in through the back door."

"What is S-3?" Forrestal asked.

Before Lilienthal could respond, the president said, "It is a unique group of people engaged in research."

Forrestal frowned, and Truman could tell he didn't like being excluded.

"I apologize for putting you in this position, David," Truman said. "I agree with your assessment and recommendation. We are all going to have to think on our feet, shoot from the hip, and do the best we can as we progress. So be ready for it." He looked at the other two men.

"The policies we create here tonight and the direction we take will set the stage for the future. Secrecy and the protection of our citizens, above all else, is your primary job. Am I clear on that point as well?" Truman asked.

All three men nodded.

Truman stretched his legs and said, "Good. I asked Mr. Clark to be here to insure we create a legal entity which cannot be discovered or forced into disclosure until the person in charge of the command, or I, deem it be made public. I want flexibility built into the policies so that information can be passed to the military, or any other federal agency, over the coming decades, if it takes that long."

Truman looked at Forrestal. "Jim, I said you wouldn't be left in the dark, and I meant it. Your first assignment is to select our first commander. Since this group will be operating autonomously for some time, I want the succession of the group commanders to be determined in advance, each one of them selected internally from its active personnel. The commander needs to have a military background, and I'm counting on you to select the right person the first time around.

"It's also important the people assigned to this command understand once they agree to join, they are there for the rest of their career. They can never discuss anything about the project—ever. This is the only way to remove any leveraging for political gain. Any disclosure of where they work or what they did even after they retire will constitute an act of treason and be punishable accordingly."

Truman glanced at his watch. "Mr. Clark, I want you to draft the documents for my signature describing the new command. I want it to be general enough in scope so we can adjust the structure over time without having to draw undue attention or having to write another confidential Executive Order.

"Gentlemen, I want the personnel assigned to be given complete presidential immunity for any and all actions they feel need to be taken as long as they're in the best interest of national security. Members of this command will have the authority to use deadly force against any enemy, foreign or domestic. I will disclose the existence of the command to the next president. Mr. Lilienthal, Mr. Forrestal, you will brief your successors. Mr. Clark, you will not need to brief your successor."

Forrestal cleared his throat and asked, "Are you sure it's wise to grant blanket immunity, Mr. President? Allowing someone to have the authority to determine the rules of engagement does not seem to be in our nation's best interest. In theory, the commander of this unit could order you killed and not be prosecuted for it. I believe some type of oversight and policy directives are warranted."

"Your point is well taken, Jim," the president said, nodding. "Very well, the commander will report directly to me. You and David will provide the necessary formal oversight associated with the general activities under S-3 operations. David, I'm authorizing you to brief Jim on what S-3 does, but I will make any major decisions related to the group's activities. I know adjustments will be necessary over the coming months. Time is of the essence, gentlemen. The important thing is to have this command up and running by the end of the month."

The three men looked as if the deadline they had just been given was a death sentence.

"That doesn't give us much time, Mr. President," Forrestal said. "Speed is one thing, but we will need time to get everything organized in order to maintain the secrecy you desire. If we just start pushing our weight around, someone will notice."

Truman looked at Lilienthal and asked, "David, what do you think about Alamogordo Army Airfield as the first physical location for the unit to operate from? You come and go from there and have a home on base, so it wouldn't be out of the ordinary for people to see you there. You'll have access to the Phoenix Two bunker that's located under the base. That would give the group commander complete privacy."

Lilienthal slowly nodded in agreement, then said, "The location works for me. I can have it operational and the commander's cover story in place in a few days. In another few months, I could have him relocated to a more remote site we're preparing in Nevada."

"Where in Nevada?" asked Truman.

"The Indian Springs Auxiliary Army Airfield north of Las Vegas. It's off Route 95, out near Yucca Flats. We've been exploring parts of the Nevada desert for future nuclear testing. The Pacific Proving Grounds are becoming too costly to use, and the surface test areas are too easily monitored."

Truman felt annoyed. "I wasn't aware we were seeking new nuclear testing grounds, but I'm sure that was just an oversight by someone on your staff." He knew Lilienthal received his not so subtle message.

Before Lilienthal could speak in his defense, Truman said, "Then in keeping with the spirit and intent of secrecy, I want all documents and records associated with the new command's activities sealed for a minimum of seventy-five years. All activities and information will be compartmentalized."

Everyone nodded in understanding.

"David, I want you to think about using one of those nuclear research contractors to funnel the group's funding. We can move any additional operational costs through them. I'm sure none of the contractors will care, considering the amount of taxpayer money flowing into their coffers already."

"I have a company in mind that has a component attached to S-3," Lilienthal replied.

"Excellent," Truman said. "I believe we should also have some kind of a cover project to draw attention away from the group. At the end of the year, I will launch the new United States Air Force. Jim, you will create a small unit within the Air Force for the sole purpose of publicly investigating unidentified flying objects. Considering the number of encounters over the last month, I'm sure people are going to want to know what we're doing about them. We'll need a public face for that new department, which we'll also use to debunk any confirmed sightings."

"You mean put a sign on the door announcing we're officially investigating UFO's?" Forrestal asked.

"I do. When the public starts asking questions, and they will, I want them steered away from the real investigative group. We will call it . . ." Truman chuckled, then said, "Project Sign."

He could tell Forrestal didn't see the humor in the name.

"How soon do all of the documents need to be ready for your signature, Mr. President?" Clark asked.

"You three must get everything drafted by the end of today. Have them ready for my signature by the time I return to Washington late tomorrow night."

Truman stood, having decided to include a secrecy oath for the three of them to take, similar to the one he had taken when he became a Freemason. "You will swear an oath here and now, before God, that under no circumstances will you ever disclose or use any of this information for personal or political benefit. Nor will you disclose any information in the future to anyone without presidential approval. So swear to me now, under penalty of death, that you will be true to the faith and allegiance under this agreement."

Each man stood and stated, "I so swear."

"Mr. Clark, please draft a nondisclosure agreement for everyone to sign," Truman said.

"Mr. President, how do you want me to refer to this command in the documents?" Clark asked.

Truman picked up the photo of the pyramid from the table and studied it for a moment. "This symbol must have some meaning to the beings that created it. It's only appropriate we use this as the insignia for the new command. In light of the fact the moon is mostly in shadow, we will call the new command … Dark Moon. Are there any objections?"

No one objected.

"Good. The *Sacred Cow* awaits me," Truman said, referring to his VC-54C twin propeller-powered airplane. It was the official presidential aircraft. "My decoy aircraft is bound for Canada already. Hard not to miss its bright aluminum fuselage, so I need to depart before anyone takes notice."

Truman walked to the door. "Well, good luck to you all," he said. "I will inform the base commander that you will be here for a while. I'll have him bring down food and lots of coffee." He opened the steel door hiding the elevator, entered, and headed for the surface. He exited the elevator that was concealed within the hangar, walked crisply toward the *Sacred Cow*, and boarded the aircraft. A few moments later, the lights in the hangar dimmed, the engines on the VC-54C came to life, and the *Sacred Cow* rolled out to the end of the runway.

As the plane lifted off, President Truman looked out the small window at the morning sky. He hoped what he had put in motion would prove fruitful. He laid his head against the headrest and fell asleep.

T W O

Washington, D.C. — January — 2022

The two-day-long blizzard had all but paralyzed Washington. Record-setting low temperatures and snowfall had forced Dulles and Ronald Reagan airports to close. The sentinels guarding the Tomb of the Unknown Soldier in Arlington Cemetery rotated their tour of duty every thirty minutes. If not for their commitment to duty and honor, the tomb guards would not have been outside at all. The wind blew with such intensity that even a polar bear would have had the sense to seek shelter in the subzero temperatures.

President Thomas Baines Collingsworth—TC to his family and closest friends—and the new First Lady, Sandra Collingsworth, had just finished their first dinner in the private dining room of the White House. The wintry storm was of no concern to them. They would stay quite comfortable in the warmth of their new home.

TC savored the ambiance of the room as he and his wife of thirty years sipped their rich Columbian coffee. The ornate mahogany chairs matched the century-old, polished table that President Teddy Roosevelt had sat at when he was in office. The finest of all things surrounded them.

His road to the presidency had been atypical. Two years ago, TC was a physics professor at Caltech. Then his old friend Jonathan Jackson, a

California congressman, asked him to be his vice presidential running mate on the Progressive Reformist Party ticket. TC accepted, but he truly believed Jackson was out of his mind. For most of his career, TC had worked in academia. He was without political affiliation or influence, so he thought he had little to offer his friend.

The two men capitalized on the Reformist movement in a time of resentment toward the bipartisan political infighting that was so entrenched in American politics. After decades of political conflict, the people were screaming for new and effective leadership. Their party offered the people an alternative, and sixty-five percent of the voting populace believed in them enough to elect them. Political power shifted overnight. Days later, TC was enlightened, or more aptly stated, *awakened* to fulfill his new role.

TC took another sip of his coffee and admired the presidential seal on the side of the white porcelain cup. It seemed everything in the residence had a presidential seal on it, even the box of M&M's on the counter.

President Jackson's abrupt resignation from office was a planned event. A year almost to the day after he became president, Jackson stepped down, citing health reasons. TC smiled as he thought of what lay ahead for the nation and the world. As president, he would oversee the greatest changes the country would ever know.

His ascension to the highest and most powerful position in the world was no accident. After all, nothing of this magnitude, with such far-reaching consequences and complexity, just happens by chance. Every move had been calculated, with no detail overlooked.

There was a new presence about TC, a magnetism and self-assurance that he knew Sandra found disturbing. When he spoke, people seemed mesmerized and found comfort in his words. TC's acceptance speech had captivated the American public and raised their hopes of a prosperous new future.

For the short term, TC needed to maintain that illusion.

The president was not a large or even handsome man. In fact, his five-foot-eight frame and small, almost feminine features would have been unremarkable but for his strangely omniscient aura of late. The wrinkles around his dark brown, almost black, penetrating eyes combined with his gray, thinning hair, did nothing to hide his age.

Over the last few months, TC's mind had developed beyond anything he expected. He'd discovered he never forgot a thing about anyone he met or what he read, and his newfound ability to sense what people were feeling was more than a parlor trick. It was a gift, and he knew exactly why he possessed enhanced intellectual prowess. He also knew his mental acuity and abilities would become even stronger in time.

He gazed across the table at his beautiful wife with a feeling of deep affection and love. They'd known each other since their junior year at Indiana University, and they had by any standard a perfect marriage. They were both vegetarians, which required a departure from the menu that had been the mainstay for several previous administrations. There were no children running around and no First Pooch for the press to spotlight on slow news days. Their two sons, Collin, who was twenty, and Thomas Jr., better known as TJ, who was twenty-two, were attending Stanford University in California.

Sandra and TC had married during their senior year. The city of Bloomington had a hometown feel, which led them to believe they would spend the rest of their life in the small community. Sandra had supported them financially while TC pursued his doctoral work in mathematics and physics.

His mentor and postgraduate advisor encouraged him to put his groundbreaking dissertation on applied quantum mechanics to use in theoretical research. TC followed the advice, and they soon found themselves living in California. For the next twenty years of his life, he taught physics and quantum mechanics. He enjoyed molding the minds of future scientists.

When he had told Sandra about his accepting Jackson's offer, she'd said he was crazy to entertain the idea of a political career, but as always, she supported him in his decision to join Jackson's crusade, even though he knew she hated the idea of public life.

"What?" Sandra asked.

"Nothing. I'm just like looking at my beautiful wife," TC replied, realizing he was staring at her.

"Oh, I almost forgot. I was organizing our personal items in the bedroom this afternoon and found something I wanted to ask you about." Sandra left the table and walked toward the luxurious bedroom.

TC admired her shapely figure as she walked away, and he laughed when she gave him an overly exaggerated wiggle. He took another sip of coffee and wondered what Sandra would think if he lit up a cigar. *Probably not a good idea*, he decided.

"This is very strange-looking," she said, walking up to the table rolling a metallic black orb from hand to hand. "I figured one of your friends or students gave it to you as a going-away present. I've never seen anything like it before. What do all these symbols mean?" Sandra asked, holding the orb in front of him.

TC tensed. He should have felt its presence, but he hadn't. His primal, instinctive response triggered the device. The orb pulsed in Sandra's hand, and suddenly a bright golden beam of light shot from it like a laser, striking him in the center of his forehead.

Sandra screamed and dropped the orb. It remained floating in front of TC, defying gravity. The light illuminated his face until he snatched the orb out of the air. Immediately, the intense golden beam ceased to exist. TC placed his coffee cup on the table and took a deep breath.

"Oh, my God! Are you all right?" Sandra asked as she gently ran her hands over his forehead, looking for any sign of a burn mark. There wasn't one. She gently kissed his forehead and sat down in the chair next to him.

He could still feel the heat and power emanating from the orb he held concealed in his hand.

"What is that thing? I am so sorry. I didn't know it would do that."

Samuel Kidd, the chief personal waiter for the White House, hurried into the dining room, a white towel bearing the presidential seal draped over his forearm.

"Everything's okay, Mr. Kidd. Sandra was just startled. Great dinner, by the way, and this is the best coffee I've ever tasted. I could use a refill when you have a chance." He was glad there were no surveillance cameras in the private quarters.

"Thank you, Mr. President. I will get you a fresh cup of coffee immediately. Would the First Lady care for another?"

"No thank you," Sandra replied.

Samuel walked back through the food service entrance.

"Guess we better remember we're never alone. Every grunt, scream, squeal, or fart is going to require someone to respond," TC said as he looked at Sandra, hoping she would find humor in his words.

"Why did that thing shoot that beam of light at your forehead? And how in the hell did it float in the air like that?" Sandra asked.

TC studied her without blinking, not wanting to miss any subtle movement or twitch as he pondered how to respond. Sandra would know if he lied to her. She had that sixth sense about her, especially after so many years of marriage. They sat in silence as Samuel brought in a fresh cup of coffee and placed it on the table.

"Thank you, Samuel," TC said, sounding dismissive.

Samuel hurried back to the serving area to afford them their privacy.

TC cleared his throat. "I'm not usually at a loss for words." He was nervous and felt a sense of guilt. "I suppose I could tell you this thing is a new toy the guys back home gave me as a gag gift or something provided by the Secret Service, but that wouldn't be true. I've never lied to you, and I'm not going to start now."

He picked up his cup and took a sip from it. "Sandra, I've been keeping something from you. Something so wonderful I often wished I could have shared it with you earlier, but I wasn't allowed." Calmness descended over him. After hiding his secret from the person he loved the most in this world, he was finally going to tell her everything, and he felt a sense of inner peace.

"I was afraid some nosy Secret Service agent would discover my gifts. I wanted to tell you as soon as I realized my new abilities, but I was afraid you wouldn't understand or believe me."

Sandra stuttered, "Te-tell me what? You're frightening me."

"Don't be frightened," TC said, trying to reassure her. "There's nothing to be afraid of."

"When that thing shot the beam of light at your forehead, it looked like your eyes darkened for a moment. How did that happen?"

He saw that she was scared and that she was trying to keep her emotions in check. She lost the battle as tears rolled down her flushed cheeks. He knew she was seeing the dawning of a new reality.

The orb flickered for a second in TC's hand. He listened for a moment to make sure Samuel wouldn't hear him. He whispered softly, "I'm a genetically enhanced human being. I've been modified so that I can accomplish a task of vital importance to the world."

A surreal out-of-body experience enveloped him. It sounded so strange to hear those words uttered aloud. He said, "I can tap into parts of my brain that usually remain dormant in most people, and I can use that ability…differently. Only certain parts of my genetic makeup are modified, that's all there is to it. You're the first to know, as it should be. This orb," he held it up in front of him, "opens a gateway that helps me focus my thoughts and receive information."

"Receive information? From what source?" Sandra asked, pushing her chair back and folding her arms.

He chose to ignore her question. She would know the answer soon enough. All that had transpired was decided long ago by those who controlled the orb. "I was awakened and given a new perspective on life. It's as if something inside of me has been turned on. I don't know how else to explain it." TC rubbed his forehead where the light had struck him. "Information is being downloaded from the orb directly into my mind."

She appeared confused and looked to be growing more concerned.

"I was frightened at first, but now I have come to understand my purpose and how best to serve humanity. That's why what I've become has to remain secret. Sandra, we are here tonight because of this gift and because of how I need to use it. You witnessed my connection to the orb once before, but that memory was erased. They wanted to protect you until you were ready to hear what I'm about to tell you."

He saw that her confusion was turning to panic. He was terrifying her. Why wouldn't she be scared, considering how crazy he must sound? He said, "I sense your fear and confusion. I imagine you're asking yourself if I've lost my mind. The answer is no. I'm still the same man you married, but now I'm connected to something that's so much bigger than anyone could imagine."

"Excuse me," Sandra said. She ran from the room.

In the bathroom, Sandra stared at her image in the mirror. Her husband, the father of her children and the man who held the power to destroy the world, was talking as if he was insane. However, the orb had floated in the air. *Is it possible he's telling the truth? He never answered my question about who they are,* she thought. *He said I'd seen the light before, but they had erased my memory. When did that happen and how?* She centered herself, blew her nose, and returned to the dining room determined to get the answers.

∞

TC heard her coming. He expected a barrage of questions. Sandra sat down in her chair and glared at him. He'd seen the look before.

"I want answers. Is that clear?"

He nodded.

"How were you genetically altered, and who are … they?"

TC smiled. "It started long ago with incremental changes being made to my mother's family DNA, going back generations. It was necessary in order for me to fulfill my destiny."

Sandra's eyes widened in disbelief.

"I know that what I'm telling you is hard to grasp, but, Sandra, I haven't lost my mind. You have nothing to fear. Let me start at the beginning."

"That would be very helpful. I still want to know how this happened and who did this to you."

TC held the orb in front of him, then released it. The orb floated above the table, once again defying gravity, as if to emphasize the power it possessed. He hoped this small demonstration would help Sandra believe what he was telling her. She gaped at the floating orb. He took another sip of coffee. "As a species, we have proven to be genetically challenging for enhancement by a species known as the Antediluvians—the Ancient Ones."

Sandra shook her head as she watched the orb.

"Let me finish. Only a select few of us have made it to the final phase of this cycle. As in any spin of the reproductive roulette wheel, not all genes passed down the way the Antediluvians needed them to. Even with their advanced abilities, they couldn't control the randomness that makes us human. It was only through additional adjustments, introduced most recently, that we were able to reach this heightened, awakened state of mind."

"Who are the Antediluvians, these ancient ones, as you call them? Are they controlling you?" Sandra asked.

"No. I'm not being controlled. They are our saviors and our future." Now, more than ever, he wanted to share everything with her. A valve turned, and the information poured from him.

"The Antediluvians were forced to wait through many generations until finally reaching this juncture. My genetic mix is optimal for what is required. There are others like me, but I was the one chosen to lead our mission. Over time, every human will connect to the Collective. It will take many more generations, but as a species we will, and must, evolve to this next level. Our friends from the stars need us to be stronger and more capable. They are relying on us for support when they arrive."

He took Sandra's hand. It felt clammy. "We have labored to create and unleash a new reality on the world. Many of the awakened hold positions of power around the globe. In time, we will bring about a wonderful and long overdue change. Jackson and I have already put the process in motion. His awakening served to place me in this position. He knew, before I did, what was to come. Jackson would have served as our leader, but his abilities weren't as developed as mine. I was selected to take his place."

"You were selected to do what exactly?"

"You've seen the look of hope on the peoples' faces. Those like me will help to ignite our collective ability to accomplish a dream long awaited—a unified and peaceful world. We can achieve immortality individually and help another species avoid extinction."

"The Antediluvians are an alien species that wants to help us, and we in turn are going to help them?" Sandra asked.

TC nodded. "If we don't succeed in altering human behavior, we will be eradicated. We cannot continue to destroy this beautiful planet and ourselves. The Antediluvians need us to survive because their world is dying, and we need them so we can evolve. It is to be a symbiotic relationship. They are a very nurturing species, and they only want to make sure we thrive. Our civilization will be a better place for all time, and I will do what I can to help them succeed."

"So the Antediluvians are going to help us create a paradise?"

"Yes, Sandra, and they're already on their way. Our grandchildren will never know the suffering of illness or old age. Our world will be one of beauty, a utopia unlike anything ever dreamed, and the people will never have to know the fear or loss associated with being conquered. What we accomplish will save billions of lives and give new hope to the Antediluvians. Humans should not fear our presence. They should embrace us. Now a new existence can dawn without panic or fear of war. Trust in us, Sandra."

"The fear of being conquered," Sandra said. "Are our children … genetically altered?"

"Our children are human. In time our sons will be tested, and if found suitable —they will be awakened. They will marry and have children of their own. We will spoil them the way good grandparents do. My mother was altered but not awakened, and never will be. This is not something to fear. It is something to be embraced."

TC felt her conflict. "Just stop and think about the historical changes over the last two thousand years, about the people who are remembered for their contribution to advancing the human race. Some of those people were different, like me, but they never fully awakened. They were individuals who contributed to the process of change, without realizing their true potential or knowing why they possessed the insights they had to offer. History remembers them as visionaries. However, they were more than that. They were the milestones that measured our progress. They helped the Antediluvians determine what we would do with the knowledge given to us.

"The Antediluvians have pushed us to achieve a higher level of intellectual prowess, waiting until we were ready for assimilation. Now we are ready to take the next leap. There will be peace and exploration of new technologies beyond our wildest imagination. Understand that what we do in the coming years will alter the direction of humanity and make it more … human."

TC cocked his head slightly, judging her reaction. She appeared focused on the orb floating in front of her. "I'm not on drugs, and I haven't been hypnotized. The orb should be proof enough for you." His tone was more insistent.

Sandra gathered her strength and stood. "I'm getting the hell out of here. I can't handle this! I think it best I return to our home in California. I need time to process what you've said. I have known you since college and have loved you for as long as I can remember. We have raised two sons together. Now, I don't know who, or more likely, what you're becoming. I need some space. Do you understand?" She took a step back from the table.

He could tell she was afraid of him. "I'm your husband, the man who loves you, and the man who will always love you. I can help you understand, but you will have to trust me."

"I can't be a part of the world you envision. It won't be the world you think it will be. People need to know what you've told me," Sandra said angrily.

TC showed no emotion. He stood and gently touched her cheek. "I understand why you are acting this way. I really do. You aren't ready to accept us, but the changes are coming with or without you. Perhaps I should have waited until they arrived to tell you. Maybe then you would have better understood."

She batted his hand away.

He frowned at her. "Go home. Take some time to think about what I've told you. I'll be here to answer your questions. You can still assist us in shaping the world's future." An involuntary spasm ran through him as the orb pulsed repeatedly.

"I know that things will never be the same now," TC said. "Your reaction has shown me that people may not be ready to welcome us. Of all the people in the world, I thought *you* would understand. It has been decided that the rest of humanity will not learn of the Antediluvians until they arrive."

TC retrieved the orb.

She backed away from him. "The human species will be lost, not reborn. I can't keep this quiet. I can't be a part it, and I will find a way to stop you."

As she turned to walk away, TC clamped a hand around the back of her neck. "TC, you're hurting me. Let go!"

His grip tightened, holding her in place. As he squeezed harder, he could tell he was hurting her. He felt her rising panic. "We can't let you tell anyone about this. I can see you won't change your mind. I sense that clearly." Fighting for control, he relaxed his grip. The orb pulsed more intensely in his hand.

"This is wrong, TC. Look what they're doing to you!" Sandra said.

TC's eyes darkened, and then his body shuddered. A golden glow appeared deep within his pupils, which dilated until very little sclera remained. The orb pulsed once more and remained ablaze.

Sandra opened her mouth to call out, but no sound came. The radiance in his eyes intensified, burning into her mind. The air seemed charged, as if static electricity on a cold winter morning had filled the space between them.

Sandra collapsed in his arms. He'd done as instructed. The secret was safe. His thoughts and feelings felt strange to him. He pushed the emergency button on his watch to summon help for her. He felt both a sense of relief and remorse. The orb went dark. He dropped it into his pocket.

He could tell Sandra was still alive, but he knew that the damage to her brain was extensive. He hadn't wanted this to happen. Perhaps when the Antediluvians arrived they could piece her mind back together, and he could once again hold her in his arms. He laid his wife on the floor and cried out like a wounded animal.

The first of many Secret Service agents burst into the room. Samuel entered through the service door and TC stood up and backed away as they tended to his wife. An agent summoned the emergency medical personnel, but he knew their efforts would be futile.

A sense of power rocked him as he understood how important he was to ensuring that the Antediluvians would not be interfered with when they arrived. He could not fail them. His actions confirmed his complete willingness to obey them. He felt their approval and appreciation and smiled.

The activity in the dining room quickened when the emergency medical team arrived. He walked to the living room and gazed out the picture window. The falling snow looked like moths flying around a flame in the high-intensity security lights as the flakes blew about in the powerful winds. He focused, trying to see each individual snowflake, testing his new powers.

He pictured each snowflake as a person. The flurries represented the people who would be scattered and tossed by the upheaval to come, and the picturesque snow-covered lawn below was the image of their remaking. After a deep breath, he cleared his mind. There was much work ahead.

He felt the presence of the Secret Service agent standing a discreet distance away. He knew the agent was waiting to assist him. TC nodded at him, then turned back to the window. The look of satisfaction on his face reflected in the glass. He could tell that the agent standing behind him took notice. He didn't care. Nothing could stop them now.

THREE

Annapolis Junction, Maryland — January 18, 2022

"What the hell do you mean it's not going to be released?" Dr. Tegan Strong shouted.

Tegan and Dr. Janet Vasine were sitting alone in a break room in the covert facility where they worked. They were discussing Tegan's newly developed programmable synthetic virus, the future of which now appeared to be out of her hands. Tegan found it hard to breathe after hearing what Janet had just revealed. She wanted to go outside to get some fresh air, but security protocols prevented it. They were several levels beneath the building, the unobtrusive appearance of which masked the work taking place there.

Tegan's office and state-of-the-art biology laboratory were underneath a sprawling advanced research and technology complex located across the Baltimore-Washington Parkway from the National Security Agency headquarters. It was supposed to be a Center for Disease Control facility.

Tegan's mission for the last three years, as far as she knew until a moment ago, was to explore new ways to combat emerging and existing viruses. Her programmable synthetic virus provided a means to develop vaccines at a molecular level.

Tegan glared at her best friend seated across the table from her. "So you're telling me all the work we've done hasn't been for a special research arm of the CDC? It's actually been for the military?"

"Indirectly. General Westfield is with the National Security Agency."

"Cecil Westfield is a general?" Tegan asked. Now it all made sense. How could she have been so naïve? She'd been blinded and seduced by the opportunity to do groundbreaking research in one of the most advanced labs ever built, and she'd allowed Westfield to take advantage of her altruistic motives.

"Maybe I shouldn't have told you. I just thought you had the right to know you will never publish your work. It will never be used the way you intended."

"So when Westfield recruited me, he knew whatever I created to eradicate disease was going to be turned into a weapon." Tegan slammed her hand on the table. "How long have you known who he is?"

"I knew just after I was recruited," Janet replied, keeping her voice low. "I'd just graduated from medical school when I was approached by a black ops group attached to the U.S. Army Biological Weapons Command. I worked there for a few months, until General Westfield talked me into coming to work for the NSA. That was more years ago than I want to think about."

"All this time you and Westfield have been lying to me."

"I've never lied to you. I just didn't tell you everything."

"That's the same thing in my book. How many others think they're working for the CDC?"

"There are a few people still in the dark." Janet looked at Tegan with sorrowful eyes. "You can't tell Westfield you know."

"The hell I can't," Tegan cried.

"You have to stay quiet, it's not an option."

"Why?"

"Tegan, my position here is unique. I'm what they call OINO—once in, never out. Once you know what's really going on here, Westfield is the only person that can allow you to leave."

Tegan shook her head. "I don't need his permission to leave."

Janet sighed. "Yes, you do. Please keep your voice down. I'm your friend, not just your boss, so try to understand the position that puts me in, especially in these circumstances. Your work is very special. You have created something that is far ahead of anything ever designed or developed before. I wish you could share it with the world, but you cannot. I wanted you to know what you were facing before you challenged Westfield when he tells you that Deep Sky won't leave the facility."

Tegan leaned forward and said, "I developed Deep Sky to cure every known virus on the planet."

"Yes, it could do just that, but not now."

Tegan took a deep breath and shook her head. "I should be making a seven-figure income and living in luxury. Instead, I'm living in a dingy two-bedroom condo, working shit hours, and now I'm being told I can't do what's right. Westfield will not stop me from publishing my findings."

"Yes, he will. Do you think Westfield will let you walk away with your knowledge of Deep Sky? Not a chance. Listen to me very carefully for a moment. If you try to leave without getting his blessing, you'll be classified as a national security threat. Even if he allows you to leave, you will never be able publish or even work in this field again. He may not even let you practice medicine."

"That doesn't even make sense." Two technicians entered the break room and sat at a table as far away from them as possible. Tegan couldn't help but wonder if they knew what was happening.

She turned back to Janet. "I know what he's planning to do with it. I have to stop him or stop working on the project."

"That won't happen, and you can't stop him. If you quit or ask to leave now, he will suspect you know what is going on here. He could discredit you, incarcerate you, or have you killed."

Tegan rolled her eyes in disbelief.

"I'm serious." Janet leaned across the table. "Tegan, this is what's going to happen. You will go back to work. Eventually, Westfield will brief you and invite you into the inner circle. The work you've done has opened that door. Then, and only then, will you have an opportunity to express your desire to terminate employment. Westfield will most likely make you wait a few months before he grants your request. You will then sign away any rights you think you have as an American, and you'll not be able to disclose the nature of your work to anyone. If you're lucky, Westfield will allow you to go home, start a family medical practice in Washington, and live a normal life. Understand, Westfield will monitor your activities, personal and professional, for the rest of your life, or until your work is declassified. If he suspects you're going to go public or you're disclosing anything associated with your work here, you will disappear."

"So I have to play along and help him test a bioweapon. Is that what you're telling me?"

"Yes, that is exactly what I'm saying. After I retire, I'll be monitored and debriefed weekly. My mail, phone calls, computer use, emails—everything—will be under scrutiny at all times. Whom I see and where I go will require approval. I'd be surprised if Westfield didn't chip me so he could track my movements."

"Does he monitor everything I do?"

"Yes. Tegan, promise me you won't tell anyone about what we've discussed. He has spies everywhere. Don't call or email anyone for advice or make any notes about this conversation. Forget it happened."

Tegan wanted to scream. All of her work, her life's ambition to help humanity, was lost. She'd made a deal with the devil, and he was going to collect his due. "I can't believe he has the power to hold me against my will. He can't put me in a cell somewhere without due process or have me killed. I'm not a terrorist."

Janet took Tegan's hands in hers. "Tegan, you have two choices. You can finish your work and wait for Westfield to invite you to join, then decline, as we discussed. As long as he's in the dark about how much you know, he may grant you your wish. Tell him you've decided you want to go home and serve your community as a family doctor. He may just buy it. If not, you will be detained and most likely be forced to continue to work for him under close supervision."

"I can't stay here and watch my work be used as a weapon. I won't complete the next phase. He can't force me."

Janet sighed. "That brings me to your second option. If you choose to leave, then you need to leave quickly and quietly. Tell no one what you're doing. Understand, though, if you decide to leave, you will need to disappear, and I mean vanish from the face of the planet. No one can know where you are. You'll have to sever all family ties and establish a new identity. You can never contact anyone you know ever again. Is that clear?"

Tegan didn't have the resources to disappear, and her family meant the world to her. She felt trapped.

Janet said, "Tegan, Westfield was here last week. When was the last time you saw him visit the lab?"

"I can't remember."

"Exactly. He shows up when we have something that interests him. Do you remember the short, stocky, bald guy that was with him?"

"Yes."

"He's in charge of security, and he makes sure everything stays in balance. He's also the most likely person to come after you if you run. If he finds you, he won't bring you back here."

Tegan shook her head in disbelief.

"Tegan, I've been in this hole far too long, and I'm burned out. If it hadn't been for your research and friendship, I would have asked to stand down long ago. If Westfield denied my request, I would have left anyway."

"You just said he wouldn't let anyone leave without his blessing."

"True. It has taken me years to put together a contingency exit strategy. I have a friend who's provided me with false identification, and I've stashed cash away. I also found a way to get out of the country without leaving a trail. If you choose to run, you would need to do the same thing, but you don't have that much time. Please stay until he asks you to join. That's your best option."

Tegan stood and looked down at the brown-haired woman. She bit her lower lip, then exhaled sharply. She'd made her decision.

"You know I can't wait years or even months. I'm taking my scheduled vacation in a few days and going home to visit my family and do some skiing. That will give me a chance to put a plan together." The determined look on Tegan's face said it all.

"Janet, I won't be returning. Thank you for your honesty. I only wish you'd told me earlier, but I'll treasure our friendship always. I would appreciate any help you can give me. I'll be in my office." Tegan walked away, understanding what her decision meant.

Once in her office, Tegan sat down behind her desk and put her head in her hands. None of the advancements she had made in her research would ever see the light of day. Westfield had given her project the code name Deep Sky. She assumed the code name referenced the scientific assumption that viruses came to Earth on asteroids and comets. Now she wondered if there was another reason.

At the age of thirty-one, she'd already contributed more to her scientific field than most scientists do in a lifetime, but no one would ever know what she'd accomplished. When it came to molecular virology and immunology, there were few in her league. She shook her head and looked at the picture of her family sitting on her desk. None of her family would ever understand what she'd done, especially her fraternal twin sister, Megan.

Tegan and Megan had grown up on a small family ranch in the Cascade Mountains of Washington, ninety miles east of Seattle. Although fraternal twins, they both stood five foot nine, had the same blond hair, and looked very much alike. William, their father, was a software designer and a career employee at a large IT company. When the girls visited their father's office in Seattle, Tegan would follow him around, asking questions about his work, while Megan enjoyed socializing with the other employees and making herself the center of attention. Their mother, Irene, was well educated, but had chosen to stay at home and raise them instead of joining the corporate scene. She was the consummate earth mother type, always on some campaign to save the planet. Her hobby was raising llamas and alpacas on the ranch. As a family, they had their differences, as all families do, but largely they were a tight-knit unit.

Tegan continued to stare at the family photograph. Her parents were always supportive of her academic pursuits and encouraged her to explore new ideas. How could she face them now? What would they think of their little girl if they learned the truth?

Her turmoil consumed her as she thought about the decisions that had brought her to this point in her life. She had graduated from high school at sixteen, entered college, and embraced the academic lifestyle. Her age, combined with her scholastic workload, kept her from having any real social life. The few men she dated in college never held her interest. The only thing that did was her thirst for knowledge.

Her sister had chosen to forgo college, opting instead to follow in their mother's footsteps. Megan wanted a family. She'd been engaged twice, with both relationships ending badly. Somehow, Megan always found someone she loved more than her betrothed before reaching the altar. Tegan smiled, remembering the chaos that ensued during the last breakup.

Tegan closed her eyes. Even doing everything right in life had taken her down the wrong path. She had earned her PhD in molecular biology at the University of Washington at the age of twenty-four. Her doctoral dissertation, based on two years of research and fieldwork, had shown conclusively that a virus was responsible for the disappearance of the Anasazi people. The once powerful southwestern civilization had vanished virtually overnight seven hundred years ago. She'd identified the genetic fingerprint of the ancient virus and had asserted that with the right funding she could reconstitute the infectious agent synthetically. That's when she first heard from Cecil Westfield.

In hindsight, the red flag of secrecy had been flying since she'd accepted Westfield's employment contract. The Center for Disease Control agreed to pay her way through the Johns Hopkins School of Medicine. The only caveat was that her contract included a nondisclosure agreement. She couldn't tell her friends about what she would be doing after graduation. It seemed a reasonable request.

She felt fortunate to accept a position with the CDC. It afforded her the opportunity to gain medical training to advance her work in virology and genetics. She'd given up any social life to stay focused on her studies and to prove she was dedicated to her work. Every night she would snuggle up on the sofa with medical textbooks and journals and study. On Friday nights, she would treat herself to a pint of black cherry ice cream while watching old movies. Her hard work had paid off. She'd graduated at the top of her class at the age of twenty-eight. Her specialization encompassed not only virology and immunology, but when it came to molecular medicine and genetics, some deemed her a savant. *Exactly the combination Westfield could exploit*, she thought. All of her expectations and plans to commit her life to public service were history.

She hadn't been allowed to tell her family about her work these past years. Westfield claimed the nature of her work would make her and her family targets for extremists. That made sense to her, so she'd lied to her family, convincing herself that it was for their own protection. Now she found herself ensnared in Westfield's web.

Tegan had created Deep Sky as a means to immunize the world's population by utilizing the most sophisticated nanotechnology ever developed. The synthetic virus was programmable at a molecular level. In time, it could revolutionize the paradigm of development and testing new vaccines against emerging and mutated virus strains. Its engineering allowed it to self-replicate like any virus found in nature. Somehow, Deep Sky had found a way to mutate on its own, which was not part of the programming. It seemed as if Deep Sky wanted to evolve and survive. It even sought ways to withstand the synthetic vaccines she introduced. The artificial intelligence program learned how to thwart the vaccines, so Tegan had to send a destruct signal to neutralize it during testing several times. Her creation was too smart, and it had taken her months to stabilize it. Tegan had resolved the last of the problems with Deep Sky just over a week ago. Now Westfield had it to use as he wished.

Until an hour ago, Tegan was looking forward to the next phase of the project. Deep down, she was grateful to Janet for telling her the truth, but she was still angry about having been deceived for so long. She thought of Janet as more than a friend. She was like a second mother. Now, Tegan wasn't sure how she felt about her.

Tegan needed an immediate exit strategy. She decided to take Janet's advice and hold her tongue. She'd play Westfield's game until she left for vacation. Maybe Janet's contacts could provide her with a new identity. Where would she go? Would Westfield monitor her family if she disappeared? How would she explain to her family that they could never see her again? Could she even tell them that much? She rubbed her knotted neck muscles, stood up, and went to find Janet.

NSA Headquarters – Fort George G. Meade, Maryland – January 25

NSA Special Director General Cecil Westfield took the last drag on his unfiltered cigarette and crushed the butt in the already half-full ashtray. He exhaled the smoke with a slight wheeze. There was a strict no-smoking policy on the NSA campus, which he ignored. He paged through the documents from the folder that had been lying amidst the clutter on his desk until he found Tegan Strong's internal security reports. He wanted to review them again, even though he'd read them three times already.

He scanned the photos taken of Tegan over the years. She hadn't aged, even with the pressures of medical school and her extraordinarily long hours in the lab. She was a dedicated and hard-working member of his team. Childless, he would have liked to have a daughter like Tegan. He thought highly of her, which was why he felt so disappointed in her now. He knew what had to be done. As he read the transcript of the recorded conversation between Vasine and Tegan in the break room, he grew angrier.

The NSA was very good at obtaining anything that was in electronic or signal-transmitted format. He monitored his people in every office, cubicle, and room by either camera or secreted microphones. In addition, the Comprehensive National Cybersecurity Initiative (CNCI) Data Center located at Camp Williams, twenty-five miles south of Salt Lake City, Utah, could remotely retrieve anything entered on any computer. The forensic keystroke algorithm software, developed and refined over the years, allowed for reconstructive data mining. The NSA could access, retrieve, and analyze any information ever entered on any computer connected to a network.

NSA cybersecurity technicians learned that the easiest way into any system was to build access into the original operating design and social network sites. In addition, the NSA embedded data-mining software into routine upgrades, which were usually daily downloads on most business and home computer systems. The challenge was accessing secure networks on foreign soil, but there were ways to crack those systems as well. As an additional access portal, the NSA had designed some of the name-brand virus protection software. No firewalls or passwords prevented the NSA from obtaining any information they desired. There were no secrets in cyberspace or in any space around Cecil Westfield. He and his team could go anywhere and do anything in the interest of national security, and they were very good at their job. His team would be eliminated if they weren't the best.

Westfield intercepted and reviewed everything his personnel entered into their computers or said over the phone, whether they were at work or at home. A voice recognition system and a special algorithm searched for keywords and phrases. Once analyzed, the information was encrypted, then forwarded to Westfield for review. He knew that some of his staff suspected he intercepted their personal communications based on suggestive comments they would send to one another. However, he never took their bait, so suspicions remained unconfirmed. He didn't particularly care to sort through the minutia of their personal life, but this was the only way to ensure the level of internal security he demanded. Those reviews contributed to his long workdays and solitary existence.

It had been during a routine wash of intercepted audio files that the system had flagged Tegan's and Janet's conversation. For some reason the conversation was not tagged as a priority intercept. Westfield had received the transcript of their conversation attached to the weekly summary review. If only he had received the transcript earlier, he would have had a different option.

General Cecil Westfield was officially assigned to the NSA, but he didn't really work for them. His commission was founded on a long forgotten, "born classified" executive directive signed by President Truman in 1947, when Dark Moon was created. True to President Truman's wishes, Dark Moon operations remained hidden from the public. Every intelligence-gathering operation Dark Moon had ever conducted remained classified.

Presidential oversight of Dark Moon had been lost decades earlier. President Truman had briefed Dwight D. Eisenhower on Dark Moon's mission parameters when he became president in 1953. Eisenhower hadn't been surprised to learn about the existence of aliens. Many years earlier, while aboard a ship, he'd reportedly witnessed a glowing blue craft rise from the ocean and disappear into the heavens. President Kennedy was the last president briefed on Dark Moon's mission. He'd taken a keen interest in the possibility of interaction with creatures from another world. He even met with Dark Moon's first commander, Colonel Alfred Schneider, several times during his first few months in office.

Colonel Schneider had grown concerned when Kennedy gave his putting-a-man-on-the-moon speech to a joint session of Congress in 1961, followed a year later by his memorable man-to-the-moon oration given at Rice University. Kennedy had pushed to have Dark Moon placed under Air Force command. Schneider had strongly disagreed, warning that

Dark Moon would face the risk of compromise. Nevertheless, Kennedy had been relentless, until his assassination in 1963.

When Westfield took command and reviewed the files on President Kennedy, he realized how much power he could use to protect the interests of the United States. After Kennedy's assassination, Dark Moon fell off the presidential radar. The Secretary of Defense and the chairman of the Atomic Energy Commission had decided that in light of recent global events it would best be kept under their control. President Lyndon Johnson never knew about Dark Moon. No requirement under the executive directive that had established Dark Moon obligated them to tell President Johnson anything. It was the duty of the outgoing president to brief the incoming one.

In 1965, the Secretary of Defense decided to modify the controlling chain of command. With the Vietnam War escalating, he exercised his authority and delegated control of S-3 operations, including Dark Moon, to the director of the NSA. The Secretary of Defense requested notification of any operational developments requiring a military response.

In 1977, President Jimmy Carter created the Office of Secretary of Energy. From that time forward, the DOE secretary and NSA director were the only people in the loop. President Truman's original executive directive granting Dark Moon's real power and authority remained hidden deep in the Department of Energy archives.

Westfield was only the fourth person to command Dark Moon, and he would choose his successor when it was time to step aside, which he knew would be soon. His age and recently diagnosed medical condition, combined with the grueling fourteen-hour days and the daily stress and demands of the job, required him to find a replacement. His lungs were failing, the consequence of smoking since Operation Desert Storm. Even after his diagnosis of cancer, he refused to stop smoking. His dark complexion and cropped gray hair helped him appear younger, but Westfield certainly felt his years. He did his best to stay in shape, exercising his six-foot frame when he found time, but he knew his lung cancer would eventually take his life. He did not intend to die in a hospital or nursing home. He was a warrior, and he would die a warrior's death, by his own hand, if necessary.

Westfield was a patriot, as was his father and grandfather. He'd grown up listening to the story of how his father had been engaged in a firefight during the Tet Offensive in Vietnam while his mother gave birth to him. His father was a Marine, as was his grandfather, so he was destined to be a Marine. At an early age, Westfield decided that since he had entered this world while his father fought for his country, he would follow his father's path and dedicate himself to the protection of this nation. That was his duty.

Westfield had graduated from the U.S. Naval Academy and commissioned a butter-bar second lieutenant in the Marine Corps. He soon found himself as a platoon leader. His first engagement in combat was during the "shock and awe" campaign to liberate Kuwait from Iraq. During an intense firefight, he realized that he was doing what he had been born to do. He enjoyed the camaraderie and the work he did in the Marine Corps. It was in his blood. It was his life.

He'd served almost ten years in the Corps when his predecessor, General Robert Blakely, recruited him to join Dark Moon. Westfield was shocked to learn that his duty was not only to protect the United States, but the entire world. The magnitude of his responsibility was daunting. No military commander had ever faced a more terrifying enemy. It was obvious from his review of the historical case files that the creatures possessed amazing technology, and they seemed to be probing the planet's defenses.

Over the years, Westfield continued to receive promotions as if he had never left the Corps. He reminded himself every day that he was a Marine and that his service in Dark Moon kept his country safe. His office at the NSA sported a Marine Corps theme, right down to the Marine Corps standard, placed next to the American flag, behind his desk. He assumed command of Dark Moon at the turn of the new millennium, just before the attack on the twin towers and the Pentagon. He desperately wanted to take revenge on those responsible, and he knew with the resources at his disposal, he could strike at the heart of the demon. It was during this time of darkness, when the country needed him most, that he felt the most impotent. Yet he understood the imperative for anonymity.

Westfield laid Tegan's file back on the desk, lit another cigarette, and took a deep drag, holding the smoke in his lungs. There was no doubt in his mind she was going to try to go off the grid. She was putting her exit strategy together, and he couldn't allow that to happen, not with her knowledge of Deep Sky. It was his responsibility to see she wouldn't become a liability.

There was a loud knock on his office door.

"Come in, John," Westfield commanded, knowing who was on the other side. He wasn't clairvoyant. John Grant was there because he had summoned him.

Master Gunnery Sergeant John Grant entered the smoke-filled room and stood at attention. Westfield told him to sit. He took a seat in an old chair opposite Westfield's oversized and scarred wooden desk. The desk was a relic left over from World War II. It was the first desk Colonel Schneider had used when he took the reins of Dark Moon.

Westfield gazed at the combat-hardened warrior for a moment. Grant's cold, gray eyes, coupled with the jagged scar on his chin and bald head, gave him a menacing appearance. Grant had reported to Westfield for over thirty years.

They had made their own rules in Iraq and in some other unfriendly places around the globe. This secret war was no different, except the enemy was harder to find. They needed an assassin, which is how Grant had earned his operational moniker, Osiris. At five foot ten, and built like a fireplug, he filled the chair in which he was sitting. He sat ramrod straight, not looking his sixty years. Westfield knew that Grant prided himself on being able to keep up with any Special Forces operator. Grant's marksmanship as a sniper would have made him a living legend if he hadn't been assigned to Dark Moon. He was a true Marine who didn't give a shit about being politically correct and got the job done at any cost.

"You wanted to see me, General," Grant stated, more than asked.

"Yes. It seems we have an internal security concern with two of our biologics. Start with Strong," he said, passing Grant the file.

"Dr. Strong appears ready to jump ship. She's on her way to her family's ranch. It's supposed to be for a family vacation, but information has come to light that indicates she intends to seek a permanent separation from service. I want you to help her in her quest."

Westfield lit another cigarette. "An accident would be fitting, I think. I'm not sure if she plans on disclosing her work activities, so her family should be considered a risk factor as well. I would have liked you to take care of her here, but I only learned of her traitorous intent a few hours ago. I want you on the company plane and headed for her ranch as soon as possible. I guess it's only fair she gets to visit her family one last time. Use your own discretion on ingress and egress from the area, and take whatever time and equipment you'll need to get the job done, quietly."

Westfield leaned back in his well-worn leather chair. The arms and seat cushion were dotted with numerous cigarette burn marks. He looked Grant squarely in the eyes. "Do you have any questions, Master Guns?"

"No, sir, I do not."

"Good." Westfield knew that Grant understood his orders—neutralize the entire family. "When you get back, we'll deal with another target."

After a quick review of Tegan's file, Grant said, "I'll make it a clean sweep. Who is the other target?"

"Dr. Janet Vasine. She has been a growing pain in my ass over the last few months. She's having a negative influence on her staff and is responsible for Strong jumping ship. I wish to make an example of her, so she will need to be done very publicly.

Westfield stubbed out his half-smoked cigarette in the overflowing ashtray. "Osiris, I've decided you won't be responsible for her termination." He knew that would ruffle his friend's feathers. "I'll make those arrangements myself. I have a recruit I want to test. We'll see if he has the balls to do this kind of work. If he does, he'll be yours to mold."

Grant nodded.

Westfield could tell what he was thinking by the look on his face. "John, it's time to start thinking about slowing down. We need to recruit our successors and give them time to absorb what it is we do. I'll need you to oversee and evaluate Dr. Vasine's termination. If my recruit does well, I'll need you to begin training him. He needs indoctrination as quickly as possible. If he doesn't live up to my expectations, you can handle the sanction. Are we clear?"

"Yes, sir."

"Tegan was a special one, with so much to offer," Westfield said in a soft, almost distant voice. "A real shame she has chosen this path. I missed the signs for a while. Now Vasine has managed to turn Tegan against me right under my nose, and at a very critical time. I will miss Tegan. As for

Vasine," he said, switching to the voice of a hardened killer, "if given the opportunity, I'd piss on her grave. Read the transcript of their conversation."

Grant pulled the transcript from the file and read. Then he studied Tegan's newest photo and her background information. He took an occasional note and then gave the folder back to Westfield.

"I will confirm the kill," Grant said without emotion. "I assume you want video for file, as usual."

"Not this time, John. Just make it quick and painless, if possible. With the family out of the picture, cleanup at their ranch should be easy. I'll handle the electronic sweep and erasure once you confirm the kill."

Grant nodded.

"Dismissed," said Westfield.

John Grant stood at attention, held it for a second, then turned crisply and left the office without making a sound.

Westfield sighed heavily. With Deep Sky stabilized, the research phase was complete. Now he needed to test the virus. He decided to skip the animal testing and move directly to human subjects. He would task one of the other, less squeamish, biologics to conduct the tests, then ready the weapon for deployment, should the need arise.

Westfield closed Tegan's file and rummaged around for the other brief he wanted to reread. He picked up First Lady Sandra Collingsworth's file. The report said that Samuel Kidd, the chief waiter, had heard her cry out just after dinner. When he went to check on her, she looked quite shaken. The president had told him his wife had been startled. Of particular interest was that Kidd reported seeing a strange yellow flash of light at the same time as the First Lady's scream, but there was no evidence of a source, and no one else had mentioned anything.

Westfield looked through the medical report one more time, feeling as if he was missing something. Mrs. Collingsworth had no signs of trauma, and the toxicology screening found no drugs in her system. Her cholesterol was normal, as was her blood pressure. She exercised regularly, had never smoked, and by all accounts was healthy. *She was not at risk for a stroke*, he thought. Yet she was at Bethesda Naval Hospital in a coma, with limited brain activity, and the doctors had no explanation for her condition. Westfield knew there was more to the story, especially in light of President Jackson's mysterious exit from office and his return to Lincoln, Nebraska.

He'd reviewed Jackson's medical files. Jackson was in good health, with no known medical condition, and even his Secret Service detail reports indicated he was fit. The public may have bought the story of his resigning because of health reasons, but Westfield didn't. There was something going on.

He couldn't quite put his finger on it, but he had learned to trust his gut instincts. The yellow light Samuel Kidd saw was an unusual detail that could have been nothing more than a simple reflection. Nothing pointed to any alien involvement, so this was more a matter of interest for him than a priority. He decided to give his subconscious time to ruminate on the incident. He knew the Secret Service and the FBI had assigned agents to investigate. He would let them dig for a while and then hack their files.

FOUR

Leavenworth, Washington — January 26 — 1000 hours

John Grant was flying to Wenatchee, Washington, in a Gulfstream G350. The whine of the jet's twin engines dropped an octave, signaling they were starting their approach to the Pangborn Memorial Airport. He stowed his MPad computer and walked to the cockpit. As an instrument-rated pilot, he admired the precision the senior pilot demonstrated as he shot the ILS approach, followed by a soft landing.

"Very nice," Grant said to the two pilots as they went through their after-landing checklist.

"Thank you, sir," the senior pilot replied.

Grant returned to the cabin and gathered up his gear. A few moments later, the jet came to a stop at an executive jet center. He was anxious to begin reconnoitering the area around the Strong ranch, but as he disembarked the aircraft, he took a moment to enjoy the crisp air and the beauty of the snow-covered mountains. He could already feel the bloodlust building just thinking about the hunt.

While the copilot offloaded the sophisticated electronic equipment and explosives he'd brought to deal with the Strong family, Grant walked across the tarmac and entered the lobby of the fixed-base operator building.

An attractive, twenty-something woman behind the counter smiled at him and said, "Good morning, sir. Did you have a good flight?"

"It was fine, thank you. I reserved an SUV. The last name is Jones," he replied, handing over his fictitious identification. Grant thought back to the days when he would have had her out of her blue business suit in less than thirty minutes. However, he had not felt that yearning for some time now.

"I have a Honda Pilot with four-wheel drive all ready for you. It's the gray one parked just to the right of the exit. You can't miss it."

Grant nodded, signed the rental agreement, and took the keys.

The copilot approached him, pulling two military-grade hard-shell cases. "Leave those with me. Go get the rest of the equipment, then meet me outside by the gray Honda Pilot."

"Do you need any help with those?" the attendant asked, smiling sweetly.

"No, I can handle them." He slung his duffle over his shoulder, grabbed both cases, and headed for the SUV.

He loaded the one hundred pound cases into the back of the vehicle and threw his duffle in on top of them. The copilot arrived and handed him two small cases.

"That's all the gear from the plane, sir."

Grant knew that the copilot was waiting for instructions. "Proceed to SeaTac, refuel, and find a place to stay near the airport. I will need extraction in a few days. I'll let you know where and when to pick me up. When I call, I want you en route within an hour." He planned to be airborne as soon as possible after Tegan and her family were dead.

"Yes, sir." The copilot walked back through the FBO and out to the plane.

Grant left the airport and headed west on Highway 97 for the forty-minute drive to Leavenworth. The small, Bavarian-themed town, nestled in the Cascade Mountains, would serve as his base of operations. This time of year, there would be tourists everywhere, and he would blend into the background. Most of the hotels were booked, but he had been able to secure a reservation at a quaint hotel on the west side of town.

Because of the intercept on Tegan's phone, he knew the location of the ski lodge where the family would be staying and that they'd be taking her father's Toyota Sequoia to get there. The only thing Tegan hadn't discussed with Megan was the route, but based on his research, he was fairly certain the family would take Icicle Road to get to the lodge.

The operational plan was simple. Using a remotely triggered explosive, he'd kill them when they were all together in the SUV while en route to the lodge. He planned to follow them until they reached the place on the winding mountain road he'd selected from satellite images, then detonate the untraceable MilEx G2B explosive devices he'd attach to the vehicle's steering mechanism and brakes before they left for the lodge. Nothing fancy or elaborate, and he could make their deaths look like an accident. The Sequoia, with its high center of gravity, would be uncontrollable after the steering and brakes stopped functioning. He hoped a little ice on the road would complete the picture for the police investigation. The fire from the explosion would hide any evidence of his handiwork.

Grant's compulsive and methodical work ethic forced him to dissect every kill he was assigned. He was always looking for ways to improve his craftsmanship and considered every possible variable before execution. As a precaution, he always had a contingency plan ready in case something went wrong. *A bullet would be so much easier,* he thought, but Westfield didn't want this to be a public execution, and he wanted to please his boss.

He'd studied the topographic map of the area around the Strong ranch and compared it to the most recent satellite images. For the surveillance of the Strong property, he'd use the new KX5 audio/video equipment concealed in the cases behind him. The distance between the Strong ranch and his hotel was twenty miles, well within the KX5's operational range. He had considered using a specialized stealth drone to orbit over the ranch for surveillance, but decided it wasn't necessary. The same was true with tasking a satellite to feed him continuous imagery, but too many people would be involved in that type of operation. Besides, he didn't need that much support for this assignment. He planned to do this the old-fashioned way. He'd have to spend some time in the woods doing the creep and peek to find a suitable site to set up the KX5, then he could watch the property remotely.

Grant found the hotel and checked in. His room was on the top floor, facing south, ideal for what he needed. He retrieved the monitoring equipment and his duffle from the SUV and left the rest of the gear in the back.

After setting up the monitoring equipment, he left the hotel and drove through the center of town. People strolled along the sidewalks and peered into the windows of specialty stores on the main strip. He wondered what it would be like to be that carefree. Maybe after he retired he would experience that sensation. He put that thought aside and headed south.

The ranch was located on the west side of a two-lane highway. As he drove by, he spotted a pickup truck by the barn, but saw no one outside. He turned around about a half mile from the ranch and drove by the property again, then pulled off at a scenic overlook about a mile north of the ranch. After twenty minutes, he was still alone in the secluded parking area. He'd counted twenty-six cars drive past the overlook, and no one noticed his Honda. He got out, transferred the KX5 to the mountain pack, hiked across the highway, and disappeared into the dense vegetation.

He moved easily across the snowless terrain, although he could see there was some in the higher elevations. He used the trees and brush for cover as he moved stealthily, circumnavigating the forty-acre property. After a few hours, he found the best location to conceal the KX5. It took him only a few minutes to assemble the camera housing and get the system sighted. The laser rangefinder indicated the house was 1,400 yards to the south and 238 feet below him. He used camouflage netting and foliage to hide the KX5, its power unit, and the satellite dish transmitter he needed for the remote data feed. The location provided him a clear view of the windows on the north and west sides of the house, the barn, the driveway, and all the exterior doors of the residence except one. There was a blind spot behind the detached garage, but he figured he could monitor any activity around the ranch with the remote motion sensors he'd place at the entrance to the driveway. The back door of the house, which was used to reach the detached garage, wasn't visible from the KX5's position either, but anyone who came out of that door would be visible as soon as they came around the corner of the garage. Once they were clear of the garage, the KX5's enhanced optics could easily identify the vehicle and its occupants. He decided this area wasn't a factor.

Sunset came early this time of year. The sky gradually turned dark while he sat next to the KX5, watching the ranch and the surrounding area. The crisp air and the thrill of the mission energized him as he observed Tegan's sister and mother walk from the barn back to the house. He noted which rooms in the house had lights on. He checked the audio reception from the laser microphone, then confirmed that the low-light and infrared images were being transmitted back to the hotel. Now he could watch and listen in the comfort of his hotel room. He made one final systems check. Finding no anomalies, he crept down to the driveway and placed the motion sensors, then headed back to his car.

In his hotel room, Grant worked the high-resolution digital zoom lens, which gave him not only great close-ups but also a wide-angle field of view of the property. He tested the infrared thermal settings, using the llamas and alpacas in the pasture as targets. The optics provided excellent imaging even in the darkness. He zoomed in to get a close-up view of a llama's head and found that even in the reduced light he could still see the animal's facial features. The system's facial recognition software could compare any photographic image with those in the NSA databanks and confirm an identity within minutes. He wondered what the software would do with the face of a llama. *Better not try,* he thought. *General Westfield wouldn't find the humor in it.*

Satisfied with the performance of the equipment, he poured himself a scotch from the small bottle he'd taken from the minibar. Propping a pillow up on the bed, he lay down with the monitor next to him and observed the activity at the ranch. Tegan wasn't scheduled to arrive until early tomorrow, so he had time to relax.

He was on his third drink when he received an electronic alert informing him that Tegan was airborne on the overnight flight from Dulles. He knew her flight number and scheduled arrival time. She would not get to the ranch until late the next morning. He muted the audio and fell asleep.

Leavenworth — January 27 — 0630 hours

Grant awakened to the sound of the alert when Megan tripped the sensor when she left the ranch and headed for the airport. He knew the round trip would take a good four hours. He showered, dressed, and left for the ranch.

Later, he was standing next to the KX5 and communing with nature. He'd just finished eating a power bar when he saw Tegan and Megan pull into the driveway. The SUV stopped in front of the house, and the happy family greeted one another. After witnessing the tearful reunion, he knew that Westfield had been right to order a clean sweep.

During the first few hours of monitoring, he'd discovered an audio black hole which corresponded with his visual blind spot. There wasn't anything he could do about it now.

He patiently monitored the family for hours, noting that Tegan never mentioned her real work. All she told the family was that she was thinking about taking a World Health Organization position in France. He could tell the family wasn't pleased to hear this news. Her pitch about experiencing a new culture and making a higher salary seemed to fall short of convincing them it was a good idea. It didn't matter. They would all be together for eternity soon enough.

The conversations he intercepted confirmed they would be traveling to the lodge the next morning as one big happy family, taking the Sequoia, as expected. He was also pleased to learn that their route was the one he was expecting them to take. Mr. Strong was attentive to details in planning their vacation activities, and apparently he liked sharing his travel plans with everyone. *Good for me, bad for them*, Grant thought.

Grant left his vantage point, returned to his car, and drove the route the Strongs would take the next day. He stopped at the location he'd selected for the accident to occur. It was on a sharp, downward-sloping curve. On the other side of the guardrail was a deep crevasse. This was where the Strong's SUV would plow through the guardrail and make the three-hundred-foot drop to the rocky floor below. Grant knew there would be no survivors.

Local law enforcement would investigate the accident and determine it was a horrible tragedy. The only variable he could not control was other vehicular traffic. Witnesses might see the explosive charges detonate under the car, but he'd deal with that if and when the time came. It took only a few minutes for him to sabotage the guardrail. Not a single car had driven past him.

When Grant returned to the ranch later that night, he saw that the Sequoia was outside the garage, which he interpreted as a good omen. He wouldn't have to break into the garage to sabotage the vehicle. In less than seven minutes, he had placed the explosives on the SUV. He smiled to himself as he jogged back to the woods. *It was a shame Westfield had not wanted it recorded*, he thought. *It was going to be a work of art.*

Leavenworth — January 28 — 0530 hours

Grant experienced the same restlessness he'd had the night before. The remote sensors had gone off several times, and each time he awoke to watch small animals and deer wandering around the property. He took a shower, shut down the monitor in the room, activated the smaller hand-held version of the remote, and stuffed it into his mountain pack. Today, he would make his kill.

Strong Ranch — 0630 hours

Tegan looked out the window as she walked into the kitchen. "Why is the Sequoia out of the garage?"

"I moved it out last night so I could get to the skis," William Strong said with a sly smile.

She looked at her mother and could tell her parents were up to something. "Okay, what's going on?" Tegan asked.

"I think you and Megan should go out and check the garage," William said. He sounded as if he was telling them to go check under the Christmas tree. Irene's smile was telling.

Tegan looked at Megan, who only shrugged, and they walked out the back door.

"Do you have any idea what they're up to?" Tegan asked her sister.

"Not a clue."

Tegan heard a car door close just as she lifted the garage door.

"Surprise!" Alessia Stryker yelled.

"Oh, my God!" Megan and Tegan said in unison.

Alessia, Tegan, and Megan had been inseparable during high school, and Alessia had spent so much time with the Strong family that she had earned the nickname the "Third Twin." Alessia's hair was long and blond, and her resemblance to Tegan and Megan was remarkable. Alessia had parked her new yellow Mustang in the garage so they wouldn't see it just moments earlier.

When Tegan turned to her parents, she could tell they were enjoying the moment. "How did you pull this off?"

"I called Alessia and made the arrangements just after you confirmed you were coming home," Irene said. "I wanted to surprise you both. I guess I succeeded."

"You certainly did," answered Tegan.

The girls talked excitedly, catching up as if they were still teenagers. Tegan hadn't seen Alessia for over three years. For a moment she forgot that her life was going to be different very soon. The look on her mother's face had broken her heart last night when she told her about moving to France. She felt the warmth of being with her family again, even if it was for only a short time, and she planned to make the most of their time together.

As the excitement abated, William asked, "Are we ready to go?"

"All I need is to get my suitcase in the car," Alessia answered.

"I just need to grab my purse," Tegan said.

"Ditto," Megan added.

"I've arranged for an early check-in so we can get some skiing in this morning," William said.

"That sounds great," Tegan said, walking toward the backdoor.

Grant parked at the scenic overlook. He pulled the handheld monitor out of his pack. He noticed that both the audio and alert tone switches were disabled. *That explains why it had been so quiet,* he thought. The switches had been accidently turned off when he put the monitor into the pack. All of the audio and video since then was lost. A design flaw he would have to mention to the engineers. When Grant turned the monitor on, he felt a jolt of panic. There was no conversation emanating from inside the house.

He zoomed in the camera and could still see the edge of the Sequoia's bumper sticking out from behind the garage. A minute later, Mr. Strong walked around the front of the SUV, and then he heard his deep voice briefly. He could tell that the family was getting ready to leave. *They're outside already. Timing is everything*, he thought.

Grant couldn't see or hear anyone standing behind the garage. The audio and visual dead zone was proving to be more of a problem than he'd anticipated. He pointed the audio laser at the kitchen window. A few seconds later, he heard Tegan and Megan talking inside the house.

"What a nice surprise," Tegan said.

"It sure is," Megan replied. "You ready?"

"I am."

Their voices dropped off as they entered the dead zone behind the garage. *I wonder what the surprise was. It doesn't matter. They will all be dead soon.* He decided to stay at the overlook, knowing the family would pass by his location. He was close enough to the road to be able to confirm all targets were in the vehicle. He would follow at a discreet distance until they reached the planned execution site and then take care of business.

Megan and Alessia jumped into the backseat of the Sequoia. Tegan was about to get in when her cell phone rang. She opened her purse, recognizing it was Janet's ring tone. She threw her purse onto the backseat next to Alessia and answered the call.

"Hello," Tegan said.

"I know this is probably a bad time, but I need some information," Janet said.

Tegan thought Janet's voice sounded stressed. Realizing her mother could hear her, Tegan walked away from the car, toward the back of the house. "Is there a problem?" Tegan asked.

"I need access to your personal files on Deep Sky," Janet replied.

"Why?" Tegan asked, feeling concerned.

"I was instructed, early this morning, to secure all information on the project, with specific instructions to get all of your personal files."

"Let me call you right back. We're getting ready to leave for the lodge. I need to work out some things here before I can talk freely."

"I understand," Janet said, and hung up.

$$\infty$$

Grant saw Tegan walk away from the garage, talking on the phone. He realigned the audio laser to get a better angle for reception, but was able to hear only the last few words Tegan spoke before she walked into the dead zone. He sensed he'd missed something important. He hit the speed dial button on his satellite phone and contacted the NSA Intercepts Officer assigned to his section. He'd soon know the identity of Tegan's caller.

$$\infty$$

Crap! Tegan thought as she walked back to the Sequoia. *Now what do I do?* She could tell that everyone was anxious to get under way. "Guys, I'm really sorry, but I'll have to meet you all there. There's an emergency at work, and I need to use my laptop. The Wi-Fi is just too sketchy and unreliable in the mountains, and this could take a while." Tegan opened the back hatch, put her phone down, and retrieved her laptop. When she turned around, she saw the disappointed look on her mother's face. She closed the hatch and walked over to her.

"I know you're all disappointed, but hey, this will give the party girls time to catch up. I don't know how long I'll be, but if I'm not at the lodge an hour after you arrive, go have fun without me. I'll find you on the slopes."

Tegan hugged her mother. As an afterthought she said, "Alessia, can I drive your car to the lodge? I really want to check out your new Mustang."

"No problem. I left the keys in it."

"Great, thanks."

Tegan waved and blew them a kiss as they left. She walked into the garage and closed the door, feeling the chill in the air. The weather was changing. Dark, ominous clouds were building to the west. She could tell there was snow in them, which was good for the slopes but not for driving.

Tegan suddenly realized she had left her cell phone and purse in the Sequoia. "Shit!" She walked over to the Mustang and saw Alessia's purse sitting on the passenger seat. *Well, at least I wasn't the only one caught up in the moment,* she thought. She opened Alessia's purse and found her phone inside. The keys were in the ignition as she had said. *Problem solved.*

Grant watched the Sequoia on the monitor and counted four heads as the vehicle drove down the driveway to the main road. The vehicle turned north, as expected. He waited impatiently for the vehicle to pass. When it did, he saw Irene and William were in the front. Megan and Tegan were in the backseat. *All were present and accounted for*, he thought. He remotely shut down the KX5, seeing no reason to leave it on, then pulled out on to the highway and followed the SUV at a discreet distance.

He planned to wait for the target vehicle to get close to the selected spot before he moved in behind it and triggered the charges. He'd decided to blow out both tires on the right side and the steering tie rods, to make sure the vehicle would hit the guardrail before anyone could react. He'd also added a little something extra next to the fuel tank to prevent anyone from bailing out at the last minute. Once the explosives detonated, the weight of the Sequoia, combined with the limited reaction time and the momentum of the vehicle, would be sufficient to carry it over the cliff. Grant's adrenaline surged into his bloodstream as the vehicle approached Icicle Road. He closed the distance.

Tegan dialed Janet's untraceable cell phone, making a mental note to make sure Janet ditched the phone, just in case Alessia got an itemized bill with the number on it.

"Yes," Janet answered. She didn't sound like herself. The stress in her voice was obvious.

"It's me. Can you talk?"

"Go ahead."

Tegan gave Janet the access codes to her files, and Janet immediately disconnected without a good-bye, before Tegan could tell her to ditch the phone.

Something was wrong. Tegan got a funny feeling in the pit of her stomach. She opened the garage door, jumped into the Mustang, and wondered if she could catch up to her family before they got to the lodge. After backing out of the garage, she closed the garage door, then jumped back into the car. When she hit the pavement, she stomped on the accelerator, smoking the tires. A wave of anxiety fell over her. It was a fear she couldn't explain, like a premonition that something bad was going to happen.

Grant drew closer to the Sequoia as it approached the curve. When he saw the SUV's brake lights, he triggered the explosives. The car jumped with the force of the blast. Trailing smoke, it swerved sharply and plowed through the guardrail. A second later, Grant triggered the fuel tank charge. The SUV, engulfed in flames, hurtled over the edge and dropped straight down the cliff to the bottom of the ravine. *I am the bringer of death*, he thought.

With no other cars on the road, he stopped and walked to the edge of the cliff. He leaned out as far as he could, but saw no sign of the vehicle. Only a wisp of dark smoke blown away by the wind marked the crash site. He was sure there were no survivors. Grant took one last look around. Mission accomplished.

The satellite phone beeped just as he got back into the Honda. He answered and listened as the technician explained that the call to Tegan originated at the Maryland biolab. The technician went into great technical detail about how they had traced the call and how it had come from an unknown burner phone. Grant wanted to know who had called Tegan, but the technician couldn't provide that information. Feeling annoyed, he hung up, pulled out on to the roadway, and dialed Westfield.

"Yes?" Westfield answered.

"Target terminated. Four confirmed."

"Any complications?"

"No, sir, it went like clockwork," Grant said, then added without emotion, "She didn't suffer."

"That's good."

"There is one thing which may require some follow-up. Tegan received a call from an undetermined source that originated at the biolab just before she left the ranch."

"That's interesting. I think I know who it may have been. Thank you, Osiris. I will take care of it."

"Is there anything else you need, sir?"

"Sweep the ranch for anything Tegan may have left behind. After that, your work is done." Westfield hung up.

Grant took a different route back to the ranch, enjoying the feeling of completing another successful op. He contacted the pilot as he drove on to the Strong ranch and told him to pick him up at the Pangborn airport in three hours. He'd sweep the ranch, retrieve the KX5, and head back to the inn to settle up.

Cascade Mountains – Ski Lodge

Tegan tried calling her mom as she pushed down harder on the accelerator. It went to voicemail. She tried all the other cells with the same result. She drove the same route she knew her family had taken. She pulled into the lodge parking lot, wondering why she had not caught up to them, then cruised around, but could not find the Sequoia. She parked in front of the entrance and walked into the lobby.

"Excuse me, has the Strong party checked in yet?" she asked the desk clerk.

The young woman smiled and said, "No, not yet. Are you with their party?"

Tegan hesitated for a moment. She didn't know why. "I was supposed to meet them here. I'll just wait outside for them, thanks." Tegan returned to the car. Something was terribly wrong. She could feel it.

She dialed Megan's cell again, and it went straight to voicemail, something that rarely happened twice. She didn't leave a message. She called her own cell phone, then her mom's and dad's again. There was no response. Panic gripped her as she sped out of the parking lot and headed back toward home. She thought back to her conversation with Janet. Her tone of voice had been unusual. *Was she trying to warn me?* she wondered. Janet hadn't used the danger code phrase they'd agreed on.

As Tegan rounded a sharp curve on Icicle Road, she noticed part of a metal guardrail was missing. She parked on the side of the road and got out. A strange odor tainted the air. She saw no skid marks, but the grass that fringed the road appeared scorched. Two distinct tread marks in the dirt lead to the gap in the guardrail. They looked as if a large vehicle had made them. Her blood went cold.

Tegan followed the tire marks to the edge of the cliff and looked down. She didn't see anything unusual. *It's not possible,* she thought. *I'm just being paranoid.*

"Hello? Is there anyone down there?" A soft echo was the only reply. She walked back to the car, got in, and sat for a while in silence. She dialed all of the cell phone numbers again, but they all went to voicemail. She tried the house number, thinking that maybe they had gone back there. The answering machine picked up. Tegan didn't leave a message.

As snow began to fall in light flutters, Tegan started the Mustang and headed for home. Alessia's cell rang, startling her, but she felt a rush of relief.

"Hello?"

"Everything okay there?" Janet asked in a hushed voice.

"I thought you were my parents. They never made it to the ski lodge. How did you get this number?"

"You called me from it earlier, and since you weren't answering your phone, I thought it was worth a shot."

"You sounded funny earlier. What's going on?"

"Where are you?"

"I'm on the road, headed back to the ranch. They aren't answering their cell phones. I'm really worried something has happened."

Silence.

"Janet, did you hear what I said?"

"Yes. I heard you. I'm very sorry. I wish you the best of luck, with all of my heart." She hung up.

Tegan's heart raced. This time Janet had used the code phrase. *All of my heart* meant that she should disappear, immediately and permanently. Tegan drove the rest of the way back to the ranch as fast as she could.

As she approached the driveway, she slowed, and was preparing to turn when she saw a gray Honda SUV parked beside the garage. Movement caught her eye. She let out a whimpered gasp. Westfield's stocky security man was walking toward the barn. She knew her family wasn't coming home.

Tegan accelerated away, driving another mile as tremors rocked her body. Fearing they would grow worse, she pulled into the neighbor's driveway. She sat there trying to regain control of the panic. She panted as she broke into a cold sweat. Tegan knew she was on the verge of a full-fledged anxiety attack and needed to find the strength to beat it back. She opened the driver's door and vomited. Her heart pounded. The pain in her chest was becoming unbearable. She focused on the center of the steering wheel and breathed slowly for a minute, counting to eight between each inhale and exhale. The pain and cramping in her chest gradually subsided, and her heart rate slowed. Her experience with meditation had arrested the attack, and her focus returned, as did the crushing reality of what had happened.

She closed the car door, her hands still trembling. There was no doubt they were dead. Tegan felt it in every fiber of her being. She couldn't stem the flow of tears, knowing she was responsible for the deaths of those she held most dear.

Tegan backed out on to the highway and headed back toward the ranch. She needed to take one more look at her home, regardless of the risk. As she passed the driveway, she could see he was leaving. She knew she'd never go back to the ranch after today. She accelerated, continuing north toward Leavenworth. She needed to find a place to stay where no one knew her. Tegan Strong could exist no more.

Snoqualmie Falls, Washington – February 7

Tegan sat on a lumpy bed in a cheap motel room, watching TV. Her shock had turned to a vengeful resolve as she listened to the news report she had dreaded. Stained vertical blinds covered the front window of the musty room. They matched the shabby look of everything else. She thought the depressing place was symbolic of her life now.

The young newswoman was reporting live from the scene on Icicle Road. Tegan recognized the spot. The reporter said that four people had perished in a tragic car accident. She gave no names, pending identification and notification of the next of kin. The newswoman said State Transportation Department workers had found the vehicle, a Toyota Sequoia, when they went to repair a guardrail. The workers had used a small drone to check the bottom of the crevasse and found the burned-out vehicle. The newswoman added that everyone inside the vehicle was ash. Tegan wanted to throttle the cold-hearted little bitch and throw her off a cliff. That was her family she was talking about, not actors in some late-night horror movie.

Tegan knew that her phone, purse, and identification were in the Sequoia. If they had survived the fire, Westfield would surely get a report listing the items, which would confirm she was one of the dead. If not, he would assume that anyway. She'd thrown her laptop into a shallow creek before she got to Leavenworth. No one would ever find that again. Tegan turned off the television and wept.

So far, she'd had no trouble using Alessia's identification and credit cards. She and Alessia looked so much alike that no one ever gave her identification a second glance. Alessia had no family. Her parents had perished in a freak motorcycle accident just after she started high school. Her great aunt had taken her in, but had thrown her out of the house the day she turned eighteen. After that, Alessia had shown up on the Strongs' doorstep, and she soon became an adopted daughter and sister.

Tegan remembered Megan telling her that Alessia had broken up with her boyfriend a few months back, so he wouldn't look for her. If Tegan was going to keep the charade going, she needed to come up with an explanation for Alessia leaving the area permanently. She wasn't sure about Alessia's social life, but with her Department of Defense clearance she would be missed at Boeing, where she worked. Eventually someone would make inquiries and file a missing person report. With Alessia being listed as a reference on Tegan's security background check, she couldn't risk Westfield making the connection.

The Strong ranch and their family possessions would no doubt end up with Uncle Curtis, her mom's alcoholic lowlife brother, since her father was an only child. Curtis lived in Portland. She was certain he and his family would move to the ranch and enjoy their newfound wealth. The thought of them pawing through her family's things made her feel ill, but she couldn't do anything about that now. No way could she go back to the ranch. The risk was too great.

Just before noon, Tegan checked out of the motel and drove to Alessia's upscale apartment complex in Redding. She figured most people would be at work at this time of day. The need for a quiet place where she could plan her future outweighed the risk of someone seeing her. She also desperately needed a change of clothes and hoped Alessia owned a decent laptop.

She pulled into the apartment complex, hoping no one would recognize the Mustang and come running over. She parked in Alessia's numbered parking space, found her apartment and used her key to unlock the door.

When she walked into the apartment, the scent of perfume overwhelmed her. She looked around for a moment. Her home was neat and clean, uncharacteristic of her friend. She checked Alessia's phone messages. There weren't any. She relaxed a little and decided to take a shower in a clean bathroom before she packed up Alessia's clothes and personal items.

After her shower, she found Alessia's passport in a filing cabinet hidden in her closet. She retrieved her bank statements and all the other paperwork with her name on it.

Posing as Alessia, Tegan called human resources at Boeing to inform them she was terminating her employment and wouldn't be returning to the area. The HR associate told her she needed to "exit clear" and return her identification badges before they would release her final paycheck. Tegan told the woman she would mail everything to them, because she was leaving for Maine immediately. After some argument, Tegan abruptly terminated the call, figuring they would get the message.

Next, Tegan called Alessia's apartment management office and told them she was going to be away a few months, but wanted to keep the apartment. She said she'd leave a check on the kitchen counter to cover the rent while she was gone.

Tegan put on a pair of Alessia's jeans and a long-sleeve shirt. She found an old leather jacket tucked in the back of the closet and decided to wear it instead of her own. Once dressed, she drove to the bank where Alessia had an account, choosing a branch away from the apartment, hoping no one there would question her identity. They didn't. She withdrew most of the cash in the account and drove back to the apartment. Tegan managed to get two of Alessia's credit card limits increased. She had the financial resources she'd need to vanish. Now she just needed to decide where to go.

An unopened bottle of Columbia Crest Merlot sat on the kitchen counter. Tegan found a glass, opened the bottle, and then sat down on the sofa in the living room. She hoped a good idea about a destination would strike her. After her third glass of wine, one did.

An image flashed in her mind—an island surrounded by beautiful turquoise water. The place seemed oddly familiar. She couldn't shake the image from her mind as a strong force welled up inside her, a sense that this was the place to go and start a new life as Alessia Stryker. The image in her mind faded as she pondered what had just happened. She looked at her wine glass. Maybe that was the reason.

Tegan moved to the desk, opened Alessia's laptop, and turned it on. She brought up Google Maps and soon found what she was looking for, guided by something she couldn't explain. The island she had pictured in her mind was before her eyes. She knew it would be her new home. Tegan wasn't a religious person, but she felt a spiritual connection to the island. It was as if something on the island was calling to her.

She brought up Expedia and booked the first leg of her flight. She planned to make multiple stops along her route just to be sure she wasn't followed. Eventually, someone would inquire about Alessia, and she didn't want anyone connecting the dots to her final destination.

Tegan went to the bedroom and sat down on the bed. Her emotions overtook her again when she realized Alessia would never sleep here again. She wept with a sense of deep grief. She knew the wounds would never heal completely. Her family and dearest friend were gone forever. When the sobs stilled, Tegan swore it would be the last time she would shed tears for them.

When she stood up, she felt a sudden change come over her. It was something primal—a yearning for revenge—and a focused hatred unlike anything she had ever felt before or even knew she was capable of feeling. Somehow, she would hunt Westfield down and even the score. She would make sure the animal that killed her loved ones would meet a gruesome end at her hands. They would all pay for what they had done to her family.

Tegan went through Alessia's dressers and closets and gathered up the clothes she thought she could use. She packed them in a red suitcase that she found in the guest bedroom closet. It was the same battered suitcase Alessia had when she moved in with her family after her great aunt kicked her out.

Over the next hour, Tegan stuffed all of Alessia's personal items into garbage bags, along with the food left in the fridge. Then she bagged all of the cosmetics and medicines and everything someone would normally take with them if they were leaving for an extended period. It took several trips to the dumpster to dispose of everything. She dropped the Boeing

ID into the mailbox slot and left the rent check and a note on the kitchen counter for the manager. She made one final check of the apartment as she collected her thoughts, then picked up the suitcase and walked out the door as Alessia Stryker.

FIVE

Washington, D.C. — February 12

Cecil Westfield sat at a table near the back of an Italian restaurant, waiting impatiently for Robert Knolls to arrive. He didn't like to be kept waiting; it was one of his many peeves. With each passing moment, he grew angrier at Knolls's lack of respect. This was their second face-to-face meeting to discuss his recruitment into Dark Moon. Knolls wouldn't know the real scope of the job until after he'd accepted the position, but that was all part of the process.

Knolls possessed an aptitude for black operations. At thirty-three, he was young enough to be of value for many years. During their first meeting, Knolls had impressed Westfield with his candor and his desire to serve his country. His intelligence background and lack of family fit the selection criteria perfectly. He was inquisitive, tactful, and a natural leader. Westfield believed Knolls might be the right person to fill his shoes when he retired. First, Knolls needed to "earn his bones" before Westfield would even think about bringing him into the inner circle, much less offering him command.

Currently, Knolls served in the NSA Gossamer Section (GOES) under Director Frank Talbot. Even with his distinguished record as an exceptionally gifted cryptographer and electronic intercepts analyst, Knolls wasn't going to move up the food chain under Talbot's command.

Talbot had risen to his position by taking credit for the work of others. Like all of Talbot's assets, Knolls was withering on the vine. Westfield had dangled the bait during their first meeting. Knolls seemed to be nibbling on the bait. Now all he needed to do was reel him in. The big question Westfield needed to have answered was whether Knolls had the stomach for the seedier side of the work. The job required doing "wet work," and Knolls had never dropped the hammer on anyone, and he wasn't battle-tested. If Knolls joined the team, Westfield would test him in short order.

Having virtually disappeared in GOES, Knolls's departure from the NSA would go unnoticed, which was exactly what Westfield needed in a new operative. While in the Navy, Knolls's work on a new cybersecurity encryption system had gained him a Pentagon assignment. He could have made the Navy a career, but instead had chosen to work for the NSA. Westfield knew why he had left the Navy. After five years of marriage and three deployments, his wife divorced him and married a Marine Corps captain, a classmate of Knolls at the Naval Academy.

Westfield checked his watch again and decided to give him five more minutes. He took a sip of his scotch. As he put his glass down, Knolls came through the front door. He took off his gray London Fog coat, revealing his solid, six-foot frame. He was the stereotypical good-looking All-American type—well groomed, with cropped, dark brown hair. Westfield refused to make any gestures to attract his attention. Recognizing that he was being passive-aggressive, he enjoyed watching Knolls fret about whether he hadn't waited for him. Knolls looked relieved when he finally spotted him in the darkened corner.

He walked up to the table and sat down across from Westfield. "Sorry I'm late, sir. Director Talbot held me up, and I missed the metro connection. I had to wait for the next one."

"I really don't want to hear your excuse," Westfield said. "I believe in loyalty first, and timeliness second. Your tardiness and making excuses is not the way to impress me. Excuses are for the weak and the underachievers that whine about not being able to do their job. The mission comes before all else. In my command, if you fail, people die. Are we clear?"

"Yes, sir."

"If you are ever late for a meeting with me again, I will kick your ass and then throw you out the door. Do you read me?"

Knolls stiffened in his chair. "Yes, sir. It won't happen again."

"No, it won't. Mr. Knolls, you have the attributes I am looking for, and I think you would be a great asset to my team. I'm willing to offer you a position—conditionally."

"What is the condition?"

"You will need to pass a test. One you may find distasteful."

"I will do my best, sir."

Westfield smiled. "I'm sure you will."

"In our first meeting you only hinted at my primary responsibilities. Can you elaborate?" Knolls asked.

"Yes. Your primary job is to keep the United States of America safe from all enemies, foreign and domestic. As to your specific function, well, that will depend on what the enemy is doing. Unlike Director Talbot, I don't want drones that do the same thing the same way every day. I want a person who can think on his feet, adapt to any situation, and accomplish objectives without question or hesitation. Most importantly, you need to take responsibility for your actions." Westfield took a sip of scotch.

"This position will require you to get your hands dirty. As we discussed, you will work as a crypto-analyst, officially. However, you will have other duties requiring extended tours in the field, sometimes in faraway lands. You will gather intelligence and develop human assets. You will make life-and-death decisions. And you may be required to kill or order someone to be killed."

Knolls didn't flinch or look away. *So far so good*, Westfield thought. "Your assignments will vary. You will receive the best specialized training possible and have unlimited resources at your disposal."

"Can you give me some idea of the scope or type of operations I'll be assigned? Am I replacing someone, or is this a new billet?"

"It's a new position. As to your duties and responsibilities, they will be assigned as you progress through your training. I will expect you to create your own mission parameters when deemed ready. You will report directly to me and to the man who will be training you. You follow orders without question."

"I understand, sir."

"We will see about that, Mr. Knolls. There is still much to discuss, but I want you to understand that if you work for me, you'll be called upon to do some very unpleasant things. This isn't a desk job. It is not a position you can just walk away from. The job is high-stress, high-adrenaline, and more importantly, permanent."

"I understand. I've been in need of a challenge."

Westfield said, "This isn't just a challenge, it's a way of life."

Knolls nodded his understanding. "Will the position require additional clearances?"

"You will be given special clearances above your current TS/SCI/TK. In fact, I have already done your background, and you are good to go. I wouldn't open my fly this much if I didn't already know you could keep your mouth shut."

"Yes, sir."

"Mr. Knolls, I need to emphasize a point here before we go any further. I want you to understand it very clearly. Once you accept my offer, there is no turning back. It is truly a permanent post. I am the only person who will allow you to resign. I will monitor everything you say and do. Think long and hard about this before you officially accept. I want your eyes wide open, because once in, you are never out," Westfield said, knowing that Knolls was ready to commit. Westfield motioned for the waiter, who had been standing out of earshot, to come and take their order.

"What do I tell Director Talbot?"

The waiter walked up and stood by the table.

"Nickolas, we would like two orders of your famous homemade lasagna, house salads with balsamic dressing, and my friend will have what I'm drinking," Westfield said. The waiter smiled and left without saying a word. Westfield gave Knolls a cold, hard stare.

"I will take care of Talbot. He won't be happy about it, but screw him. He's an idiot. Once you accept the position, you will go dark and won't officially exist anymore. You will be required to terminate all relationships with other NSA personnel and friends. You will drop off the radar, except for when you need to be visible. Do you have any questions?"

Knolls took a deep breath and said, "I understand. I don't need to think about it any further. It sounds like an exciting opportunity to serve my country, and that's all I need to know."

"Are you sure about this, son?"

"Yes, sir."

Westfield leaned toward Knolls and said, "Any attempt to leave the command will meet with dire consequences. Are we very clear on this point?"

Westfield thought about Tegan. He hadn't given her this speech, because her assignment had been different. He wondered if she would have signed up if she had known. Probably not. She did not have a need to know about Dark Moon. Knolls, on the other hand, would.

"I understand, sir. I'm ready."

"Well, then, welcome to S-3," Westfield said, extending his hand across the table.

"Thank you, sir. I won't disappoint you," Knolls replied, shaking Westfield's hand.

Westfield smiled. "I know you won't. If you do, I *will* kill you."

Knolls leaned back and nodded.

"Mr. Knolls, you will never speak of our command designator to anyone. Our code of conduct forbids any action that will endanger the command in any way. S-3 doesn't officially exist. Its funding is well cloaked. Our work is off the grid, so much so that even the president has to have a need to know before he gets a look-see, and then only by my granting him permission."

Knolls nodded.

Westfield drained his glass and said, "I have the authority to take any action I deem necessary to protect the interests of the United States. I will give you a better history lesson when we next meet, but for now, all you need to know is that we get whatever we want, when we want it, without question. S-3 has absolute power in every sense of the word."

Nickolas returned with the salads and drinks.

After the waiter left, Westfield said, "When we finish lunch you will go directly home, pack, and call no one. You will be moving to a new address, and you will assume a new identity tomorrow. I will call you in the morning to tell you where and when to report. Talbot may try to contact you. Do not speak with him again, unless I tell you it's permitted. There will be no need for a debriefing by GOES because you don't exist any longer. Do you understand?"

"Yes, sir."

"Good." Westfield had his new man. He would know shortly if he would keep him. He took a bite of his salad.

Baltimore, Maryland — February 26 — 1800 hours

Last week's snow had turned to a cold rain. Robert Knolls sat alone in the driver's seat of a black van, waiting for his target to arrive home. The raindrops sparkled on the windshield in the headlights of a passing car.

"How has it come to this so quickly?" he asked himself. It had been only two weeks, and already he was in the field, assigned to make his first kill. He remembered that Westfield had called it "earning his bones."

His training thus far had been intense by any standard. It included firearms, explosives, and close-quarter-battle tactical work. He had also spent two hours per day at the gym for strength training. It was a very structured regimen, much like what he'd experienced at the Naval Academy.

Every night after an evening meal, he sequestered himself in his new abode to study required reading material. Most of the books dealt with the psychology of killing, surveillance tactics, and warfare, including *The Art of War*, written more than two millennia ago by the Chinese general, military strategist, and philosopher Sun-tzu. In addition, Westfield wanted him to have rudimentary language skills in Russian and Chinese within a year. He would be required to learn Spanish, Arabic, and German the following year. Learning so many languages in such a short time was going to be more than challenging.

Westfield had briefed him earlier in the day about his target—Dr. Janet Vasine, whom he called a traitor of the worst kind. Westfield didn't tell him the specifics of her actions, because he didn't need to know them. Westfield had ordered him to kill her and to make it overt, and that was precisely what he planned to do. Westfield told him he needed to send a message to other S-3 members. Knolls didn't know everything S-3 was responsible for yet, but it obviously included eliminating internal security threats, especially one of their own.

Now here he sat waiting for a person he had never met. When she arrived home, he would drive up next to her and shoot her to death. He wasn't supposed to feel any emotion when he did it. He wasn't sure he could do that. Was it cold-blooded murder or just his duty? Either way he was going to kill a human being for the first time. He needed to believe his actions would serve a greater good.

The rain tapped gently on the roof of the van, creating a meditative, peaceful sound. He would have liked to know more about Vasine's subversive activity. Maybe then he wouldn't be so apprehensive about killing her. But that really didn't matter. He had his orders, and he would execute them.

Knolls had studied a photograph of his target, and he knew the make and model of her car. He also knew when she should arrive home. Westfield had given him the untraceable Glock 45 lying on the seat next to him. His orders were to make sure she was dead before he drove away. Knolls knew that meant he would see her face and have to look into her eyes, witnessing her moment of terror before he pulled the trigger.

The contents of his stomach roiled as he picked up the semiautomatic handgun, his patriotic fervor gone. He understood the warrior mindset, and he was an excellent marksman. He had no doubt that his skills would ensure a clean kill. However, this time his target wasn't paper or steel. It was a human being, a person with a past, a family, and friends. In her photo, she looked more like a grandmother than a traitor.

Knolls breathed slowly and visualized how the event would unfold. He pushed the negative thoughts from his mind and focused. He needed to maintain his fine motor skills. He knew that elevated stress and adrenaline would change his trigger pull. *Squeeze the trigger, don't snatch it. One clean shot to the head. Remember she is just a target, the enemy,* he repeated to himself. Knolls took a deep breath and let it out slowly. Just then, an older model black BMW pulled to the curb and stopped in front of Dr. Vasine's residence. She had returned home for the last time. Knolls started the engine and lowered the driver's window.

Dr. Vasine struggled to open her car door against the wind. Once out of the car, she opened an oversized bright red umbrella, then reached back into the car to get something. Knolls checked for potential witnesses in the residential neighborhood. Seeing none, he pulled slowly away from the curb.

As he closed on Dr. Vasine, he felt the rush of adrenaline. *Not too fast, not too slow. She is just a target.* He took another deep breath to slow his heart rate. He wiped his sweaty palm on his pants, moved the gun to his left hand, and raised it to the edge of the window frame. He made a final check of the area. He had a clean shot. All he had to do now was pull the trigger.

Dr. Vasine turned toward the sound of the approaching vehicle. A gust of wind caught her umbrella, forcing her to turn away as she struggled to keep it under control. Knolls felt relieved as he pulled up beside her, knowing he wouldn't have to live with seeing the look on her face before he pulled the trigger. He pointed the Glock out the window, lined up the shot, and squeezed the trigger three times. He felt the concussion in the van with each round he fired.

The first round struck Dr. Vasine in the back of the head, a perfect kill shot. The next two rounds struck her in the back. She dropped onto the pavement facedown. He stomped on the accelerator. In the side mirror, he watched her umbrella blowing down the slick street behind him, bouncing in the wind, carried away like the soul he had just taken. The ringing in his ears didn't help distract him from the knowledge he had been successful. He dropped the gun onto the seat next to him, slammed on the brakes, and vomited out the window.

To the east of Dr. Vasine's residence, Osiris watched the kill from his GMC Yukon. He had recorded the event with his digital camcorder. Grant shivered with the thrill of having seen a life taken. Killing fed his spirit like raw meat thrown to a ravenous tiger. This time he had only watched from the sidelines. Still he had the satisfaction of knowing that if Knolls had balked at the assignment or missed, he would have had the pleasure of killing both of them.

Grant had smiled when he saw the muzzle flashes explode from the driver's side of the van. The zoom feature on his camera helped penetrate the rain as he documented the termination with an up-close and personal view. He drove slowly past Dr. Vasine's prone body, recording as he went. Her blood streamed into the gutter. Grant knew it would wash away soon.

Knolls pulled the van into the parking lot of a small shopping center and parked next to a slate-gray Toyota pickup truck left for him. He wiped the van down as instructed, but he knew he didn't have to worry about fingerprint comparisons or DNA linking him to the shooting. He no longer existed in any database. He dropped the firearm into a plastic bag, tucked it under the seat, and exited the van.

The smell of the rain helped clear away some of the stench of his own vomit, some of which was still on his sleeve. He found the keys to the Tundra on the right rear tire where Westfield said they would be, got in, and started the engine. He sat there for a while, hoping his hands would stop shaking. Just as he put the truck in gear, a black Yukon pulled into the parking lot and sped toward him.

When the SUV pulled up next to him, Grant motioned for him to lower his window.

"What are you doing here?" Knolls asked.

"Making sure you did your job. You did well, except for the puking. If you don't have the stomach for killing, don't eat beforehand."

"Westfield had you follow me?"

"I wouldn't put it that way. I was your backup on this op. I confirmed the target is dead and recorded the whole thing. I keep a recording of all my kills to see how I can improve the next time, so it's available if you want to study it. You always remember your first kill." Grant smiled. "I called Westfield to let him know you completed your assignment successfully. He asked that I convey his congratulations for a job well done. He wants you to call him."

Knolls looked into Grant's cold, hard face and wondered if that was what he would become in a few years. Grant spoke about killing as if it was a common occurrence.

"Will do," Knolls replied, not really knowing what else to say. He pulled away, his hands still shaking as he dialed Westfield's number.

Elbow Cay, Abaco, Bahamas — March 01

Tegan took her time getting to the Bahamas. After leaving Alessia's apartment, she stayed in Eugene, Oregon, for a week, where she sold the Mustang for a ridiculously low price to a less than reputable dealership. While in Eugene, she learned that she'd been listed as one of the victims in the accident. The television news reported that a steering failure had caused the accident. Tegan knew that the steering had not failed on its own. Since she was officially dead, she thought her new identity as Alessia Stryker was secure.

The following day, she flew to Phoenix, Arizona, where she stayed one night, then continued on to Asheville, North Carolina, where she spent five days at the historic Biltmore Estate. Ft. Lauderdale, Florida, was her next stop, where she enjoyed walking on the beach in the warm weather. Then it was on to Nassau, Bahamas. Alessia's passport would leave a trail, but once in the Bahamas she planned to disappear for good.

Her flight to Nassau arrived late, and by the time she cleared customs, she had missed the connecting flight to Marsh Harbour, her ultimate destination. Since the next available flight didn't leave until late afternoon the following day, Tegan decided to take advantage of the delay and see some of the sights. Perhaps this would give her some insight into why she felt drawn to the Abacos. She had never been to the Bahamas, had never thought about going, yet the islands seemed oddly inviting and familiar.

Tegan shared a taxi van with a newlywed couple for the drive to Paradise Island. The driver took the scenic coast road into downtown, where the newlyweds disembarked to do some shopping, giving the driver an extra twenty dollars to drop their luggage at the Atlantis Resort. Alone in the van, Tegan gazed at four large cruise ships docked in the port and thought about how easy it would be to disappear on a ship. The hotel she'd chosen was one that belonged to the Atlantis property. She checked in, paying cash in advance for the one night, and was pleasantly surprised her room had an ocean view.

The next morning, she took a taxi downtown and wandered through the myriad of shops along Bay Street. She mingled with the crowd. Families strolled up and down the sidewalks, window-shopping. Bumper-to-bumper traffic inched along the narrow street, and the sound of beeping horns echoed off the buildings. After shopping, she went back to the hotel, showered, put on a pale blue sundress she'd purchased, then checked out of the hotel and headed for the Nassau airport.

The flight to Marsh Harbor was bumpy, but fortunately, Tegan wasn't prone to motion sickness, which was more than she could say for the man in the seat in front of her. Marsh Harbour International Airport was smaller than most of the airports she'd visited. She left the terminal and hired a taxi for the short drive to the marina, where she would catch the water ferry to Hope Town and stay there for the night.

When Tegan arrived at the docks, a small ferry was getting ready to depart. She hurried to the boat. "You have room for one more?" she asked the captain.

"We're pretty full, but I could be persuaded, if the price is right," the skipper replied.

"I see the price posted on the board," Tegan said, gesturing at the sign. "Isn't that the right price?"

"It could be," he said, eyeing her. Tegan felt her skin crawl.

"I'll pay double the fare if you stop undressing me with your eyes. I'm tired, and I don't need your shit. It isn't going to happen."

The passengers that heard the verbal exchange broke into laughter and clapped. The skipper apologized, accepted the standard fare, and helped her with her suitcase. She took a seat at the back of the ferry. The smell of the sea air lifted her spirits as the boat motored away from the dock.

When she arrived at Hope Town, Tegan realized she was hungry, so she decided to grab a bite before finding a place to stay for the night. A small restaurant that overlooked the docks and a small bay looked promising. The sound of lively Caribbean music and the aroma of grilled food drifted her way from the Shark Fin Bar and Grill. She walked down the dock toward the restaurant and saw a handwritten sign stapled to a piling.

Experienced crew needed
Inquire on the S/V Whispering Winds

Tegan was low on cash. Working on a local yacht would give her the mobility she needed, as well as provide an income. She could blend into her new surroundings while she determined her next course of action. Now all she needed to do was persuade the captain to hire her.

With her blond hair blowing gently in the breeze, she stepped off the dock and stood under the canvas roof of the bar. "Afternoon," she said to the bartender. "Do you know where I can find the skipper looking for crew on the *Whisper Wind?*"

"That would be the *Whispering Winds*," said a man sitting at the bar with his back to her. Hunched over a chart spread out in front of him, he was making marks on it with the stub of a pencil. He picked up his half-full Corona from the bar and took a swig before turning around.

Tegan couldn't miss the surprised look on his weathered face. He slowly scrutinized her slim physique, as if he was eyeing the graceful lines of a new boat.

"Sorry," Tegan said. "The *Whispering Winds*. I saw your sign on the dock. I need a job."

The man looked as if he had forgotten how to speak. It was nice to know she could still render a man speechless with her looks.

"Do you still need a crew member?"

He took another swig of beer and cleared his throat. "Yes, I still need a mate. You know anything about sailing?"

"My dad taught me how to sail when I was a little girl," she lied. "And I'm a respectable cook," she added, realizing she sounded overeager.

He gave her a crooked smile. "Do you have any references?"

"No one you would know. I'm from California."

"Come sit down," he said, gesturing to a worn bar stool next him. "Have a beer with me so I can get to know you a little before deciding whether to trust you with my livelihood in these treacherous, shark-infested waters."

"How do I know you're really the skipper and not just some drunk trying to pick me up? Have you got anyone who'll vouch for you?"

He smiled at her and said, "Well, you got me there. Most of these reprobates would tell you they don't know me just so they'd have a chance to buy you a beer. I guess you will just have to trust me. Come on, sit down. I'll buy."

The beer-bellied bartender chuckled. "If Cal's buying anyone a beer as broke as he is, he's telling you the truth."

She looked at the skipper. "Really, you're broke? How do you intend to pay me, with beer?"

"I'm not that broke," he said with an indignant look.

Tegan lifted an eyebrow and looked at the bartender.

"He's okay, miss. I've never known Cal not to pay his debts. It may take some time, but he always comes through."

"Well, then I guess you've been vouched for." Tegan extended her hand. "I'm Alessia Stryker."

The skipper stood and stretched to his full, imposing height. He took her hand and said, "I'm Calvin Locke. Call me Cal. Nice to meet you. When was the last time you were on the water?"

Tegan could tell by the way he held her hand that he probably knew she had never handled a line in her life. She felt a quiet strength in this man. He appeared kind, gentle, and seemed to have a sense a humor. He might have been someone she would have found a distraction when she was in college.

"It's been a while," she lied again.

"Okay. You said you can cook?" he said, finally releasing her hand.

"I've never had any complaints. With a bottle of wine and some spices, I could make your deck shoes taste good."

Tegan judged Cal to be in his mid-thirties. His dark brown hair was disheveled but cut neatly over his ears, and he had incredibly deep-blue eyes. The one-size-too-small, blue T-shirt with a Shark Fin logo on the front pocket emphasized his muscular six-foot-four frame. Both the shirt and stained shorts had seen better days, and his old deck shoes were speckled with varnish. She thought he was the very picture of a sailor. A warm feeling went through her as she sat on the barstool.

"What can I get you?"

"A Corona would be fine."

"John, a Corona for the lady, if you please," Cal said with an overly dramatic aristocratic-sounding voice.

"It will be a pleasure," John replied. "In fact, for such a beautiful lady, it's on the house."

Tegan's face suddenly felt hot. This place and these people felt right somehow.

"I'm John Parker," he said. "If Cal had any manners he would have introduced us. I own the Shark Fin."

"It's nice to meet you, John."

"A good Corona must always be accompanied by a lime and be drunk from the bottle," John said, placing the beer on the bar in front of her.

"Thank you. I agree." Tegan took a long pull from the bottle. Beer had never tasted so good.

"Let's talk about your salary and your duties, just in case I decide to hire you. How soon would you be available?" Cal asked.

"Immediately, if the salary is acceptable."

"Great. The job pays twenty-five percent of the charter. Any tips you receive are yours to keep. I take fifty percent, and the boat gets the other twenty-five. The Mulligan family is arriving from Detroit in two days for a two-week charter. The fare is $15,000. You'll get paid when we get back. Is that acceptable?"

"Yes," Tegan said, knowing she would have worked for room and board.

"Good. We will need to provision the boat, so I'll show you the lay of the land. If you work out, provisioning will be your responsibility. You'll be expected to cook and clean up after all meals, clean the cabins and heads. It'll be your responsibility to come up with different recipes for the fresh catch daily. My clients are my livelihood, so we'll cater to their needs to make their trip worth remembering. Does that sound okay?"

"Yes, worth remembering," Tegan repeated, nodding like a student listening to a professor's lecture.

"That's so they come back again," Cal added. "I'll count on you to handle the lines and the helm when needed. We only sail during daylight, and we'll either anchor or dock at night. You won't have to stand watch or work split shifts. We rise early every morning before the clients, usually before sunrise, and we only go to bed after they do.

"Before sunrise and after dark. Got it. Separate beds, right?"

"Are you making fun of me?"

"Not at all," Tegan replied, taking a sip of beer. "I just wanted to establish boundaries."

"I understand. I'm the captain, and at sea my word is the law. There will be no questions or talking back in front of clients. Any suggestions you might have, keep them to yourself."

"What if I think the boat is about to run aground? Should I just stand there looking obedient?"

Parker laughed so hard it brought tears to his eyes. Cal frowned at him.

When Cal returned his attention to her, he said, "There will be no flirting or sex with the passengers. That's bad for business. That is why I need a new mate. On the last charter, my mate decided she wanted to make a little money on the side, and the man's wife damn near threw her overboard."

Tegan smiled. "I believe in keeping my business and personal life separate. I assume I'll have my own cabin."

Cal grinned. "Yes, you'll have your own stateroom. You haven't seen the *Whispering Winds* yet, have you?"

"No, I haven't. She can't be a very big boat if I'm all the crew you need."

"The *Whispering Winds* is a modified Lagoon 440 catamaran sailboat. She has four staterooms, two in each hull, fore and aft. She's configured for charter work, so she has a head in both guest staterooms on the port side. Unfortunately, your stateroom has no head, and part of it is being used for storage."

"I'm sure my quarters will be adequate. Anything else I need to know?"

"Yes, one other thing. No charters are clothing-optional. You'll have to refrain from skinny-dipping or wandering around naked," Cal said with a twinkle in his eyes.

Tegan smiled, feeling the beer eroding her inhibitions. It had been a long time since she'd flirted with a man. "That won't be a problem. I don't do those things, at least not very often. And since we'll be sharing a head, any accidental entry while I'm using it will result in your ass going over the side, after I have thoroughly kicked it."

Parker broke into laughter again and said, "Well, now, she's not the usual mate you're used to, is she? She has class and sass. I like her." He put another Corona on the bar in front of her. "This one's on the house, too. You deserve it if you plan on sailing with this pirate."

"Shut up, John," Cal said without looking at him. Parker only chuckled.

"You'll need to get acquainted with the boat. We will get an early start in the morning to find provisions. I'll swing by and pick you up. Where are you staying?"

Tegan looked at Parker and said, "John, do you know of any good hotels nearby?"

Parker shrugged and gave Cal a knowing look.

"You aren't staying on the island?" Cal asked.

"No. I just arrived this afternoon."

"That explains the suitcase. You can stay aboard the *Whispering Winds* tonight if you like. That'll give you time to get settled and get a feel for her, and we can get an early start."

Tegan thought it over for a moment, not wanting to seem too eager. "I guess that means you're offering me the position. Alright then, I accept your offer," Tegan said, holding up her beer.

"I'm happy you accept," Cal said. They clanked bottles. "Are you hungry?"

"I'm starving. I haven't eaten since breakfast in Nassau."

"John, the lady is hungry. Bring us two grouper sandwiches and an order of sweet potato fries."

"Good choice, sir. I will add two bowls of my famous conch chowder as an appetizer." He turned and headed for the kitchen.

"So who are you?" Cal asked her.

Tegan had prepared to answer these types of questions, so the lies rolled off her tongue with ease. "Not much to tell, really. I grew up in Oregon and northern California. Graduated from Stanford with a business degree and went to work for a pharmaceutical company. I made a good living, selling drugs, but the doctors were a pain to deal with, if you know what

I mean. I'm not sure what was worse, the constant dinner invitations or their arrogance. But, it paid the bills, at least until the company was sold and my job was eliminated."

Tegan took a swig of beer.

"After losing my job, I decided to see the world while I was still young enough to enjoy it. I guess you can call this my midlife adjustment before I go back to the grind. I jumped on a plane to explore the world and found myself here." Tegan decided to add a bit of truth to her tale. "I have no family. They recently died in a car accident. I have no children, no ex-husbands, and no commitments."

"Wow, so much for small talk. I am sorry to hear you lost your family. When did it happen?"

Tegan remained silent.

"Sorry, I shouldn't have asked."

"It's alright," Tegan said, feeling melancholy. "My parents and twin sister died a few months ago."

"I'm very sorry."

Tegan decided to change the subject. "Tell me about you. I showed you mine, now you have to show me yours," she said with a grin, really feeling the effect of the beers on her empty stomach.

"Okay," Cal said. "Stop me when you've heard enough. I grew up in Florida and graduated from the University of South Florida. I love the sea, so after college I joined the Coast Guard, went through Officer Candidate School, and received my commission. My first duty station was in Miami assigned to a 110-foot cutter as the executive officer. Over the next three years, I visited almost all of the islands in the Caribbean. Mostly what we did was drug interdiction, a lot of it off the coast of South America. I fell in love with the Abacos, so I vowed to live here when my military career ended. After my sea duty, the Coast Guard decided to assign me to a JOART."

"What's a JOART?"

"It stands for Joint Operations Action Response Team. I was one of a handful of personnel from the Coast Guard assigned to a special team composed of Navy SEALS, MARSOC Raiders, and Army Rangers. I went through some very intense training, and then operated in faraway lands gathering intelligence and executing operations that I can't discuss."

"Like James Bond or something?"

"Far from it. I was mostly involved in counterterrorism operations with a focus on narco-terrorists. We were there to reduce the flow of drugs, which curtails the primary source of income that supports the terror organizations. Without funds, we can deprive them of the ability to buy weapons. Most of the work I did is still classified"

"That sounds exciting."

"It had some interesting moments."

"So how did you end up here?" Tegan signaled Parker to bring them another round of beers.

"My promising career ended about five years ago when I stepped on my dick, if you'll pardon the expression, while I was in Washington. After my separation from the service, I came to this tranquil place and found the *Whispering Winds* beached on Great Guana, her starboard hull holed from striking rocks during a storm. I tracked the owner down and learned his insurance had lapsed and bought her from him. I spent the next year and a half fixing her up so I could run charters. Now I am up to my eyeballs in debt and forced to put up with the likes of John here. But I do enjoy my life."

"Ever married?" Tegan asked, biting her lower lip after the question left her mouth.

"I was, once upon a time. Emily was a great woman, but she couldn't adjust to me being deployed. Our marriage only lasted a year. We parted as friends. She lives in Cocoa Beach near my parents with her new husband. He's a doctor, and they have two little kids. I'm very happy for her."

"So how did you step on your dick?" Tegan asked.

John delivered the beers and the conch chowder, which smelled wonderful. Parker grinned at her question.

Cal squirmed a little on his bar stool. "I was in Washington and had some time to kill. As the old story goes, I met a lady. I use the term loosely. It turned out the woman was a congressman's wife, and he found out about our affair. I didn't know she was married, much less married to a congressman. As fate would have it, he happened to sit on the Military Appropriations Committee.

"That wouldn't be good."

"No. A week later, I learned of my reassignment to Kodiak, Alaska. They also gave me the option to resign my commission. I don't like cold weather, and I knew my career was at an end, so I left."

Tegan chuckled. "Didn't know she was married, huh?"

"Nope."

They talked for nearly two more hours while they ate. John brought them fresh lobster tails to go with the grouper sandwiches. Tegan ate everything put in front of her.

She felt comfortable with Cal. They bid Parker farewell and strolled down the dock so Cal could retrieve the help-wanted sign. Then they walked to the end slip on the dock where the *Whispering Winds* was berthed. The vessel was impressive and not what she had expected. The white-and-blue-striped hulls, joined by an elevated, broad-beamed salon, offered a 360-degree view through large glass windows. A flybridge was above the salon, just behind the seventy-foot aluminum mast, and trampoline netting was tied between the hulls in front of the salon. The vessel presented a larger outside profile than what she would soon discover inside. She fell in love with the boat almost instantly.

"She's beautiful," was all she could say. She turned toward Cal.

"Yes, she is," Cal replied, looking deeply into her eyes.

SEVEN

Maryland — March 15 — 1000 hours

NSA Director Lieutenant General Steven Bishop sat across from his subordinate, Gossamer Director Frank Talbot. He couldn't remember ever seeing Talbot this nervous at a meeting before. Talbot wrung his hands over the conference room table and ground his teeth, making a noise that annoyed him. Talbot was only five foot five, lacked muscle definition, and weighed barely 130 pounds. He looked like a little kid sitting in his father's chair. His narrow, freckled face, red hair, and round, red-rimmed glasses did nothing to diminish his childish appearance.

Bishop had been the director of the NSA for just over two years. He was the first African-American to hold the post. He stood a foot taller than Talbot and outweighed him by over a hundred pounds. He had grown to detest the little man, not just because he reminded him of a clown, wearing those silly glasses, but also because he was such a stickler for following the rules. It irritated him that Talbot enjoyed pointing out the deficiencies of his fellow employees. He knew that most people under Talbot's command found it difficult to take him seriously, but they also feared him, which wasn't a bad thing in this job. Talbot would have been better suited working for the IRS. In the intelligence business, rules needed to be overlooked at times, and Talbot didn't like operating in gray areas.

He knew that Talbot hated direct confrontation, preferring to snipe at people by putting his complaints in writing. However, today Talbot had asked for a face-to-face meeting with General Westfield to discuss the death of Dr. Vasine. Since both Talbot and Westfield reported to him, and knowing the general as well as he did, he figured he should be present when Talbot confronted Cecil about his failure to report her death.

In addition to code-breaking, disinformation, and cyberwarfare, GOES was responsible for conducting internal security investigations for the agency and for reviewing and analyzing any NSA member's death to determine if their demise was work-related and whether their death posed a security threat. It was a perfect job for Talbot.

Because of Westfield's cloak of secrecy and his ability to ignore and circumvent the rules over the years, Bishop understood that Talbot wanted Westfield to feel the heat for a change. The two men hated each other. It was a wonder that Westfield hadn't killed him already. Talbot had never had the opportunity to take a shot at Westfield, but the unreported death was a breach in protocol, and that gave him some advantage in trying to crack Westfield's armor. Any formal investigation would require access to Westfield's section, which Bishop wasn't going to allow, but he needed to play along for the time being. The harder anyone looked into Westfield's operations, the more obscure they became.

Cecil Westfield entered the conference room wearing a warm smile and extended his hand to Director Bishop. "Hello, Director Bishop," he said, and sat down in the chair next to him, ignoring Talbot completely.

Talbot gave Westfield an icy stare.

Bishop said, "Cecil, Frank has some questions concerning Dr. Vasine's death and you not reporting it to GOES. He asked me to sit in on this meeting."

Bishop knew why Westfield hadn't reported it to GOES. Talbot may think this was the first time someone in Westfield's section had died, but Bishop knew otherwise. This was just the first one that Westfield apparently wanted others to know about. Bishop continued, "I have reviewed the reports Frank provided, and I have to agree with him. This doesn't look like a street crime. The shot placement and circumstances indicate a professional hit rather than a random act of violence."

Talbot asked, "What do you know about the murder of Dr. Vasine, and why didn't you report it?"

Westfield looked from Bishop to Talbot and back again. Bishop could tell Westfield understood the game they were about to play.

"I'd like you to provide me with a full accounting," Talbot added.

"Director, are you sure you want me to answer his questions?" Westfield asked.

"I think Frank is owed an explanation."

"As you wish," Westfield replied. He turned to face Talbot. "I didn't report it to you because I didn't feel it was important enough to waste your valuable time. Dr. Janet Vasine was killed in front of her home in Baltimore during an attempted robbery."

Westfield stood up and walked to the credenza, where a pitcher of water sat. He poured a glass. "Director, can I get you some coffee or water while I'm up?"

"No, thank you. Please continue."

Bishop wanted to laugh at Talbot's expression.

"Dr. Vasine was outspoken to a fault," Westfield continued, "and I discovered that she wasn't happy working for the NSA. She lost her temper often, was *short* with her staff, and seemed on edge most of the time. Her behavior was creating an uncomfortable work environment, a morale problem, and her attitude was interfering with productivity."

Bishop didn't miss that Westfield's emphasis on the word *short* was a jab at Talbot.

Westfield walked back to the table, sat down, and said, "Dr. Vasine was working on some very special projects. I overlooked her behavior because the work she did for us was valuable. I cannot discuss the specifics of her work. You're not cleared, Frank."

Talbot slammed his fist on the table. "Director Bishop, GOES is responsible for conducting an investigation anytime a member is killed under suspicious circumstances. I demand to have access to General Westfield's staff so that I can conduct the necessary interviews. I need access to Dr. Vasine's work area—wherever that might be. I have to determine if records were compromised. I need a list of all personnel she supervised, as well as a list of all projects she was working on and access to her computer and mainframe files."

Director Bishop turned his head slightly so Talbot wouldn't see him smile and said, "Let's hear what else General Westfield has to say before making demands."

Westfield turned to Talbot and calmly said, "I really can't offer anything further. That is all you need to know, Frank. Case closed."

Before Talbot could respond, Westfield added, "Frank, I have already looked into the shooting and determined her death was not agency-related. It poses no security threat to the country. All of her classified files are secure.

"Director Bishop, Janet gave much of herself to protect this country. I see no reason to waste Frank's precious time investigating this tragic incident, which is why I didn't bother him," Westfield said.

Bishop waited for Talbot's reaction. The man's face flushed with anger.

"Cecil," Talbot began, "You failed to contact my department, which is a violation of policy and an internal security violation. Dr. Vasine's death wasn't an attempted robbery. It was a professional job. There were two shots to the body and one to the head. I've also been informed that another member of your staff is missing. I demand access to investigate both of these matters."

"I don't answer to you, Frank, and I don't care for your tone." Westfield smiled and added, "As to someone else being unaccounted for, well, you will need to be a little more specific. To my knowledge, no one is missing. You're not going to get a license to go fishing in my pond based on unsupported accusations. I will not release any of Vasine's files or anything else on your list of demands."

"Director Bishop, I demand access to Westfield's command structure immediately," Frank shouted. His face was a light shade of purple. "I want to know who works for him, what they do, and everything else I need to know to conduct a proper investigation, as per policy."

Bishop sat back in his chair, pretending to consider his request. Frank looked as if he was going to explode at any moment.

Talbot said, "Hell, Cecil, all I know of your section is its official name, Special Operations and Technology Development. No one in the agency has ever heard of any technological developments your section has been involved in or, for that matter, ever received an intelligence briefing from anyone under your command."

Westfield raised his eyebrows slightly. "Good, that means my security is tight."

"Your section seems to be a one-way street," Talbot said. "I understand the need for secrecy, but you have to admit it's awfully suspicious that nothing comes out of your section's black hole. With that in mind, my investigators will conduct a full inspection of your section, including interviews with members of your staff to determine if there are any … discrepancies.

"I also want to see the report of the death investigation you claim you conducted. It will help to expedite our investigation. Oh, and Cecil, maybe the other person isn't missing. Perhaps there's another death we should be looking into."

Talbot had crossed the line. Westfield's stare turned predatory. If Talbot kept pushing, *he* would end up missing.

Westfield pushed his chair back and stood. His command bearing projected a powerful image. Westfield was battle-tested and hardened by his years in the Marine Corps and his work in Dark Moon. Talbot's demand was hardly a threat. No one spoke. Tension hung in the air while Westfield stared at Talbot. Bishop wasn't sure what was going to happen.

Westfield turned to Bishop. "Director, you know where I stand on this matter. There is nothing more Frank needs to look into."

Talbot stood up and said, "That's hardly reassuring. Director, if you would please remind Cecil I have a job to do. I also don't appreciate his pilfering talent from my team. Robert Knolls just up and disappeared. I was in the dark for several days. Cecil finally notified me of Mr. Knolls's transfer after I'd already opened an investigation into his disappearance and was actively searching for him."

Westfield smirked. "That is very true, Director Bishop. I didn't call Frank for a few days. I didn't see the need."

"What is Knolls working on? Talbot asked.

"Nothing I can tell you about. I do know he's happy not having to look behind him to make sure you aren't checking to see if he wiped his ass properly."

"I have had enough of your shit, Westfield," Talbot shouted. Spittle shot from his mouth and landed on the highly polished table.

"Good. Stay out of my business, and I won't have to shit on you."

Bishop stood up. "Alright, that's enough. Frank, we're done here. I see no reason for further inquiry. If General Westfield says all of his people are accounted for and he has looked into Dr. Vasine's death, then the matter is closed."

Westfield smiled and turned to leave the room.

"I'm not through talking to you, Cecil," Talbot shouted.

Westfield stopped at the door and turned. "Frank, I believe Director Bishop has indicated we're finished. Let me explain this as clearly and as succinctly as possible. I answer to only one person in this agency, and he's standing next to you." Westfield took a step toward Talbot, clenching his fists.

"What I do, or how I do it, is scrutinized by Director Bishop. He's all that stands between me and God. I operate by the authority and power of a directive way outside of your need to know, you little prick. As to my means, my associates, my recruitment tactics, my subordinates, or anything else you might want to take up with our boss, feel free. My job is to insure the safety of this country, and I will not have an incompetent micromanager get in my way. With your permission, Director Bishop, I would like to get back to work."

Bishop nodded. Westfield turned and left the room, closing the door softly behind him.

Talbot took a step toward the door as if he was going to follow Westfield. "Wait a minute, Frank," Bishop said. "Sit down."

Talbot walked back to the table, fuming, and sat down.

"This is about as angry as I think I've ever seen you," Bishop said.

"Director, I apologize for my actions. I don't mean to cast aspersions on you, but that son of a bitch needs to be taken down a peg or two, and you don't seem to want to do it. I'm not the only one who thinks so. The others are just too intimidated to speak up when it comes to Westfield."

"Frank, don't you think how he does his job is up to me to evaluate?"

"Yes, sir. I mean no disrespect, but something isn't right here. If someone else is missing from his staff, I believe it needs investigating. If you don't authorize it, well, quite frankly, I may need to explore other options."

Director Bishop frowned and clenched his jaw. "Let it go. You don't need to poke around in things that are not your concern. I will talk privately with Cecil and determine if someone else is missing from his command that he hasn't reported. If I find anything, I will be the first to initiate the inquiry, and I will give you authorization to proceed. Is that clear?"

"Yes, sir. You're the boss."

Bishop decided to let it drop. He needed to get back to matters that were important. He stood up to leave.

Talbot turned to him and looked up. "Director, what directive was Westfield referring to?"

"Don't go there, Frank. You may not ask about or even mention that again. You got the better of Cecil today, whether you know it or not, and you certainly got under his skin, which I'm certain was one of the things you hoped to accomplish. I'll speak with Cecil. In the meantime, let's try to remember we all work on the same team." Bishop decided to put the issue to rest. "Frank, I'm issuing you a direct order to stand down. Do not mention this matter to anyone or snoop around trying to determine where his authority rests. Are we clear on this point?"

"Yes, sir."

"Good. Then we're done here."

Talbot left the conference room, still seething and even more curious about what it was Westfield really did for the agency. This pill was not going down easily. Westfield was someone who exercised his power with impunity, which wasn't acceptable. He knew that Westfield was involved in something beyond his scope and that intrigued him. Dr. Vasine's death somehow figured into whatever it was Westfield was hiding, and Director Bishop was covering for him.

For the first time since joining the NSA, he made a decision he knew could end his career. Talbot decided he was going to go after Westfield against Director Bishop's order. He knew there wouldn't be a happy ending, but it was the right thing to do.

Capitol Hill – 1025 hours

Frank Talbot called Senator John "Woody" Woodsman on his cell phone.

"Hello," Woodsman answered.

"Hello, senator. This is Frank Talbot at the NSA. I apologize for calling you on your personal line, but I have a concern we need to discuss, *privately*. It's of the utmost urgency, and I didn't want to leave a message of record at your office."

Frank hoped he'd developed a strong enough relationship with Senator Woodsman over the last year to approach him. He saw Woodsman monthly at the intelligence briefings he gave the Select Intelligence Committee. He was certain Woodsman could pave the way for him to meet with President Collingsworth, without Director Bishop's knowledge.

Like the president, Woodsman was a member of the Progressive Reformist Party. Everyone thought well of him on the Hill, and knew he was one of the president's favorites. The young senator had already earned a solid reputation for being honest and direct.

"Frank, if it's that important, come by my office at the Hart Building in about an hour."

"No, sir, that isn't a good idea. I don't want to alarm you, but this is an NSA internal security concern that may require an investigation. I have exhausted all other means available to me. This matter will require some clout for it to be investigated discreetly and properly. I have a serious problem. Director Bishop may be involved, which is why this issue needs an external review." He tried to keep his emotions in check, knowing he could be committing political suicide.

"Okay, Frank. Where's a good place to meet?"

"The west end of the Vietnam Memorial should give us privacy."

"That's fine. I need a walk anyway. I'll see you there in an hour."

NSA Headquarters – 1130 hours

Director Bishop had called General Westfield after Talbot left, asking him to meet him back in the conference room. Westfield arrived five minutes early for the meeting. Bishop was already there.

"Cecil, you lost your cool, and that isn't like you. To make matters worse, you disclosed that your operational authority is different from the rest of the NSA. That's not good, especially when it comes to Frank. Was Frank on the mark with his allegation that someone else has disappeared? Do I have a problem?"

General Westfield didn't respond.

"Cecil, I'm responsible for any mess you create, and I won't be able to defend you, or myself, if I don't know I have a problem. Any blowback will hamper our collective effectiveness. The last thing I need now is a congressional inquiry."

"I understand. To answer your questions, yes and no," Westfield stated, without emotion.

"Yes to Frank was on the mark with you having another member of your staff missing, and no to me having to worry about it?"

"That is correct, sir."

"Enlighten me further, please."

"We had an internal security threat with two of my biologics. The one who created the new synthetic virus, Dr. Tegan Strong, is not missing."

"She's dead?" Bishop asked.

"Yes. I had every indication she and Dr. Vasine were going to go public with the synthetic virus."

"So you killed both of them?"

"Yes. Strong was sanctioned quietly, the other publicly to discourage others from having similar treasonous thoughts."

"Is there anyone else involved?"

"No, they were the only ones. There will be no fallout for the NSA, or for you."

"The virus is only going to be used on nonhuman threats, correct?"

"Yes, sir. As you know, Deep Sky is programmable, so we can launch combinations of infectious agents at any alien threat. It truly was a work of genius by Dr. Strong."

Bishop stood and paced. "Can you assure me there hasn't been a breach? Deep Sky won't be made public?"

"No information has been leaked. What do you want me to do about Frank?"

Bishop knew that Westfield did not need his permission to eliminate Talbot, but it showed his respect that he asked. He could tell that Westfield wanted to kill Talbot. "I would like you to do nothing at all. I can handle Frank. I need him where he is, at least for now. Unbelievably, I need his expertise. I gave him a direct order to forget your faux pas on disclosing the existence of a classified directive. I would like you to avoid him for a while. I know that isn't the option you would prefer, but I'm asking it as a favor. Can you do that?"

"I won't cause you any headaches," Westfield said. His cell vibrated.

"Thank you, Cecil."

"Excuse me, sir." Westfield answered the call.

"Yes, John." A moment later Westfield said, "Are you shitting me?"

Director Bishop raised a questioning eyebrow.

"Okay, stay with Frank and let me know of any developments as quickly as possible. Have Knolls keep an eye on Senator Woodsman. We may have to become proactive, John." Westfield disconnected.

"What did Frank do?" Bishop asked.

"Sir, you may want to start handling Frank. He's meeting with Senator Woodsman right now. They are standing at the Wall, whispering sweet nothings into each other's ears, and I don't believe I have ever known Frank, or Woodsman, to hold any meeting outside of a secure conference room. So I can only guess I'm the focus of their discussion."

Bishop scratched his chin. "*That's* an interesting turn of events. I certainly would not have expected Frank to be that impulsive. He actually disobeyed a direct order. I guess he does have a set of balls."

"And I'm going to cut them off. I have a feeling Frank is trying to get a line on the directive I mentioned, using Woodsman's pipeline to President Collingsworth. His game will not go anywhere, but it will put me on President Collingsworth's radar. This is my doing, and I will clean it up." Westfield stood to leave.

"What makes you think it needs to be cleaned up?" Bishop asked.

"It requires a response. If Frank is out of the picture, Woodsman won't have anything to take to the president."

"True. But I have an idea that I'm sure you won't like."

"When you start out like that, I probably won't. What is it?"

"I suggest we let Frank play his hand. You keep them both under surveillance and see what we can learn. I'm afraid if we react too strongly, it may make Woodsman and President Collingsworth more inquisitive. You know they won't find anything even if they look. If I'm asked about the directive, I'll disavow any knowledge of it. If pressured, we can up the ante."

"I don't like sitting and waiting for the enemy to spring an ambush. But I suppose monitoring will suffice for now."

"I know what you really want to do is put a bullet in Frank's head. But with a little subterfuge we can make Talbot look like a crazy man and discredit him."

"That makes sense. I'll try it your way."

"Then we are in agreement?" Bishop asked.

"Yes, sir."

EIGHT

Director Bishop sat in Senator John Woodsman's reception area, knowing why the senator had requested his presence. He was on a fishing expedition for information. Westfield had called him earlier in the day to tell him to expect a summons. Bishop knew that the senator had come up empty with his inquiry into Westfield's operations. He also knew that Woodsman had met with President Collingsworth and Melvin Kotter, the Director of National Intelligence. He wasn't concerned about Kotter. The DNI knew nothing about Westfield that would be of value to them.

Bishop anticipated that Woodsman would play the duty, love of country, and presidential cards before the meeting was over in an attempt to gain insight. To put an end to this foray into Westfield's operations, he was prepared to offer certain tidbits of classified information in hopes that when he left the senator's office the investigation would be finished.

Over the last six weeks, the surveillance of Talbot and Woodsman indicated the two men met twice a week and always away from the Hill. Their phone conversations were limited, cryptic, and usually ended the same way. *Nothing new to report.*

Westfield had provided Bishop with updates on the information they had collected thus far. Woodsman had been pressing Talbot and his other sources about the directive. The inquiries seemed aimed more at finding out about Westfield than about Vasine's death. Bishop knew that Westfield had been disseminating false leads to confound them. Woodsman was spending more time and effort than should have been warranted, so he had to be acting at the direction of the president. *But why would the president care?*

Senator Woodsman's assistant looked up from her computer screen and smiled. Bishop returned the smile, knowing that the senator was on his way. A moment later the tall office door opened and the forty-one-year-old senator greeted him with a friendly handshake, and then led him into his office.

"How can I be of assistance, Senator Woodsman?"

"Please, sit down and call me Woody when we're in private."

They sat facing each other across the conference table.

"I have a problem I hope you can help me with," Woodsman began.

"Explain the problem, and I'll see what I can do for you."

"I've received some disturbing information from people within your agency that I can't ignore. I was informed that Dr. Janet Vasine, a member of General Cecil Westfield's staff, was killed a couple of months ago. I was also told that a proper investigation wasn't conducted to determine if her death was work-related. I've also been advised by a source that another member of Westfield's staff is missing. That all of these people risked their career by coming to me gives weight to their concerns. I have to ask you if there is any validity to these accusations."

Bishop leaned back in his chair and asked, "Who brought this to you?"

"I don't want to say. I normally wouldn't involve myself in something like this, but President Collingsworth requested I conduct an investigation after he met with Director Kotter."

"I wasn't aware Dr. Vasine's homicide was of such importance to the president. Director Kotter never mentioned he had any concerns about the police investigation or my internal findings."

"They were meeting on another issue, and the president asked him about the investigation as a favor to me."

"I see. You should have called me sooner with your concerns. I looked into Dr. Vasine's death. The investigation was properly handled. Her death was not related to her work and posed no security threat."

Bishop decided to dispense with the game playing. "Woody, I know you only have one source. It's Frank Talbot. To put your mind at ease, I also looked into his allegation that someone had disappeared from Westfield's command. No one is missing. Frank and Cecil despise each other, and I'm afraid you've been dragged into their conflict. I believe Frank took this opportunity to try and get at Westfield because he had circumvented protocol for the sake of efficiency."

"Let's cut to the chase then, shall we?" asked the senator. "Mr. Talbot said that General Westfield's operations are authorized by a directive that doesn't seem to exist. President Collingsworth has asked that I determine the scope of this order."

Bishop nodded, but didn't respond.

"I've had people trying to ferret out this secret for weeks, without success," Woodsman added. "Can you verify its existence?"

"I'm sorry you wasted so much time, Woody. I now understand why the DNI asked me about it. As I informed him, there is no secret document governing General Westfield's operations within the NSA." Bishop was not lying. The Department of Energy held the directive.

"General Westfield is still a Marine officer, and he *is* assigned to the NSA?"

"Yes." Bishop chuckled at the absurdity of the question.

"Director Bishop, do you find this inquiry funny?"

"Yes, sir, I do. I'll make this easy for you. There's nothing I can tell you about Cecil Westfield's operations."

"You are responsible for Westfield's conduct and his actions, are you not?"

Bishop decided on a little misdirection. "We can sit here and play this game all afternoon, but I believe strongly that this issue needs to be put to rest. In the best interest of our country and in the spirit of cooperation, I'll tell you what I can."

"Alright, let's hear it."

"First, I want your word this will be the last anyone hears about this."

"Agreed."

Bishop could tell he was lying, but then, so was he. "Westfield's operational mandate was born classified many years ago."

"So you lied to me. There *is* a directive."

"I didn't lie. Woody, there is no directive governing Westfield's operations within the NSA or the DoD."

"Then where is it?"

"As I said, it was a mandate that was born classified. I can't tell you any more than that."

"What's born classified mean?"

"It's a classification developed in the 1940s, created with the assumption that some information is too important to national security to risk disclosure before it could be formally evaluated for classification. In other words, Westfield's operation was born secret. Operations under this classification restrict access to only those who have a need to know. Much of General Westfield's work falls into this category. It's a security classification above TS/SCI/SAP/TK and is considered ORCAN from conception. Frank Talbot is frustrated because he can't have access to Westfield's operations. He's using you and the president to continue his vendetta."

"I see. Can you explain ORCAN?"

"It means the originator of the information controls its dissemination. Cecil Westfield has the legal authority to protect the interests of the United States, using any means he feels are necessary, and he's the only one who can grant authorization for the review of his operations. Even I don't have access to everything."

"Are you serious?"

"Yes. Frank Talbot disobeyed my direct order. He violated his secrecy agreement by coming to you. However, considering he made the disclosure only to you, I'm willing to forgo a drawn-out formal investigation and his subsequent prosecution, provided that he resigns immediately. I'm sure you could use him on your staff."

Woodsman stared at Bishop for a moment. "I'm sure that Mr. Talbot's actions in this matter were indeed honorable, and yes, I will find a place for him. However, I still have lingering questions about General Westfield. Does Westfield report to anyone in the Marine Corps?"

"Not to my knowledge."

"If you don't have the authority to access Westfield's operations, and he's not reporting to anyone in the Marines, who's watching over him?"

"I am responsible for oversight of most of his actions. I trust him implicitly to handle those things to which I'm not privy."

"I find that unacceptable."

"It really doesn't matter what you think," Bishop replied. "I've disclosed everything that I can legally tell you about this matter. Not even President Collingsworth can compel General Westfield to disclose any information about his operations. That's just the way it is. I'm asking you to keep your promise and drop this inquiry."

Woodsman sat back in his chair and sighed. "At least you've confirmed there's something being hidden from us. No one can act without legal authority, especially with the level of secrecy you've described. If General Westfield can do anything he wants, without the knowledge or approval of anyone, there must be a directive governing him somewhere."

Bishop didn't respond.

"I have never heard of anything like this before. The president always has the need to know on all intelligence issues related to national security. Everyone in this country reports to somebody. It's called checks and balances."

"Not always, Woody. President Clinton once made an inquiry into operations deemed ORCAN and learned he didn't have access. At times, the intelligence community is sanctioned to operate without disclosure to any governing body. Whether you like it or not, that's a fact of life. Most politicians are grateful for the distance between them and the dirty work. It provides plausible deniability. You should let this go."

Senator Woodsman drummed his fingers on the arm of his chair. "You having disclosed all of this makes me want to dig deeper. President Collingsworth has every right, under law, to know about any subject related to national security. He's chairman of the National Security Council, for Christ's sake. Perhaps we should make this a test case and let the Supreme Court decide."

"It has already been decided." Bishop decided to soften his approach. "Please understand the work being done by General Westfield is incredibly sensitive. Believe me, you do not want to know what he is doing. What little I do know about, I wish I didn't."

"Well, let's say for the sake of argument that I want to forge ahead."

Obviously, Woodsman wasn't going drop the subject. He leaned forward in his chair and said, "Senator Woodsman, you will not inquire any further into General Westfield's operations. You will not, and I emphasize *will not*, conduct any further inquiry—*period*. If you do, you will be considered a threat to national security and be dealt with accordingly. You can run and tell the president, and the DNI, exactly what I just said. It won't make any difference to the outcome. Have I made myself clear?"

A vein on Senator Woodsman's temple throbbed. "You son of a bitch! Where do you get off threatening a United States senator? I will crucify you for this. I will see to it that you're out on your ass."

Bishop raised his hand, and Woodsman took a breath and stopped his tirade.

"Let me be very clear. You have no authority in this matter. The president has no authority is this matter. Westfield is immune from any criminal prosecution or other punitive actions. It's been this way since President Truman was in office. In other words, Westfield has absolute power, and if his command is threatened, he has the authority to do anything he feels is necessary to keep his operations from the public. I operate under the same cloak of protection. If you persist in this inquiry, I'm telling you that you will be eliminated. That's a promise, not a threat."

Woodsman stared at him, aghast.

Bishop eased back. "Woody, there are many days that I wish it could be different. I really do, but these are the cards I've been dealt. It is my duty to comply with the mandates entrusted to me. Even if President Collingsworth fires me, I have no other legal option. I cannot disclose any additional information. Do you understand?"

Bishop pushed his chair back and stood up. He looked down at Senator Woodsman and added, "Let it go. Someday maybe you will understand what kind of personal sacrifices Westfield has made for our country. His operation will be kept off the radar, one way or another. Do not speak of this again. Do not tell Frank anything other than how nice it is to have him as a member of your staff. Do not utter another word about this subject."

Senator Woodsman stood and adjusted his two-hundred-dollar tie. "I don't believe you or Westfield has that much authority. You are telling me to keep my nose out of something that I believe needs to be exposed. You come in here and threaten me without any evidence to support your claim. I guess I'm supposed to take all this on faith, huh? Well, you can kiss my ass."

Bishop sighed. "I'm trying to protect you and the interests of our world." Bishop knew instantly he'd made a slip.

"Our *world* you say? Well, that certainly does open up a completely new can of crackers. What are you saying? Is Westfield the only person that can save us from our evil ways, or little green men, or some cataclysmic environmental event that could destroy our planet? Perhaps Westfield is Christ reborn, sent here to save us all. This is such bullshit."

Bishop turned to leave.

"We are not done here, Bishop."

"Yes, we are, Woody. More than you can imagine. If I get wind of anything other than you telling Frank to shut his hole, I will take the necessary actions to protect Westfield's operation, and you really don't want that to happen." Bishop opened the door and walked out, leaving the door open. He knew that Westfield would kill Woodsman, Talbot, or anyone else, including President Collingsworth, if they didn't stand down.

Senator Woodsman walked to the door, watched Bishop leave his reception area, and willed his blood pressure to return to normal. He laughed to himself as he removed the recorder from his coat pocket. The irony of the situation amused him. He'd secretly recorded the director of the NSA using an old-fashioned, low-tech device. Woodsman picked up the phone and called the office of the president. He had the feeling he knew what Westfield was investigating. It was all about little green men, only they were gray, and President Collingsworth would not be happy to hear the news.

Bishop knew he'd failed, and that didn't sit well with him. He hoped he wouldn't have to expand the target list, but that was Westfield's decision to make. Bishop walked to the underground parking garage. His driver opened the rear door of the black, standard-issue Chevy Tahoe as he approached. Bishop got in and took a breath. Then he dialed Westfield's private number from his secure encrypted phone.

It rang two times. "Yes, sir," Westfield answered.

"I believe I have complicated matters. Woodsman and the president are going to be a problem. It's your call on how to deal with them or anyone else you feel is a threat to keeping the lid on this thing."

"We're already on it. Woodsman called POTUS the minute you left his office."

"I'm sorry, Cecil. I thought I could reason with the man. When that failed, I threatened to kill him if he pursued his inquiry. He's either too stupid to save his own hide or just too stubborn."

"I will deal with it."

Bishop stretched his legs out and disconnected. Killing a United States senator was not what he wanted, but he knew it wouldn't be the first time a high-ranking official had been terminated to protect Dark Moon. Bishop was aware that Colonel Schneider was responsible for several deaths, including Secretary of Defense James Forrestal. He'd made it look like Forrestal had committed suicide by jumping from a sixteenth-floor window, but that was far from what really had happened.

The Tahoe pulled into traffic. Bishop gazed out the window at the Washington Monument. *There is something driving Woodsman and the president to be this relentless*, he thought. He knew what his next action had to be.

Senator Woodsman contacted the president, and less than an hour later he was with President Thomas Collingsworth in a secure White House conference room. After a Secret Service agent secured the door, Woodsman said, "TC, Bishop confirmed that Westfield is operating under a secret mandate or directive of some sort. I think he's actively searching for alien life."

"That could explain why you haven't found anything. Do you have any proof?"

"Bishop claimed the operation was 'born classified' during Truman's presidency. We know the significance of what happened then. Listen to this." Woodsman played the recording of their conversation.

TC listened to the recording. When it ended, he said, "That tells us nothing. Do you think Westfield's focus is on discovering our existence or just alien life in general?"

"I'm not sure."

"Don't you think that's important?" TC asked, sounding as if he were speaking to a child.

"Yes, of course it is. I believe the creation of Westfield's group was in response to the crash in 1947. It explains why the Kawich incident never became public. They're hiding the crash and everything they recovered from it."

"Probably, but how does that concern us?"

"You heard Bishop threaten to kill me if I continued to dig."

"I did."

Woodsman said, "We need to be very careful going forward in light of all that's transpiring."

"I agree, Woody. We must remain vigilant in our efforts to remain hidden until the Antediluvians arrive. I don't believe Westfield is of any immediate threat to us. You asking Bishop about Westfield will have put him on alert, so he will monitor you more closely. I think you should drop the matter as Director Bishop suggested. I appreciate your efforts. It's certainly nice to know who might be hiding in our backyard."

"I understand, sir. I will limit my inquiries."

"No, Woody, you will stop altogether. Let's not antagonize Director Bishop. I will see if I can introduce one of my people into the NSA. Let her do some digging and see what she turns up. Is there anything else?"

"No."

Three hours later, Westfield briefed Bishop about Woodsman's meeting with the president.

"I expected as much," Bishop said.

"We don't know what was discussed. It was a short meeting," Westfield said.

"I believe Woodsman told the president there's a secret directive governing your actions and that I threatened to kill him. My guess is that Woodsman will stop making inquiries and that the president will activate someone else to do the digging." Bishop sighed. "It's time to initiate Operation Flash Burn."

"I'll see to it that all Dark Moon personnel are airborne as soon as possible."

"I'm sorry, Cecil." It's been an honor working with you."

"Likewise, sir. I'll be back where Dark Moon began by tomorrow."

"You're going back to Alamogordo?" Bishop sounded surprised.

"Yes, sir. It's the last place anyone will look for us."

Bishop smiled. "Be safe, and good hunting."

PART TWO

"All that we are is the result of
what we have thought."

DHAMMAPADA

Calvin Alexander Locke surfaced from the depths of the turquoise Bahamian water. He closed his eyes, tilted his head back, and soaked up the warmth of the sun. The *Whispering Winds* rolled gently in the low swells off the north tip of Great Guana Cay. He was very close to where he'd discovered the abandoned and wallowing catamaran. A hurricane had driven the boat onto the rocks, holing her starboard hull. He'd purchased the boat for fifty thousand dollars, about ten percent of her value, from the previous owner. The extensive damage had taken Cal and Garth Aldeberie, a close friend and master boat builder, longer than expected to repair. He was down to the last of his savings by the time the *Whispering Winds* was ready for charter.

Today he'd been near the end of his dive when he spotted a pair of spiny lobsters. They'd scurried into hiding beneath a large outcropping of fire coral. After several attempts, he finally managed to capture them, checked his gauges, and ascended.

At the surface, Cal pulled the fish bag up out of the water and looked at the two lobsters. They were admittedly a bit on the small side, but they would keep his reputation intact. He let some air out of his ancient but reliable Dacor buoyancy compensator. With the fish bag trailing him, he began the swim back to the sailboat, which lay at anchor a hundred yards away.

Cal reminisced as he swam through the gentle waves. He'd proposed to Alessia after only a few months of them being together, and to his surprise and delight, she agreed to marry him. He'd felt the connection to her the first time they met. A long engagement seemed silly, so they set the date for the twenty-sixth. Cal called his oldest friend, Alexandra Hutchins-Winslow, and invited her and her husband, Nate, to witness their nuptials.

Cal and Alex had met the summer before their senior year in high school. They'd been best friends ever since. They went to the University of South Florida together, and their friendship grew as they each tried to find their calling in life. Alex had double majored in cultural anthropology and archeology. She had a thing for ancient civilizations, and she liked exploring ruins and digging in the dirt. After graduating from USF, she earned her Master's and a PhD in archeology from Northern Arizona in Flagstaff. She was currently a professor at Arizona State University in Tempe. Cal knew the pay was poor, but he could tell she was happy, and that was all that mattered to him.

They had never been romantically involved, which had allowed them to grow close without the baggage. He loved Alex like a sister. She was only five foot three and a bit plump around the middle. Her only vice was indulging in sweets. She was a tomboy and nerd at heart. She seldom bothered with cosmetics, and the only dress Cal had ever seen her wear was her wedding gown. He'd walked her down the aisle five years before when she'd married Nate. Alex's father had died during her first year of college, and then her mother died the following year. He'd been there to pick up the pieces, and he would always be there for her.

Alex flew out to meet Cal's future bride a few days ahead of Nate. She claimed Nate had to work, but Cal knew what she really wanted was some time to determine if Alessia was right for him.

Tegan was living a lie. She hoped Alex's probing questions would only reveal the background she had created for Alessia Stryker. She'd not been able to bring herself to tell Cal who she really was or anything about her past, believing the less he knew about her, the safer he'd be.

She didn't like it when Cal dove alone, but Tegan reluctantly agreed to stay behind, knowing that Alex wanted time with her. They sat in the salon talking. Tegan had taken a liking to Alex. She told her about her supposed life, and Alex shared stories about Cal when he was younger. She felt comfortable around Alex. She seemed like someone she had known for a long time. Tegan was disappointed when they had to stop telling Cal stories, but it was time to pick up Nate at Marsh Harbour, and first they needed to stop at Man-O-War Cay. Realizing that Cal was overdue, she left Alex in the salon to check on him. She went to the stern, gazed across the water, and saw him swimming toward the boat. She sat down to wait for him, soaking in the sun's rays.

When Cal reached the stern, Tegan pulled the starboard dive ladder out of the hidden transom compartment. Cal pulled the fish bag out of the water as he climbed up the ladder, beaming at her, and teased, "See what I caught?"

Tegan knelt on the step above him and kissed his salty forehead, then took the bag from him. She walked back to the open cockpit, examining the lobsters in the shade of the hardtop, then put them in the wet bar sink. She said, "These are a good start."

"Did you and Alex have some quality girl time? She really is sweet, isn't she?"

"We had a great talk." She pulled her hair back behind her ears, walked back to him, took his tank, and put it in the storage rack. "I'm going to take the lobsters inside to show Alex what you brought us for dinner." She grabbed the bag and ducked into the air-conditioned salon.

Alex put down her romance novel and slid out from behind the chart table. "Is that all he got us?" Alex asked, looking at the tiny lobsters in the galley sink.

"That's it."

"I guess hunting isn't one of Cal's strengths."

"He usually does better," Tegan said, coming to his defense.

"Well, Alessia, at least they'll make good appetizers."

"You think they're big enough for that?"
They both laughed.

$$\infty$$

Cal looked out at the peaceful panorama as he listened to the sound of the waves lapping against the twin hulls. He checked his watch. They needed to get going. He stood and turned only to find both women standing there. They each had a smug look on their face.

"Nice catch, Captain," Alex said, "but what else do you plan to provide for dinner after we eat these scrawny appetizers you brought us?"

"Hey, all I promised was that I'd find us some lobsters. I didn't say how many or how big." He brushed past them and walked to the open cockpit, then turned around. "I need you to rinse and stow the gear so we can get going."

"You're the captain," Alex replied. "But I think it's gone to your head. I need to show Alessia how to knock you down a peg or two."

Both women laughed as Cal entered the salon.

$$\infty$$

"Your equipment is rinsed and stowed," Alex said, walking into the salon a few minutes later.

Cal handed her a bottle of water. "What do you think of Alessia?"

"She's attractive, has a mind of her own, a strong will, and appears to have been blessed with a keen intellect. It's a mystery what she sees in you. She isn't anything like the other women you've been attracted to, or the last one you married," she teased.

"Do you like her?"

"Very much. I enjoy her company. She's well read, has diverse interests, and she's what I would call a closet academic. I think she's smarter than she wants me to know."

"She's very smart."

"Any skeletons in her closet?" Alex asked.

"None that I know of. Why do you ask?" Cal said, watching Tegan walk toward the bow.

"I just get the feeling she's hiding something. The way she talked about her past seemed rehearsed. Did you do a background check on her when you hired her?"

Cal cocked his head. "No. Alexandra, I think you would find fault with anyone I wanted to marry."

"Probably. I'm just looking out for you."

Cal smiled and said, "Mrs. Winslow, the sooner we get under way, the sooner we'll get you to your hubby. You'd better get cleaned up."

"That's Hutchins-Winslow," Alex said, flipping him the finger on the way to her cabin.

Cal left the salon, climbed up to the flybridge, and sat down at the controls under the small Bimini top. When he got a thumb's-up signal from Alessia, he turned on the electric winch and raised the anchor. With the anchor locked in the chocks, he started the two forty-horsepower diesel engines. A few moments later, he pushed the throttles forward. He felt the wind on his face as the *Whispering Winds* reached her top speed of just under nine knots and set a course for Man-O-War Cay.

TEN

Vice President Stacy Preston felt TC's mental presence reaching out to her seconds before her assistant told her that he was on the private line. Preston picked up the phone.

"Yes, Mr. President."

"Stacy, Sandra is dead." His voice held no hint of emotion.

"I'm sorry, TC. I know you once cared for her, but you had no other option."

"There will be the usual media circus. I need you to be prepared. We haven't officially made the announcement, but there are rumors being leaked from the hospital."

"I'm here for you. I'll do whatever you need me to do."

"I know you will."

The president had visited his wife at the Bethesda Naval Hospital four times a week over the last six months. The visits were made for the sake of public appearance. The time he'd spent there had interfered with the preparations he'd needed to make for the arrival of the Antediluvians. After receiving his instructions, he'd gone to the hospital, waited for the hospital staff to leave her room, then placed his hand over hers and sent the final charge into her body, ending her life. Anyone watching the monitors at the nurses' station would have only noticed the president holding his wife's hand when her heart stopped.

TC's powers had grown stronger over the last few weeks. He could sense others like him awakening all over the world. After hundreds of generations and numerous iterations of genetic alterations, the Awakened were nearly ready for the Antediluvians' arrival. TC's ancient ancestors were the first ones genetically augmented. Now he was to lead the Awakened. TC welcomed those fully awakened, reaching out to each of them with the aid of the Orb. When his neural pathways were better developed, he would no longer need the Orb to communicate with them.

Unfortunately, not all of the awakenings had gone as planned. TC found that some could not respond to his contact. The psychic link they needed to connect to the collective whole was missing, leaving them struggling to understand what was happening to them. Just as with wiring that has not been connected properly, the incomplete synapses of some of the awakened had shorted out. Many claimed they were hearing messages from God. The result was a spike in unexplainable mental health facility admissions and suicides.

Stacy Preston, awakened a year ago, had quickly learned the role she was to play in the future of humankind. TC had chosen her to be his vice president shortly after his inauguration. No one questioned his choice. Stacy had impeccable credentials. A congresswoman for over twelve years, representing the state of Maine, she was well liked by all parties. She was elected to her first term in Congress at the age of thirty-six. Now, at forty-eight, she was in the position she'd been destined to hold. Stacy stood five foot six inches and had the beginnings of a middle-age spread. She hid it well in her custom-made dark business suits and dresses. With her gray eyes and black-dyed hair, she projected a commanding appearance.

Over the past few months, TC and Stacy had spent more time together than should have been necessary as they prepared for the Antediluvian arrival. They could not afford any unforeseen problems. They bounced every possible problem they could think of around and then developed contingency plans for every one of them. Their private meetings had drawn attention from staff. Rumors were circulating.

The White House planned a news release for 1700 hours, announcing the death of Sandra Collingsworth. Also included was the fact that the president's two sons would soon join him. The press release also requested that everyone remember the family in their prayers and give them privacy.

Man-O-War Cay – July 22 – 1600 hours

It was a short and pleasant trip to Man-O-War Cay. The weather was postcard perfect. Small cumulus clouds dotted the sky as the gentle tropical breeze pushed them westward. Cal decided to take the *Whispering Winds* through the narrow inlet on the western side of the island. He listened as Alex and Tegan chatted in the salon. He couldn't hear everything they were saying, but they were obviously talking about him.

Nathan Winslow was arriving at the Marsh Harbour airport in an hour, which gave the women time to freshen up before they caught the ferry. The ferry was usually on time, so Cal figured it would be easier and faster than sailing the *Whispering Winds* to Marsh Harbor. Dock space was always at a premium there, especially for a wide-beam catamaran. While the women went to get Nate, Cal planned to buy additional provisions for the coming days at sea. He had decided to get fresh mahi from Miles Fish and Bait store, and he hoped to grab a few loaves of Maggie Aldeberie's famous day-baked bread. Cal wanted to have a nice welcoming dinner aboard for Nate, and he planned to anchor in Bakers Bay before nightfall.

"Hey, stop gabbing and prepare for docking," Cal yelled from the flybridge.

Cal always found it challenging to navigate the narrow passage because of the strong current that raced through the gap. He made a sweeping turn and slowed the *Whispering Winds* to maneuvering speed. Luckily, the current was running with him into the harbor, which would make for a faster and safer passage. Not seeing any vessels in the channel, Cal entered the inlet.

A moment later, he spotted a large motor yacht coming toward them. It was still far enough away that its captain had plenty of time to give way. Midway through the passage, the motor yacht accelerated as if they weren't even there. From his many years of traversing the channel, he knew that the water to starboard was deep, so he steered that way to avoid an imminent collision. He pushed the throttles all the way forward and straightened out at the last second to avoid a submerged rock outcropping. At the same time, the captain of the motor yacht veered away, cut his engines, and let the large boat settle. The vessels passed each other just feet apart.

"Hold on!" Cal yelled, seeing the large wake the motor yacht had created.

The wake rocked the *Whispering Winds*, nearly causing Alex to fall as she left the salon.

"What the hell?" Alex said.

"Big boats make big wakes," Cal replied. "The captain of that boat should never have been going that fast."

"No shit!" Alex cried.

Garth Aldeberie watched from his chair on the lookout deck atop the marina office as the two boats nearly collided. He could see the outbound skipper gesturing at Cal. Garth knew that most captains would not have been able to avoid a collision as adeptly as Cal had. Cal was a deliverer of miracles.

Man-O-War Cay had been Garth's home since his birth in the old family clapboard house fifty years ago. He was five-ten and a little overweight for his height, but looked younger than his age even with his full head of gray hair. He had a great sense of humor and keen business acumen. Maggie, his wife, ran a small bakery on the island. They could have made a small fortune if they had expanded her operation, but already having a net worth in the millions, they didn't need to increase their wealth. Garth and Maggie preferred the simple life, and they enjoyed living in their modest home, which resembled a New England saltbox cottage. The yellow house, surrounded by a white picket fence and nestled among the many brightly painted homes that overlooked the harbor, had been passed down from generation to generation.

The Aldeberie clan was a quiet, unpretentious, hard-working family. Their daughter, Jessica, was the youngest at nineteen. She still lived at home. Their son, Edward, at twenty-three, ran a fledgling ferry service and lived in Marsh Harbour with his soon-to-be fiancée, Sara Pinder.

Jessica grudgingly helped in the family businesses, spending most of her time running their dive shop and tending to their vacation home rentals. She had a knack for entertaining the tourists. Jessica was opinionated and strong-willed, not unlike her father, and was eager to start her own life away from the Abacos, which scared Garth to death. She had a good heart and an inquisitive soul, but possessed an innocent view of the world. Jessica had expressed a desire to attend college in America, and he knew the time would come when they would have to let her go out on her own.

Garth figured that Edward would stay rooted in the islands. He didn't have the wanderlust his sister did, for which Garth was grateful. He wanted to help Edward build his own empire in the Abacos and knew that it was dependent on the success of Edward's ferry business.

He checked his watch and noted that Edward should have arrived by now. He wondered what was keeping him. Garth went down the stairs and walked around to the front of the dive shop, then waved as the *Whispering Winds* approached the dock. "Hey, there, you two, uh, three," he said after he saw Alex standing in the cockpit. "Nice bit of seamanship there, Cal," Garth added with a light Bahamian accent as he approached them on the dock.

Garth was dressed in his usual attire, a pair of faded khaki shorts with a tan polo shirt and his trademark varnish-stained boat shoes, which he had worn for the last ten years. He cast Alessia a smile, his pearly teeth in sharp contrast to his suntanned face. He snagged the line she threw him and tied it to the dock cleat.

"Goodness, Alessia, look at you. You are the most beautiful creature on this island," Garth said.

"And you will be in big trouble when I tell Maggie you're flirting with me again."

"Maybe so, but I still think we'd be great together. All you have to do is dump that underachiever husband-to-be of yours." Garth smiled up at Cal.

"If you two don't mind, I'd like to get this boat tied up sometime today," Cal said.

Garth took the stern line from Alex and secured it.

Cal asked, "What's Jessica up to these days?"

"Jessica's going stir-crazy. Chompin' at the bit to get off this rock and see the world. Any chance you can take her along on your next charter and tell her about the big bad world out there? She won't listen to us anymore, but for some reason she believes what you and Alessia tell her."

"Sure, it would be fun to have her with us."

"I don't think you'd have to pay her anything. I only request you don't let her scamper off."

"We would be honored to watch over your daughter. Where's Edward? I thought he'd be at the dock by now."

"He's late. You can't build a ferry business if you get a reputation for not staying on schedule." Garth shook his head.

"Garth, the ladies want to grab a ride back to Marsh, if there's room," Cal said, jumping to the dock and helping Alex off the boat.

"He'll have room for sure. Now who is this fine young lady?" Garth asked, looking at Alex.

Cal introduced them, then added, "Garth's Loyalist relatives have been living in the Abacos since the Revolutionary War. They haven't been allowed back in America since then."

Alex smiled.

"Don't listen to him, love. He's been at sea too long, and the sun has fried his brain," Garth countered.

"Alex is an old friend," Cal said. "Her husband, Nate, is arriving at the airport this afternoon. They need a round trip to Marsh Harbour."

"Will they need to rent one of my cottages?" Garth asked, rubbing his hands together.

"No, they'll stay with us on the *Whispering Winds*. Alex is going to be my best man at the wedding." Cal turned to Alex. "And Garth is going to marry us."

"Your best man?" Garth asked. "I think you need to get your eyes checked. Are you all heading back out today, or do you need a slip for the evening?"

"I plan to head to Bakers Bay, but those plans could change. Can you leave dock space open?"

"No problem. Stay as long as you like." Garth excused himself.

ELEVEN

Man-O-War Cay — July 22 — 1645 hours

Edward Aldeberie stood at the helm of the *Alde I*, struggling to keep his temper under control as he bore the brunt of an elderly gentleman's tirade. Edward was the same height as his father but thirty pounds lighter. His hair was a youthful light brown. He owned the *Alde I*, a thirty-eight-foot Wagner Custom. It was the only boat in his fledging ferry service. He hoped to have a second boat running soon.

The hull of the *Alde I* was white, with distinctive bright red accent stripes down the side, making it stand out from the crowd. It could seat twelve passengers comfortably. Unfortunately, the passenger area lacked air-conditioning, but its design provided good airflow, which kept his passengers cool once the boat was under way.

Edward's hazel eyes stared straight ahead as the man jabbed his finger against his shoulder.

"If I ran a business like this back home, Eddie, I would be out of business," the elderly man yelled. "No air-conditioning on this tub in the middle of July. I can't wait to see the dump of a place we rented on the island." The man walked back and sat down next to his wife.

Edward hated being called, "Eddie." He was behind schedule because he'd waited for the old man and his wife as a favor to Fran Cottingham, the owner of the Go Native motel.

Less than eighteen minutes after leaving Hope Town, Edward steered the *Alde I* through the narrow passage to Man-O-War. As he turned toward the docks, he spotted the mast of the *Whispering Winds* standing tall against the blue sky. He motored to the marina and docked directly behind her.

Garth met Edward at the dock and helped him secure the lines. Two young couples disembarked. They thanked him and offered praise for his seamanship and patience, giving him generous gratuities. Edward directed them to the rental office at the dive shop. The elderly couple was the last to leave his boat. The old man gave Edward a hard, hateful stare, forgoing any gratuity. Edward decided he could find the rental office on his own.

"Jessica is going to love them," Edward said to his father once the elderly couple couldn't hear him.

"You're late," Garth said quietly.

"I know."

"I need a favor from you, and then you and I are going to have a little talk."

Edward grimaced.

"You won't mind doing this favor. Alessia and her friend, Alex, need a ride to Marsh Harbour. They're picking up Alex's husband at the airport. Cal asked if you'd wait and bring them back."

"No problem. For Alessia, I'll even stay overnight here with you and mom, if that's okay." He knew what his father wanted to talk to him about, and it wasn't going to be a pleasant discussion.

"Fine by me, son, but what about Sara?"

"I'll give her a call. I'm sure she won't mind."

"Look at that," Garth said. "Alessia sure cuts a fine figure. Look at those legs."

"Careful, father, you don't want mother learning you're crushing on her."

"I don't have a crush on her," Garth snapped. "She could be my daughter and your older sister. But there's no harm in admiring beauty."

"Whatever you say. Hey, there," Edward said as the women approached. "I hear you need a water taxi to Marsh and back." Edward noticed Cal standing in the cockpit of the catamaran and waved to him. Cal smiled and waved back.

"We do indeed," Tegan replied. "Edward, this is Alex, a friend of ours. We would dearly appreciate you waiting for us while we get her husband at the airport. We shouldn't be too long."

"He won't leave you stranded," Garth said. He left them to go and tend to the new arrivals.

"Are you here on holiday?" Edward asked Alex.

"Yes, and for their wedding."

"Alessia, you and Cal are getting married?"

"Yes. I thought you knew."

"Nope."

"Edward, Cal and I haven't told many people. We asked your parents not to say anything. I guess they thought that meant you, too. I'm sorry. You know you're welcome to attend."

"Does Jessica know about the wedding?" Edward asked.

"I think so, but if you didn't know, I'm not sure. I'll have to ask her when we get back from Marsh."

"I don't think she knows," Edward said. "She would've said something to me about it. I'd be honored to attend your wedding, Alessia. May I bring Sara?"

"Absolutely," she replied.

"We better get going," Edward said, boarding the *Alde I*.

The women helped with the lines and boarded.

Marsh Harbour — 1715 hours

It was a quick ride to the island. After arriving at the dock, Tegan and Alex took a taxi to the airport. They found Nate standing in the shade of a palm tree just outside the terminal entrance. Tegan's first thought on seeing him was that he looked like the poster child for the ugly tourist.

Nate stood six feet tall but weighed only one hundred and forty pounds. His thin, white legs looked like toothpicks sticking out from the bottom of his navy colored shorts. The Hawaiian shirt he was wearing hung on him like a tent. A white Panama hat covered his thinning brown hair.

"What *are* you wearing?" Alex asked, giving him a hug and kiss.

"Comfort clothes, with a hint of Bahamian flare," Nate replied.

"Nate, this is Alessia Stryker. Alessia, this is my style guru and loving husband, Nate."

"I'm pleased to finally meet you," Tegan said. "Alex has told me a lot about you over the last few days."

"All good, I hope," Nate replied. He picked up one of his suitcases, then asked, "Where's Cal?"

"He stayed on MOW to rustle us up some dinner," Tegan said. "We're going to eat on the boat tonight. I am guessing it will be some sort of fish on the grill.

"And a lobster tail appetizer," Alex added.

Nate looked puzzled. "What's MOW?"

Tegan grinned. "MOW is what we call Man-O-War Cay."

"We have a ferry waiting," Alex said, putting her arm around his waist. "If you have everything, we should be back on MOW in less than a half hour."

Man-O-War Cay — 1750 hours

Cal was waiting on the dock, talking with Garth and Maggie when the *Alde I* arrived. Maggie was holding her husband's hand. She was shorter than Garth by five inches and didn't look her fifty years of age. Her light brown hair was cut short, and her slender build didn't fit the stereotype of a baker or the mother of two adult children.

"Hey, Nate, it's good to see you. It has been too long," Cal said, taking a line from Edward.

"Same here."

"They don't let you out much in Arizona, huh?" Cal said, spotting Nate's white, spindly legs.

"Occupational hazard. Unlike you guys who get to sail the ocean as carefree as you please, I'm tied to a desk all day."

"Nate, this is Garth and Maggie Aldeberie. You already met their son, Edward."

"It's a pleasure to meet you," Nate said, tipping his hat.

"Come on," Cal said. "Let me show you the *Whispering Winds*, your home away from home for the next week."

Nate and Alex boarded the *Whispering Winds*. Cal hung back and watched as Edward and Garth argued, which was unusual.

"What do you think that's all about?" Tegan asked.

"I don't know," Cal answered, noting Maggie was doing her best to referee. "But it must be serious. Garth seems worked up."

Cal and Tegan boarded. The women walked into the salon and sat on the couch behind the chart table. Nate looked around the spacious salon at the furnishings. The couch wrapped around the oversized chart table in a half-moon arc, offering a panoramic view through the large windows. The stairs leading down into both hulls were made of highly polished teak. The boat was immaculate, and it showed little sign of wear.

"Wow, this is nice!" exclaimed Nate. "It's bigger than I thought it would be. So this boat was really sunk when you found it?"

"In a manner of speaking. The starboard hull suffered extensive damage and had a hole in it. Garth helped me rebuild her and get her seaworthy again. To your left, please," Cal said, motioning toward the stairs.

They descended into the port hull and turned aft. "This is your stateroom," Cal said, opening the door. "Each stateroom on this side has its own head. The starboard side mirrors this one, except there is only one head. Alessia and I share the aft stateroom. Our supplies usually end up in the forward cabin."

"This is beautiful. What does something like this cost?"

"New, about three quarters of a million. I obviously got this one for a lot less. We put a lot of labor into her to make her suitable for chartering. She may be only forty-four feet long, but she's very seaworthy. I modified her during the rebuild so our guests and clients would be more comfortable. Alessia and I spend most of our time topside or in the salon. The beauty of the sea and the smell of the fresh salt air melt our troubles away. You and Alex should buy a boat, retire to the islands, and live the good life with us. You could use some sun."

Nate chuckled. "Do you know of any good sailboats for sale? I'd love to join you in the vagabond life at sea, but I'm not sure I could get Alex to leave Arizona."

"There are quite a few for sale on Treasure Cay. If you're serious, we can swing by sometime during the next few days and take a look. Who knows, maybe Alex will like being on the water instead of digging in the dirt. By the way, thanks for being here. It means a lot to us."

"Thanks for inviting us. How long has it been since we last saw you?" Nate asked.

"It's been way too long, that's for sure."

When Cal and Nate returned to the salon, the women had already opened beers and snacks for them.

"Nice," Nate said. "This day is getting better and better. I've wanted to get away from the office and see something other than the desert for some time now. It's quite a contrast."

"Yes, it is," said Alex. "Wait until you're out at sea."

"How many more guests are you expecting for the wedding?" Nate asked.

"It's only going to be Garth, Maggie, and their daughter, Jessica. Alessia, do you know if Edward is coming?"

"I just found out he didn't even know we were getting married. He looked hurt, but I explained we were keeping it very private, and we had asked Garth and Maggie not to say anything. I guess now we know they can keep a secret. I'm not sure if Jessica even knows. I told him Sara was welcome."

"Come to think of it, Jessica hasn't said anything about it either," said Cal, noticing Edward walking toward the boat lugging Nate's suitcases. Cal excused himself and went to meet Edward.

"Thanks, Edward," Cal said, taking Nate's suitcases. "Is everything alright?"

"It will be. My father found out I had inquired about a job running a fishing charter out of Green Turtle Cay two days a week to earn some extra money. He doesn't think it's a good idea. He says I need to stay focused on the ferry service."

"I think you should listen to his advice. He's very wise."

"Sara and I want to get married."

"Wow, that's a big step. Are you guys ready to settle down?"

"Definitely. I want to squirrel away some extra cash to buy a house. I can earn twice what I make running the ferry during those two days. My father offered us a house to live in here, but I want to do this on my own, without his help."

"I understand."

"I just heard you and Alessia are getting married. Congrats."

"Thank you. We're sorry for the late invite. I hope you and Sara will be able to attend."

"No problem. We'll be there," Edward said, then turned to walk back down the dock. "You guys have a good evening."

When Cal entered the salon, he saw that the lobsters had been dispatched and were laid out next to four pieces of mahi. They were all seasoned with a special blend of herbs and ready for the grill.

"Cal, Nate's a bit tired," Alex said. "Can't we spend the night here and get an early start tomorrow?"

Cal nodded. "Not a problem. Let me show you what we have planned for you guys tomorrow, then I'll start the grill." He pulled a chart of the Abacos from the overhead rack and spread it out on the chart table.

"The Abacos are the northeasternmost islands in the Bahamas," Cal said. "The Sea of Abaco is fairly shallow, but once you head east of the islands, the depth drops thousands of feet in just a few miles." He pointed to the depth markings on the chart. "These are in fathoms, so multiply that number by six, and you have the depth in feet. The reef along this outer bank is the third-largest in the world, and it extends over a hundred and fifty miles to the south."

"Wow," Nate said.

"Tomorrow, we'll sail around the island and anchor here," Cal said, pointing at a spot on the chart. "It's about a mile and a half south of the northern tip of the island."

"Sounds good to me," Nate said.

"There's a pristine reef there that disappears into the abyss that I know you both will love."

"That sounds exciting," Alex said.

Cal said, "I'd like to be away from the dock by nine at the latest. We should be wet just before lunch time."

"About that abyss, how deep are we diving?" Nate asked.

"We aren't going very deep," Cal said. "No deeper than ninety feet. I'm not a big fan of using exotic gas."

"Don't worry, honey. I'll hold your hand if you get scared," Alex teased.

They all laughed.

TWELVE

Alamogordo, New Mexico — July 22 — 1730 hours MST

Deep under the New Mexico desert, Cecil Westfield was reviewing the latest intelligence reports and internal security threat assessments. A medical report was included which said that Sandra Collingsworth's cause of death was the result of a massive stroke. Of particular interest to Westfield was that Mrs. Collingsworth's heart rate and brainwave activity had spiked, as if she had grabbed onto a live electrical wire just before she died. The confidential brief said the president had been holding her hand when the heart monitor alert sounded. He hadn't responded to the alarm, never sought help, and had just sat there until medical personnel arrived. The president had left the hospital while the medical team was still trying to revive his wife. It seemed as if he already knew her fate and didn't care.

Westfield concluded that the events associated with her coma and her death were all too suspicious, regardless of what the final medical report indicated. He knew President Collingsworth's behavior was abnormal, especially in light of the president's curiosity in his command.

The classified brief also reported that the first responding nurse told a doctor that as she entered the room she heard the president speaking softly to himself, as if he was in a trance, chanting in a strange language.

The oddest thing was that she also told the doctor that when the president looked up at her, his eyes appeared larger than normal. She described them as being black with a golden glow, and that his eyes abruptly returned to normal when he saw her looking at him. The report attributed the nurse's vision to the lighting in the room. *Smoke and mirrors, shadows and lights,* Westfield mused. He needed to dig deeper, and Woodsman was the weak link to the president he needed to exploit.

Westfield then read a series of psychological profiles about Collingsworth, prepared by the Defense Intelligence Agency, which said the president had been more irritable and short-tempered recently. His demeanor didn't match his psych profile from a year earlier, which raised questions within the DIA about whether the president was becoming unstable. From all indications, the president saw his wife's condition as an imposition and that he was only pretending to be a caring and loving husband. The profile also said the president appeared preoccupied, but there was no reference to what would be important enough to distract him, except possibly Vice President Stacy Preston.

The CIA reports noted that for the last several weeks the president had met daily with Preston, always behind closed doors. All of the meetings lasted more than an hour, and most were unscheduled. The president left standing orders that they were not to be disturbed unless there was an act of war. Senator Woodsman joined them on occasions. The purpose of the meetings was unknown.

Westfield rubbed his chin. *There is more to it than a simple tryst,* he thought. He closed the file and lit a cigarette.

The underground sanctuary where he sat, located nearly three hundred feet below Holloman Air Force Base, was where Westfield had moved operations the day after he left NSA headquarters in May. Flash Burn had been a success. All electronic signatures, including files and gateways, had been deleted so that there was no record that Westfield or any of his teams had ever been in Maryland. As gifted as NSA technicians were at forensic data mining, they would still never find a trace of any of his operations.

General Westfield, along with Knolls and Grant, had flown to New Mexico. Dark Moon, Signal Intelligence Analysis (SIGINT), Human Intelligence (HUMINT), and Technical Intelligence (TECHINT) staff had followed at intervals, arriving at different locations around the Southwest. Then the teams had traveled to Alamogordo by different routes.

The Medical, Biological Research, and Genome Team (MBRG), based at Annapolis Junction, had moved Deep Sky and all its operations to the Los Alamos National Laboratories facility in New Mexico. Los Alamos was three hundred miles north of Alamogordo and had nearly ten thousand employees working at the sprawling facility. MBRG was operational just days after the move from Maryland. They were utilizing a medical facility that had been vacant for years. The team was posing as a medical research company doing contract pharmaceutical work for the government.

Westfield had decided to leave the reverse-engineering unit, hidden within the National Air and Space Intelligence Center at Wright-Patterson, alone. It had been functioning without issue since the spacecraft wreckage was taken there in 1947. Back then, the NASIC was known as the Foreign Technology Division.

He'd left his cybersecurity team attached to the Comprehensive National Cybersecurity Initiative data center in place in Utah, even though he knew they'd be compromised eventually. However, they had no other place to go and still be of value. They were his weakest link, but the technicians operated as a blind cell, so they couldn't provide any information about his operations, and none of the information transmitted could be tracked.

For now, the new headquarters for Dark Moon remained hidden from prying eyes. Westfield was back where it had all started, inside Phoenix Two. He knew that the first Dark Moon commander, Colonel Schneider, had once sat in this office after he relocated from Fort Bliss. The underground complex had undergone many upgrades over the years, but his office still retained its late-forties feel.

No one was going to think twice about a new group of people occupying the old five-thousand-square-foot building on the outskirts of the base built during World War II. Hidden in a bomb shelter under the old building, protected by a sophisticated biometric and electronic security system, was the entrance to his underground labyrinth. Officially, the building above him was a Department of Energy research facility. His people were there under the guise of being employees of the Alternative Energy Group, a research company contracted and funded by the DOE.

Westfield could no longer hide or rely on funding from the NSA, so he'd shifted his funding sources back to the DOE. He was certain Woodsman knew how to follow a money trail, but thanks to General Bishop's work, Woodsman's efforts to find them had been in vain. The Department of Energy received funding for S-3 operations through private contractor earmarks. It had been that way ever since conception.

Woodsman was still trying to pierce their veil of secrecy. His program that allowed him to track black ops funds would not provide the results he sought. However, if Woodsman expanded his funding search to classified earmarks, it could become a problem.

As a way to explain Westfield's sudden disappearance from the NSA, Director Bishop told Senator Woodsman that General Westfield had been killed during a covert operation in Hawaii. Woodsman hadn't believed the story. After the ruse failed and Bishop refused to answer the president's questions about the operation, he'd been forced to retire. Then Bishop disappeared.

Director Bishop had sacrificed his career to keep Dark Moon off the grid. Westfield knew that Bishop's replacement, appointed by Collingsworth, would never learn about Dark Moon. The Secretary of Energy, Timothy Stoltz, was the only one who remained in the oversight loop. Westfield knew that Stoltz wouldn't disclose the existence of S-3 operations to the new NSA director without his approval, which wasn't going to happen.

With everything that had happened, Westfield believed he was becoming a liability to Dark Moon operations, and that needed to change. The mission always came first.

This would be his last posting. His health had declined dramatically over the last two months. He knew it was time to pass the torch, and he had decided Robert Knolls would replace him. He recognized many of his own attributes in Knolls. He was ideological and focused, and he always finished what he started. Knolls had matured quickly and had thrown himself into his work, striving to perform at the optimal level on every project assigned to him. Knolls possessed the leadership qualities needed for being the next commander of Dark Moon. The only deficiency Westfield found, and one he couldn't change, was that Knolls wasn't a Marine.

He lit another cigarette and leaned back in his chair. As he inhaled deeply, there was a knock on the door. "Enter," Westfield commanded.

"You wanted to see me, sir?" Knolls asked.

"I did," Westfield replied, noting that Knolls was a few minutes early for their meeting. He pointed to a chair at the small conference table.

"Rob, I feel you're ready to take the next step."

Knolls looked a bit apprehensive, but only Westfield would have noticed. "I'm always ready for a challenge. You know that."

"Yes, I do, and that's why I'm about to give you the challenge of a lifetime. It's an opportunity to carry on a tradition passed down since the days of President Truman."

Westfield took a drag on his cigarette. "Rob, I've decided to retire. I need someone to fill my shoes and carry the torch. That someone needs to put country and mission before all else, and I believe that person is you."

Knolls appeared stunned.

Westfield joined Knolls at the conference table. "I think it's time for you to know everything." Westfield leaned in. "For the last twenty-four years, I have commanded a group known as Dark Moon. Thanks to Senator Woodsman, I've become a liability. Dark Moon, the group you really work for, is now vulnerable to discovery. This is something that simply cannot happen, as I will explain in detail.

"President Collingsworth and Senator Woodsman are determined to find out what secrets I hold and what it is that I do. If they are successful, they will uncover Dark Moon. Director Bishop tried to protect us, and it ended up costing him his job. Woodsman and the president didn't buy the story of my death, so they upped their game, which I find very interesting. Most politicos run from knowledge about secret organizations in order to protect their careers. President Collingsworth and Senator Woodsman are different. We'll talk more about my suspicions on that subject later, but first . . ."

Westfield took another long drag on his cigarette and coughed. "The tradition and the protocol for the transfer of command of Dark Moon come from a classified presidential order signed by President Truman. It is the responsibility of the outgoing commander to select the incoming commander of Dark Moon. It will mean a lifetime commitment to the cause. You won't have a personal life, and in all likelihood you'll never be married again. Kids are out of the question even if you do get married. They would be too much of a liability. Before you accept my offer, I want you to think it through."

Knolls still looked stunned, but managed to say, "It would be an honor to follow in your footsteps, sir."

"Good. Osiris will be retiring with me, although he doesn't know it yet. You will need to find his replacement as soon as possible."

Westfield stood and walked to his desk. He picked up a dark navy binder, along with a very old green metallic folder, which had a lock on the front. He walked back to the table and handed Knolls the green folder and a key.

"Rob, what you are about to read explains why Dark Moon was created. I know you have suspected for some time now that our true mission was not just internal security and counterterrorism operations. The documents in the folder are the originals, signed by President Truman. Less than three dozen people in the world have seen this folder. There are no copies, and only one key. Guard them well. That document is your license to operate. It grants you unconditional immunity for your actions."

Knolls started to open the folder, then stopped and gave Westfield a deadly serious stare. "This is way beyond national security, isn't it?"

"Yes, it is. It's about the security of our planet and our way of life."

"Are we talking alien encounters?"

"That is exactly what we're all about. However, we call them Nonterrestrial Intelligent Beings, NIBs for short. Take a few minutes to read the documents, and then we'll get into the nuts and bolts of operations."

Knolls used the key to open the metal folder. Inside was a World War II security binder labeled, "Dark Moon - Eyes Only - by Presidential Authority." At the bottom of the front cover was a security classification he had never seen before: "Born Classified." The next page, titled "Executive Order 47001," bore the signature of President Harry S. Truman at the bottom of the page. Next to his signature was the date, July 28, 1947.

The names and signatures of everyone who had reviewed the file to date filled the next two pages. Only three presidents had reviewed the document. The last was John F. Kennedy. The names read like a who's who of former secretaries and directors. Director Bishop's signature was the last one on the document.

The next page listed the previous Dark Moon commanders. Commander Robert Knolls's name was there, as was a place for his signature just below Westfield's signature, where he had signed it in 2000. Knolls's hands trembled as he turned to the next page.

"That's the Dark Moon emblem," Westfield said. "A pyramid with an ankh symbol affixed to the side, with a crescent moon in the sky above it. It was the symbol found on a piece of the Kawich wreckage. You'll read about it in a few minutes. Read the maxim below the pyramid."

"We stand silently to serve all of humanity." Knolls looked up at Westfield. "You knew I would accept the position?"

"Yes."

"You have me listed as a Navy commander. Why?"

"Because the leader of Dark Moon has to be a military officer, I had your commission reinstated with a promotion. You're the first commander of Dark Moon from the Navy. All the other commanders have been Marines. Keep reading. I'll be back in a minute." Westfield left the room. He was sure Knolls would have questions when he came back.

$$\infty$$

Knolls turned the page and began to read.

The scope of Dark Moon's mission was straightforward. The primary objective was to ascertain the motives and intentions of the alien beings exploring Earth and to determine if they posed a threat to humanity. Dark Moon was authorized to investigate and reverse-engineer any non-terrestrial intelligent beings' technology and to exploit that technology for the benefit of the United States. Dark Moon personnel were to develop and engage in countermeasures, including disinformation, to protect the public from the truth about the alien presence. They were to determine if any other nation was engaged in activities with alien beings and take all appropriate measures.

The last paragraph of the document caused Knolls to break into a sweat. It said that the commander of Dark Moon had authorization to carry out these directives, with prejudice, by any means necessary, including the use of nuclear weapons.

Knolls sat back in his chair as he realized that Westfield could actually start a nuclear war, which meant that in a few months, he would be one of the most powerful people in the world. He was going to direct all operations and become the filter through which all threat assessment information flowed. In essence, he was the singularity around which all decisions, plans, and operations were executed.

The extent of the power he would have was intensely disturbing. Knolls knew he lacked the experience and knowledge to hit the ground running, and that frightened him. As he read further, he discovered there was very limited oversight. After President Kennedy's assassination, no other president ever knew Dark Moon existed. The Department of Defense had given oversight to the NSA.

Knolls read on. He reviewed the organizational structure of Dark Moon and saw how it fit with S-3. President Truman had been insightful in the way the organization was structured and hidden. There were S-3 members embedded in almost all facets of government without the parent agency knowing they were there. S-3 had layers within layers to provide intelligence to Dark Moon.

S-3 looked for threats that other government agencies weren't chartered to conduct or were prohibited from doing by law. It was the mortar between the bricks, a government within the government, and he would be in command of the flagship. Knolls finished reading the mandate and fully understood his role.

Westfield walked back into the office and lit a cigarette, then asked, "What's your first impression?"

"General, I knew there was more to what I was working on, but this is … staggering. The magnitude of operations and the nature of it … well, I don't know what else to say. How have you managed to run all of this by yourself all these years?"

"Easy. By picking the right people, compartmentalizing everything and everyone, and eliminating anyone who threatened our existence."

"Like Dr. Vasine?"

"Yes. Rob, you will be the only person that will know the identity of the personnel associated with Dark Moon and S-3 operations. You will compile all the intelligence gathered and decide what is relevant, what is actionable, and assign personnel to the various operations. In other words, you are the central repository of all knowledge. You won't have a personal life. I work twelve to fourteen hours a day, and for the next several months you will be working eighteen-hour days."

Westfield lit another cigarette. "As you have read, Secretary Stoltz is the only oversight we have now. I just informed him you would assume command when I retire or die. If anything happens to you, Stoltz would inherit Dark Moon, so stay alive. Bishop had been my backup." Westfield wheezed, then took another drag on his cigarette.

"There was a trilateral command structure originally. Following President Kennedy's assassination, Colonel Schneider decided to keep President Johnson in the dark. It would have been Kennedy's duty to brief the incoming president anyway. I guess a presidential assassination wasn't something President Truman had considered.

"Colonel Schneider had learned that Kennedy was about to expose Dark Moon to promote his own political agenda and to rub salt in the wounds of the then Soviet Union following the Cuban Missile Crisis. He couldn't allow that to happen."

Knolls said, "Are you saying Kennedy was killed by Dark Moon?"

"Not directly. Schneider saw it coming, knew it would serve his purpose, so he didn't stand in the way. By the way, Oswald didn't act alone. There was a second shooter."

Knolls rubbed the base of his neck while turning his head from side to side. "Get used to it, Rob. From here on out every day will be worse than today." Westfield knew what Knolls was feeling. He'd had the same reaction when he took command.

"Rob, Secretary Stoltz doesn't want to know what we're doing. He understands the need for S-3 and Dark Moon, but he prefers to keep his distance. I don't anticipate anything will change with you in command. The good thing is he understands the covenant of secrecy that protects all of S-3, and I've seen nothing to indicate he'd violate his oath. The oversight he's supposed to provide is nonexistent. My concern is who will replace him when the time comes."

"When I take command, I will be the only one who knows what threats exist, and any actions I take will be my sole responsibility?"

Westfield nodded. "That is correct. Bishop was the last true oversight. If you feel the need, you can try to keep Secretary Stoltz more informed, but I wouldn't recommend it. I'm sure you're on Woodsman's radar. If you're seen with Stoltz, he'll connect the dots. Dark Moon has its ass hanging out, and we don't want someone taking a bite out of it. Times have changed since the 1940s, when secrecy meant something. Now it seems like anyone with a kernel of information is trying to sell it for a profit and their fifteen minutes of fame. We live in a world of accessible information unlike any time in the past. Now when classified information is leaked it spreads so fast that there's no chance of containment."

Westfield suddenly felt an intense pain in his chest and could barely breathe. He tried to hide his weakness by pretending to look for something in the blue binder. Westfield inhaled with a wheeze. As the pain subsided, he passed the binder to Knolls and said, "I can offer you only this small piece of advice. First, you must understand. Read everything you can that's in the files. Learn all there is to know about Dark Moon's activities. All of the intelligence files are yours to review. You need to understand the playing field and see how nebulous it is at times. The blue binder contains all the access codes and contacts you'll need to operate."

Knolls opened the binder as if it were the Holy Grail. "Rob, there's a wealth of information in the files, but we're still far from understanding the NIBs' intentions. If I were you, I'd start reading everything in the archives first, then move on to the more current information. Ask me anything you like, anytime."

"I appreciate that, sir. What about Talbot and Woodsman? Shouldn't they be removed from the equation?"

Westfield gave Knolls a genuine smile. "I like the way you think. I've given Frank and Woody a whole new set of problems to deal with in their not so distant future. The CNCI gurus that I'll introduce you to in a few days planted photographs in Frank's personal and office computers that aren't politically or morally correct. These photographs will become the focus of a criminal investigation when they surface. I have no doubt Woodsman will distance himself from Talbot for self-preservation. I'm hoping the scandal will slow them down and give us some breathing room."

"What about President Collingsworth?" Knolls asked.

"The president seems preoccupied with something else right now." Westfield rubbed his chin. He decided against telling Knolls about his suspicions. "There is something that bothers me about Collingsworth, but I want to explore it further before I brief you."

Westfield stood. "I suggest you get started on your reading. We'll meet here tomorrow at 0700 hours for your next history lesson. I suspect you'll have a lot more questions by then."

"I'm sure I will."

"I want you to think globally as you process the material. Thank you, Rob. You are dismissed."

Knolls left and walked down the hall to his office. His head was spinning. *Unbelievable* was the only word he could think of to describe today's revelations. He now knew beyond any doubt that nonterrestrial beings existed. Knolls always thought that other intelligent life existed in space, but he figured it would be an anticlimactic discovery. He expected radio astronomers from NASA or SETI to announce they had intercepted radio signals broadcast from an alien world, but it would be too distant to travel to the source within the human lifespan. More likely, he thought they would find microbial life like that found on Mars. He never imagined direct contact.

He entered his small office and sat down at his desk, opened the blue binder, found the access code to the archive files, and entered it on his computer. A multitude of files appeared on his screen, listed by date. He decided to start his history lesson by reading the files in chronological order, as Westfield had suggested. He opened the first file and began reading what he thought should have been titled "The Greatest Story Ever Told."

Four hours later, he had managed to digest the report summaries and technical findings of the two major crashes in 1947. He had reviewed several other reports of unverified events that had occurred over Alaska during the same period. The most detailed reports were about the Kawich crash and the alien biological specimen recovered there. The specimen was with the MBRG team at Los Alamos. The metal fragments and assorted debris from the crash remained housed at secure facilities in Ohio and Nevada. Knolls decided he would visit those places soon. He wanted to see the alien artifacts and the biological remains in person.

THIRTEEN

Like a cat waking from a long nap, President Collingsworth stretched his arms in front of him, arched his back, and pushed himself up off the exercise mat. He looked at his reflection in the floor-to-ceiling mirrors that covered one wall of the gym. TC wondered what he'd become. He looked the same, but he felt so much different within his being.

He was at peace for the first time in many months. His wife was dead, and all he felt was a sense of relief. After the public memorial tomorrow, she would no longer be a distraction. Sandra was the fourth First Lady to die while her husband was in office, and TC had to follow protocol. Staffers were handling the arrangements. Normally, such preparations took several days, which gave dignitaries and other guests time to arrive. TC would follow protocol only so far. He was tired of wasting time.

His sons would be in Washington later in the day. Both of them were angry with him for rushing everything. He didn't care. It was important to keep them in the dark about who he was becoming. TC planned to spend as little time with his sons as possible. Knowing he wasn't the man they once knew, he was afraid his change would be noticed, and he couldn't afford anyone taking an interest in his new persona.

After the memorial, he and his sons would fly to California, where they would hold a private service. Sandra had already been cremated, and he planned to scatter her ashes in the Pacific Ocean, as was her wish, then return to Washington. It was the least he could do.

He sensed Senator Woodsman and Vice President Preston waiting quietly just inside the gym doorway. With his abilities growing more acute, he'd been able to follow their movement the moment they arrived at the White House. He hadn't even needed the Orb. Not only was he now able to sense the presence of an Awakened, but he could also discern their identity.

When TC finished his Tai Chi workout, he motioned for Preston and Woodsman to join him and dismissed the Secret Service agent standing near the door.

"What new information do you have for me?" TC asked.

"We've learned very little," Stacy answered quietly. "Westfield hasn't resurfaced."

TC pulled the Orb from his pocket and allowed it to float free. His eyes enlarged, and his gaze bore into them. A few seconds later, a golden glow radiated from the Orb. Without uttering a word, he transmitted his disappointment. Any unforeseen variable could derail the operation. Westfield needed to be located and then eliminated. "What have you learned from our operative inside the NSA?"

The Orb rotated as it hovered in the air between them.

Woodsman said, "The NSA is a dry well. No one knows anything about what Westfield did there. From our interviews, all we were able to determine was when Westfield was posted to NSA headquarters."

"That's it?" TC asked. "Anything from our insiders at the Pentagon?"

"No, sir," Woodsman answered. "We've been at this for months. It's as if he never existed."

"He is but a whisper," TC said softly. "It seems General Westfield was very thorough in covering his tracks. What about Talbot's informant?"

Stacy and Woodsman looked at each other.

"Talbot is a dead end," Stacy said. "He claims his source has disappeared."

"And Bishop?"

Woodsman said, "I received a call from the DNI a few hours ago. He seemed truly perplexed by Bishop's disappearance. He's treating the situation as if Bishop was a foreign agent. They're investigating everything he was involved with and everyone he had contact with over the last twenty years. I'll be advised of their findings as soon as their investigation is completed. He's as much a ghost as Westfield."

The Orb pulsed. TC looked at Woodsman. "You have more to add?"

"We discussed this earlier. You know my feelings."

"Yes, I do. We all know an Antediluvian scout ship crashed in Nevada in 1947."

The Orb grew brighter.

TC smiled as the Orb expanded its glow and embraced all of them, and then he said, "The question remains, how much does Westfield know? We don't believe he has learned who we are or of the Antediluvians' pending arrival. No military or intelligence traffic indicates that anyway. What is still of concern is what information Westfield may have amassed and where his base of operation is now located. We know he has the remains of the 1947 crash hidden somewhere. What we don't know is what he has discovered from the crashed craft that could be used against the Antediluvians."

"Agreed," said Stacy. "Woody has been searching for the craft, Mr. President."

Woodsman cleared his throat, then said, "We've checked all military and private corporate facilities and all labs connected to government contracts since that era. So far, our search criteria have only singled out Wright-Patterson."

"I know that," TC said.

Woodsman continued, "We searched the facility two days ago, but found nothing there. The Nevada test site and our secret base in Utah held promise, but I've been assured they are only being used to develop advanced military hardware. I've checked out military installations all over the world for any hint of Westfield using other facilities. Nothing stands out."

"There are a host of black ops government facilities and contractors located around the country," Stacy offered. "But gaining access to them has been difficult. Senator Woodsman's committee could focus on identifying private contractor redundancy and financial earmarks as part of their efficiency management initiative. That could lead us to a hidden thread. We may just stumble onto the giraffe hiding in the shoebox."

"I'll give you my support to expedite the initiative," TC said. "You should have thought of this sooner." He looked at Woody. "Let's hope you find Stacy's giraffe before it finds us."

TC stood and retrieved the floating Orb, signaling the meeting was over. The golden glow disappeared, and TC's oversized eyes returned to normal. He walked them to the door, opened it, and thanked them both for their time loud enough for the agent to hear him.

When he was alone, he thought about another option. If Westfield's operation was looking for signs of extraterrestrial life, he may have to provide him with something that would draw him into the open. He would check to see if it was worth the risk to the Antediluvians. He sat down, released the Orb, and opened his mind.

The Orb was his portal to knowledge and an interpretive conduit to his Antediluvian controller. He'd been shown what was to come. His genetically altered brain absorbed everything they wanted him to know. It was as if his mind was a massive Cray supercomputer that stored and analyzed information every nanosecond of the day. At night, when his body rested, his mind processed the images that had exploded and imprinted themselves on his brain when he was awake. His mind was no longer under his control. He was a vessel, a tool for what was to come. He could do nothing to change that, and he didn't want to. He'd been genetically programmed to respond to the Antediluvians' demands from birth.

His rapid metamorphosis was a challenge for him to control. He found it difficult not to use his new gifts instinctively, feigning ignorance as he interacted with other humans. The Antediluvians did not want people to think he was different, at least not yet. Too much rested on his ensuring a nonconfrontational response when they arrived. If anyone suspected what he was, his mission would end in failure.

TC didn't know that Antediluvians were devoid of any sense of individuality, nor was he privy to their true aspirations. He'd been told that the Antediluvians enjoyed a long lifespan, and with his help, extending the human lifespan was possible. The technological advancements they offered would revolutionize human existence, pushing it thousands of years into the future, which is what TC believed needed to happen. He'd been told that they needed human beings to evolve to a higher state of intellectual acuity. They even gave him a glimpse of the symbiotic relationship the future promised, and he believed them.

The Antediluvians' civilization was like a living machine. Only the collective mattered, and every Antediluvian served to provide a greater good for their kind. As their home world's habitat and resources dwindled, the Antediluvians found it necessary to maintain a static population. Reproduction was restricted to replacing only those that expired or could fulfill a specific purpose. However, that would change once they were on Earth. They would once again know the grace of life, because science would no longer be their only reason for existing. The Monan, their sovereign, would see to it that her subjects thrived.

The Earth was a sanctuary rich in nitrogen, oxygen, and water. The frigid polar regions provided a place for them to live. Their home world's red-dwarf star, Kapteyn, in the Pictor constellation, was thirteen light years from Earth. It had been only seven light years away when they first discovered Earth and sent an expeditionary force.

Eight thousand years ago, the small expeditionary force had tried to subjugate the human species, and then another alien race intervened, giving the peaceful humans the knowledge of waging war. The human bands joined forces, took up arms, and forced the Antediluvians to withdraw. From that experience, they knew a direct confrontation would prove too costly in casualties if faced with the same human resistance, especially with their more advanced weapons. This was why they had developed a strategy which would not spark any human, or alien, retaliatory action.

A second expeditionary force came to Earth and began genetically modifying small numbers of humans. The genetic restructuring would produce a more intelligent, less hostile, and controllable human. Over thousands of years, they abducted small numbers of people from around the world for testing. The people found to have the traits they needed were enhanced and returned to breed. The modified DNA strands passed down from generation to generation were adjusted until their awakening.

The Antediluvians had existed for hundreds of thousands of years, traveling from one planet to the next. Their planet, KTAR, had been their home for the last twenty thousand years. Its darker environment had forced them to adapt their physiology. Their pupils had enlarged, and their visual spectrum had increased. The exposure to lower gravity had reduced their bone density and muscle tone, but those things would change on their new world.

KTAR was moving rapidly away, along with many of the other stars and planets locked together in a retrograde orbit in the Milky Way. It was now a frozen world incapable of sustaining life, cast in a perpetual twilight of mauve and violet starlight. They'd abandoned KTAR and were traveling toward their new home on massive interstellar ships. There was no turning back from the path chosen. Earth was their future, offering them a stable environment for billions of years to come. They had at last found a permanent home, and their nomadic lifestyle would end.

When their armada arrived, they would be welcomed, without loss of Antediluvian life and without other alien interference. TC and the other Awakened would ensure that the Antediluvians remained unharmed as they settled in the frozen wastelands of the planet. Once their bases were established, subjugation of the human species would begin. The Xunta, their newest weapon and creature of destruction, would see to it that the humans they allowed to live would provide for their every need. A new era was about to be born.

FOURTEEN

As the *Whispering Winds* rounded the north end of Great Guana Cay, Cal marveled at the calm Atlantic waters. With just a hint of gentle swells and a breeze from the west, he sailed south toward the dive site. If the wind and sea conditions held, it would be a fantastic day for diving. *Little Breeze*, their fourteen-foot, rigid-hull dinghy, was tethered behind them. *Little Breeze* was unsinkable, had virtually no draft, and was powered by a fourteen horsepower outboard motor. It was fast and reliable, and it offered a way to explore places in shallow water that the *Whispering Winds* couldn't reach.

The reef began only yards from the beach and descended into the depths. From the shallows along the eastern shore of Great Guana, the fragile coral was visible as a dark outline beneath the turquoise surface until the sea turned to cobalt blue. Cal knew from experience that the beauty and variety of marine life swarming the reef would be something Alex and Nate would never forget.

Preset mooring buoys marked the location where snorkeling gave way to scuba diving. Cal and Garth had set moorings at many of the best diving sites along the reef to protect it from the anchors dropped by weekend diving enthusiasts.

Cal hoped they could get in at least two morning dives and another one in the afternoon before sailing back to Bakers Bay. He planned to anchor in the shallow water on the west side of the island for the night. Even when the Atlantic was calm, it was always smarter to anchor on the protected side of the island. There would be a new moon tonight, so the heavens would be aglow with the soft light of billions of stars and cosmic gas clouds.

They'd left the dock fully provisioned for the next week. The wedding was only three days away, and Alex and Nate would be joining them on their honeymoon cruise. He planned to sail the Abacos, showing Nate and Alex many of the islands. They had never been to the Abacos before, so it was going to be great fun watching them discover the beauty of the islands.

Cal looked longingly at Alessia as she stood on the bow. She was wearing a skimpy, bright yellow bikini, one of his favorites. Her back was to him as she waited to retrieve the line from the mooring buoy. He loved her, and not just because she was easy on the eyes. She was the love of his life, and he would do anything to make her happy. She leaned over the railing to catch the line with the boat hook in her hand.

He smiled.

Alex, seated next to Cal on the flybridge said, "You're enjoying the view, aren't you?"

"You know it," Cal replied.

They both chuckled.

"Hey, am I missing something?" Nate asked, poking his head up from the cockpit. "Nope, it doesn't concern you," Alex said.

After tying off to the buoy, the *Whispering Winds* was a little over a half mile from the beach, stern to the island, and the water beneath the keel was invitingly clear. Tegan could see the coral below from the bow. She looked out on the horizon at the ocean. Sailing around these islands was something she could do forever.

Tegan had fallen in love with the Bahamas as her life had normalized over the last few months. She'd found the man she wanted to spend the rest of her life with, and she wished she could share her happiness with the family she'd lost. Tegan was going to become Mrs. Alessia Locke in three days. It would be her second name change in less than a year and hopefully her last.

She dreamed about having children, raising them in this peaceful place, away from the evils of the world. She really wanted the life Maggie and Garth lived. Tegan envied the Aldeberie clan and their having ancestral roots in these islands. She felt a sadness gnawing at the edges of her heart. Her children would never meet their grandparents or their aunt. They would live in the false world she had created. Her only solace was in knowing that her children would be safe with loving parents.

Tegan worried that she'd overlooked some detail and that Westfield might still be looking for her. She'd been careful not to have her picture taken with clients, fearing they would appear on a social media site. With all of the surveillance cameras along her route to the Bahamas, it was possible that one of them could have caught an image of her face. If Westfield discovered she was still alive, she knew he would come after her again. She felt a pang of guilt, knowing she was concealing a dangerous past and living a lie. She wanted to tell Cal the truth, but knowing him, she was afraid he might do something stupid, like trying to confront Westfield. It was best to let things be.

Tegan walked back to the cockpit and smiled at everyone. "If you guys want to get a dive or two in before lunch, go for it. I'll whip up some sandwiches and keep an eye out for you—just in case I need to come to your rescue."

"That sounds good to me," Cal said. "I know Alex is in. What about you, Nate?"

"No thanks. I think I will stay here and help Alessia with lunch. I'll take the plunge later. What do you mean by rescue them?"

"Sometimes the current can pull you away from the boat. After a long dive it's hard to swim back against it, so I bring the boat to you. That's why we always leave someone topside."

"Great," Nate said. "All I thought I had to worry about was sharks, barracuda, jellyfish, and the abyss. Now I learn there's a current that can drag me out to sea. Any other dangers I need to know about?"

"I think that about covers it," Cal said. "Let's get wet, Alex."

Cal removed the dive gear from the storage bins. He connected the regulators to their tanks, tested the airflow, then loaded them into their buoyancy compensator vests. He carried the tanks to the starboard stern dive platform. Cal drew air from the tank, inflated the BCDs, and tossed them into the water one after the other. Alex brought him their power fins and booties. He put his fins on, grabbed his mask, and then dove off the boat into the warm water. Alex jumped in after him, slipped into her BCD, put on her mask, and cleared it like a pro.

"We'll see you in thirty minutes or so," Cal shouted.

Alex put the regulator into her mouth and dropped beneath the surface. Cal followed her down.

Water visibility was over a hundred feet in all directions. The sea life was abundant, just as Cal had hoped it would be. A small cluster of clownfish darted around the coral as Alex approached them. A large parrotfish and several triggerfish leisurely swam around the various corals and brilliantly colored sea fans. Cal could see that Alex hardly knew what to look at first, her head moving back and forth so often it reminded him of a bobble-head doll. He pointed out an outcropping of the fire coral he'd warned her about earlier, and she waved an acknowledgment of the danger.

They stopped their descent at twenty feet and hovered above the marine growth, allowing the current to pull them slowly along the reef. Even with the regulator in her mouth, Cal could tell she was smiling as she gave him the thumbs up sign.

He looked down and saw a large piece of coral that had broken away from the reef. It had taken part of the rock face and other marine growth down with it. The chunk of coral rested on a small ledge about fifty feet below him. He tapped Alex on the leg to get her attention and pointed down at the ledge, indicating he wanted to check it out. Staying at that depth for only a few minutes would not cause them any decompression issues. Alex gave him the okay sign, and they headed down, clearing their ears as the pressure increased with depth.

About thirty feet down, Cal caught sight of a glint of metal. There was something shiny embedded in the sedimentary rock where the chunk of coral had broken off. The break was obviously recent. *This is exactly why I put down the anchor moorings*, he thought. He had seen anchor damage to the reef before, but anchors usually didn't cause this much damage.

Cal swam closer to the exposed piece of gold-colored metal. The metal had retained a remarkable luster, considering that coral had covered it for a long time. From what he could see, the piece of metal was flat, slightly rounded at the edge, and far too brilliant to be gold bullion.

Alex swam over to him. Cal checked her air gauge and was pleased to see she still had some bottom time left. He turned back to the embedded metal and pulled his large, orange-handled dive knife from its sheath, which he always kept strapped to his right calf while diving. He lightly tapped the plate with the butt of the knife, and it sounded solid. It appeared as if the coral and sedimentary rock had encapsulated it over a long period. Cal touched the golden finish with his gloved hand, noting the rich amalgam, but he still couldn't determine the type of metal. It looked as if it could be the end of a marker of some kind.

The broken chunk of coral resting on the ledge below was over three feet across. Cal traced the outline of where it had been with the tip of his dive knife, brushing away some of the loose rock and debris to expose a little more of the metal. It looked as if the metal disappeared into the rock with more of it concealed beneath the sediment. He couldn't begin to guess how big it was, but from what he could see, the metal had been manufactured and embedded there for some reason.

Alex swam closer as Cal brushed away some more of the loose sediment. What looked like a raised symbol appeared. He pointed the symbol out to Alex. She eagerly ran her hand over the smooth metal plate, using her fingers to probe under the marine growth to expose more of the metal. She traced the markings as if she was reading braille. Then her eyes grew large, and she pointed toward the surface.

When Alex surfaced, she spat out the regulator. Cal swam up next to her and signaled Nate that they were okay.

"Have you ever seen anything like that before?" Alex asked.

"No. That break in the coral is new. Whatever is under the marine growth and rock has been there for a very long time."

"Do you have an underwater camera onboard?"

"Yes. It's an older Nikon digital, but it works great. Was that writing on the metal?" Cal asked.

"I'm not sure. I could feel raised edges, but it felt more like a symbol than a letter. It could be the beginning of a cartouche or a hieroglyph." Alex smiled, showing Cal the goosebumps on her arm. "I have the feeling I get when I've stumbled onto something of significance. I'd like to scrape away more of the marine growth. I need to see what's written on it."

"Okay, let's head back to the boat. We can replace our tanks, and I'll have Alessia come back with us to take photographs."

They submerged and swam for the boat. Cal figured they had found something very special and thought that Alex's vacation was going to turn into work. Maybe Nate and Alex would have to buy a boat to live on while they worked on the site. He'd be happy to have them around more.

When they reached the boat, Nate and Tegan helped them get their gear onboard. Tegan could tell something was going unsaid as Cal boarded. "Okay, guys, spill it," she finally said, tired of watching Cal and Alex look at each other with obvious excitement.

Cal said, "A large chunk of coral broke off the reef about thirty feet down. It's about three feet in diameter."

"Why are you smiling?" Tegan asked. "That's horrible. What do you think caused it to break away?"

"I don't know, but it exposed part of a metal plate or a marker that's embedded in the rock. Judging by the amount of growth around it, I'd guess it was affixed to the rocks hundreds of years ago. It has what appears to be some type of a symbol on it. The portion of the metal that's visible is only a few inches across, and it's incredibly smooth. Almost like a piece of wood that had been finely sanded—slick like a nonstick surface."

"The symbol could be a hieroglyph," Alex added, looking excited. "Considering where we are and the age of the coral, it could be Mayan or from an undiscovered civilization. I know this is a significant find. I feel it in my bones."

"Uh-oh, I've seen that look before," Nate said. "Once she picks up the scent of an archeological find, nothing else matters."

"What look?" Alex asked, frowning at him.

"You know perfectly well what look. The last time you were this excited, I didn't see you for months."

"This time I can't go anywhere, so you needn't worry."

"If the plate is Mayan, how could it be in such pristine condition?" Cal asked.

"Maybe microorganisms protected the surface," Alex replied.

"I've never heard of any marine microorganism that could do that," Cal said. "What do you say we grab a bite to eat and get back down there? Alessia, we'll need you to take photographs."

"Sounds good to me," Tegan said. "Nate, can you handle the boat?"

"No problem. I'll be your safety guy."

After eating, they swapped tanks, and Cal, Alex, and Tegan were in the water. They swam north on the surface using their snorkels so they could save the air in their tanks for the dive. When they reached the area, they swapped their snorkels for regulators and started down.

Tegan took pictures as they approached the site. The panoramic shots would provide a wide view of the area they could study later. She could see the broken piece of coral lying on the ledge below and decided to get some close-up shots of that first. She motioned to Cal to let him know she was going deeper and then descended along the vertical wall face to the ledge. Checking her depth gauge, she noted the ledge was just over seventy feet down. As she photographed the coral, she heard a dull metal-on-metal thudding sound. She looked up and saw Cal tapping on the metal plate above her. After taking a few more close-up photos of the broken coral, she flipped the heavy coral chunk over and photographed the other side, then headed up to rejoin the others.

Cal took off his dive glove and touched the metal with his bare fingers. The surface felt finely polished. Any metal he knew of would pit or corrode quickly in this environment. He gingerly pried the remaining sediment and rocks away from the metal plate to give Alex a better view. He heard the sound of Alessia's bubbles grow closer and saw the reflection of the flash of the digital strobe as she took pictures near him.

After a few minutes, Cal had managed to scrape away enough of the loose debris to see several symbols. He realized the plate was larger than he had first imagined. He could tell Alex was growing impatient waiting to see what he'd uncovered. He inserted his dive knife into a small crack in the rock about eight inches from where he'd already dug. He probed until the point of his knife struck metal again. Cal worked the knife gently upward along the crack and pried a basketball-size chunk of rock loose, letting it drop away. His digging had exposed more of the metal plate—and more symbols.

Cal moved back to let Alex get directly in front of the marker. She waved her hands to clear the silt, then reverently touched the newly revealed raised hieroglyphic-like symbols. He could tell by Alex's reaction that the marker was something very special. She carefully examined the exquisite artistry and the intricate detail of each symbol.

After Tegan looked at the marker, Alex pointed up, and they all headed for the surface.

Alex took her mask off and said excitedly, "Wow! None of those symbols represents any language I've seen before. They aren't Mesoamerican or Egyptian hieroglyphs, but still, there is a familiarity about them. They remind me of cuneiform, like ancient Sumerian text, but more detailed."

"Is it a marker of some kind?" Cal asked.

"I'm not sure what it is. We need to expose more of it so I can see the whole thing. I could feel more metal beneath the marine growth. There is something quite unique about the markings."

Alex knew whatever the language was, it was old, *very* old, so this site could be of great historical significance. Her mind raced as she thought through the possibilities.

"What do you want to do now, Alex?" Cal asked.

"I want to go back down and get good close-up pictures of what we have excavated already. I need to see how big the marker is and if there are additional symbols."

"I'm going to need more than my dive knife to get behind all the rock and marine growth."

"Okay. Let's get pictures of what we've exposed and then head back to the boat. I need time to ruminate on it anyway."

"How many pictures do you want and from what distance?" Tegan asked.

"As many as you can take at varying distances. They will give me an overall perspective. I want each symbol photographed separately so I can see as much detail as possible."

"You got it," Tegan said.

They dove and Tegan moved in front of the marker. When her forearm grazed the metal, a cold chill ran up her spine. She didn't see the pulse of blue light ripple across it at her touch. A deep, primal fear came on suddenly and built within her as she took pictures of every symbol on the marker. Tegan breathed faster, not understanding why. She tried to keep calm, but she couldn't shake the feeling there was danger here.

She felt Cal's touch and looked into his eyes as he took her by the shoulders. She screamed through her regulator, as if she had come face to face with the most horrible creature imaginable. The sound of her scream pierced the water. Tegan pushed Cal away and swam for the surface, rising faster than she should have, leaving a trail of bubbles behind her.

Cal and Tegan broke the surface at almost the same time. She ripped off her mask as if it were on fire. Her face was pale. Without a word, she dropped her mask and swam hard for the boat. Cal grabbed her mask before it sank, stuck his face back into the water, and saw that Alex was only a few feet down and rising. He didn't wait for her to surface.

Cal caught up with Tegan when they reached the stern of the *Whispering Winds*. He helped her out of her BCD, and pushed it toward Nate. She swam to the dive platform on the other hull.

"Alessia, what's wrong?" Cal asked.

She didn't answer. She scrambled out of the water, throwing her fins onto the deck.

"Something I should be worried about?" Alex asked, breathing heavily as she came up behind him.

"I don't know," Cal said.

Cal took off his BCD and stepped up onto the dive platform. "Alessia, are you okay? Answer me."

"I'm fine," she replied. "I'm sorry. I don't know what happened down there. I just felt I needed to get away from that place. I am sorry I left you. It doesn't make any sense, but I had a feeling of impending doom, and I panicked. I can't explain it."

"You're okay now?" Cal asked, walking into the cockpit.

"Yes, really I'm fine." Tegan took the camera from around her neck. "I'm just embarrassed." She sat down on the seat in the cockpit and wrapped a towel around herself, shaking.

Cal knew she wasn't cold. He sat down beside her and took her hand. He didn't say anything until the shaking stopped.

When it appeared she'd recovered, Cal asked, "What happened down there?"

"I told you, I don't know. I looked at those symbols, and something inside of me just snapped. I can't explain it. I saw images of places and things I didn't recognize. I had the strongest impulse to flee. I wasn't in control. It wasn't until I was back on the boat that I even thought about you. I don't understand."

Cal held her and said, "I'm here. Nate and Alex are here, and everyone is safe."

Tegan leaned against him and wiped the tears from her cheeks. "You're right." She stood up and threw her towel onto the seat cushion. "But I still need to understand why this happened and why I saw those images. Sorry I scared you all. I'm fine now."

∞

Tegan went into the salon and downloaded the pictures she'd taken to the laptop computer that was on the chart table. She breathed deeply as she tried to figure out what had triggered the panic attack. She hadn't felt like that since the day her family was killed. The images must have been a hallucination caused by her panic. The deeper she searched for an answer, the more she realized that the marker and the symbols meant something to her, but she didn't know why.

The others walked into the salon.

"Alessia, please show Nate how to operate the camera," Cal said.

"You're going back down, aren't you?"

"Yes. Nate and I are going to look around. Alex will stay here with you."

Tegan nodded. She couldn't think of a reason for Cal and Nate not to go back to the site. "Please be careful. I had the most intense feeling there was danger associated with the marker."

"We'll be careful," Cal said. "I learned long ago to trust your instincts, but I saw nothing around us that posed a threat. I'm taking the underwater metal detector with me. I want to map what's under the coral. We need to know the size of the marker and if there are any more of them down there."

Tegan and Alex sat at the table in the salon with a view of the dive site. They hadn't said anything since Nate and Cal left. Both were absorbed in their own thoughts. Tegan felt she should know what the marker represented. She looked at the symbols Alex had drawn in her journal from her photos. "What do you make of them?"

"I'm not sure," Alex replied. "Some of the symbols look like Sumerian cuneiform, but not entirely. This one symbol looks a little like it could even be Jiahu, but I need to see more of the symbols to draw any conclusions. The bigger questions are why it's thirty feet below the surface on an island in the Bahamas and who the hell put it there."

"How old do you think it is?"

"It's hard to say. I'm not sure there's any way I can date it exactly. I could carbon date the coral, but that would only tell me how long the coral has been growing."

"What about the metal? Any idea what it is?"

"Not a clue. All I can tell you is it's highly refined, based on the striations of the mixed materials I could discern, but the exact composition will have to wait until I can take a sample and have it analyzed."

Tegan sat back, still maintaining her vigil over the dive site, then said, "The Sumerian civilization predates the Egyptians by thousands of years. How could the symbols possibly resemble Sumerian?"

"I don't know. I'm not even sure it's related, but the symbols do have a cuneiform style, and that really interests me. The Sumerian civilization is one of the oldest and most advanced societies of its time. As far as we know, the Sumerians were the first to develop a written language, which is another reason I'm intrigued by the symbols."

"Cuneiform is unique to Sumerian?"

"For sure," Alex said. "Linguistically speaking, it's what we call language isolate, meaning it belongs to no other known family of languages. It's based on morphemes, not whole sentences, like in analytic languages."

Tegan raised her eyebrows and cocked her head, feigning ignorance.

"Perhaps I'm not doing a very good job of explaining. Morphemes are simply units of meaning. That's why Sumerian is so difficult to read and understand. There isn't any real grammatical structure to the language, at least like we're accustomed to seeing." Alex turned her journal around. "Sumerian cuneiform symbols are wedge-shaped, similar to this one, but as you can see it's not exactly the same. That's why it's so interesting."

Tegan looked at the symbol and wished she could pry her gaze from it. When she finally looked up, Alex appeared to be lost in thought.

"Alex, the Sumerians lived in southern Iraq seven thousand years ago."

"That's correct."

"So how could there be a resemblance to their language form?"

"I haven't a clue," Alex answered. "The Sumerians were an incredible people. Did you know they invented the wheel and mathematics and studied and mapped the stars?"

"I didn't know that." Tegan lied. She had studied Sumerian history and their accomplishments, as well as many other ancient civilizations, when she was doing her doctoral studies.

"The Sumerians were first in many things. They created the first truly structured military with delineated specialized units. They were the first civilization to have a codified legal system, and they even held formal judicial proceedings. Of course, their legal system was based mostly on their religious beliefs, which isn't all that surprising, considering they were a religion-based society. They even developed the first city administrative systems which are believed to have been the models used for running the Greek and Roman Empire cities built thousands of years later." Alex paused.

"We also know the Sumerians created the first school system and were also the first to develop advanced agricultural and irrigation systems to optimize crop yield. And let's not forget that they were making beer long before the Egyptians."

"For which Cal and Nate are appreciative," Tegan said. "It sounds like they were an amazing people. You said they were a religious society. What gods did they worship?"

"The Sumerians believed in over three thousand deities. They wrote one of the first religious texts, titled *The Epic of Creation*, and they believed the gods had created man out of clay so he could serve their needs. Alessia, I'm not an expert on Sumerian religion, culture, or language. I probably know just enough to get into trouble, but I do know the markings on the plate have Sumerian overtones."

"What happened to the Sumerians?"

"They thrived for thousands of years and eventually merged with another civilization, the Akkadian, who lived in northern Mesopotamia."

Tegan scanned the dive area. She was too far away to see Cal's or Nate's bubbles. "How were they able to develop all these things?"

"That is a curious thing. All of their advancements seemed to have sprung from nowhere, almost as if their priest kings had found a DIY guidebook. They succeeded in shaping the future of human development, even though some of the knowledge they passed down wasn't accurate."

"For instance?" Tegan asked. Just talking seemed to be having a calming effect on her.

"Well, for starters they got their astronomy wrong. The Sumerians believed that the Milky Way was a flat disk encased in a universal bubble."

"That's not so far-fetched," Tegan said. "If viewed from another galaxy, the Milky Way would appear flat."

Alex nodded. "True."

"You know, M-theory postulates we could be living on a flat plain in a dimensional multiverse, like in a bubble." Tegan stopped before she expounded on the theory, having noted the twinkle in Alex's eyes. She needed to be more careful, but she enjoyed the intellectual stimulation she got from talking to her.

"True again, but I doubt they would have understood quantum physics in ancient Sumer. Alessia, I think you are better educated than you let on."

"Not really. I read a lot."

"Uh-huh. There are a few things that can't be explained, such as how the Sumerians were able to discover and document many of the planets in our solar system without the use of a telescope. There is even documentation they knew about Neptune, Uranus, and Pluto. In some of their writings, they referred to Uranus and Neptune as the 'Watery Twins.'"

"So you're thinking that someone provided them with the knowledge of the planets. You mean like aliens?"

"I won't go that far."

"Could the marker have been put there by a culture that interacted with the Sumerians?"

"You read my mind, Alessia. From what little I saw of the marker, I can tell it shouldn't be there. The Sumerians were the first to work in bronze, but that plate isn't bronze. It's a finely crafted metal of some other kind. The symbols are an extension of the metal, formed when the metal was still hot."

"Could they be from a more advanced Sumerian society?"

"I'm not sure of anything right now." Alex pointed at a page in her journal. "See these markings in this symbol?"

"Yes," Tegan replied.

"This one is much like the Sumerian symbol for Anu, and the one next to it looks like the symbol for Ki. They aren't exact, but they are close."

"And Anu and Ki are…?" Tegan asked.

"Anu and Ki are gods. Anu is the god of heaven or sky. Ki is the goddess of the earth. Is there any Internet access here?" Alex opened the laptop and found the pictures of the symbols.

"Ever since Hurricane Chantal roared through in June, the Internet has been a bit sketchy. I'm sure you'll be able to get a connection at the marina. Would you like something to drink?"

"A bottle of water would be great, thanks."

"Did Akkadian eventually replace Sumerian as the language of the time?" Tegan asked, placing a bottle of water on the table.

"Yes, but Sumerian was still used for religious, scientific, and ceremonial purposes. Some form of Sumerian was actually used until the first century CE in Mesopotamia."

"Could the Sumerians or Akkadians have sailed across the ocean?"

"Anything is possible, I suppose. The Sumerians used boats on inland waterways, but had no oceangoing vessels. I can't imagine them sailing here from Iraq. More importantly, where would they develop the technology to forge the metal we found? And why put it underwater?"

Tegan glanced out the window again. There was still no sign of Cal or Nate.

"But you could be right about the symbols being more advanced," Alex continued. "The more I look at these, the more I think they could be a precursor to Sumerian cuneiform. Perhaps the Sumerians adopted these symbols from an undiscovered and more advanced civilization."

"That would certainly be significant. Maybe we got it wrong. Perhaps Europeans didn't discover the Americas. Maybe it was the other way around."

"Now *that* would stand the world on its head, for sure." Alex took a sip of water. "I know this discovery is going to be of great significance. I can feel it. And if it pans out, you may be seeing more of me after the wedding than you planned."

"That would be wonderful," Tegan replied.

FIFTEEN

Great Guana Cay — July 23 — 1400 hours

Cal saw that Nate had adjusted quickly to the underwater environment, considering he hadn't been diving for some time. They carried extra gear, including Cal's old reliable Pirate Pro underwater metal detector. The two extra bags Nate had strapped to his dive vest made him look like an underwater Sherpa.

When they reached the site, Cal watched as Nate ran his fingers over the symbols. He knew if this turned out to be an archeological mystery, Alex was going to remain at Great Guana Cay until she solved it. He was sure Nate would stay with her for as long as he could. Maybe they would end up buying a boat.

Before they left the *Whispering Winds*, Alex told them the first order of business was to survey the site and determine the exact size and shape of the metal marker. She stressed the need to keep the site as pristine as possible. They knew that divers occasionally anchored in the area, so all they could hope for was that no one stumbled upon their discovery.

Cal extended the metal detector's arm to its full length, turned it on, adjusted the control settings, and moved the detector over the edge of the marker. He received a loud and sustained tone from the exposed metal. He calibrated the sensitivity, then worked the metal detector back and forth over the rock face and coral. The signal remained strong and steady as he found the edges of the artifact under the marine growth. Nate outlined the marker using the orange-colored line they had brought, and then they began taking measurements. At its maximum height, the marker was about three feet from top to bottom and four feet across. It was football-shaped. Cal knew from the pulse intensity on the detector that the marker was one solid piece. The more he looked at it, the more he realized how unique the metal appeared. *What in the hell is this thing?*

Nate took several pictures of the outline of the marker from varying distances while Cal continued sweeping the nearby rock and coral to determine if there were other markers hidden there. After nearly twenty minutes, he'd found nothing else.

Cal dove deeper, and when he reached the piece of broken-off coral, he worked the metal detector around the area. Again, he found nothing. He checked his air supply and had Nate do the same. After a quick calculation, he was confident they had at least five more minutes at this depth. Cal motioned for Nate to stay on the ledge by the coral, and he swam away from the reef. He didn't usually venture far from the reef, because there wasn't much to see, but visibility was excellent today. When Cal looked back, he saw it.

The coral and assorted marine growth camouflaged it up close, but the shape was unmistakable. He hadn't noticed it in all the years he had been diving here. The elongated ledge jutted out uniformly until it disappeared into the more irregular-shaped rock at both ends. The ledge appeared to be at least seventy feet across and ten feet high. Cal moved back another thirty feet until the coral was in shadow and Nate was barely visible. The ledge looked like the base of a massive pier. There were unnatural vertical lines extending upwards at each end of the ledge. It looked as if a concealed doorway lay hidden behind the rock and coral.

Cal swam back to the ledge. Nate pointed at his air gauge and drew a finger across his throat. Getting the exact measurements of what they had found would have to wait. They were both getting low on air. Cal had them stay ten feet beneath the surface as a precautionary decompression stop as they swam toward the boat. It also would serve as a way to stay hidden from the prying eyes of anyone on the beach. He knew what they had found was indeed significant, and his paranoia was on the rise.

$$\infty$$

Tegan was there when they surfaced directly behind the stern of the *Whispering Winds*. She had tracked their air bubbles as they approached. She reached down and took Cal's tank from him, then glanced at the air gauge and saw that it was almost empty. She saw that Alex had the same concern about Nate's tank.

"Learning bad habits from Cal, I see," Alex said.

"Absolutely. It's all Cal's fault," Nate said, climbing onboard.

"Thanks, buddy," Cal said.

"Well, are you going to keep us in suspense or are you going to tell us what you found?" Alex asked.

"Let's get the gear stowed, then we'll look at the pictures," Cal replied, handing Tegan the camera.

She took the camera into the salon and downloaded the digital photos. A few minutes later, they were all huddled around the laptop. She scrolled through the photos until reaching the picture of the ledge Cal had described. The shape was distinctive.

"So you think this wasn't made by nature?" Tegan asked, looking more closely at the photos.

Cal said, "Look at the depth of the ledge. It reminds me of a large pier used to berth a cruise ship. The rock face from the marker down to the ledge looks like a big door to me."

Alex leaned in and said, "I agree. The area doesn't look like a natural geological formation. The Abaco islands are composed mostly of limestone and calcium carbonate, and that would erode evenly, along the lines of the slope, like these. I wonder if it was constructed by the same people who left the marker."

Everyone sat in silence.

"If I had to guess," Tegan said, "I'd say there's a structure buried under the island, and Cal found the entryway to whatever it is."

Alex nodded. "Possibly. I wish I could get a ground-penetrating radar system out here so I could see what's there. Cal, could you get your hands on a system for me?"

"Not likely. Garth could order something for us, but it would take days, if not weeks, to arrive. How long do you plan to stay?"

"As long as it takes," Alex replied, looking at Nate.

"I knew it," Nate said. "Cal, I may need to buy that boat we talked about earlier."

"I was thinking the same thing just a little while ago."

Alex shrugged and went back to looking at the pictures of the marker. "Look at the detail of the symbols. There's no doubt in my mind that they are an ancient form of writing. My gut feeling is that they are a precursor to the Sumerian. It could take me years to figure all this out. Cal, can you knock the marine growth and sediment away from the rest of the marker?"

"I don't see why not. The chunk of coral that fell away, and the area where it was attached, is dead anyway. It shouldn't take too long to expose the rest of the metal."

Alex said, "I think the sedimentary rock is mostly oolite, and from what I saw, it may only be a few inches deep."

"Do you think you can decipher the symbols once it's all exposed?" Tegan asked.

"I don't know, but what I do know is I can't do much with what I can see now. I'll need the whole marker exposed to tell you for sure. If it's a new language, it may take years to decode."

Cal said, "Why would anyone build something underwater?"

"Could it be a submarine pen left over from World War Two?" Nate asked.

"I don't see how," Cal replied. "The folks that live here, unless they were all blind and deaf, would've known something this large was being built. Believe me, it wouldn't have stayed a secret."

"I'm just trying to keep it real, before you guys go off exploring far-out ideas about ancient civilizations," Nate said.

Alex looked at him with disdain at his comment. "I appreciate you keeping us all grounded, but I'm the scientist here, and I'll find the truth."

"Let's not get into who's got the bigger set," Nate countered.

"I think we all know who that is," Alex said.

Tegan laughed, then said, "So is this how couples talk to each other after being married a few years? Maybe we should postpone the wedding. What do you think, Cal?"

"Not a chance," Cal replied. "So what's next, Alex? This is, after all, your expedition, you being the scientist and all."

Alex acknowledged the barb. "Alessia, will you be able to take the pictures when we uncover the marker? I mean, are you up for this?"

Tegan took a deep breath and said, "I'm good to go."

"Then let's get to it," Cal said. "Nate, you'll be staying here."

Thirty minutes later, Cal hovered in front of the marker, with Alex beside him, while Tegan remained behind them. He inserted a small crowbar beneath the rock adjacent to the marker, tapped it in gently using the heel of his hand, and pulled it downward. A large section of rock came loose, creating a cloud of silt around him. As the particulates cleared, Tegan swam up, took a picture, and retreated. Cal went to work on the next piece. After a few minutes, only a few fragments remained. Tegan photographed the progression, but always moved away after she snapped a quick shot. It didn't take long for Cal to reveal the oval-shaped piece of metal. It shimmered, reflecting the sunlight shining down through the water.

Cal moved aside as Alex ran her hands over the surface of the metal, brushing away the remaining sediment until numerous symbols and the uneven coloring of the metal appeared. There were darker patches, but they didn't appear to be from any damage he'd done with the crowbar. The pattern and color changes in the metal appeared deliberate in design. Alex examined the six dark patches on the metal that varied in size and shape. He could tell she was in awe of the strange symbols.

There were nine large, intricately designed symbols on the marker. Three of the large symbols were spaced equal distances apart across the bottom center of the marker. A large symbol was on each side of the centerline at the marker's edge. The largest of all the symbols was at the top, just beneath one of the dark patches, which appeared to cap the marker. There was an oddly shaped, dark circular symbol in the center of the marker. It didn't look like the other symbols. Extending outward from the center were darker shades that tapered to points a foot on either side. Bracketing the circular symbol were two more large symbols, one above and one below.

Cal counted forty-nine smaller symbols scattered across the face of the marker, all just as intricate as the larger ones. The smaller symbols were uniformly spaced vertically, and if traced horizontally from end to end, they formed nine different planes across the marker. They varied in complexity of design and detail, and none of them looked alike.

Alex ran her hand over the raised symbols again, then pumped her fists up and down. Cal could tell she was excited. He knew this was far different from any of the sites Alex had worked before.

Tegan swam up to the marker and took pictures from every angle, trying to capture the shadows and small indentations that might reveal some significant clue about its origin. When she touched the marker, she felt a charge of static electricity building around her. She quickly swam back a few feet, and the sensation faded. The scientist in her needed to know what was happening. Tegan moved forward again, touched the face of the marker with her hand, and left it there. The reaction was immediate and intense.

A blue glow appeared under her hand. Keeping her emotions in check as the strong current flowed through her, she tried to pull her hand away. Like someone holding a live electrical wire, her hand wouldn't move. She turned to Cal, fear evident on her face. She felt a strong sense of power emanated from the marker.

Cal reached out to grab her, but his hands stopped, as if something surrounding her arm had prevented him. Tegan waved Cal away and stopped struggling. She gave Cal the okay signal and turned back to the marker. She touched it with her other hand. The blue aura appeared beneath that hand as well. A calmness descended on her. The static charge she'd felt was gone, as if the electrical current running through her had been grounded. She sensed something in the current, a presence, a form of intelligence.

Tegan slid her hands over the marker, and the light followed her movements, the bluish glow sparkling as she moved her fingers across the different symbols. She ran her hands over every inch of the marker, sensing changes in what she was feeling with each symbol and area that she touched. She took a deep drag from the regulator and braced herself, then lifted both hands away at the same time and floated free. There was no resistance, and the blue aura disappeared.

Alex swam up next to Tegan and motioned for her to touch it again. Tegan looked at Cal, and she could see he wasn't thrilled by the idea, but she reached out anyway. The bluish glow reappeared beneath her hand, but the electrical current felt different this time. She removed her hand without difficulty. Alex touched the marker where Tegan had just had her hand. Nothing happened.

Cal tilted his head toward the boat. Tegan understood he wanted them to head back. She tapped Alex on the arm, and they swam away from the marker.

As Tegan swam, her fear returned and became stronger the further she got away from the marker. She grabbed Cal's arm and pulled him along. She was sure he understood. Cal motioned for Alex to follow.

When they reached the *Whispering Winds*, Tegan left her tank and buoyancy compensator floating in the water behind the boat, threw her mask and fins up into the stern, nearly hitting Nate in the face. She climbed the boarding ladder, pushed Nate aside, and hurried to the trampoline at the bow.

Cal unbuckled the straps to his BCD and handed his gear to Nate.

"Did it happen again?" Nate asked, putting the tank down on the deck.

Cal rushed to the bow without answering him as Alex retrieved Tegan's gear and passed it to Nate.

"Did it happen again?" Nate asked a second time.

"Not exactly. This time the marker reacted to her," Alex said.

Nate raised his eyebrows. "What do you mean it reacted to her?"

"I mean it responded to her touch."

Cal walked forward to the trampoline. Tegan sat there rocking back and forth, holding her knees under her chin like a child. Cal sat down next to her and examined her hands and arms. There were no burn marks or any other signs of damage to her skin.

Tegan looked at him and said, "What is that thing, Cal? Why did it react to me?"

"I don't know."

"I felt something that was beyond explanation. This time I wasn't afraid until I swam away. It was as if the marker was there to protect me. The further away I got, the more frightened I became. It was as if it wanted me to come back."

"Do you still feel scared?"

"No. The sense of panic stopped just before I reached the boat. That thing was holding on to me. I couldn't let go. Cal, how did it do that?"

"I don't know."

"Hey, is anyone going to tell me what is going on?" Nate asked. He dropped Alex's gear among the other equipment scattered over the deck.

"Let's go forward," Alex replied. They went forward and sat down.

Alex said, "That was a little strange, but very interesting."

"Alex, do you know what happened down there?" Cal asked. "Why did it only react to Alessia, and how could it keep me from touching her and keep her from removing her hand?"

"She couldn't remove her hand? I have no idea. We can rule out a static charge, although the onset was similar. The bluish glow and Alessia not being able to let go of the marker is unexplainable. Do you have any lotion on your hands? Maybe it chemically bonded to the marker."

"That isn't it," Tegan snapped.

"Alessia, what did it feel like? Help me understand," Alex pleaded.

Tegan sighed. "It didn't feel like anything I can explain. I felt power, like a current of some sort, but I know it wasn't electricity. There wasn't a shock of any kind, but I did feel a slight chill running through me. It wasn't an unpleasant feeling, just strange."

"You couldn't move your hand from the marker, which is more than strange, and something physically blocked me from touching your arm. Why?" Cal asked.

Tegan looked at Cal. "How the hell do I know? I'm just as baffled by what happened down there as you are."

"Tell us everything you felt," Alex said.

"When I touched the marker, I felt … at peace. The feeling is hard to describe. I felt safe, like a child would feel holding a mother's hand."

"Did you have any other feelings, sensations?" Alex asked.

Tegan hesitated. "This is going to sound really weird. There was a moment when I felt like it was intelligent, like it wanted to communicate with me."

"What?" Cal and Alex yelled at the same time.

"I can't explain it any better than that."

"Alessia, how exactly do you feel intelligence?" Cal asked.

"Cal, if I could explain it, I would."

"Was the sensation coming from the marker, the symbols, or was it in the blue energy field?" Alex asked.

"The sensation was more psychological than physiological. You're going to think this is crazy, but I sensed it was welcoming me home. That somehow, this was a sanctuary from the dangers in the world." Tegan looked up to find them staring at her. "It was Zenlike. It evoked an inner warmth and peace."

"Was it like you were drugged?" Cal asked.

"No. It wasn't like that at all. Like I said, I can't explain it," she added, sounding frustrated.

"Did you see images like last time?" Alex asked. "We never really talked about them."

"That's because there isn't anything to talk about. Why don't you get that I can't explain what it is that I felt?" Tegan snapped.

Tegan sat as if frozen in time, staring out at the water. She wondered if her reaction was post-traumatic stress coupled with her desire to see her family again. But why was she thinking of them?

"Hey, are you still with us?" Cal asked, touching her elbow after a minute.

Tegan looked at Cal. "I think we should head back to MOW for the night. I don't want to stay on the open water." She looked at Alex. "I hate to spoil your cruise, but I believe what I felt after I swam away from the marker, was . . ."

"Was what?" Cal asked.

"Primal. I felt like a predatory animal was stalking me. The flight or fight syndrome kicked in, and I ran. It was a predator-versus-prey instinctual feeling, and I felt like the prey." Tegan looked up at Cal. "I don't want to be out here in the open if we're the prey."

"I understand," Cal said.

"I need to think this through and figure out exactly what I'm feeling and what I experienced, and I want some distance between me and the marker."

"Alessia, you're safe now," Cal said, rubbing her back. "I saw nothing down there that resembled a predatory animal or anything else that was hunting you. It's just a piece of metal."

"That glows when I touch it," Tegan snapped. "Cal, I also felt like I was being challenged, as if the marker was trying to determine who I was. Maybe the sense of peace was its way of controlling me while it decided what to do with me. I really need time to process all of this, and I want to go back to MOW."

"Alessia," Alex said, "this isn't a science fiction movie where a scary monster is going to rise from the depths and grab you."

"Let's hope not," Nate said.

Alex continued, "I'm sure there's a good explanation for what happened. I still think the blue glow was a chemical reaction to something you had on your skin."

"The reaction was *not* from something I had on my hands," Tegan snapped. "It wasn't superglue that held me to that thing and kept Cal from touching me."

"Well, I don't think we should leave the site," Alex said. "I'm afraid someone will stumble onto it. This is just too important a discovery to leave unattended."

"No one else reacted to the marker like I did, physically or emotionally. I don't frighten easily, Alex. I can tell you there's danger here. You need to pay attention to what I'm telling you."

Alex turned to Cal. "I still don't think we should leave it unguarded. I'm sorry, Alessia. I know you think there's something bad down there, but I can tell you there's always a logical explanation for the mysterious."

"There *is* something down there, goddamn it!" Tegan shouted. "I don't know what it is, but I can feel it in every fiber of my being."

"Sorry, Alex, but I agree with Alessia," Cal said. "We don't know what that thing is, and quite frankly I'd prefer not to anchor on top of it tonight, especially since we woke it up. I doubt seriously that anyone else will discover it. We'll come back tomorrow, after we've had time to think this through."

Alex nodded. "Alessia, I apologize. You're right. I'm just really excited by this find, and sometimes I can get too focused on a project and forget about other people's feelings. Just ask Nate. I can work on deciphering the symbols from the photos and make some inquiries when I can get access to the Internet."

"Come on, Nate, help me get under way," Cal said.

Tegan looked out over the water, then looked back toward the site. *There is something there. I know it. I was guided to this place for a reason, and by a power I don't understand, and that marker is connected to it all.* She knew her thoughts and the images she'd seen shouldn't be shared with the others, at least for now.

When the engines started, she knew that was her cue to cast off the mooring line. After untying the line, she joined Cal on the flybridge and took his hand. As the boat turned, Tegan looked down and saw the magnetic compass slowly tilting from side to side, as if they were in heavy seas, but there was very little wave action to cause the compass to react as it did. As the *Whispering Winds* turned to the north, the compass spun one complete revolution. She tapped Cal on the leg to get his attention and pointed at the compass. As they passed over the site, the compass spun wildly. Once past the dive site, the compass's magnetic indicator stayed glued to the bearing of the site. Tegan squeezed his hand and stared at the compass.

"There's something odd about this place for sure," Cal said. "I'm glad we're leaving."

"That's never happened before. The only thing that's changed is our making contact with the marker."

"True. Hey, Alex," he called. "Check your cell phone service."

"No signal," she yelled from the cockpit.

Cal looked at Tegan. "Maybe we just solved the mystery of the Bermuda Triangle."

"That isn't even remotely funny," Tegan said, squeezing his hand tighter.

When they reached the northern tip of Great Guana, the compass swung back around and returned to normal. Cal had Alex check her phone again. She had service.

"You want to tell them, or should I?" Cal asked.

"You go ahead. Alex thinks I've lost it," Tegan replied.

Cal called Nate and Alex up to the flybridge and explained what had just occurred. Nate's eyes went wide, and Alex looked stunned.

"Could be electromagnetic interference," Alex suggested. "Let's go back and see if it does it again."

"I'm not going back there today," Cal said. "We're headed for MOW. We can see if it reacts again tomorrow when we come back."

"Sounds good to me," Nate said.

Tegan knew that Garth would wonder why they had come back so soon. "Hey, guys. Going back to MOW will make Garth ask why we cut the trip short. Should we tell him what we found?"

"No," Alex snapped. "We can't tell anyone what we found."

Cal said, "Alex, Garth can be trusted, but I see your point. Until we know what's down there, the fewer people that know about it, the better."

"If anybody cares about my opinion, I have to agree," Nate offered.

"Then we keep a lid on it. What's our cover story for coming back?" Cal asked.

"Blame it on me," Nate said. "You could say I got seasick. That's the most plausible reason, and it will require the least amount of explanation."

Alex gave Nate a kiss on the cheek. "I love you. So secure in your self-esteem that you'd sacrifice your ego to help out."

"Damn. If I had known I could get lucky by playing the wimp, I would have used that ploy years ago."

"You already have been, dear," Alex replied.

SIXTEEN

Man-O-War Cay — July 23 — 1700 hours

Garth Aldeberie met the *Whispering Winds* as it docked. Cal had radioed ahead to let him know they were returning because of Nate's seasickness.

"How was the trip?" Garth asked.

"Great," Cal replied. "We managed three dives and explored the reef on the east side of Great Guana. Nate enjoyed one dive before he turned green on us." He hated lying to Garth. "It's probably a good thing that Nate's condition required we come back. We went through more air than I anticipated. If I could get the tanks refilled in the morning, I'd really appreciate that."

"No problem. I'll leave Jessica a note to fill them first thing. I got your guests set up at the Ashley House." Garth looked at the boat. "I don't see much salt spray on the windows."

Cal got the dig, as did Nate, who was standing next to him.

Nate said, "Actually, I think it was more a combination of the heat, lunch, and the gentle rolling action of the boat. I'm feeling much better now. Thanks for getting us a place for the night. I'm sure I'll be good as new and ready to go again tomorrow."

"Glad to hear it. I blocked out the rental for the week, but I gave you a discount, so it'll only run you two-thousand. You can pay me later," Garth said with a straight face.

Nate looked stunned, turned, and walked back into the salon without saying a word.

Cal said, "Thanks, Garth. I'm assuming the door is unlocked and you were only joking about the rental fee."

"It is, and I was. I'm not sure if the door even has a lock that works. It's not one of our better properties, but it offers character."

Tegan walked to the railing. "Hey, Garth. Good to see you."

"Afternoon, Alessia. Nice to see you, too."

"Garth, what did you say to Nate to make him turn green again?"

"I told him about the weekly rate on the house he rented. I'm a bit of a kidder. Let him know it's free for as long as they need a place to stay."

"Thanks. I'll tell him. Say hello to Maggie for me."

"I will. I'm going to call it a day," Garth said. "I'll see you two love-birds later."

When he was gone, Tegan and Cal stepped into the salon. "So far, so good. What's our next move?" Cal asked.

Nate stood by the chart table and asked, "Did he really say two-thousand dollars?"

Cal said, "He did, but I got him to give it to you for free, as a personal favor. You owe me, buddy."

Tegan elbowed Cal in the ribs. "Nate, Garth and Cal are messing with you. You don't owe them anything."

Nate shot Cal an evil glance, then smiled and said, "Always with the jokes."

"We wouldn't kid you if we didn't love you. Feeling the love yet?" Cal asked.

"Oh, yeah."

"Knock it off," Alex said. "I want to get back on the site as soon as possible tomorrow, but I want to get an opinion from a colleague before we leave."

Tegan looked at Alex. "I thought we were going to keep this quiet."

"We are. Professor Brian Lee is a friend and an expert on ancient languages. I may need his expertise to decipher the symbols. Brian won't say anything to anyone."

"It's your project, Alex, but I have an idea, and I'd like your feedback before you contact him," Tegan said.

"Sure, I can always use another perspective."

"What's your idea?" Cal asked, intrigued.

"Let me review the photos and pick Alex's brain a bit before I go out on a limb. You'll understand after you hear what I'm thinking."

Cal said, "This should be interesting. You want to go over the pictures here while we eat or look at them up at Ashley House?"

"Both. Alex and I can run through the pictures now if you make us some sandwiches."

Following dinner, everyone walked to the spine of the island, where the Ashley House was located. The cottage was small, even by island standards, but it offered a view of the harbor. The one-bedroom, one-bathroom home was a century old. The yellow paint was peeling from its wooden frame.

"Well, at least it's clean," muttered Alex, as she walked around the cramped interior.

Alex and Tegan sat down at the small dining table, which had to be as old as the cottage. Alex connected her MPad computer to the outlet to recharge the battery.

Everyone sat quietly watching Tegan scroll through every picture again, zooming in and out repeatedly.

"You haven't said a word since you began reviewing the pictures." Alex finally asked, "So what's your idea?"

Tegan looked up and saw everyone looking at her expectantly. "Alex, you said you think the symbols, and the marker, predate the Sumerian civilization, right?"

"That's my hypothesis at the moment."

"Do you believe it's possible an ancient people traveled from here to Europe, taking the language of the symbols with them to pre-Sumerian culture?"

"That's a very remote possibility. All archeological evidence points to the inhabitants of these islands being primitive Indians. The native populations didn't have vessels that could cross the Atlantic or the knowledge of metallurgy to create the marker during the Sumerian era."

"Alex, is there any evidence of a civilization developing in these islands or anywhere in the Americas with origins in the Middle East or Africa during that era?"

"No."

Tegan smiled and said, "So how do we explain what's down there? If a civilization didn't migrate eastward, and no known civilization traveled here until well into the last millennium, who made the marker and left it here?"

"I don't know."

"Then bear with me a few minutes while I brainstorm aloud. Assume the marker was left here before the Sumerian civilization developed, which would have to make it around five to six, possibly as long as eight thousand years ago, correct?"

"Correct."

"What if an unknown, more advanced civilization found their way to Sumer, before the Sumerian culture blossomed? Wouldn't that explain why they made all the sudden advancements you told me about?"

Alex sat thinking about that for a moment. "That would mean this unknown civilization would have to of developed over ten thousand years ago."

"Actually, I think the marker was attached to the site at least twelve thousand years ago."

Alex looked stunned. "That's absurd. How did you arrive at that date?"

"Hang in there," said Tegan. "First of all, the marker is at a depth that would have been exposed twelve thousand years ago, when sea levels were lower. Back then, the Abaco islands were all a part of Great Abaco. In fact, most of the Little Bahama Bank would have been dry land, and you could have walked to Grand Bahama island from anywhere in the Abacos. The marker would have been well above sea level, and the ledge that's seventy feet down would have been accessible from the sea."

Tegan looked at Cal and could tell he was intrigued.

"So you think the marker was placed here during the last ice age," Cal said, "and the civilization disappeared, leaving the marker behind."

Alex said, "I'm not buying it. There's no evidence of any advanced people living in the Bahamas."

"Maybe we just found it," Cal said.

Tegan put her hand on Cal's forearm. "Alex, most of these islands have no underground freshwater source. People rely on rainwater-filled cisterns for their water. If the climate changed and the rainfall diminished or stopped entirely, whoever inhabited the islands would have been forced to move."

"Plausible foundation for an argument," Alex said. "I will give you that."

"The Wisconsin Ice Sheet was at its zenith about eighteen thousand years ago, correct?" Tegan asked.

"Correct, again. It covered most of North America, Europe, and part of Asia. Sea levels would have been at least a hundred feet lower than they are today, probably more. I'm not an expert in the topography or tectonic movement of these islands, so I can't say exactly what the sea level was back then around the Abacos."

Cal said, "Not to sound like a geek, but I know these islands have remained virtually unchanged, at least tectonically, for over a hundred thousand years."

Everyone turned and looked at him as if a great ape had uttered its first word.

"Why are you looking at me like that? I have an education."

"I know you do," Alex said. "I was there when you got it. But you didn't study earth sciences."

"Garth and I heard that the Azores could slide into the ocean, which would create a tsunami large enough to destroy the Bahamas, like the one in Japan a few years ago. When I checked, I found the information on the plates."

"Okay, I'll take your word for it, geo-boy," Tegan said, smiling at him. "That rules out a shift in elevation caused by tectonic plate movement, which means the ice melt caused the marker to be submerged."

"Only if our starting point is twelve thousand years ago," Alex said. "It could have been placed there after the water rose."

"I don't think so." Tegan looked at the screen and brought up the picture that Nate had taken of the area from a distance. "Let me take you deeper into my rabbit hole. Look at this picture. Do you see where the marker is in relation to the ledge?"

"Yes," Alex replied.

"I think Cal is right," Tegan said. She pointed at the edge of the picture as she zoomed in. "This is too level. That's not something nature made. That means its upper edge could have been at least twenty feet above sea level twelve thousand years ago, give or take a thousand years. This ledge could be a pier."

Alex leaned back in her chair. "There's still no hard evidence to support this line of thought."

"True." Tegan pointed to the large area above the ledge. "I still think this is an entrance to something not yet discovered under the island."

Silence.

Tegan said, "For whatever reason, the civilization that lived here abandoned the site. It could have been the lack of freshwater, the rise in sea level, or any number of other reasons, but I believe they left the marker, and whatever lies beneath Great Guana, to be found by a future generation."

"Are you thinking this was the Atlantis Plato described?" Nate asked.

"No, it's not Atlantis," Tegan replied. "Alex said there's no evidence of an advanced civilization in this area, but no known natives could have forged that marker either, especially one that can do what it did to me. That leaves only one option." Tegan looked at all of them for a moment, then decided to take the plunge. "I think it was left by beings from another world."

"What?" Cal cried.

The others shook their head in disbelief.

"I told you I was going out on a limb," Tegan said.

"I love you, but I think you just fell out of the tree," Cal said.

Everyone laughed, except Tegan.

"Thanks for your support."

"Are you serious?" Cal asked.

"Yes, I am. Listen, I know it sounds crazy, but think about it. If an alien species came to Earth in ancient times, they would've selected an area devoid of human inhabitants or one with a minimal number of people."

"Maybe, maybe not," Alex said. "It depends on what they wanted to do. Maybe they left the marker as a declaration of their visit. It could be a beacon for humankind to discover when we could better understand what it meant."

"Like the marker the crew of Apollo Eleven left on the moon," Nate said.

"Exactly," Tegan said. "Isn't it possible the visitors built a base in these islands, then moved on to the Middle East and Europe? Perhaps that explains the sudden advancement in the early Sumerian culture and light-skinned people appearing in Europe."

Alex said, "But why would aliens come here and do that? Why wouldn't they want to stay and see how their assistance helped us develop? Why would they go to such extremes to hide their presence? Why not build a massive monument to tell us they had been here?"

"I'll get to monuments in a moment," Tegan replied. "You said the similarity of the symbols to Sumerian cuneiform is remarkable. I've read books and watched programs about the possibility of ancient aliens visiting Earth. This may be the hard scientific evidence everyone has been looking for to prove that."

"A marker stuck in a rock doesn't prove anything," Cal said.

"You're right, it doesn't," Tegan replied. "But think about all of the huge structures around the world that many believe couldn't have been built without help from a more advanced civilization. I think the idols on Easter Island, Stonehenge, and the many pyramids are the monuments they left behind. These structures all show signs of a common influence upon human culture. For example, the great pyramids of Egypt were built to align almost perfectly with true north and with the stars of Orion during the time of their construction."

"Alessia, what does any of that have to do with the marker?" Cal asked.

"Please, just keep an open mind for a little longer. Alex, aren't there pyramids all over the world that align with celestial bodies and with the four true compass headings?"

"Yes. The pyramids of Mesoamerica, like the Sun and the Moon pyramids, align perfectly to the east and west. Different civilizations built many types of pyramids throughout history. There are mound pyramids in the American Midwest and Southwest. A pyramid was even recently found in Croatia." Alex paused, then added, "All of them have earthly explanations for their design and construction. None of the over 350 known pyramids date back twelve thousand years or show any evidence of being built by an alien species, and they certainly don't have anything to do with the marker. There's no way to show a correlation."

Tegan tucked a strand of hair behind her ear and said, "Haven't archeologists discussed how the stones found off Bimini have a striking resemblance to the casing stones found at the Great Pyramid in Egypt?"

Alex chuckled. "You are well read, Alessia. Yes, some have noted how the Bimini Road stones have the same angle of cut as the casing stones found on the Great Pyramid, although they are much smaller. However, geologists are convinced the Bimini stones are a natural phenomenon created by wave action over the limestone beach rocks. It's only a coincidence they look similar."

Alex looked as if she'd suddenly remembered something. "Interestingly enough, though, the Bimini stones are in about thirty feet of water, and they are arranged in a J pattern."

"What's that mean?" Nate asked.

"It means they could've created a breakwater to make a safe harbor, providing that sea levels were low enough."

Tegan smiled, looked at Alex, and said, "Haven't J-pattern breakwaters been found in the Mediterranean?"

"Yes, that's true," said Alex.

Alex brought up the search engine and typed in an inquiry. "I thought I remembered something else about Bimini. There's a place called the 'Rectangles,' where they've found a large slab of highly polished white marble underwater. It's embedded in the sea floor. Some archeologists think it was built by an advanced civilization that lived near Bimini long ago." Alex looked at Tegan and added, "Human, not alien."

"I've never heard of the Rectangles. Have you, Cal?" Tegan asked.

"No, but it sounds like it would make a great charter destination. Where exactly is it located?"

Alex said, "It's seven miles north of Bimini. Very little has been published about it. Some claim the marble may be the top of a temple, but no serious excavation of the site has been done, which is surprising."

"How deep of water is it in?" Cal asked.

Alex scanned the rest of the article. "Ninety feet."

"Close to the same depth as the bottom of the ledge," Cal said. "There's no marble in the Bahamas, so how would it get there?"

Alex said, "Marble is made of limestone, which is prevalent in the Bahamas. In order to turn limestone into marble, it needs exposure to high temperatures and pressure. Any marble in the islands would be buried thousands of feet beneath the ocean seabed, and it certainly wouldn't be polished."

"Anything else?" Tegan asked, seeing the odd look on Alex's face.

"Yeah, there is. This archeological journal article claims the Rectangles may have been built … twelve thousand years ago."

"Okay, that raised the hair on the back of my neck," Nate said.

Tegan's excitement grew. "The time certainly matches. Alex, if an alien civilization lived here twelve thousand years ago, is it reasonable to assume they had the technology to convert limestone into marble?"

"Who knows? We're drifting far from science and jumping to conclusions based on hypothetical inference."

"Why would an alien species need to build a harbor?" Nate asked.

Alex shook her head. "I don't know that they would. This is crazy."

Nate asked, "Are there any other unexplained civilizations that emerged around ten to twelve thousand years ago where structures were built beyond the believed technological ability of the people living then?"

After a minute, Alex answered. "There's a place in Bolivia called Puma Punku. It's near Tiahuanaco." She went back to her computer.

"Here it is," Alex said as she read. "There are three structures built there, the Akapana pyramid, the Kalasasaya platform, and a subterranean temple. It's estimated that Puma Punku was built twelve to fourteen thousand years ago … it's believed to be the oldest man-made structure on Earth … thought to have been built beyond the abilities of the indigenous population of that era."

"The plot thickens," Nate said.

"The buildings at Puma Punku are really different. They're constructed of stones that weigh many tons each. One of the stones weighs nearly eight hundred tons. The stones used in the construction were quarried more than ten miles away. No one can explain how the primitive inhabitants moved the massive stones across that distance." Alex paused for a moment as she read. "It seems they were cut so precisely that when assembled there wasn't a need for mortar. The stones weren't just chiseled out of a quarry and crudely stacked on top of one another, they were finely cut, smoothed and polished and bored precisely to interlock with each other. Some of the structures at the site are four stories high, and even using current construction methods they would be hard to replicate today."

"Cut and polished, like the marble at the Rectangles and the marker?" Tegan asked.

"The marker is made of metal," Cal said.

"Yes, but it's polished," Tegan replied.

"So are my dress shoes," Cal quipped.

Tegan knew she wasn't swaying them to look at it from her viewpoint.

"How did they cut and move the stones at Puma Punku?" Nate asked.

"You weren't listening, were you?" Alex said. "No one knows how they did it. There are no written records, and there is little known about the culture that built them. What is even more interesting is the stones quarried and used to build their structures are made of granite and diorite. The only thing harder is a diamond, and diamond-cutting tools weren't around back then."

"Where would they get the tools to cut granite and smooth the surface?" Cal asked.

"I think both of you are brain dead. No one knows!" Alex shouted.

"My question was rhetorical," Cal said. "Is there any record of other civilizations working with any type of metal twelve thousand years ago?"

"No," Alex replied.

Tegan smiled and said, "We're avoiding the real issue. Nothing explains the blue light that appeared when I touched the marker."

"As I said, I think the light was a chemical reaction to something you had on your hands," Alex replied.

"And the fact I couldn't touch her to pull her away?" Cal asked.

"It could have been an electrical discharge that linked her to the marker. An electrical field might have been momentarily created to keep you away. When enough of the charge dissipated, she was able to let go."

Cal said, "I don't think so. That was different from anything I've ever seen. It wasn't normal, and don't forget what the compass did when we left. It reacted like we went through an electromagnetic field."

"All very good points geek-boy, which leads me to my next theory," Tegan said.

"Uh-oh," Nate said.

Tegan glanced at Nate. "I believe the marker reacted to my touch because of my genetic code."

"You mean your DNA caused it to change color?" Alex asked.

"Yes. I'm wondering if it could be an alien biological receptor of some kind."

"You really are hung up on this thing being an alien artifact, aren't you?" Alex asked.

"You think you're an alien?" Nate asked.

"No, but it's possible that one of my ancestors could've been in contact with whoever left the marker, and it was coded to react to their genetic signature. The marker simply recognized it from long ago."

Alex dropped her jaw and looked aghast. "So you think this marker has been waiting for you to discover it? No offense, but I think we need to circle back to reality. I'm willing to say we can look at an advanced human source, but I want to discard anything alien."

"Alex, I'm not saying this thing has been sitting here waiting for me to stop by," Tegan replied. "I just think it may have been waiting for someone with the right genetic code to unlock it. It's possible it was programmed to work like a biometric lock."

Alex shook her head.

"Alex, there was nothing on my hands. It was not a chemical reaction. You have to discount that as a possibility. Can anyone think of a better explanation for why the marker only reacted to my touch?"

No one answered her.

"What's the source of power that created the glow and the electrical field?" Tegan asked.

"Bioluminescence could create the glow," Alex answered. "The power could be from an electrical buildup created by wave, current, or tidal action. That makes more sense to me than aliens."

"You're grasping at straws," Tegan said. "Follow the path of least resistance. I believe genetics is the cause. Human DNA is our basic genetic composition or trademark. We all carry the same phosphates, sugars, and bases arranged in a double standard molecule, or helix."

Nate, Cal, and Alex exchanged glances.

Tegan saw the looks and added, "We all learned this in basic biology classes in high school. Come on, you all remember there are four different bases—thymine, guanine, cytosine, and adenine. Adenine joins with thymine, and cytosine and guanine are together. Both pairs intertwine across the two sides of the strand. When DNA replicates, these two sides are broken, and new nucleotides join to the strand. Mutations occur when something goes wrong or when something is deliberately introduced to the sequence, then a new base is substituted in the sequence. Every human carries this basic sequence, but we all have some type of variance, which makes us who we are as individuals. Each of us also has what was thought of as junk DNA, but we're learning that this unused DNA may have a use, or it had one at some point in time."

"You think I remember any of that from my high school science class?" Cal asked.

Tegan ignored Cal's comment. "Over millions of years, our DNA has allowed us to adapt, become smarter, and survive at least two near-extinction events. As we became smarter, we became self-aware and learned to reason, further separating us from other species. We can trace human evolution back along the phylogenetic tree, some fifteen million years. Think about the number of humanoid species that branched off the tree only to go extinct and the genetic changes we experienced as modern humans in order to survive.

"Whether we were helped by friendly beings from another world, I can't say with any certainty, but I don't think we can dismiss it entirely, especially in light of what we found. Maybe, just maybe, some of my junk DNA left over from an ancient ancestor has a purpose."

Cal asked, "If we all came from the same tree, shouldn't we all carry that ancient junk DNA sequence?"

Tegan stood and paced. "Not necessarily. Scientists traced our specific mitochondrial DNA back two hundred thousand years to a female who lived in Africa. She's known as Mitochondrial Eve. She is truly the mother of all of us. We all carry her DNA." She stopped and faced everyone. "Wait, what if there were new strands introduced more recently—say ten to twelve thousand years ago?"

Alex moaned, "Now we're back to aliens again."

"What if an alien species altered our DNA or mated with humans to produce hybrid offspring?" Tegan asked. "Either way, the altered DNA would have been passed down through the generations, perhaps fading out in most people entirely after enough pairings. Throughout our evolution, our DNA has mutated, creating different branches of the hominid tree, until we became the sole surviving form of our genus. Maybe one of my maternal ancestors passed down a strand of DNA that contained the alien genetic sequence. Millions of people could be carrying an ancient genetic anomalistic trait the marker would recognize. I just happen to be the only one among us that still carries the gene."

"You're saying that you believe around twelve thousand years ago an alien species purposely altered or interbred with our ancestors to create a new DNA string that was passed down to you?" Alex asked, shaking her head in disbelief.

"Surely you must find it interesting that light-skinned humans just suddenly appeared in Europe about eight thousand years ago," Tegan said. "I won't go into the probabilities involved in such a sudden genetic change, but most geneticists believe it was too quick for it to have occurred naturally. I find it damn coincidental that there were so many significant events happening all over the planet during the same time period that propelled human development forward so rapidly."

Tegan paused, then asked, "Alex, weren't the remains of the first known religious structure built found in Turkey? Didn't it date to around twelve thousand years ago?"

"Yes, that's true. The most current information about Gobekli Tepe confirms that the temple was built then."

"You said Puma Punku was constructed around that time as well. Isn't it possible that humans could have had contact with an advanced species and been genetically altered during that time period?"

"I respect your passion, but there isn't any proof," Alex said.

"Are you sure?" Tegan asked, growing frustrated. "The marker could be the key to proving why humans all over the world changed so quickly."

"Who would have thought my wife-to-be was an ancient alien theorist," Cal quipped.

"So you think an alien species guided our evolution?" Nate asked. "I'm having a hard time buying this theory."

"I understand, but I don't think we should ignore the possibility," Tegan said. "Humans have simply made too many leaps forward over too short a period of time, and they all occurred around the same time when contact between civilizations across the oceans wasn't thought possible. We really shouldn't be as genetically advanced as we are today, considering the historical timeline of our development."

"But why would an alien species go to all the trouble to change us, then never bother to say hello?" Nate asked.

"I don't know." Tegan had kept these thoughts bottled up inside for years. She had always believed a species capable of space travel could have altered the human genome. She also thought an alien species could have been the source of viruses, not comets and asteroids.

Cal pointed his finger at her and said, "Lucy, you got some splainin' to do," imitating Desi Arnaz's accent. "How do you know so much about genetics and ancient civilizations?"

Tegan feared she'd exposed too much of her knowledge on the subject. "Not much to explain. I worked at a pharmaceutical company peddling drugs, remember, and I received a very good education to help me do my job. I also took biology classes in college."

Tegan thought Cal and Alex saw right through her veil and knew she wasn't being completely forthcoming. She hoped they wouldn't push her. Fortunately, they didn't.

Finally, Alex said, "Okay, so we have Alessia's theory on the origins of the marker and human development, which, after some consideration, I can't dismiss entirely. I suppose it is possible that an advanced *human* civilization, not aliens, existed in Peru or Bolivia. They could have migrated to the Bahamas for a climate change, then moved to the Middle East and Europe after the last ice age. A more advanced human civilization could have developed a technology which was lost over time that allowed them to create unexplainable structures. The marker, and whatever may lie beneath the island, could hold the key to allowing us to link it all together."

"Thanks for not discounting my idea *entirely*," Tegan said.

"We need to decipher the meaning of the symbols on the marker to get more answers, but I suspect when we do, we'll end up with a lot more questions," Alex said, standing. "How about I email copies of the photos of the marker to Brian? He has a knack for cracking ancient languages.

If anyone can decipher what's on the marker and confirm the age of the symbols, he can."

"Why not just call him, Alex? He's hours behind us in Arizona," Nate suggested.

"I suppose I could do that, but let me send him the photos first. Brian may give us insight into what we're looking at and how we should excavate the site. It has certainly been an interesting day of speculation so far," Alex said.

$$\infty$$

Alex composed her email, attached the photo file, and sent it to Dr. Lee. Then she dialed his number.

Dr. Brian Lee answered after the third ring.

"Hello," Lee said.

"Hey, Brian. I hope I didn't catch you at a bad time."

"Not at all. We just finished an early dinner," Brian replied, then yelled, "Crystal, it's Alex."

"Listen, I want to get your opinion on something, if I may," Alex said, getting right to business. I just sent you an email with a photo file attached. I've run across some very interesting symbols that I can't decipher, and I was hoping you might take a look at them."

"Hang on a minute. Let me pick up in the study. Crystal, please hang up for me."

Alex looked at the others and said, "Crystal is Brian's wife. They have the cutest little girl."

"Hi, Alex," Crystal said. "It's been a while since we spoke. I hear an echo. Am I on speaker?"

"You are. I'm here with some friends. I need Brian's advice on something we've discovered."

"Okay, Crystal, I got it," Lee said, sounding dismissive. "Are you still there?"

"I'm still here," Alex replied.

"Well, Alex, I guess that's my cue. Let me know when you are back in Phoenix so we can get together for lunch or shopping. He's all yours."

"What can I do for you?" Lee asked.

"I guess you haven't opened the file yet, because it should be pretty evident."

"I'm doing it now. I see what looks like underwater photos."

"Yes, they were taken between thirty and seventy feet down. What I'd like you to focus on are the symbols on the metal plate."

"I see them. Yes, they are interesting. What type of metal are these markings on?"

"We don't know. I'm mostly interested in the language. I believe it may be pre-Sumerian."

"I'm zooming in now. Yes, they could possibly be pre-Sumerian. Where did you find this?"

"I can't tell you that, Brian. I'm sorry to be so secretive, but I think I should keep the location a secret for now."

"I understand. I hope you don't want an immediate translation. I'm good, but not that good."

"I need it as soon as possible. I have limited time to work on the site. I'd appreciate you not sharing what I've sent you."

"I understand, Alex, but this may take a while. I'll start with the premise that they're a precursor to Sumerian cuneiform and see where that gets me. If I knew where the site was, I might be able to give you a faster answer. But you have never been someone to make my life easy."

"That's because I know how much you like challenges. Thanks, Brian. I'll call you tomorrow. If you come up with something before then, you can reach me on my cell or my tablet if you want to video chat."

"I'll try to call you no later than noon my time," Lee said. "This is fascinating stuff. Crystal isn't going to be happy with you. I have a feeling I'm going to be up all night."

"Tell her I'm sorry. This discovery could be of major historical significance. You'll get full credit for being involved. Talk to you later." Alex hung up.

"I recommend we all get some rest and be ready for an early start in the morning," Cal said.

"Sounds good to me," Nate said, yawning. "It has been a long day."

"That's my adventurer," Alex said.

They all said good night.

Tegan and Cal headed for the *Whispering Winds*. A few minutes into their walk Cal said, "You took us all by surprise tonight with your depth of knowledge in genetics and ancient history. I know you impressed Alex."

Tegan took Cal's hand, knowing what he wanted. He deserved an explanation. "I know you want to talk about this, but I don't. Not tonight."

"I'm just curious. I know you're keeping something from me."

"I have a secret, Cal, and someday I'll explain everything to you. But I can't right now. I hope you will respect that."

"Okay. Tell me when you're ready."

"Thank you." Tegan leaned against him and squeezed his hand, then thought about the marker. She knew it was biogenetically responsive and that no human civilization could have ever developed the technology, which meant the marker was of alien origin.

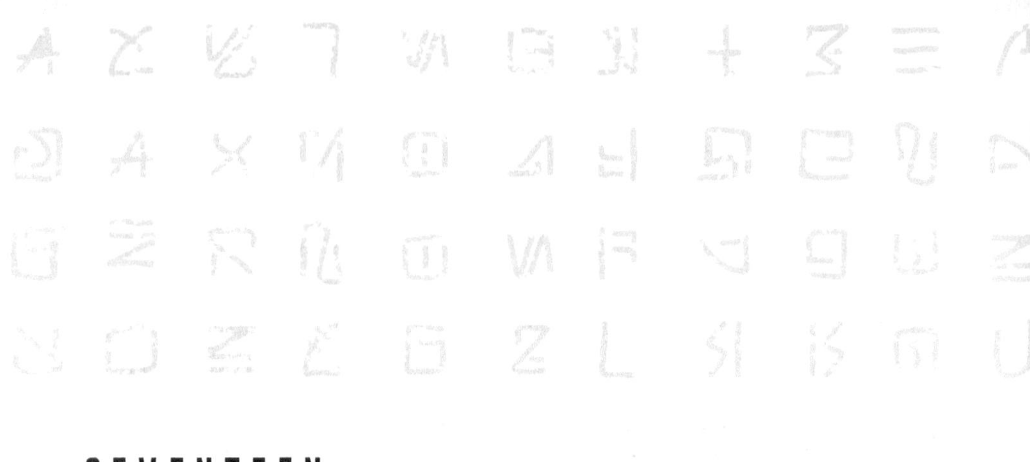

SEVENTEEN

Alamogordo, New Mexico — July 24 — 0030 hours MST

Westfield awakened to the alert tone on his computer, indicating he had received a priority action message, which was a common occurrence. He rolled out of bed and rubbed the sleep from his eyes. The alert tone sounded again. The insistent alarm would chime every fifteen seconds until he punched the acknowledge button. He pulled the laptop from the night table, typed in his security password, and waited while the encrypted message ran through its software filters.

He spent most nights in the room adjacent to his office. Under the circumstances, this was not only practical, but also allowed him to remain unseen, except by his own people. Westfield opened the file. He noted it had been sent from CNCI in Utah, and it was marked "Urgent—Immediate Action." Not many files were marked that way. He checked his watch. It was just past midnight.

Westfield threw on a pair of slacks and a white V-neck undershirt. The day had started early. He carried the computer to the small work desk in the corner of the room and sat down to read the file. The message-opening prompt brought up the contents of a signals intercept that met the search criteria he had put in place long before. He noted the intercept had occurred earlier in the evening. The point of origin was in the Bahamas, and the receiver was located in Arizona. He opened the attached original email transcript and photo file. Dr. Brian Lee, PhD, had received the file. His attached bio said he was an archeology and linguistics professor at Arizona State University.

The sender was another professor, Dr. Alexandra Hutchins-Winslow. Her bio and specialization were also included. The message referred to photographs of symbols from a language never seen before. According to the report, shortly after Dr. Lee received the email, Professor Hutchins-Winslow called him. The transcript of the telephone conversation revealed little actionable information. The call originated in Man-O-War Cay, Abacos, Bahamas. Next, he opened the attached photograph file and was amazed to see the symbols. He felt certain they were alien. He forced himself to take his eyes off the symbols and speed-dialed Robert Knolls.

"Hello," Knolls answered, sounding as if he had been in deep slumber.

"It's me. I need you in my office now," Westfield said, and hung up.

Westfield contacted the analyst who had sent the information and told him to monitor all calls, emails, and anything else they could get from either of the parties. The analyst advised that intercept tracers were active. Westfield ordered the analyst to notify him immediately of any additional SIGINT intercepts and to relay them in real time.

Next, he contacted an analyst who worked for him at Los Alamos. He forwarded the photograph file and ordered him to use the DOE's supercomputer, known as "The Beast," to decipher the symbols. He didn't think it would take long to have answers.

Feeling he'd started the ball rolling, Westfield finished dressing, lit a cigarette, and took in the first good drag of the day. He coughed, sounding like an out-of-tune bagpipe, and walked to his office.

Just as he arrived, the computer chimed its annoying alert sound. The message alert was from Los Alamos. He opened the communiqué and was disappointed to see there was no substantive information to report yet, and there was no estimate of when the translation would be complete. The only information the computer could provide was that the language was unknown and that it may have its origins in the ancient Middle East.

Robert Knolls arrived fifteen minutes later, dressed appropriately for the day ahead, and appeared eager, as always.

Westfield pointed to the chair behind his desk and motioned Knolls to sit down. Knolls looked confused. "You want me to sit in your chair, sir?"

"Yes, or I wouldn't have pointed to it. Mr. Knolls, I know you like exploring the mysteries of the unknown and the hunt for answers. Well, this is a real mystery. I received this action alert a little while ago. Our people can't identify the symbols. What do you make of it?"

Knolls read the email, followed by a quick review of the bios on Hutchins-Winslow and Lee. He then opened the photograph file and scrolled through the pictures, taking his time looking at the symbols. "Interesting pictures. It looks like a submerged marker of some sort. I have no idea what to make of the writing."

"What would you suggest for our next course of action?"

"I'd recommend we have the Beast take a shot at deciphering the language. That will help us decide if the marker warrants our time."

"That has already been done. The computer is still working on a translation. So far, the analysis indicates the language is unknown. What else?"

"Judging by their conversation, they appear to be friends, but Dr. Winslow doesn't want anyone jumping her claim. Since she needs Dr. Lee's help with the translation, I think we have the edge in getting this translated first."

"Never assume anything," Westfield said, lighting another cigarette. "I did some quick research while I was waiting for you and found that Dr. Lee is considered somewhat of a savant when it comes to ancient languages. He's been consulted on numerous archeological projects over the years. He's the expert other experts turn to for help in deciphering ancient languages." Westfield wheezed.

Knolls scrolled through the pictures again. "We need to understand what the symbols mean before the eggheads do. I think we need to develop a disinformation plan if it looks like it's of NIB origin."

Westfield nodded his approval and motioned for Knolls to get out of his chair. "Where are you in your history lesson?"

"I've worked through the 1970s, and I'm about halfway through the '80's."

"That's impressive, considering the volume. Did anything of interest jump out at you? Find any patterns?"

"I found several things of interest. First, people are reporting similar types of alien spacecraft. The most prevalent are the saucer-shaped, triangular-shaped, and cigar-shaped types. There are a number of UFO sightings involving only lights. Most of the reports are of little value, except those reported by military personnel near their installations. Second, the physical description of the alien beings is similar. They seem to fall into distinct categories. The most prominent are the short, gray creatures with dark eyes."

"So from what you've learned so far, which species left the marker in the Bahamas?"

"That's hard to say. None of the symbols in the photos resembles anything I've seen in any of the files. I can't draw any conclusions as to whether they're related to any other reports. I can't even say if the symbols or that marker are of alien origin."

"That's true, but I'm telling you the marker was left by an NIB. So it appears you have some work to do to prove, or disprove, my belief. I want you in the Bahamas by this afternoon. I'll send you the translation as soon as I get it. Hopefully, that will give us a better idea of what we're dealing with and tell us whether the site is still active."

"You want me to find and retrieve the marker?" Knolls asked.

"Find, yes, retrieve, not yet. Let's wait and see what the Beast can tell us. Who knows, I may be wrong, and this could just turn out to be of terrestrial origin, maybe ancient Mayan or some other ancient language. If that's the case, then the archeologists can enjoy their discovery."

"Understood. Is there anything else, sir?"

"I received information that Senator Woodsman's half-assed effort to ferret out the source of our funding is progressing. I've decided that the senator needs to go. I'll pick the time and place and take care of it myself."

"Yes, sir."

"That is all. Dismissed."

Man-O-War Cay — 0430 hours

Alex's cell phone jolted her awake. When she looked at it, she saw Brian's number displayed. "Morning. I hope you have a good reason for waking me."

"Yes, I have a very good reason. I haven't gone to bed yet, and I thought you'd want to know I've made some headway with the symbols. Since you're still in bed, I know you're not in the Mediterranean."

"I apologize for my snippiness. I'm not a morning person. No, I'm not in the Med. What did you find?"

"The symbols could very well be the root language for Sumerian cuneiform."

"Anything else?"

"Yes, but I want to see the look on your face when I tell you."

"Seriously? It's that important, or are you just trying to find out where I am?"

"Yes and yes."

"Okay, give me a few minutes to put some clothes on. I'll video-Zon you back so you can see my sleepy face." Alex elbowed Nate in the ribs to rouse him.

"You're going to love this," Brian said, "and I expect you to tell me where you are, because I intend to make a house call."

"Okay, if you insist. I'll call you in twenty."

"Sounds good," Brian said, and hung up.

Alex looked at Nate lying beside her. He hadn't moved, so Alex elbowed him again, harder this time.

Nate moaned. "What is it?"

"Get dressed. We got news from Brian, and I want Cal and Alessia to hear this firsthand. Brian seemed pretty excited about it, so get your ass in gear."

Nate looked at the clock and said, "You are kidding, right?"

"No, I am most certainly not kidding. Now call Cal and tell him we're coming over." She got dressed while Nate grumbled.

"Get your ass up. Let's get going!" Alex shouted, ignoring his whining.

"Yes, your royal highness."

Ten minutes later Nate and Alex joined Cal and Tegan in the salon on the *Whispering Winds*.

"What's up guys?" Cal asked. "I know I said we'd get an early start, but this is a bit too early."

"We need to connect with Brian Lee for a video chat on Zon."

"You got us up at this time in the morning so we could watch you make a video call?"

"Cal, I got a call from him a few minutes ago. He said he has some information for us, but wanted to see my face when he told me the news.

I thought you'd want to be there when he briefed us. I now have seven minutes to make the call."

"Or what? He turns into a pumpkin?" Cal joked.

"He might. Brian said he'd been up all night working on deciphering the symbols. It has to be something monumental or he would have told me over the phone. Can we get on with why we came here?" Alex asked, setting the MPad on the table and opening it to make the call. The signal strength was weak and intermittent. "Shit, doesn't anything electronic work out here?" She couldn't sustain a connection on the MPad from the boat. "What the hell is the problem?"

"I told you," Cal said, "ever since the last hurricane, wireless service has been sketchy. Guess we were lucky we got Nate's call before you surprised us. Well, it looks like we got up for nothing. I'm heading back to bed for a few more hours of sleep. You can let yourselves out."

Alex ignored Cal and muttered, "The signal strength is fine back at the house."

"Then let's go back there," Nate said.

"Damn it, we don't have the time," Alex said.

There was a knock on the side of the boat's hull. "Hey, there, you guys are up early," Garth said.

Cal opened the salon door and walked out on deck. "Yes, we are, and so are you."

"I couldn't sleep," Garth said. "I have too much on my mind. What's your excuse?"

"Alex needs to video conference with someone, but she can't get a good signal. We were just heading back to bed."

"They walked all the way down here, at this hour, to make a call?"

"It's an important call."

"I can see that," Garth said as everyone walked out on deck.

"Good morning, Garth," Tegan said with a big smile.

"Morning, all," he replied.

"Garth, can we use your office to see if we can get a signal?" Tegan asked.

"I thought we were going back to bed," Cal said.

"Alex needs to make this call right away. Garth's office is on the second floor, so she might get a good connection there."

"No problem. I'm opening up anyway," Garth replied.

Garth led the way to his office, opened the door, and turned on the window-mounted air conditioner. The room smelled musty from years of continuous exposure to high humidity.

Alex pulled the MPad out of its case.

"What's so important that you need to call someone at this hour?" Garth asked.

"That's personal, Garth," Alex said, seeing she had a good signal. When she made the connection, Brian's smiling face appeared on the screen. "And it's private," Alex added, looking at Garth.

"I understand. I'll wait outside."

When Garth was gone, Cal said, "Alex, we'll need his support if this thing comes to fruition. Moreover, it is his office. Garth can keep a secret, trust me on this."

Alex frowned at Cal, then let out a heavy sigh. "Okay, okay already. Go get him and bring him back here. Just a second, Brian."

When Garth returned, Alex said, "You need to hear this, too, but you are sworn to secrecy."

"What's going on there?" Brian asked.

"We've just added a new member to our team. I have a small group here that has been working with me on the discovery. We're all excited to hear what you have to say." Alex panned the MPad around to show Brian everyone who was present.

"You certainly do have a bunch of people there. The only one I recognize is Nate."

"Circumstances require it." She introduced everyone to Brian. "These are the only people who are aware of the discovery. I'd like to keep it that way."

"What discovery?" Garth whispered to Cal.

"Just listen. I'll fill you in later," Cal said.

Alex said, "Sorry, Brian. Okay, what's the news?"

Brian pulled a white board with symbols on it into view. "Can you all see this?"

"Yes," Alex answered for everyone as they all crowded together.

"I can conclusively say that these symbols are not only a precursor to ancient Sumerian, but they are possibly the root language for others. It's a language I have never seen before."

"That's great news, Brian."

"You woke us all up to tell us that?" Nate asked. "I thought you had something for us."

"I do."

Alex gave Nate a quick withering look, then said, "I've learned over the years not to question you, but are you absolutely certain? You've only had the pictures for a few hours."

"I am very sure, and I'll show you why in a minute. It's going to be, at the very least, an unknown language worthy of my time to help you, and I thank you for including me."

"You're welcome."

"I think you've stumbled onto something incredible. For these symbols to be a root language, they have to be over seven thousand years old, maybe older than that. Where did you say you were?"

Alex smiled. "Okay, Brian. You win. We're in the Bahamas on Man-O-War Cay."

"The Bahamas! In that case, if this turns out to be as old as I think, we are going to rewrite history. How did you find it? And just so you know, I'll be coming there."

"I expected that. We found it by chance," Alex explained. "Now explain your findings, please."

Brian moved the white board closer to his computer. "These symbols are unique." He pointed to the larger symbols at the base of the marker. "These appear to form context. Now look at these symbols." He pointed to two of the smaller symbols. "These are not just wedged-shaped cuneiform symbols. They actually have some characteristics of Vinca."

"Really?"

"Yes. As you know, it originated in southeastern Europe more than six thousand years ago. Some of these symbols could even be the root structure for Chinese Jiahu symbols."

"Do you know what any of them mean?"

"Not yet. But I think this symbol near the edge looks like both the Sumerian symbols for Anu and Ki, but its structure is more complex."

"That was my first guess as well. It is a puzzle, but I know you can decipher them. You're the best."

"I know I am, but my ego needs reassurance every once in a while, so thanks. Alex, you know you can expect to find changes in writing and the meanings of symbols over time. The early cuneiform writing of the Sumerians was in flux for thousands of years.

"Alex, I believe some of these symbols could be logosyllabic-style writing, like that of Asian languages. However, something doesn't quite fit the mold. Each symbol appears to be unique and doesn't repeat anywhere on the marker. It's going to be a bitch to decipher. I see root structure for many ancient languages in these symbols."

"Can't you work forward from the Anu and Ki symbols?"

"I tried that already."

"Who is Anu and Ki?" Nate asked.

"The Sumerians believed Anu was the god of heaven or of the sky," Lee said. "Ki is the goddess of Earth. By extension from that interpretation, these symbols don't make any sense."

"Where do you plan to go from here?"

"I'm not sure. Probably to bed so I can sleep on it. I'll work on the assumption the symbols are a precursor to Sumerian and Vinca. I want to see if any of these symbols could be from the Levant area. I really think this language may have laid the foundation for all the languages found in the region, and possibly even Asia, but I may be stretching at this point."

"Could there be a correlation with anything found in Mesoamerica?" Alex asked, wondering what Brian would think of a west-to-east migration of human civilization. She didn't want to mention the extraterrestrial theory yet.

"You're thinking that whoever left these symbols brought their writing from your island across the Atlantic and introduced it to the rest of the world?"

"That's one of the ideas we've discussed. If you find that the symbols are a precursor to all writings throughout Europe, Asia, and the Levant region, with an origin in Mesoamerica, we'll have something really exciting."

"I'd say. When do you think you will be able to date the site?" Brian asked.

"I'm not sure, and I don't even know if I can. The marker is some type of a metal alloy, so standard carbon dating is out. I'll see if there's any material around the marker I can use uranium-thorium for dating. I may have to resort to looking at the geological composition of the area for some clues, but that will be speculative."

"It's always difficult working in a fluid environment. Forged metal with the intricacy of those symbols would require technology far beyond anything known in that era."

"That's for sure," Alex replied.

"I just thought of another work to compare your symbols to. It's been a puzzler since it was found in 1926, one I've been asked to consult on."

"Are you talking about the Sitovo inscriptions?"

"Yes. As you know, they are about three thousand years old. The inscriptions are much larger than the symbols you found, and they're inscribed in stone on a cave wall. But they may be of interest for comparison."

Alex nodded in agreement.

"If memory serves, the Sitovo symbols are very intricate. Excuse me for a second." Brian went off camera. When he returned, he was holding a large hardcover book. He flipped through the pages until he found what he was looking for. "Here it is. There are fifty symbols at Sitovo, and each symbol is sixteen inches high. What are the dimensions of your symbols?"

"There are forty-nine small symbols measuring two inches square and eight larger symbols that are four inches in diameter. The center symbol, a very curious one, measures six inches across, two inches high at the center, and tapers off at the ends."

"I was thinking that if I wanted to duplicate the detailed symbols you found there, without having the ability to forge metal, I could copy them onto a stone medium."

"I can't remember what the Sitovo symbols look like, so I'll do some research on my end while you get some sleep."

"Thanks. I am a bit tired."

"We all thank you for your time, Brian."

"Wait a minute. I need directions to your location."

"All we've done so far is preliminary work. You don't need to come here yet."

"Yes, I do. This could be an epic discovery, and seeing the site firsthand may help me decipher the symbols." Alex looked at Cal.

He gave her an approving nod.

"Okay, Brian. We can work out the details later. But it won't be until the end of the month at the earliest."

"Why so long?"

"We're here to attend a wedding, and we may not be back to Man-O-War until then. Communications are sketchy, so if you can't get me, keep trying."

"Okay. In the meantime, I'll keep digging."

"Get some sleep and give my best to Crystal."

"Thanks, I will. It was good to meet you all, and I look forward to working with you." Brian disconnected.

"I think we should get out to the site as soon as possible and see what we can find," Alex said.

"Who put you in charge?" Cal asked.

"I did," Alex said, grinning.

"Could it wait until after breakfast? The tanks haven't been refilled yet."

"Breakfast sounds good," Garth said. "I work better with a full belly."

"Breakfast it is. I'll get it started," Tegan said, heading for the door.

Garth said, "Cal, tell me more about this discovery."

Alamogordo, New Mexico — 0330 hours MST

When Westfield received another alert, he keyed in the access code and opened the file. He saw that Dr. Lee had placed a call to Dr. Winslow, and twenty minutes later she had called him back on Zon for a video chat. The Zon call was image-captured. He picked up the phone, summoned Knolls to his office, and started the video recording.

As Westfield watched the group introduced to Dr. Lee, his blood went cold. *It couldn't be,* he thought. She stood slightly behind a rugged-looking, tall, dark-haired man. He took a breath, then replayed the video, freezing the best image of the woman's face. He fixated on the image, wondering how she could be alive. The professor had introduced her as Alessia Stryker, but he knew she was Tegan Strong. Her height and weight looked the same as he remembered, as did the blond hair, although it was longer. She was tan, but her smile was something he would never forget. He had no doubt about who was standing there.

He tore his eyes from the screen and read the accompanying intelligence summary. The facial recognition search matched the names of all the others introduced perfectly, except for Alessia Stryker. There was only an eighty-five percent probability the woman was her. With no official photographs of Tegan in any public or classified data files for the system to compare, the software could not have identified her as Tegan. A brief bio of Alessia Stryker indicated she had a last known address in Seattle. Her security file from Boeing, where she had once worked, contained a photograph. He looked at it carefully. Alessia Stryker looked remarkably similar to the woman in the video, but Westfield could see the difference. He gripped the arms of his chair so tightly that his fingers turned white.

A few minutes later, there was a knock on Westfield's office door, and Knolls walked in.

"Son of a bitch!" Westfield shouted, reaching for his phone. "Sit down, Knolls. There's a change in plans."

"What's wrong, sir?"

Westfield called John Grant's quarters in the facility.

Grant answered on the first ring. "Yes, sir."

"Osiris, we have a problem. Get your ass to my office immediately." Westfield slammed the receiver into the cradle so hard that some of the plastic on the phone broke away and fell to the floor.

Westfield chose not to tell Knolls the reason he was so angry. He was going to wait for Grant to arrive to enlighten him. Westfield watched and listened to the recording again. Two minutes later, Grant rapped on the doorframe and requested permission to enter.

"Enter," Westfield replied, and stopped the recording.

Grant entered and stood at attention. "Reporting as ordered, sir."

"Master Gunnery Sergeant Grant, you were assigned a mission to perform in Washington several months ago. Do you remember the assignment?

"Yes, sir."

"You confirmed the target had been eliminated, and I closed the file on it. Do you remember that as well?"

"Yes, sir, I do."

"Are you sure that you eliminated the designated targets?"

"Yes, sir."

"Then perhaps you can explain to me why Tegan Strong is alive and living in the Bahamas."

Westfield saw the smallest twitch under Grant's right eye. He could see Grant was confused.

"Sir, Tegan Strong was in the family SUV when it went over the embankment. I put additional charges on the vehicle to ensure her death. I saw the vehicle explode and the cabin become engulfed in flames when it went over the cliff. I saw her die, and the police report confirmed her death."

"Come here and look at this."

Grant walked around the desk and stared down at the screen. He looked dumbfounded.

"I have no explanation, sir. I saw Tegan Strong in the SUV. I followed it until I blew it up. That cannot be her. It has to be someone who looks like her."

"I hope that's true. However, I don't think so. I've watched the way she moves in the recording. I know that is Tegan. John, I think you have gone soft on me. Is that what has happened? Are you too old to perform your duties?"

"Sir, I did my duty. I eliminated the target." Grant didn't move as he continued to stare at the frozen frame. "I still don't think that's her."

"I don't give a shit about what you think, Osiris. I want to know if you screwed up. I want to know if the woman in this picture is the target you were supposed to have terminated."

Westfield showed Grant the Boeing security file. "Alessia Stryker is from Seattle. I don't think this is a coincidence. You will accompany Mr. Knolls to Man-O-War Cay, and you will confirm whether that woman is Tegan Strong. Is that clear?"

Westfield turned to Knolls. "I'll forward this to you. You will familiarize yourself with the Strong sanction and her previous work history. You will take the lead on this op. I'm not sure I can count on Osiris anymore. If this is Tegan Strong, *you* will see that she is *properly* disposed of this time and find me that site. I want a lid clamped down on their discovery. We have to find and control that site." Westfield stopped to catch his breath and wheezed. His computer chimed.

Westfield opened the new file and read it. "Goddamn it! I knew it. Guess who is listed in an old background file I kept as a personal contact?"

"Alessia Stryker?" Grant responded.

"Osiris, I'd bet my pension you'll find Tegan in the Bahamas and up to her neck in this discovery."

He pulled up another file and read it. "According to Boeing, Stryker quit her job around the same time you killed the family, and she hasn't been seen since. How interesting. This is not a coincidence." He softened his tone. "John, I can see why you could have been mistaken."

Westfield turned to Knolls. "We have an asset stationed at AUTEC on Andros Island in the Bahamas. She may be of value to you in the search. I'll put her on notice. I want you to leave within the hour. You're both dismissed."

EIGHTEEN

Cal was at the helm as the *Whispering Winds* left the dock loaded with additional tools and extra scuba tanks and diving equipment. Included with the gear was a brand-new digital underwater video camera with battery-powered lighting, and three of the latest diver's full-face mask communication units, complete with a surface base station. Garth had provided all of the equipment, but it had come with a request. He wanted Jessica to accompany them on the trip. He hoped that having an adventure close to home would curb her wanderlust.

Jessica was an accomplished diver and boat operator and would be a welcome addition to the team, so Cal agreed. He knew that Garth had already told Maggie about their discovery, so he found no reason not to include Jessica in the dives, and no one objected. He also knew that Maggie had conspired with Garth to get Jessica to accompany them.

Secrets are never secret for long, Cal thought. In the last twenty-four hours, the number of people who knew about the discovery had doubled. Cal hoped the trend didn't continue.

Once they left the dock, Tegan briefed Jessica on what they were really doing at the site and the need for the discovery, and its location, to remain a secret. Jessica swore not to say a word about it. He could tell she was excited to be going on an adventure with them.

They would need to train with the new masks, and that would use up some of the air. Even with the additional scuba tanks aboard, Cal knew they would not have enough air for the number of dives they planned. He was certain they would be returning to MOW the next morning, which wasn't such a bad thing. There were always last-minute wedding preparations to make, and Jessica would probably be bored by then anyway.

Tegan was more spiritual than Cal, and neither of them had any organized religious group affiliations. Tegan followed the Taoist teachings with a dash of Buddhism thrown in, and was only religious about her meditation. Cal was a lapsed Catholic. Their wedding was going to be a civil ceremony. Cal felt as if they were already married, and Tegan agreed. But they needed to make it legal under Bahamian law. Fortunately, Garth could legally officiate.

As the *Whispering Winds* sailed through the gap between Scotland Cay and Great Guana, Cal was pleased to see Jessica and Alessia laughing as they sat on the trampoline. He could tell Alessia was enjoying Jessica's company. She was good with kids, especially teenagers, and someday they would have children of their own. He wanted a real home for her so they could raise a family. However, for now, the *Whispering Winds* would have to do.

Skirting Great Guana Cay on the outside, heading north, Cal could see that the Atlantic was not as calm as yesterday. The higher swells wouldn't prevent them from diving on the site. As they approached the anchorage, Cal was relieved to see there were no other boats in the area. Jessica enthusiastically secured the *Whispering Winds* to the mooring buoy with the energy of a nineteen-year-old. He still thought of her as being younger, and many days she acted that way. Today, she appeared grown up. Once he turned off the engines, everyone met in the salon.

Alex explained the priorities for the next series of dives, including the type of samples she needed taken in order to date the site. After much deliberation, she had decided to cut a small fragment or obtain metal scrapings off the marker in order to determine its composition. She gave specific assignments to each team member. Everyone felt it was only fair to have Alex be in charge, considering this was her field of expertise.

On the first dive, Alex wanted them to set up perimeter grid markers so they could precisely map and measure the area. That was going to be a challenge because the area was vertical, not a flat sandy bottom.

"Jessica, you will be our underwater photographer," Alex said. "Alessia, you will help me lay out the grid and record the measurements. Cal, I want you to dive to the ledge and scout for anything of interest, then come back and help us with the measurements. And Nate, you will remain aboard the *Whispering Winds* as the safety officer."

"As always," Nate grumbled.

"Jessica," Cal said. "Have you trained with these new masks?"

"Yes, and I don't care for them. The nose plugs are a pain to use to clear your ears, and the battery life isn't all that great. I'll stick with a regular mask and regulator, if that's okay."

"That's fine. I like a traditional mask, too, but under the circumstances, it will make it easier for us to communicate. Nate, I need you to monitor the receiver after I get the transducer into the water. Our voices may sound strange, but you should be able to understand us. Garth said these models are the latest and have a two-hundred-meter range. You should be able to hear us from the site."

"That would be nice," Nate said.

Cal picked up the cobalt-colored mask and put it on. "To clear, push up from the bottom of the mask. It is push-to-talk. Just remember to release the button to listen. That's all there is to it. Any questions?"

Alex asked, "Where's the regulator?"

"It's built in. Just breathe normally. It's almost impossible to flood the mask, and you won't get jaw fatigue, unless you talk a lot."

"Very funny," Alex quipped.

"If you have a problem, just yell. Alessia, I've given you the emerald mask to match your eyes, and Alex, you get the pink one."

After twenty minutes of practicing with the masks on the boat, the four of them entered the water, submerged, and Cal led them to the site. Cal checked communications with Nate. The connection was good, although the signal grew weaker as they moved farther away from the boat.

Once over the site, Jessica swam to the marker and ran her hand over it. When she turned toward them, Cal could see by the expression on her face that she was beyond excited.

Cal and Jessica dove down twenty feet past the ledge to look around. When he looked back up at the bottom of the ledge, he could tell it wasn't a natural formation. It appeared as if someone had carved the ledge out of the rock and squared off the edges.

Cal signaled Jessica to start up. He checked her air supply, as he had done for years. Jessica snatched the gauge from Cal's hand and gave him a look that said, "Duh, don't you think I know how to do that?" Both of them ascended to where the women were working.

"Cal, the grid markers aren't going to work," Alex said.

"I didn't think they would," Cal replied.

"Let's use the orange line to divide the area into four squares. Cal, have Jessica video while you and Alessia measure the area. I'm going take a closer look at the symbol Brian mentioned."

Cal motioned for Jessica to video and they began laying out the grid.

Alex said, "The more I look at the marker, the more detail I see in the symbols. I didn't notice this yesterday. There are small faint dark anomalous lines etched into the metal running between some of the symbols. I wonder what those could be. Alessia, get the camera from Jessica. I need someone to be able to hear me. I need close-up video of these dark lines."

Tegan swam over to Jessica and took the camera from her and then joined Alex.

Alex asked, "Do you see the lines?"

"Yes," Tegan replied. "I didn't see them yesterday. Are they new?"

"I don't know. Maybe they formed after the marker was energized." Alex reached into her buoyancy vest pocket and removed the metal snips. "I'll take a sample of the metal while you record."

Alex ran her hand along the marker. "There aren't any exposed edges. I'll have to dig out part of the rock."

Cal moved closer.

"It looks like the surface of the metal turns from the polished gold to a rough-looking black material." Alex rubbed it with a finger. "It isn't rock, and I don't think it's metal or plastic."

She dug deeper into the rock until she exposed a smooth edge between the marker and the new material. Cal could tell that there was no way to take a sample using the snips. He looked at Alex, who held out a small metal file.

"Will you do the scraping for us?" Alex asked.

Cal took the file from her and went to work scraping the upper edge of the marker. Alex stayed next to him, holding a small plastic sample bag beneath the area to catch the metal shavings as they sank. The sound of Cal running the file over the metal sounded like fingernails on a chalkboard. After a minute of work, Cal stopped. There was no sign of damage and no shavings.

In a stroke of genius, or madness, Cal handed Alex the file, retrieved his dive knife, and stabbed the face of the marker.

"What are you doing?" Alex shouted, grabbing his arm and stopping him.

"There's no damage," Cal said. "Not even a dent, and the tip of my hardened steel dive knife is blunted."

Cal secured his dive knife and pulled a small crowbar from the tool kit attached to his waist. He inserted it between the rock and the marker and worked it deeper. He could tell the black material extended farther back into the rock, and it was just as impervious to damage as the marker. He realized the marker wasn't affixed to the rock. The marker appeared to be anchored to the strange material. He ran his fingers over the seam between the black material and the metal. It was definitely one solid piece. Cal dug deeper into the matrix and managed to gouge out about eight inches of it along the edge of the marker. He could see that the composite material continued deeper into the rock.

He was about to start working his way around the edge of it when he felt a slight tug in the mask, telling him his air was getting low. "Time to head back to the boat," Cal said, making a circular motion with his hand, indicating they needed to surface. He began his ascent, with Alex right behind him.

"I want to touch the marker before we head back," Tegan said. When she touched it, the soft blue glow danced under her fingertips.

Cal looked down and saw that Jessica had gone back to join her. "Not too long, Alessia," Cal said.

∞

The blue light followed the movement of Tegan's fingers. When her fingers moved over the darker lines, the color of the light changed to a darker hue. It was subtle, but Tegan saw it. Jessica began recording. Tegan repeatedly ran her fingers over the different areas so they could get good video of the color changes. This was a new development.

Tegan put her dive glove on and touched the marker. Nothing happened. No matter where she touched it, there was no reaction. Tegan motioned for Jessica to place her hand on the marker. As with the others, nothing happened. She was certain the marker was reacting to her genetic signature. This had to be a biometrically operated system. She took off her dive glove and traced the symbols again, but this time she didn't take her hand off the marker. She followed the fine dark lines from the large symbol at the top down to a smaller symbol. Fear began to creep up her spine. She had no doubt. The marker not only reacted to her touch, it caused an emotional response.

Each contact Tegan had with the marker was different. Sometimes it created a sense of well-being, and sometimes it produced a fear response. She had no idea what it all meant.

When she removed her hand, a ghostly impression of her hand remained on the marker. It glowed for a few seconds and then faded. Tegan swam away from the marker, feeling normal. She motioned for Jessica to follow her up.

∞

Cal floated at the stern of the *Whispering Winds*, waiting for them to surface. "Alessia, do you copy?"

"Yes, Cal. We're on our way."

When they made it back to the boat, Cal asked, "How did it go?"

"Cal, did you know that the marker sends out a blue light when Alessia touches it?" Jessica asked as she climbed the ladder and handed her gear to Nate. Jessica had never called him by his first name. He was always Mr. Locke or Captain Locke. Cal figured she must be feeling a bit older. He decided not to comment on it.

"Yes, Jessica, we did," Cal replied. "Alessia, did you discover anything new?" He believed she was being reckless interacting with the marker without him being there. He passed his gear up to Nate, then leaned back and floated in the water.

"I learned if my glove is on when I touch it, the marker doesn't react."

"What does that mean?"

"In my humble opinion, it confirms that the marker is reacting to my genomic signature." Tegan passed her gear up to Nate, but stayed in the water.

"So it's definitely reacting to your DNA?"

"Yes. I get the feeling the marker senses me, but I don't think I'm giving it what it's looking for in return. I think it's like an alarm. Punch in the wrong code, and it goes off. Only in this case it sends a signal that makes me feel an emotional response. I'm wondering if the symbols could be a keypad to a biometric lock."

Standing at the stern of the boat, Alex said, "Interesting thought. You think if you push the symbols in the right sequence using your DNA signature that it will respond."

"I think it is possible. I felt as if it was looking for something, but I didn't know how to respond. I know that sounds crazy. How could an inanimate object stimulate me to have an emotional experience?"

"I thought we were looking for an ancient ruin or something," Jessica said. "If that marker has power, it can't be an ancient ruin."

"We really don't know what is generating the light," Tegan said.

"Could it be from another world?" Jessica asked, wide-eyed.

"Out of the mouth of babes," Nate mumbled.

Alex interjected, "That's one possibility, Jessica. We are exploring others. It could be a rare bioluminescent reaction to Alessia's body chemistry."

"Cool. This is getting better and better."

Once the gear was secure, they all went into the salon.

∞

"I take it you all want to pursue the ancient alien angle as our primary theory and forget the real science," Alex said.

Tegan sighed. "Alex, I've given the marker a lot of thought. In my opinion, it's the only thing that makes sense. Let me recap what we have seen, which will bring Jessica up to speed. We know of no ancient civilization capable of producing the marker. We don't know what it's made of and, I'm sure you will agree, it's unlike anything any of us has seen before. You couldn't damage it. The seams where the composite material meets the marker aren't welded like you'd expect to see, and they appear to be one piece."

"What composite material?" Nate asked.

Cal briefly explained what he'd unearthed.

Tegan said, "What *human* civilization could have produced something like that and also biometrically coded it to react to a specific genetic signature? Our biometric systems are just now capable of recognizing genetic signatures."

"And don't forget the power source," Jessica added.

"Yes. Without power, it couldn't generate an electromagnetic field or produce a sustainable light. Where is it drawing its power from? So what else does that leave?" Tegan asked.

They sat in silence for a while.

Cal said, "Alex, I'm with Alessia. The only other explanation I can come up with is that a person traveled back in time, built this thing, and left it to tell whoever found it that they had been here."

"This is just great. Now you're getting into fantasyland," Alex said. She shook her head and turned to Nate. "What do you think?"

"Based on what I've seen and what you guys just said, I'd say we aren't in Kansas anymore. Alex, my love, I know you are not going to like this, but I don't think that marker was left by a lost human civilization. I'm in the alien camp."

Alex looked at Jessica. "You're a member of the team now. Do you have an opinion?"

Jessica looked around the room. "I have to agree with Alessia. I think it is alien."

"You all have a majority vote. However, for now, I'm going to stay in the minority just to keep things real. I want to disprove all other options before they lock us away and label us as crazy.

"I see my academic career going down in flames. Let's all agree not to mention the ancient alien theory until we can prove it. That goes for you too, young lady," Alex added, pointing a finger at Jessica.

"No problem. I'll make like a clamshell." Jessica smiled.

"What do we tell Brian?" Nate asked Alex.

"We present him with the facts and see what conclusion he comes to. If we tell him it's an alien artifact, he may think we're messing with him. I don't think he'll want to commit academic suicide with me, even if he can't find a terrestrial explanation. Aliens. I must be crazy."

"Then we all are," said Cal.

Marsh Harbour Airport – 1300 hours

The Gulfstream G350 jet landed on the six-thousand-foot Marsh Harbour airport runway and taxied to the terminal. At just below Mach speed, they had made the trip in just under four hours.

Knolls had rented a house for a week on Man-O-War Cay. From his brief research on the area, he had learned that almost all of the transportation in the out islands involved ferry service. Even though the ferry schedules seemed adequate, he had opted to rent a small boat on Man-O-War Cay to give them flexibility.

Even before the plane stopped at the terminal, Grant was waiting by the cabin door with his military duffle in hand. As soon as the plane stopped moving, he popped the door and extended the ladder, letting the hot, humid air and the sound of the turbine engines winding down invade the cabin. Grant slung the duffle over his shoulder, walked down the stairs, and headed straight for customs. The weapons they'd brought remained concealed in special compartments on the Gulfstream, and they would remain there until the aircraft cleared customs and they could determine a way to retrieve them. The pilots were to stay at a hotel near the airport.

Grant hadn't spoken a word on the plane, except to answer direct questions, and Knolls had watched him studying the copy of the intercepted video over and over again.

Knolls collected his overnighter, computer, and satellite phone and left the aircraft as the Bahamian authorities approached the pilots. Grant was already in the terminal. He knew that Grant wasn't going to wait for him. Knolls caught up to him at the customs counter, where their fake identification elicited no scrutiny. They took a taxi to the docks and boarded a ferry to Man-O-War Cay.

They were the only two passengers aboard the ferry. Grant ignored the skipper's best attempts to engage him in friendly conversation. Knolls explained to the skipper that his friend wasn't very sociable because he had lost everything in a divorce settlement. The skipper told him they had come to the right place to forget their troubles and suggested they do some diving, recommending Aldeberie's Dive Shop to rent their gear. It was the same place Knolls had rented their boat from and where he would retrieve the keys to their rented house.

When they arrived at the Man-O-War marina, Knolls gave the skipper a healthy tip. Grant leapt off the ferry with his duffle in hand without saying a word. When Knolls caught up to Grant, they walked down the dock to Aldeberie's Dive Shop and went inside. After looking around, Knolls knew they could get everything they needed in the shop. He signed the rental agreement for the boat and the house and then received directions to the house from the friendly woman behind the counter. She introduced herself as Maggie Aldeberie, although no introduction was necessary. Knolls knew who she was. If needed, he would use her to find the woman they sought. He could tell that Grant wanted to extract the information from her now.

"Let's go," Grant said as he walked out of the dive shop, leaving Knolls inside to apologize again for his friend's abruptness.

When Knolls caught up with Grant, he said, "I recommend we get a feel for the area while we walk to the house."

"Agreed. It looks like the primary mode of transportation on this rock is by golf cart or on foot."

As they walked up the narrow street, Knolls could tell that it was going to be difficult to blend in if they needed to do active surveillance. They were going to need a reason to wander around asking questions. He knew from his research that only about four hundred people lived on the tiny island. The tourists stood out from the natives, and both of them would stand out even more if they stayed together. The rental house overlooked the beach on the east side of the island. Knolls thought it was as picturesque as the travel guide had described. The house had two bedrooms and two baths, a spacious living room with a full kitchen, and it offered a nice view of the ocean from the raised deck.

"What do you think?" Knolls asked.

"It'll do," said Grant. He entered the first bedroom he came to and dropped his duffle onto the bed. "I'm going for a walk."

"Hey, nothing overt," Knolls said, knowing that Grant wasn't going to rest until he knew if Strong was alive.

"I know how to do my job," Grant said, and walked out the door.

Knolls telephoned Westfield, gave him a status report, and told him about Grant's demeanor. Westfield didn't sound concerned by the news. He told Knolls to give him some room and to report back as soon as they were able to confirm the woman was Tegan Strong.

It had been a long time since Knolls had been outside during the day and even longer since he had seen an ocean. *At least the operational area has a good view,* he thought as he watched the seagulls float on the warm currents of air above the surf.

Great Guana Cay — 1400 hours

On the first dive of the afternoon, Nate and Alex collected samples of the marine growth above the marker and took a piece of the broken coral still resting on the ledge. Cal carved more of the rock away, exposing a larger section of the black material. Every time Cal dug into the rock around the marker, he hit the strange material. He was beginning to think this part of the island had formed around it.

"Hey, guys. The composite-looking stuff that's attached to the marker goes back under the rock toward the island."

Alex said, "How far back do you think it goes?"

"I can't even begin to guess."

"Nate, take pictures of the area Cal has excavated," Alex ordered.

"Your wish is my command," Nate replied.

The material absorbed the light from the camera flash. "Are you seeing this, Alex?" Cal said.

"I am. Things keep getting stranger and stranger."

"I'm running low on air," Cal said. "We need to start back. Alessia, do you copy?"

"I copy," Tegan replied from the boat. "Jessica and I will prep our gear for the next dive."

"See you in a few minutes."

Tegan took her mask from Nate, adjusted its six straps, and inserted a new nose clamp. After Cal swapped his tank, he was ready to go. Jessica had decided to stay with the traditional regulator. They tested the gear, then went over the side leaving Nate and Alex behind.

A few minutes later Tegan and Jessica explored the shallow water near the shore. The marine life was abundant. A brightly colored parrotfish took a keen interest in their work. So did a four-foot barracuda. It watched them for a minute, then shot off into the depths.

Tegan and Jessica dove down to where Cal was working. When Tegan saw the large area Cal had exposed, she knew that the marker and ledge were just the tip of whatever remained hidden here. She decided to try to see if she could coax the marker into giving up more of its secrets.

Hovering in front of the marker, she was sure it was more than just a sign announcing someone had been here before, especially in light of what Cal was uncovering. Tegan motioned for Jessica to begin recording. She touched the symbols in order, starting at the center and working outward, then from top to bottom. The intensity of the blue light under her fingers remained constant no matter how hard she pressed on the symbols. She didn't linger on any of the symbols very long, treating the marker like a keypad. She knew even if the symbols worked like a biometric combination lock, finding the right sequence would be nearly impossible with all the permutations possible.

Running her hand over the dark-shaded areas, Tegan felt the fear begin to build. When she took her hand off the marker, the fear abated immediately. She placed both of her hands over the length of the center symbol. Almost immediately, she felt a sense of serenity envelop her, and she continued to press the symbol.

Suddenly, the area beneath her hands began giving off intense pulses of light, each lasting for several seconds. Every time the light pulsed, she saw the outline of the bones within her hand. When the blue light returned to normal, the sense of euphoria left her. Then a strange sensation enveloped her. It was different from anything she'd felt before, but still gave her an emotional feeling.

Tegan removed her hands from the marker and turned to face Jessica. She could tell Jessica was frightened, but she was still recording. Tegan motioned for her to stop recording and to place her hands on the marker. Jessica swam up beside her and courageously placed her hands on the center symbol without hesitation. Nothing happened.

It was time to try another approach. The marker didn't react to Tegan when she wore gloves, but since humans were good conductors of electricity, she wondered whether the marker could sense her presence through Jessica. She placed her hands on the back of Jessica's hands. The blue light arced out around Jessica and encapsulated Tegan's hands without touching Jessica's hands.

Jessica looked both amazed and fearful. She slowly pulled her hands away. Tegan knew that no biometric system could operate the way the marker did. It had detected her essence through Jessica and had isolated Jessica from the conduit. The marker had actually sought her out.

"Cal, can you come over here?" Tegan asked.

There was no response.

"Cal, can you hear me?"

Again, there was no response.

Tegan took her hand off the marker and drifted back. The glow of ghostly handprints lingered for a moment, then faded away as it had done before.

Tegan said again, "Cal, do you copy?"

Cal stopped digging at the rock face. "Yes, I copy."

"Come over here. I want to show you something."

Tegan had Cal place his hand on the marker and repeated the exercise. The light sought her out.

Cal said, "That's amazing!"

After a few more minutes of exploring, they all swam back to the boat.

Huddled in the salon around the table, they all looked a bit bedraggled from the repeated dives and stress of the day. Tegan briefed everyone on what she'd experienced. She told them about the different sensation that had come over her.

Alex listened quietly, watching the new recording Jessica had made of the pulsing light beneath Tegan's hands. Bioluminescence would not produce the intense pulses of light. She racked her brain for a possible scientific explanation, but came up empty. She also knew the light was not the result of any hand lotion after seeing the light reach around Cal's hands and find Alessia. *What was providing the power to the marker, and why was Alessia so special?*

Alex had more questions than answers, which wasn't unusual during the exploration phase of any discovery, but they were the type of questions which made her wonder if the others may be right about the origin of the marker. She had to admit her hypothesis of an advanced human civilization having built the site and leaving a powered biometric system in place was difficult to reconcile with the evidence at hand. Cal's time-travel theory was an even more ludicrous idea to explore.

The symbols on the marker held the key. Alex knew that nothing of this magnitude had ever been unearthed before. It was like discovering an airplane under the Great Wall of China. There was no way to map the size of the structure beneath the coral without a ground-penetrating radar system or digging it out of the rock. She wasn't sure what to do next. She was beginning to feel as if she'd been given part of the answer to a riddle but was missing key pieces of the question. Alex looked at the faces of everyone sitting around the table and decided she needed to approach the problem from a different perspective. She could not believe she was going to go down the alien path, but it was the only path available.

"I want to try and prove the alien hypothesis," she announced. "But I want to take a different approach."

"So we've made a believer out of you," Nate said.

"Not entirely, but I can't rule it out unless I challenge it."

"Challenge away," Cal said.

"Since I can't date the site accurately and I'm unable to obtain a sample of the marker or the material around it for chemical or microscopic analysis to determine its composition, I want to explore the possibility of alien interaction by examining religious texts, folklore, myths, and legends. I want to see if there is a common frame of reference, or any reference, to what we have found. I want you all to evaluate the stories to see if they have any bearing on what we are seeing down there. I want to work backwards, using a qualitative analysis approach."

"Sounds like a reasonable plan. Where do we start? Tegan asked.

"Let's think globally, but I want to start with North America."

"Maybe someone should take notes," Jessica offered.

"Good idea. Are you up to the task?" Alex asked her.

Jessica smiled. "I will do my best."

"That's all we can ask for," Cal said, passing her a notepad and a pen.

"Alright, Jessica, label the first group as North American and Mesoamerican civilizations," Alex directed.

"Done."

Alex said, "Few Native American tribes developed a written language, while Mesoamerican, Middle Eastern, European, and Asian civilizations did. I have always wondered why. Let me brainstorm this aloud for a bit, walk you through some of the legends, and see if we can find anything related to the marker. Remember, nothing is off the table for now."

"And she's picked a topic I've heard so much about at home," Nate added under his breath, drawing a chuckle from everyone. "But to be fair, she's very well versed on this subject."

"Thank you, my dear. Now bear with me, and if I go too fast, Jessica, just say so."

"Okay."

"Maybe we can find a logical connection between what we found here and whoever could have influenced the developing civilizations in the region. Sometimes just talking it through provides a different perspective."

"Logic would be a good place to start," Cal said. "We're all ears."

"Cute," Alex said, understanding the reference. "Let me start with Native American folklore, which is rife with tales of sky people and star beings. Most of the best legends come from the western tribes, but the stories are prevalent in almost all of the tribes found in the Americas. But no such legends or stories have ever been attributed to the indigenous tribes of the Bahamas."

"At least not yet," Cal said.

Alex ignored him. "The tales were passed down from generation to generation by oral tradition. As in any tale retold numerous times, I suspect that stories have been embellished, but from a certain perspective, there are alien overtones and connections between the stories told by the different tribes of North America."

Jessica poured herself an adult glass of the Pinot Grigio from the bottle sitting on the table and curled up with the notepad on the bench seat behind the chart table.

No one said anything.

Alex said, "Native American tribes all have stories about creation and how the gods descended from the heavens and brought life to Earth. The Pawnee Indians, also known as the Star People, were infatuated with the stars. They created very accurate star charts and packaged them together with sacred ceremonial objects in what they called 'sacred bundles.' Pawnee legend claims the objects stored in the sacred bundles were magical and had been brought to Earth by heavenly beings."

"Okay," Nate said. "But how does that apply here?"

"Let me finish. A select group of warriors always guarded the sacred bundles. No one but the shaman of the tribe could touch the bundles or even look at them until blessed by otherworldly beings. The legend claims beings descended to Earth from time to time to determine if the tribe still possessed the magical items they'd left behind. Once the beings saw that the tribe was faithful, they provided their blessing, and the shaman would invite the tribal elders to join him to converse with the gods from heaven. The beings taught the tribal elders how to use the magical objects to ensure their food supply remained plentiful. The beings also taught them to heal those who had a disease, wounds, or broken bones. They spoke of an intense blue light that pierced the skin and healed the afflicted."

"A blue light is interesting … and finally relevant," Cal said.

"An advanced alien race would seem like gods," Jessica added, taking a sip of wine. "Were the Pawnee Indians the only tribe that met with the heavenly beings?"

"No. Apache Indian legends tell us they interacted with Gehe. These beings supposedly dwelled deep within the mountains of the Southwest. The Chiricahua paid homage to the Gehe or 'Gray Ones' by holding spiritual dances. They would dress in different colors of clothing and headdresses to represent the different points of a compass."

"How would they have known the points on a compass?" Cal asked.

Alex leaned in and said, "Legend says they were shown a magical instrument with a needle that spun as they faced different directions."

"Like the compass on the boat," Tegan muttered.

"Exactly," replied Alex. "The Gray Ones were powerful beings and were held in the highest esteem, above all other beings because of their magic."

"That's pretty amazing. Tell us more," Jessica said.

"The Pueblo Indians believe in kachina spirits who are all-powerful and are considered the rulers of all things. The Hopi Indian legends describe spirits descending to Earth in flying shields."

"Like a flying saucer," Jessica said.

"Possibly. The most interesting stories I know of come from the Lakota Sioux legends. The Wakinyan Tanka or great thunderbird is a flying craft that looks like a giant winged bird. The Wakinyan Tanka is said to shoot blue lightning from its eyes to kill its enemies."

"Like the pulses of light that shot out from under Alessia's hands, only more powerful," Jessica said.

Alex nodded. "Some Sioux myths speak of Wakonda, the great spirit that holds the universe in balance. Like in the Pawnee legend, the Wakonda would come to Earth and visit with the shaman of the tribe. During these encounters, the shaman received great wisdom and knowledge. The Wakonda revealed secrets about life and the workings of the universe."

Alex poured a glass of the Pinot Grigio. "The Sioux legends closely match those found in the Iroquois Nation. The Sioux lived on the plains of North America, while the Iroquois tribes lived in northeast America. They were separated by what would have been a great distance back then, and there's no evidence the tribes ever met."

"What was the Iroquois legend?" Jessica asked.

"The Iroquois believed in the Hino, who were also thunderbird gods thought to be the guardians of the skies. They believed that thunder was made when the Hino flapped their wings, and like the Sioux Wakonda, they flashed lightning from their eyes."

"Isn't that an interesting coincidence," Nate said.

Alex said, "There are many more legends with similar stories. The Cherokee Indians believed in the moon spirit, Geyaguga, who possessed great magical powers. The Blackfoot Indians spoke of the 'above' or 'sky' people. The Blackfoot thought of the above people not as gods but as a distinct race that lived above the clouds in an isolated society."

"I'm seeing a pattern here," Cal said.

Alex took a sip of wine. "Then we have the lost civilization of the Hisatsinom, who some believe began dwelling in the Four Corners area of the Southwest as far back as the time of Christ. Discoveries that are more recent push the date back even further, possibly as long as seven thousand years ago, but that hasn't been verified yet. With so many small nomadic bands living in North America back then, it's hard to draw any definitive conclusions about exactly when they emerged as a civilization."

Tegan whispered, "The Anasazi."

Alex smiled. "Yes, the Anasazi. Translated from the tribal languages in the area, it means 'ancient ones,' 'ancient strangers' or 'ancient enemy,' depending on the tribe. The Anasazi were an advanced civilization for their time."

"Like the Sumerians were in theirs," Tegan said.

"The Anasazi disappeared suddenly around the thirteenth century. The Navajo, Hopi, and Zuni Pueblo Indians, who still live in the area, are their ancestors. Many of the ancient legends associated with flying shields of fire were thought to have originated with the Anasazi."

"I think I've heard this part before," Nate said.

"Yes, you have. Most archeologists refer to the Hisatsinom, or Anasazi, as the original ancestral pueblo dwellers, while others still refer to them as the 'ancient people.' Regardless, they were responsible for passing on the tradition of carving cities out of the sides of cliffs. During their era, they built great roadway systems throughout the Southwest, facilitating trade between the various settlements."

"I've seen pictures of those cliff cities," Jessica said. "They're amazing."

"Recent satellite imaging has revealed eight distinct roads running in different directions, like the spokes of a wheel, from the main city in Chaco Canyon. Referred to as 'spirit lines,' the roads are straight, are more than thirty feet wide, and cover more than four hundred miles. Excavation of the roads revealed that they were once perfectly smooth, and only a few hundred yards separates two of the main roads. No one has yet explained why they would build two straight roads so close together or why the roads had to be free of debris. It's not like they had motorized vehicles."

"Straight lines and smooth surfaces," Nate said. "That sounds like the Nazca lines in Peru."

"Yes, the construction of the Nazca lines is similar, but the Anasazi roads don't form images like the lines in Peru or the ones found in Blythe, California. However, the Anasazi roads have a creationist connection, especially the Great North Road. That road is supposed to represent a connection to the Shipapu, the place where modern Pueblo Indians believe their ancestors appeared on Earth.

"The Anasazi were a peaceful people. They farmed the land, traded goods, hunted, and developed a deeply religious culture. Then one day they abandoned their homes and lands, leaving behind pottery and household items—items they would normally have taken with them if they were just moving to a new location. It's still a mystery why they left so suddenly."

"The Anasazi were decimated by a virus far worse than any ever encountered by the human race," Tegan said. "The only thing that remains a mystery is the origin of the virus."

Alex had heard this theory before, but did not support it.

"The Anasazi who contracted the virus died quickly, mostly from respiratory failure," Tegan said. "The speed at which death took their lives may have actually saved the greater population and their descendants from complete eradication. The virus was highly contagious and spread as both an airborne pathogen and by physical contact. The reason archeologists have found human remains in nontraditional burial places is because as soon as someone became ill, they would be quarantined to specified buildings to await death."

"Do go on, Alessia," Alex said, wondering why she would know so much about the virus and the Anasazi.

Tegan nodded. "The civilization ultimately fragmented to avoid contact with one another, leaving everything behind they believed was contaminated. The Anasazi believed the deaths were the result of them angering their gods, and rather than staying and facing any further wrath, they left everything they built and took refuge in small caves throughout the area. They stayed in hiding for many years and never returned to the cliff cities they had built. They were afraid the gods would return and bring back the invisible death."

"Disease is only one theory," Alex stressed. "I read an abstract written by a grad student from a northwestern college years ago that supports what you just said. Although the research was sound, I didn't find it conclusive. You sound like you know it to be a fact."

"It *is* a fact, Alex," Tegan said. "Think about it. What makes more sense, a virus decimating a civilization or a prolonged drought that forced them to abandon their cities?"

"Most archeologists believe a drought forced them to leave," Alex said.

"Why would they abandon their personal possessions and flee?" Tegan asked. "Why would they live in caves in smaller groups and stay hidden for so many years? And why did they never return to inhabit the cliff dwellings which were already built and were easily defendable even after the drought ended?"

Alex didn't answer. She was trying to remember the name of the graduate student that wrote the paper.

Tegan said, "The Anasazi were frightened by something they didn't understand, and they ran, literally, from their villages. If thousands of your family, friends, and elders all died within a few days or weeks and you believed your gods were responsible for unleashing a disease, you wouldn't want to wait around for death to come knocking on your door either. Think Ockham's Razor, Alex,"

Alex knew that researchers had fought for years for the acceptance of a theory. They were always passionate about their beliefs, and that passion seemed to be surfacing here. Why was she defending the theory?

"What's Ockham's Razor?" Jessica asked.

"Ockham's Razor is a law of succinctness." Tegan replied. "The principle dictates that when given competing hypotheses, the one that makes the fewest assumptions should be selected. In this case, a virus has a greater possibility of being correct than drought."

Everyone stared at her. "Come on, guys. Just because I'm a blond doesn't mean I'm stupid. I heard it defined in a sci-fi movie I watched a long time ago."

Alex smiled at her, then said, "That isn't exactly the line used in the movie *Contact*, which happens to be one of my favorites, to describe the principle. In the movie, the version of the principle used specified that if all things were equal, then the simplest explanation is correct. Alessia, you used the academic definition of the principle."

Tegan bit down on her lip.

"I guess I should have gone to work selling drugs instead of going to graduate school," Alex said, noting her reaction. "It seems your education was just as good as mine and far less expensive."

"Alessia was a drug dealer?" Jessica asked, sounding shocked.

Cal said, "It wasn't the kind of drug-dealing you're thinking about, Jessica. She worked for a pharmaceutical company. She peddled prescription drugs … legally."

"Let's move on," Tegan said. "Alex, in all of your research is there anything that we could use to tie any of these Native American legends together?"

"There are only similarities in their stories and the era when they were first told. Nothing directly links any of the myths to a common event."

"Alex, didn't you say the Nazca Lines had similarities to lines found in California?" Cal asked.

"Yes, the Blythe geoglyphs were found by a pilot in 1932 as he flew between Las Vegas and California. There were dozens scattered across the desert. Some of the geoglyphs formed human figures that were only identifiable at higher elevations. A labyrinth was also discovered, which is believed to have been constructed for some type of ritual."

Jessica scribbled a note on the pad. "What's a geoglyph?"

"It's a large design created when the upper layers of rock and soil are removed to reveal a different shade of dirt beneath. The contrast when seen from the air is quite striking."

"When were the Blythe geoglyphs created?" Nate asked.

"It's believed to be about a thousand years old, but there are some who believe the glyphs could date back to almost ten thousand years. They can't be dated precisely, so the date is based on artifacts found in the area, which is similar to what we're faced with on our site."

"Just out of curiosity, how large are the Blyth glyphs?" Cal asked.

"The largest human figure is over 170 feet long."

"Wow, who made them?" Jessica asked.

"It is believed they were created by the Quechan Indians. But there are other geoglyphs scattered around the desert, so it isn't certain that they were the only group creating them."

"When were the Nazca lines created?" Cal asked.

"They were made around 500 to 650 CE."

"That's way after the time we think the marker was left," Nate said.

"And let's not forget the material surrounding the marker doesn't reflect light. So where does that leave us?" Cal asked.

Alex shook her head. "I'm not sure. Many ancient myths around the world claim that beings came to Earth and interacted with humans. Even the Bible refers to angels riding across the sky in fiery chariots, which is not all that far from the legends we talked about already. Many cultures around the world have creationist stories. Many of them speak of the Great Flood occurring during the same timeframe."

Tegan said, "Isolated civilizations that all share similar experiences, or have the same delusion, can't be coincidental. The Native American civilizations all describe magical lights and beings from the sky in their stories they passed down. There has to be a reason."

"I don't see it," Alex said. "Maybe this exercise was a waste of time. There are similarities in all the stories, but that could have nothing to do with what we've found."

Tegan smiled. "It wasn't a waste of time. All of the stories you talked about point to the possibility of an ancient alien presence. I believe what we found down there may very well be the cornerstone of the puzzle and concrete proof that alien beings have guided our primitive human ancestors to a better way of life for thousands of years. They could even be the founders of our religious beliefs."

"You're saying what we found here is somehow connected to aliens coming from the heavens and educating our ancestors?" Cal said.

"Yes," Tegan replied. "Alex's colleague may be able to shed more light on the subject of ancient writings. Think about it. All of the known written works arose in a short period of time during a global growth spurt in human development. I believe the symbols we found are a link to the ancient writings discovered in Europe and the Middle East. Almost all of these civilizations developed independently. There are the cuneiform symbols found in Sumer, which Alex and Dr. Lee believe have some characteristics in common with those found on the marker. There are hieroglyphs in Egypt, calligraphy in Asia, and the Mayan inscriptions of Mexico. So why did they all develop at around the same time?"

"Alien intervention," Nate said. "Makes sense to me."

"Alex, weren't there symbols found on Easter Island that haven't been translated?" Tegan asked.

"Yes," Alex replied.

"The idols they created there still can't be explained. Isn't that true?"

"Yes. Where are you going with this?"

"There has to be a common denominator," Tegan said. "I know there aren't any local legends or stories about the marker. Perhaps the builders sought out a secluded place to build a base of operations, then visited the various groups of humans around the world, while keeping their base secret. It could have served as the nucleus for their work."

Alex knew there was certainly more to Alessia's background than her being a pharmaceutical sales rep and having watched shows on television. Sometime in her past she had researched this subject for a reason. She wanted to return to a more scientific approach. "We're making quantum leaps about the connection to aliens and the marker based on stories and drawing conclusions according to what we want it all to mean. All we know is there is something unexplainable below us."

"Something that glows when Alessia touches it and causes compasses to spin without any reason," Cal proffered.

"We keep coming up with more theories than answers," Nate said.

Tegan nodded in agreement. "The human species has made incredible evolutionary jumps over the millennia, and it has come back from the brink of extinction more than once. Each time we were a new and improved model, so to speak."

"What are you getting at now, Alessia?" Alex asked, growing weary of this discussion.

"Since we are brainstorming, I submit it's possible we were genetically enhanced or reengineered by an alien species."

"Oh, for heaven's sake!" Alex cried.

"Alex, people have been reporting alien abductions for years. Isn't it possible that the shamans of the Indian tribes you talked about were abducted, enhanced, then returned so they could perform their magic? Can you explain the rapid changes in population density, mental acuity, and all of the diversity we now have on the planet?"

"Random acts of nature," Alex replied.

"You can't be serious!" Tegan exclaimed. "Alien involvement in our development could also explain why buildings like the pyramids are found all around the world and how writing developed."

Alex felt flushed. "Really, that's quite a leap in connecting the dots. We have no scientific evidence to support your views. First, you think you have alien DNA, and now you are advocating aliens abducting and modifying our DNA to make us smarter. Alessia, you have gone from myths and legends to the twilight zone."

"Alex, all of the answers to the questions about our past, present, and future wait for us down there. I know it, as sure as I know I'm the genetic anomaly who can unlock those answers."

Maybe it was the second glass of wine, but Alex couldn't hold back any longer. "Alessia, I've only known you for a few days, but during that time I have seen that you are a well-intended, good person, and most importantly, you love Cal. I'm truly happy for you both, but I have an itch that needs scratching, and if Cal won't address it, I will.

"There's more to you than what you have been leading us to believe. You're much better educated than you let on. I don't know what you're hiding, but I think you know more than you are telling us. I think you are afraid to tell us what you know."

Alex could tell she had struck a nerve by the look on her face.

"Listen, Alessia. We are all friends here. Whatever it is you are afraid of, we can help you. Why don't you tell us your secret? If not all of us, at least tell Cal. He has a right to know."

"That's enough, Alex!" Cal said. "We aren't going to discuss anything about her past. We've all had a long and tiring day, and maybe that thing down there has us all a little bit spooked and edgy. I know I am on edge. Just drop it, Alex."

Tears came to Tegan's eyes, as if a river had been unleashed, and she didn't try to hide them. She wiped the tears from her cheeks, grabbed a napkin from the table, and blew her nose.

"Alessia, I'm sorry," Alex said. "I shouldn't have been accusatory and tried to pry into your life. I thought it might help if you could share your burden, that's all. Please accept my apology."

Tegan walked out of the salon without saying a word, closing the door quietly behind her. She was living a lie, and Alex was right. Cal deserved to know the truth before they were married. Thoughts of her parents and her past life flooded over her. She knew they would be alive today if it wasn't for what she'd created. The ache in her chest was crushing her spirit more than she realized during these past months. She didn't want to put anyone else at risk.

She trusted everyone around her. Perhaps they could help her unlock the mystery of why she felt an unnatural connection to this place. The more she thought about it, the more she believed the marker had somehow drawn her to the islands.

She loved Cal with all her heart. It was time he knew the truth. Maybe everyone had a right to know. Tegan walked to the stern, stepped onto the dive platform, and sat down. The warm water caressed her legs as she gazed up into the sky. Would he forgive her when he learned the truth? She heard the sliding glass door open and close behind her. Tegan looked back at Cal. The decisive moment had arrived.

PART THREE

"The advance of scientific knowledge does
not seem to make either our universe or
our inner life in it any less mysterious."

J. B. S. HALDANE

NINETEEN

Man-O-War Cay — July, 24 — 1730 hours

"Find anything of interest on your excursion?" Knolls asked, seeing Grant was still in a foul mood.

Grant grunted something unintelligible, walked into his bedroom, and slammed the door.

Knolls walked to the bedroom and banged on the door with his fist. "Hey, asshole. I need to talk to you."

Grant opened the door and asked, "What is it?"

"I want to go over some ideas I have for our reconnaissance and what contingencies we need to have in place before disposing of Strong—if we find her. We just can't walk up to her, ID her, and kill her. So do you want to hear my ideas or do you want to sulk in your room like a petulant child?"

Knolls thought Grant's smile was more of a smirk.

"Let's hear your ideas, boss," Grant said. He shouldered Knolls aside, walked to the kitchen table, pulled out a chair, and sat down. "I'm all ears."

"Mr. Grant, you need to stow the attitude. General Westfield designated me as the alpha on this op, so you need to get your head in the game. Is that clear?"

Grant replied, "Very clear." Grant puffed out his chest like an angry ape, then said, "The only person that has earned the right to speak to me in that tone is General Westfield. I didn't think you had the balls to stand up to me. Good for you, but you'd better temper that newfound positional power of yours or you'll be picking your ass up off the floor. Is *that* clear?"

Knolls knew that Grant was testing him, but at least he'd gotten his attention. He clenched his fists, locked his jaw, and inhaled deeply. "Get on your feet and we will see who ends up on their ass."

Grant slid his chair back and stood, his arms at his side. "I'm on my feet, as you requested. Now what?"

Knolls walked up to Grant and glared at him, their noses only inches apart. The height and age advantage went to Knolls, but Grant had the experience and the training. He knew if it came to a fight, Grant would win, but Grant respected strength, so as long as he made a good showing, he figured he would respect him for standing his ground.

Grant didn't look the least bit intimidated or concerned, and his face showed no sign of fear. "Are you going to hit me or kiss me, sir?" Grant asked. "Make a decision. Hesitating could get you killed someday."

Knolls didn't back away. "Under different circumstances, I'd kick the shit out of you and then have you court-martialed, you disrespectful dinosaur. You've gotten lazy and accustomed to being stroked and fawned over by General Westfield. Well, that ends now. You got that, Marine?"

Grant leaned slightly back as a few drops of spittle struck his cheek, but he didn't wipe them away. "General Westfield would have knocked the shit out of me by now and then bought me a beer. You need to stop thinking about playing by the rules."

Knolls wanted to deck him. "If you have a problem working for me on this op, feel free to leave anytime. The reality is you may have missed a target for the first time in your distinguished career, and that doesn't sit well with you. Your crappy attitude is only compounding that error. We need to remedy the problem, not make it worse. Knocking the shit out of each other will accomplish nothing."

Knolls stepped back and tried to calm down. "John, this is a small island, and the locals know each other. Your hostile demeanor isn't going to win you any friends. These people will clam up as soon as you start asking questions. You can rest assured they will relay any questions you ask to the person we need to find. If Strong is alive and she hears we are looking for her, she will disappear. You get me?"

"I hear you."

"Damn it, John, this isn't a village in some third-world country with people you can intimidate. We're not in a war zone. People here expect tourists to be relaxed, happy, and friendly. We have to be subtler in our approach. General Westfield chose me to be his successor, so you'd better get used to it. I expect to be shown the same respect you would show him."

"What's your plan?" Grant asked, sitting back down in the chair.

"We know the woman is here and that she's engaged to a boat captain named Calvin Locke. Our best chance at identifying Tegan is down at the docks, probably near the dive shop. That is where the video call came from. If we have to, we will use Maggie Aldeberie as leverage, but only as a last resort. Her husband will give up Locke in a heartbeat. By the way, I told the ferryboat captain and Mrs. Aldeberie that you had just broken up with your wife to cover for your shitty behavior. So if anyone asks how you're doing, play along, and put on a happy face."

Grant snorted. "Put on my happy face? I don't have one."

"Then find one," Knolls said, sorting through the supplies Grant had bought. "No beer or other spirits?" Knolls asked, lightening his tone.

"It's a dry island," Grant said, giving Knolls an exaggerated smile. The facial expression was actually scarier than his scowl.

"If that's your best happy face, we're in deep trouble. I say we start by getting to know the people at the dive shop, rent some fishing gear, buy some bait, and then do some fishing around the docks. The boat I rented is there. If we stay close to the dive shop, we can keep an eye on the marina as boats arrive."

"What do you think I was doing while I was out?" Grant asked. "I've already checked the dive shop and the rental. I walked around the docks to get a feel for the place. I met Garth Aldeberie. His son, Edward, runs his own ferry service in the islands. His daughter, Jessica, is away with some friends, scuba diving."

Knolls nodded. "That's a start."

"It's more than you've managed to do. I also spoke with some of the locals down at the marina and learned Locke and Alessia Stryker run their sailboat charter mostly out of Man-O-War. I confirmed their boat is the

Whispering Winds. The locals told me the best places to shop for food on the island, and I also learned which restaurants have the best cuisine."

"Did you ask the whereabouts of Mr. Locke or Alessia Stryker?" Knolls asked, concerned that Grant may have pushed for too much information.

"Not directly. I asked about taking an island charter, and Locke was the first on everyone's list. Mr. Aldeberie was very helpful. He showed me how to operate the boat we rented. I gave him a list of the diving and fishing equipment we'd need and told him we would be taking the boat out tomorrow morning around ten. Mr. Aldeberie provided a chart with the best areas to scuba dive marked." Grant pulled a small touristy-looking chart out of his back pocket and threw it onto the table. "He was also kind enough to circle the best fishing holes."

"Anything else?" Knolls asked, picking up the chart.

"It probably isn't a part of your master plan, but yes, I did learn a few things about the island. The marina is the hub of activity. Nine small boats stopped at the marina to take on fuel in less than thirty minutes, and I saw several yachts leave the harbor. I didn't see anyone else from the video, except Mr. Aldeberie. I don't think the others are on the island right now."

"Good job."

"Yeah, I thought so. I say we eat out tonight. You can make us a bag lunch for tomorrow, and then we can scout the waters around the islands. There are a lot of motor yachts and sailboats in the area. I'm thinking our best chance of finding Tegan, or her look-alike, will be searching for the *Whispering Winds* around the dive sites Mr. Aldeberie provided. If we don't find her in a few days, I think we should head back to Marsh Harbour, retrieve our weapons, and press Aldeberie for the answers."

"Let's hope we don't need to resort to that. I apologize for speaking to you the way I did, but you pissed me off," Knolls said.

"Never apologize, Commander. It is a sign of weakness. I know my job, so just watch and learn. And by the way, I really don't give a shit how you speak to me, so long as we accomplish our mission."

"I agree, Osiris."

Great Guana Cay — 1800 hours

"Alessia, are you alright?" Cal asked, sitting down behind her on the dive platform. He placed his hands on her tan shoulders and rubbed gently.

"I'll let you know in a minute. Cal, I need to tell you something I should have told you long ago. I only hope it won't change the way you feel about me."

"I love you, Alessia Stryker. That fact isn't going to change, no matter what secrets you keep."

Tegan stood, and so did Cal. She took a deep breath and turned to face him, then took both of his hands in hers. "No questions until I finish, okay?"

"Okay."

"First of all, you are not in love with Alessia Stryker." She felt him flinch. "My name is Tegan Strong, and I'm a medical doctor. I also have a PhD in microbiology. My specialization is in genetics and virology." Tegan stopped and looked at the growing confusion on Cal's face.

"I worked for the United States government until the end of January. I was involved in some *very* secret research. After the project was completed, I learned my work was going to be weaponized, and I left my employer without authorization."

Cal's look turned to one of deep concern. She knew he wanted to ask her a hundred questions.

"I'm not a criminal or a traitor, and I'm not on any wanted posters, at least none that I know of, and I'm not working for any foreign governments. But there's still someone who would try and kill me again, if he knew I was still alive."

"What do you mean try to kill you *again?*"

Tegan looked down to hide her tears. With a cracking voice, she said, "If they knew they hadn't been successful the first time, they would come after me again. If they thought you knew my secret, they would kill you."

"Someone in our government tried to kill you?"

"Yes, Cal. General Cecil Westfield tried to kill me. Now let me tell you what I have to tell you." Tegan wiped the tears from her cheeks. "He's responsible for ordering the murder of my family and my best friend, Alessia Stryker."

Tegan waited a second before going on, giving him time for the information to sink in. "I think the assassin thought Alessia was me. We looked a lot alike."

She took a deep breath. "Our family car was forced off a cliff. The news reported that I was one of the dead. I can only assume Westfield believed that I was in the Sequoia. After a few days, I came out of hiding and went to Alessia's apartment. She lived in Seattle close to where I grew up. I took her clothes, her passport, and her credit cards."

"The story you told me about your family being dead is true?"

Tegan nodded. "We owned a small ranch in the Cascade Mountains. By coincidence, I had Alessia's purse and wallet because of a mix-up before they left to go skiing. I was supposed to be in the Sequoia with them, but I received a call from someone I worked with that delayed me." She paused and wiped the tears away again. "They were found at the bottom of a ravine, burned beyond recognition."

"I'm sorry," Cal said.

"With Alessia's identification, I was able to assume her identity. For some reason I was drawn to these islands. That's the short version of the story."

Cal hugged her, and she hugged him back, hard.

Cal said, "If you keep squeezing me like that, you'll break one of my ribs."

Tegan relaxed her death grip and sobbed for several minutes. Cal touched her face. "I'm sorry. I should have told you sooner, but I didn't want to put you in harm's way. I understand if you want me to leave. This isn't your fight." She looked up into the most loving and kind eyes she could imagine.

"If you leave me, I will hunt you down and drag you back here. We're getting married the day after tomorrow, Tegan Strong, and nothing is going to stop us."

It felt strange hearing him call her by her real name.

Cal said, "I love you more than life itself, and spending my time with you over the last few months has given me a new perspective on what love really can be. This is just the beginning of our journey together, Alessia, I mean, Tegan."

Tegan smiled up at him. "That's going to take some getting used to."

"Yes, it is, but rest assured, if anyone tries to harm you, I'll deal with them," Cal said in a soft, soothing voice.

Tegan leaned against him, never wanting to let go. "Cal, the marker and the discovery of the site will bring public scrutiny."

"Then we'll stay out of the limelight."

"If General Westfield finds out I'm still alive, he'll come for me. Promise if it comes down to it, you will let me die. I couldn't live with any more guilt."

The sliding door opened. Alex stepped out on deck. "Is everything okay out here?"

"We're fine, Alex," Cal replied. "We'll be back inside in a minute."

Alex went back into the salon.

Cal said, "First of all, you are not responsible for your family being murdered. You shouldn't feel guilty about that. Second, you are the love of my life, and I'll protect you at any cost."

Tegan could tell he meant it.

"Now may I ask some questions?" Cal asked.

"I'm sure you have a few."

"You said you were drawn to the islands. Why?"

It wasn't the first question Tegan thought he would ask. "I'm not completely sure. I've never been here before. I had to decide where to run, and somehow I just knew I'd be safe here. The more I think about it, the more I wonder if it has something to do with the marker."

"I don't know how the marker would have anything to do with it, especially if you were in Seattle when you felt the need to come here. How does this General Westfield fit into this?"

"He's with the National Security Agency. When he hired me, I thought I was going to work for the Center for Disease Control doing biological research. Then I learned that I was really working for the NSA. Westfield tricked me."

"The NSA is tasked with signals intercept, not bioresearch."

"So I have been told. Cal, I worked in a subterranean lab for three years, which just happened to be located across the street from NSA headquarters. Why I didn't make the connection, I don't know."

"A general asks you to work for him and you don't think it might be military related?"

Tegan stiffened. "I'm not that obtuse. I didn't know he was a general until Janet, my boss, told me just before I left."

"What kind of research did you do exactly?"

"Mostly virology and immunology, but I also conducted molecular genetics research. My efforts resulted in the creation of a programmable synthetic virus at the molecular level. It was to be used to develop a vaccine for anything nature or man created. I thought it would save the world, but instead it turns out I created a weapon of mass destruction."

"Wow. How exactly did you get involved with Westfield?"

"It all started when I demonstrated how the virus that decimated the Anasazi civilization could be reconstituted and synthesized during my doctoral studies."

"That's why you knew so much about the Anasazi."

"Yes, I studied the Anasazi culture, or what little is known about it, and did field work in Chaco Canyon. I was part of a team working with archeologists when a mass gravesite was unearthed. I was able to extract DNA from the mummified remains. Alex knew about my work."

"So that was your paper she was referencing? No wonder you got upset."

"It was childish to let her get under my skin."

"Tell me more about your work," Cal said. He rubbed her shoulder.

"I was able to map the DNA of the virus. I published my findings as part of my dissertation. General Westfield read it and recruited me. He paid for my medical training at Johns Hopkins. After graduation, he provided me with a researcher's dream lab. Three years later, I was able to produce a programmable virus medium."

"And the NSA tried to eliminate you because of what you know about the virus?"

"They came after me because they didn't want me to leave. Cal, the virus that decimated the Anasazi has a common genetic link to other viruses we see emerging today. I believed the Anzi-13 was to the world of virology what Mitochondrial Eve was to human evolution."

"It sounds like you did humanity a great service by isolating it."

"Yeah, right. I resurrected a virus that could kill billions of people if the military decides to unleash it on the world again. Cal, the programmable aspect gives them the ability to modify it on a molecular level. The medium can test vaccines for every possible permutation you can think of, and it gives Westfield a weapon of unbelievable power. It will never see the light of day for medical advancement."

"If they use the virus as a weapon, it's not your fault. You do know that, right?"

"It *is* my fault the government has the ability to reproduce it in the first place. If I hadn't figured out a way to synthesize it, it would still be lying dormant under the New Mexico desert, my family would be alive, and I would be teaching at a university somewhere. I can be so naïve at times."

"No, just trusting," Cal said.

"Janet Vasine was not only my supervisor, but a friend. She told me that Westfield planned to immunize as much of the United States population as possible against the Anzi-13. Of course, no one would know it. I can only guess the reason he would do that."

"How could that happen without people knowing?" Cal asked.

"The nanoparticles can be added to other vaccines people receive every year. No one would ever know about the immunization. Westfield was preparing to start human trials. I didn't want to be involved. I couldn't do anything about it, so I left the agency without being cleared."

"And that's when they came after you?"

"Yes. I went back to our ranch to spend time with my family before I disappeared for good. I told my family I was taking a job overseas. I told them I would be gone for a while. I had hoped that once the NSA realized I wasn't going to go public with my work that they would back off and allow me to go home."

Tegan saw the disbelief on Cal's face. "I know, I know. But at the time, I thought they'd just debrief me and maybe detain me for a while. I never imagined they'd actually try to kill me."

Cal said, "So you're a medical doctor and you have a PhD. Quite the egghead. How old are you?"

"I really am thirty-one. I didn't lie about my age. Alessia and I were the same age. I flew through my undergrad and graduate work, and I skipped the internship and residency requirements after med school. I was only going to conduct research, so I didn't need to fulfill that requirement for my medical training."

"You said you worked in a lab near Fort Meade."

"Yes. Funny you should call it that. I worked at a very advanced lab. Anything I needed I received without question, no matter the cost."

"Is this where you synthesized the Anzi-13?" Cal asked.

"Yes."

"I'm assuming the Anzi-13 is highly contagious."

"Yes. Both my synthetic and the real virus are highly infectious. They are transmittable like the common cold or flu. Once infected, a person will be dead within a few days. Unlike most viruses, this one thrives in any temperature or environment. My synthetic version behaves the same way, with one major difference. It will remain viable on objects for weeks, and when airborne it can live for hours. What that means for our government is they now have a weapon they can launch simply by infecting a single person. Without the vaccine, millions would be dead in a week, and billions within a month."

"I can see why the government would want to add it to the arsenal. Dispersal would be easy, and it could wipe out a population center or a military unit before the virus could be isolated and identified. Exposure would allow the host to spread the virus before dying and without raising an alarm. By the time everyone became seriously ill, there would be no stopping the spread of the disease. Those not infected would be too afraid to go outside or take up arms for fear of exposing themselves."

"Exactly, and regular antiviral drugs are useless. The United States could deliver a first strike anywhere in the world, inoculating only those people they wanted to remain alive. It would be worse than a global Ebola outbreak."

"Who else knows about this project?"

"Janet knew about it. Westfield and anyone else in his chain of command surely knows. I'm sure someone at the CDC is involved, and the pharmaceutical company the CDC or NSA selects to do the mass production of the vaccine would have to know."

"What happened to Janet?"

"I learned that she was killed during a robbery, but I know that Westfield was responsible. Janet told me she was known as an OINO, and I guess Westfield saw to it she remained that way."

Cal nodded his understanding of the term. "Once In, Never Out."

Tegan looked at him in surprise. "How do you know that?"

"I have secrets too."

Tegan raised her eyebrows.

"Let me explain. While serving with the special operations team, I was apparently good enough at what I did to attract the attention of an agency. They recruited me to operate off the grid on an OINO team. It required I commit myself to the program for the remainder of my career. On the surface, it sounded like a romantic and elite lifestyle, but other things occurred that thankfully removed me from their favor, and they withdrew the offer."

"You mean you having slept with the congressman's wife?"

Cal gave her a sheepish look.

"Everyone has secrets, don't they?" Tegan said.

"You're positive it was Westfield that ordered them killed?"

Tegan stiffened. "Yes. I saw Westfield's security man at our ranch the day my family went off the cliff. I'm not completely sure about Janet, but it had to be his doing."

Cal nodded.

Tegan looked into his deep blue, understanding eyes and said, "I found you and fell in love, and as time went by, I just couldn't bring myself to tell you. I'm sorry I deceived you."

"I understand why you did, I really do. Now I also understand why you don't like having your picture taken. If the discovery of the marker goes public, Alex can take all the credit. We will move as far away from the excitement as possible. We can run charters out of the Virgin Islands until everything settles down."

"That may be more difficult than you think," Tegan said. "The media, all the governments involved, and the academics will swarm over the island wanting to get all the details. Eventually, they'll find out we were involved."

"We'll deal with that if it happens. Tegan, we need to tell the others about what's happened and who you really are."

"If we do that, they could be targeted."

"If you don't tell them and you're discovered alive, they won't be able to defend themselves. Westfield will assume that anyone associated with you knows the truth. Better you tell them so they can be prepared."

"I understand," Tegan said.

"You know I'll marry you by any name you want me to call you," Cal said, hugging her again.

"I'm happy you still feel that way. I should have told you sooner."

Cal motioned toward the salon. "You ready to face the music?"

"Ready as I'll ever be."

Cal led the way back into the salon.

Over the next thirty minutes, Tegan revealed her identity and explained her story to them. The response was better than she expected. Everyone was shocked, but supportive, and they all agreed the marker would remain a secret until she decided how best to proceed.

Tegan felt a sense of remorse for having dragged them into this mess. Everyone around her was in danger. She vowed to sacrifice herself before she would allow anything to happen to Cal or any of her friends. She would find a way to protect them.

TWENTY

Great Guana Cay — July 25 — 0600 hours

After spending the night anchored at the site, Tegan woke up early, put on her red bikini, and covered it with Cal's blue Ron Jon T-shirt. She left the stateroom and went to her favorite spot on the forward edge of the trampoline to meditate. She focused on the watery horizon, where the first glint of the sun's corona appeared. As the weak rays of light intensified and the shadows of the night slowly disappeared, Tegan breathed rhythmically and meditated.

When she opened her eyes, the vivid colors of dawn painted the eastern sky. She thought about her dreams during the night and remembered the vision of a blue light enveloping her and watching people as they walked across a foreign landscape. She felt she knew them, but they were different from her. Images of symbols and equations still pervaded her thoughts. It was as if something had invaded her mind and left her messages she was supposed to comprehend. The detail of the images was stronger than in any dream she could remember.

She inhaled deeply and listened to the sound of the birds squawking overhead. She felt at peace. No longer did she have to hide the truth from the one person she loved the most in the world. All was as it should be.

She stood up and walked back to the cockpit, entered the salon, and found that Jessica had started breakfast for everyone.

"Morning, Jessica."

"Good morning, Tegan. Does meditation really help you?"

"It helps center me for the day, gives me energy, and makes me more aware of the world around me." Tegan realized she had not heard her real name used in a long time, and last night that was all she had heard. They had agreed it was best to keep calling her Alessia in public. The official wedding documents would also reflect her assumed name.

"Remember, Jessica, in public I'm still Alessia," Tegan said, wondering if she should just have everyone stick to calling her Alessia all the time.

"Got it," Jessica replied. "Can you teach me how to meditate? My father says I need to find a way to be more focused."

"I'd love to teach you. Meet me on deck before sunrise in the morning and we will work on it. What's for breakfast?"

"Scrambled eggs and toast. I checked the fridge for strawberry jam, but I didn't see any. Toast is always better with strawberry jam."

"If there isn't any in the fridge, then we're out. How about I make us some bacon and buttermilk pancakes to go along with your eggs?"

"That sounds good to me."

Tegan felt the tug of her past. Memories always snuck up on her when she was doing the simplest things. She and Megan used to make breakfast for their parents, and standing here with Jessica brought those blessed times flooding back. They seemed like meaningless moments at the time, but as she grew older they attained a completely new level of importance. They were good memories, and today she was making new ones. She would not take this moment for granted.

The smell of sizzling bacon permeated the enclosed areas of the boat like an invisible fog, and like Pavlov's dogs the others found their way to the salon. They all gorged themselves on the hearty breakfast.

Alex said, "I need to complete some research on an idea, and I can't get a wireless connection to contact Brian."

"We can head back to MOW," Cal said.

"That's a good idea," Tegan said. She saw Jessica's look of disappointment. "Jessica, you can come back here anytime."

"Great," Jessica said.

Tegan knew when they docked that she would have to face Garth and Maggie, and that was not going to be pleasant.

Man-O-War Cay — 1000 hours

The *Whispering Winds* was a beautiful sight under sail. She was often the photographic subject of tourists. This morning was no different. As they approached the northern inlet to Man-O-War, several small motorboats left the harbor. As they passed by, people waved at them and took pictures. Tegan waved back at them from the cockpit.

She went forward and kicked the fenders over the side in preparation for docking, then walked back to stand by the flybridge, where Cal sat. Another small motorboat ahead of them suddenly stopped dead in the water. There were two men in the boat. The one with the baseball cap had a camera with a long telephoto lens held in front of his face. Tegan tensed.

Expecting the small boat to continue toward them, she decided it might be best to change clothes, but then the outboard motor came to life, and the boat headed back toward the marina at high speed. She ran back to the cockpit and grabbed the binoculars from the storage compartment, then stabilized herself against the boat's roll to get a better view of the occupants. There was a stocky man looking back at her, and a tingle ran up her spine.

Cal yelled, "What's the matter?"

Tegan climbed to the flybridge and sat down next to him. "I guess I'm feeling paranoid after dredging up everything yesterday." She set the binoculars down next to her. "The guys in that boat don't look right."

"It looks like they forgot something," Cal replied.

Tegan didn't think so.

The electric winch retracted the sails as they approached the dock and Cal started the engines. Tegan went forward to handle the bowline. The motorboat was tied up at the dock, but no one was aboard. Dive gear and fishing rods were stowed in the back of the boat. *Maybe Cal was right,* she thought.

Garth waved at them from the dock. As Cal expertly maneuvered the boat, putting the port side against the dock, Tegan threw Garth a line.

Jessica jumped off the boat with a stern line in hand, and said, "Hey Garth." Her shoulder-length, strawberry-blond hair blew across her face.

"Jessica, did you just call me, Garth?"

"I did," Jessica responded without batting an eye.

Garth said, "Alessia, I let you take my little girl out for one night, and this is what happens." He turned to Jessica. "I'm your father, and I'd appreciate it if you addressed me that way."

Jessica smiled.

"Did you have fun?" Garth asked her as he secured the line to the cleat.

"More than you can imagine. I'll tell you about it later." Jessica jumped back aboard and walked into the salon.

"Alessia, it looks like the little adventure has made a world of difference in Jessica's demeanor."

"She was a big help. Did you see the two guys who were in that boat?" Tegan asked, pointing at the small boat.

"Yeah, they're in the dive shop. They claimed they forgot something, but I can't imagine what else they'd need. I think they did enough preparation and planning before they left to launch a rocket from Cape Canaveral. You should have seen the checklist they went over. They stood dockside for twenty minutes before they finally left. They were gone maybe fifteen minutes before they came roaring back."

"Seems odd they would have forgotten something," Tegan said, growing suspicious.

"Odd is a good way to describe them. The young man says his older friend just got divorced. Both of them have been very inquisitive about the island, more so than the usual tourists. I watched them exploring the island from my office. It looked more like reconnaissance, almost as if they were searching for something. Maybe they want to buy some property. Why are you so interested?"

"I'm not sure, but I have a bad feeling about them. When did they arrive?"

"Yesterday. Rumor has it they flew in on a private jet. You look a bit on edge. Is everything alright?"

"I'm fine, Garth," Tegan said, staring down the dock toward the dive shop, feeling worse by the minute.

"The two guys are spending lots of money, so I'm not complaining. Maybe they are mobsters. You think I should keep an eye on them?"

"I'm not sure," Tegan replied. "But it couldn't hurt. Is anyone in the shop with them?"

"No. I left them to look around when I came out to help you tie up. They didn't look like they'd steal anything. They have lots of cash."

"Cal and I'll check on them after we drop the tanks in the refill rack," Tegan said, jumping to the dock. She picked up two tanks that Cal had placed there.

"Are we going to check them out?" Cal asked, picking up two more tanks.

"I think we should," Tegan replied.

"I'll go with you," Jessica said, grabbing another tank.

As the trio approached, Grant positioned himself just inside the front door of the dive shop. He had a perfect view of Tegan. It was definitely her. He nearly fractured some teeth as he ground his jaws together in anger.

"I take it from your reaction that it's Strong," Knolls said.

"It is. They're going around back."

"Good. Let's make a quiet exit out the front door and head back to the boat," Knolls said. "We can reacquire her after we retrieve our weapons from the plane. We need to do this without witnesses."

"No," Grant declared. He had only one thing on his mind, and nothing else mattered. He walked to the back of the dive shop and hid behind a rack of clothing, then looked down the hallway at the side entrance. Tegan was placing tanks in the rack next to the air compressor. He wasn't sure if Tegan would recognize him, but if she did, he wasn't going to let her go.

"Grant, we need to go," Knolls whispered.

"No, we don't!"

"I'll be right back," Tegan said. "I'm going to check on those guys in the shop." Cal objected, but she knew he was going to be only a minute and decided to go anyway. She walked down the long hallway toward the merchandise area. When she walked into the shop, a man stood at the front door. She didn't know him, but she could tell by the look on his face that he knew her. As she turned to run, she caught movement in her peripheral vision.

Grant stepped from behind a rack of T-shirts and blocked her exit. "Hello, Tegan. Don't scream or I'll have to kill your new friends too." He reached for her arm.

Tegan spun and yanked a shirt rack between them. With anger welling up within her, she yelled, "You will never harm another person I care about … you worthless piece of shit!"

Grant smiled. "I told you not to scream." He looked at Knolls. "Reposition, take the spot where I was hiding. Her boyfriend will be headed this way."

"You're a dumb-ass," Knolls said. "You've exposed us. There's going to be serious collateral damage from this."

"I don't give a shit," Grant said, then turned back to Tegan. "So you know who I am and that I'm the one who killed your family?"

"Yes, you sick bastard! I saw you at the house after you ran them off the road."

"I didn't run them off the road. I blew them up and then watched them burn to death. General Westfield thought you would like some company in the afterlife. If you had followed protocol, they would still be alive, and so would Janet. You know that, right?"

Tegan could tell that Grant was looking for an opening to grab her, but she kept the rack between them.

"It was clever assuming your friend's identity. That girl sure looked like you, but now she's dead, just like everyone else you cared about. I listened to them all scream on their way to the bottom of the ravine. Sad really, you should have been there, but then I wouldn't get the chance to kill you with a more personal touch."

"Shut your hole!" Tegan screamed at the top of her lungs.

Grant's smile only grew larger.

"Cal, look out!" Tegan shouted as he burst into the shop. Knolls emerged from the shadows and tackled him from his blindside. Cal hit the solid oak counter hard and took two quick punches to his kidneys. She screamed when he collapsed onto the floor.

When Grant glanced back over his shoulder, Tegan bolted toward the end of a large merchandise counter to get what she knew was there.

The moment she rounded the counter she pulled a large diver's knife from its sheath and tucked the six-inch, stainless steel blade behind her upper thigh. She angled her body to conceal it.

Grant stepped around the counter, his predatory eyes narrowed and his smile was gone. He slowly inched toward her.

"I want to savor every moment of this," Grant said. "I'm going to enjoy killing you, and then I'm going to kill all of your new friends. I only wish you could feel the pain of losing everyone you care about before I snap your neck."

Cal waited for Knolls to bend down to check to see if he was unconscious, then he launched himself from the floor as if propelled by a released spring. He caught Knolls under the chin with the back of his head. He pumped a fist into Knolls's groin. Knolls howled, grabbed his testicles, and fell to his knees. Then he slammed Knolls's head into the side of the counter.

Fights are never like the ones seen in the movies. They are usually over in a few seconds, providing the combatants know what they are doing. Cal knew exactly what he was doing.

The sound of Tegan's chilling scream reverberated through the shop, turning his blood cold. It was primal, not human.

Tegan stood her ground as Grant advanced toward her, his hard, cold eyes reflecting his sadistic desire to kill her.

Grant stated, "I want to feel the life leave your body. I want to hear the tearing of the cartilage and tendons in your neck. I'm going to mount your head on my office wall."

When he grabbed her shirt, his cold fingers brushed the skin on her neck. Tegan stared into the eyes of the man she swore she would kill. Something inside of her took over, and her world slowed down. She heard her own scream, but it wasn't a scream of terror. It was one of utter rage— the grief and anger pent up far too long, all of it rising to the surface and exploding like a volcano. She knew exactly what she needed to do.

Tegan yanked Grant's left arm down, catching him off guard, and used his forward momentum to her advantage. She took pleasure in knowing he couldn't protect himself. She hoped he felt the terror his countless victims had felt before they died at his hands.

With one swift motion, Tegan whipped the blade across his throat, slicing through his trachea and severing his carotid artery. Grant's eyes widened. He released his grip on her shirt. His blood spurted out, soaking Tegan and splattering the diving equipment across the aisle. He grasped his neck, trying to stop the flow of blood, and gagged. He stumbled forward trying to grab her.

Tegan couldn't understand why he was still standing, but she had the advantage, and she wasn't going to relinquish it. She took a step back, grabbed his powerful forearm as he reached for her, and pulled. Blood still squirted from his neck. She braced herself, then drove the knife down through the top of his skull with such force that she buried it to the hilt.

He crumpled to the floor.

Fighting the fog that had filled her mind, she snatched another knife from the shelf, spun to go help Cal, and nearly skewered him as he rushed around the counter.

Cal looked down at the nearly decapitated body lying on the floor, the dive knife sticking out of the top of the man's head. He couldn't believe Tegan had overpowered her would-be killer. *The power of rage, intellect, and determination can overcome brute strength every time*, he thought.

"You alright?" they asked each other at the same time.

Tegan said, "Yes. Where's the other guy?"

"Taking a nap," Cal replied. He looked at the blood covering Tegan's shirt and face, then out the window. Garth and Nate raced at full speed toward the dive shop. "Here comes the cavalry, albeit a little late. Looks like Jessica went for help when you screamed."

Garth burst through the door. "What in bloody hell happened here? Alessia, are you alright?"

Tegan was still clutching the knife.

Cal said, "Garth, it's a long story with a short ending."

Nate pushed past Garth, with Jessica and Alex on his heels. Cal tried to block them from seeing the carnage, but he was a second too late.

Alex shrieked, and Jessica looked as if she didn't know what to say.

Tegan edged past them and approached the man writhing in pain on the floor by the counter. Cal noted that her movement was smooth and determined.

Tegan yelled, "Nate, get Alex and Jessica out of here."

Nate ushered them out the front door.

Tegan found Knolls still holding his groin and moaning. She knelt next to him, grabbed his hair, jerked his head back, and placed the knife to his throat. "Who are you?"

He grimaced.

"I'm not going to ask again. Who are you?" She nicked his skin with the razor-sharp blade, drawing blood.

"I'm here on vacation. Where's my buddy?"

"He's dead and hopefully walking into hell. Now I am only going to ask this one more time, and then I am going to send you to join him. Who are you? I know you work for Westfield."

At hearing Westfield's name, Knolls hesitated for a moment. Cal could tell that Tegan hadn't missed his reaction. He knelt beside her and grasped her knife-wielding hand. "Tegan, you can't kill him. We need information from him, so stand down," Cal said, slipping into his former military vernacular.

She didn't pull the knife away. "Did Westfield send you here to kill me?"

Knolls didn't respond, but Cal could tell that Tegan had seen the answer in his eyes.

"That's all I needed to know. Say goodnight, asshole." Tegan sliced deeper into his skin.

Tegan fought against Cal's restraint as she increased the pressure of the knife blade against Knolls's throat. In her rage, she couldn't understand why Cal wouldn't let her finish him. "Let go of me! These people are here to kill me, and probably all of you. Let me finish this."

Cal's hand tightened on her wrist. "Stand down, Tegan Strong. He isn't going anywhere."

She became aware that Nate and Garth were watching her beg Cal to let her kill a man, and she realized that for a moment, Westfield had turned her into one of them.

"You're right. He isn't going anywhere," Tegan said. She relaxed her muscles and allowed the rage and adrenaline to ebb. "Westfield sent them, and maybe others, and if he knows where I am, then he probably knows who all of you are. Cal, we need to send him a message. We need to return his killers to him in a box, preferably cut up in little pieces. I'm not going to let him hurt or kill any more of my loved ones without receiving payment in kind. And as I see it, I still owe him three more bodies."

Cal said, "I'm not going to let harm come to you or anyone we know, Tegan. This son of a bitch can be of better use to us than turning him into fish bait. Now let me have the knife."

Tegan stared into Cal's eyes and saw the resolve in them. She loosened her grip and handed him the knife. Nate moved in and tied Knolls's arms behind him with a line from a bait bucket.

"I want answers," Tegan said to Knolls, "so don't think you're going to walk out of here alive unless I get what I want." Tegan turned to see Alex and Jessica standing just outside the front door. Both were staring at her with their mouths agape. She winced at what they must think of her, and she began to shake uncontrollably.

Garth knelt to look at Knolls's neck wound. "It's superficial. He'll live. Jessica, stay outside and don't let anyone in."

Jessica nodded and turned away. No one spoke for a moment.

Nate broke the awkward silence. "Lord, don't ever let me piss Tegan off."

Garth turned to Tegan and said, "So is anyone going to tell me why these two guys wanted to kill you and why everyone is calling you Tegan?" Garth asked.

"Garth, my real name is Tegan Strong. They want to kill me because I used to work for the government."

His eyes went wide. "Are you some kind of a spy?"

"No, I'm a doctor. The guy with the knife in his skull murdered my family and a friend of mine. He thought he'd killed me at the same time.

I came here to disappear from the world. I don't know this guy." Tegan attempted to kick Knolls, but Cal blocked her.

"You mean you're a medical doctor?"

"Yes, Garth, I'm a medical doctor."

"Alright. However, I think I will need a more detailed explanation later. So now what do we do?"

Alex, standing just inside the door said, "We leave the guy with the knife in his head where he is, and the other one we keep secured until the Bahamian police arrive."

"Nope, that isn't going to work," replied Garth as he stood. "Jessica, come back inside. Lock the door and wait in my office."

"Why shouldn't we call the police?" Alex asked.

"Well, from what Miss … Tegan said, I'm not sure having the constables here is our best option. Cal, what do you think we should do?"

Cal looked around the room and said, "Calling the police will expose Tegan. These are American agents sent to kill her. So for now, I say we put the dead one in the icebox in back. Then we scrub the place down and keep the guy holding his balls secure until we have a chance to figure out our options."

"Alex," Garth said, "you and your hubby take the dead guy in back like Cal said. Cal and I will take the live one upstairs. While you are back there grab the bleach, mops, buckets, and towels from the storeroom. Tegan, you need to clean up. Take one of the shirts off the rack and throw your bloody one into the chum bucket on the dock."

"If this one doesn't answer our questions, then we'll have two bodies to add to the chum," Cal said, and then winked at Tegan. "Sorry, but it would cost too much to mail them both back in a box. It will be much easier to let the fish dine on their remains and let their disappearance remain a mystery."

Tegan felt as if what was happening around her was surreal. She was glad that Garth had taken charge of the situation. He was calm and matter-of-fact in his directions, as if this was an everyday occurrence. Everyone was helping her. She took a shirt off the rack and walked to the restroom.

When she looked at herself in the bathroom mirror, she saw the blood-covered face of a warrior. She felt no remorse for killing Grant, only relief, and she wished she could have killed Westfield and ended the nightmare.

Tegan came out of the restroom as Nate and Alex dragged Grant's body past Knolls. The knife was still protruding from the top of his skull. She was sure Knolls would talk eventually.

She and the others spent nearly an hour cleaning the dive shop. When Garth reopened, Jessica went to work as if nothing had happened telling everyone that there had been an accident. Tegan was glad to see that Jessica was stronger than anyone would have guessed. She was certainly getting an adventure, but was equally certain it wasn't the kind that Garth and Maggie wanted her to have.

Grant's body, neatly wrapped in multiple layers of plastic and stowed in the large freezer tucked behind cases of frozen shrimp, wouldn't take long to freeze.

Garth called Maggie and told her what had happened. Tegan could tell by his reaction that she hadn't taken the news well.

Garth's office — 1115 hours

Bound and seated in a chair in Garth's upstairs office, Knolls sat without saying a word. He couldn't say anything because of the gag. Cal had gone to see what the two had left at the rental house. He'd made Tegan promise not to execute him while he was gone.

Before long, Cal returned to the office carrying the pair's personal items. Tegan had kept her word. He dropped a box onto the table in front of Knolls and removed his gag. "Let's see who these guys have been talking to," Cal said.

He picked up an expensive satellite phone. After a quick check, Cal could tell that the satellite phone was code-locked. "Nice piece of hardware. It's locked just like their cell phones."

"Not much help without the access codes," Tegan said.

"I'm guessing they're all GPS-tracked. We'll have to move them around the island to keep up appearances." Cal turned to Knolls. "I'm sure you have to provide status reports, and most protocols require that after two missed reports, someone will come looking to find out why. Am I right?"

Knolls just glared back at him.

He wondered how long it would be before Knolls folded. Cal pulled an iPad from the box and was surprised to find it wasn't secure. Then he checked the two identifications from their wallets. "It says here that you are Mr. Samuel Adams and your dead friend is John Jones. That's not very original. We both know those aren't your real names."

Knolls squirmed in his chair.

Cal said, "Have to pee, buddy? Well, go ahead, because until we start getting some answers, that chair is where you are going to sleep, shit, and piss until we take you out on our boat and drop you over the side. Then we will see how adept you are at swimming with a chair attached to your ass. So if you have anything to say, now is the time to start talking."

"Go screw yourself!" Knolls shouted.

"He wants to play the tough guy. I can do that," Tegan said. She walked out of the room.

Cal looked at Knolls and said, "That's not a good sign. You should start saying your prayers."

He opened a file. It was a brief, complete with Tegan's picture and biographical information. Cal's heart skipped a beat when he saw the next brief. There were complete bios on Nate, Alex, Dr. Brian Lee, the Aldeberie clan, and him. He scrolled through the assortment of images from a video chat signals intercept. *That explains how the NSA identified Tegan and determined her location*, Cal thought. Whoever was pulling this guy's chain now knew everyone Tegan was associated with, at least at the time of the call, which meant they also knew about their discovery.

Cal turned to Knolls and said, "So the NSA intercepted our video chat with Dr. Lee. It looks to me like someone has done their homework."

Tegan came back into the office carrying a small filet knife. She stopped in front of Knolls. Cal braced himself, hoping she didn't really plan to kill him, but decided he wouldn't stop her if she did. Tegan squatted in front of Knolls and said, "As you know, I'm a medical doctor."

"I know you're a traitor."

Tegan pointed the knife at Knolls and said, "I'm not a traitor. All I did was walk away from the agency—an agency I didn't even know I worked for. My family knew nothing about my work, and yet Westfield decided to kill them. General Westfield is pure evil. The question is how deep you're involved in all of this?"

Knolls said nothing.

Cal knew he needed some incentive to open up, which was exactly what Tegan was going to give him.

"I will be succinct," Tegan began. "This is what I'm going to do if you don't answer my questions truthfully and fully. I'm going to skin you alive. I'll start with your feet and work my way up to your face. I will keep you alive and conscious so you feel every slice. I assure you, before I am done, you will tell me what I want to know. Cal, why don't you leave us alone for a few minutes while I start my live autopsy. This could get messy."

Cal didn't move.

"Suit yourself." Tegan removed one of Knolls's shoes, gripped his duct-taped ankle, and said, "I think I will start with an incision along the top of the foot, right here." Tegan jabbed the knifepoint into his flesh and made an incision down the top of his foot. The wound barely bled.

Knolls rocked back and forth in his chair, sweating and panting, trying to break his bindings, but he never screamed.

"You have something you want to share?" Tegan asked.

Knolls closed his eyes and nodded.

Tegan backed away, keeping the knife visible. "So here's my first question, which I already know the answer to. You work for General Westfield?"

"Yes." Knolls replied. He looked at Cal. "Is this your version of good cop, psycho cop?"

Cal said, "No, Mr. Adams. For the record, we both know your parents didn't name you after a beer, or one of our nation's founding fathers. Let me be honest with you. I didn't even know my soon-to-be wife's real name until last night, and today I watched her nearly decapitate your friend. Her actions tell me she must have a very good reason, and I will support her, no matter the cost."

"How do I know if I answer your questions you won't kill me anyway?"

"I'll make you a promise," Cal said. "I won't kill you if you answer our questions, but Tegan *will* kill you if you don't. So why don't we continue and see how it goes. Tell us about the intercept in the file."

"What about it?"

"How did you come by the information?" Cal asked.

"I don't know exactly."

Cal knew that Knolls was still playing the game. "Stop stalling and tell us the truth, or I'll let Tegan filet you."

"Whatever," Knolls said.

Cal could see he was making a great effort to hide his fear. "Listen up, tough guy. The only reason you are alive now is that I saved your ass, so start telling us what we need to know. This isn't survival school where you get to go home once you've experienced the sensation of being held captive. Were you sent here to kill her?"

Knolls glared at Cal, then said, "We were sent here to see if Tegan Strong was still alive."

Tegan said, "You didn't really answer Cal's question. You were going to kill me if you found me, weren't you?"

Knolls stared at her and said, "There are a number of people waiting for us to confirm she's alive. If confirmed, they'll tell us what we're supposed to do with her."

"That's a bunch of bullshit." Tegan knelt, drew the knife, and grabbed his ankle again.

"Stand down, Tegan!" Cal yelled. She glared up at him and didn't let go of Knolls's ankle. "What's your real name?" Cal asked.

"Robert Knolls. I am a naval officer assigned to the National Security Agency. Tegan is a traitor and a threat to national security. My associate, Mr. Grant, thought he had successfully terminated her. General Westfield recognized her from the intercept and we were sent to confirm if she was alive."

"Were you with him when he killed my family?" Tegan asked.

"No. I was briefed about the action recently." Knolls looked at Cal. "Apparently we were both in the dark. I only learned about Tegan yesterday."

"And Mr. Grant also worked for the NSA?" Cal asked.

"Yes. Now I've cooperated, would you please tell this crazy bitch to put away the knife?"

"Don't ever call her that again or I'll kill you." Cal moved closer to him. "What's your rank in the Navy?"

"Commander."

Tegan said, "General Westfield sent you to kill me and anyone with me, didn't he?"

Knolls shook his head. "No. As I said, he sent us here to make a positive ID. He wanted to be sure that it was you. When Mr. Grant confirmed you were alive, he lost it."

"He's giving us only half-truths, stalling for time," Cal said. "What's the password to the sat phone?" Cal asked.

A second later, the phone beeped.

"Interesting timing," Cal said, moving the phone in front of Knolls. "Well, are you going to tell me how to unlock it, or does Tegan begin the slice and dice?"

"That will be General Westfield," Knolls said. "Do you want me to tell him you're willing to come back, or are you planning to stay rogue and endanger everyone around you?"

Tegan felt the sting of the question. She knew she was endangering Cal and the others, but she could never go back. "Answer it," Tegan said. "Tell him I want to meet with him."

Knolls nodded and gave Cal the code.

Cal entered the numbers and put it on speaker.

"Hello, boss," Knolls answered cheerfully.

"How's the fishing?" Westfield asked.

"Fishing isn't going so well."

Tegan had heard enough. "Hello, General," Tegan said, trying to keep her anger under control. She hadn't heard his voice for a while, but she would recognize it anywhere.

"Hello, Tegan. I didn't expect to hear your voice again, but it's good to know you're well."

"I hoped to never hear your voice again. I didn't like having to play dead all this time. Guess it must have been a shock to learn Grant hadn't killed me."

"Yes, it was quite a shock, but quite frankly, I'm glad he didn't."

"General, I was just telling Tegan she needed to come back to work and all would be forgiven," Knolls said.

"We can certainly use your help again. I'm sure Mr. Grant has expressed his regrets for the collateral damage. I'm truly sorry for your loss."

"Really? That is all I have to do? Just come back to work and you will forgive me, and no one else gets hurt, right?"

"You know there would be more to it than that. A lot depends on what you've told the others about your work."

"I'm sure." Tegan's mind raced, searching for how best to proceed.

"Your family's death was an unfortunate mistake in judgment on my part."

"That's what you call the murder of innocent civilians? You're as sorry about their unfortunate accident as I am about your loss," Tegan said, wanting Westfield to take the bait.

Silence.

"Are you still there?" Tegan asked.

"I'm here. What do you mean by my loss?"

Knolls said, "I'm sorry to report that Mr. Grant was killed today."

The silence lasted longer this time.

Tegan thought this news must have hit him hard, and she was elated to know she had caused him pain.

"John is dead?" Westfield asked.

"He was killed in action a few hours ago," Knolls replied.

Tegan laughed. "Tell him the best part about the *unfortunate* event. Tell him who killed him."

Knolls looked up into her hate-filled eyes. "Tegan killed him."

The loud sound of a crash told her that Westfield must have thrown something heavy against a wall.

"Are you still there, General?" Tegan said. She enjoyed knowing he had no control over the situation. He'd lost someone who meant something to him.

"I'm here," he finally said. His voice was hard now, nothing like the friendly tone he'd used before.

"It hurts, doesn't it?" Tegan asked. "And that piece of trash wasn't even family. I gave you the means to prevent a disaster of biblical proportions, and you turned it into a bioweapon. My family wasn't just collateral damage. You gave the order to have them killed, and I killed the man who butchered my loved ones. The only thing I wish is that you had been here with him so I could have cut your throat as easily as I did his." She wanted to slice Knolls's throat just so Westfield could listen to him die.

Cal said, "General Westfield, this is Cal, I see from the dossier we found with Commander Knolls that you know who I am and who our friends are. As you can tell, Tegan is a bit angry right now. So I'll try to be the voice of reason and at the same time keep her from killing Commander Knolls. You okay with that?"

"I'm assuming Commander Knolls is your prisoner, so I suppose it'll have to be."

"He is, albeit a little damaged and in some pain. Tegan was going to filet him, but I've persuaded her to hold off for now."

"Is this true, Rob?" Westfield asked.

"Yes, sir. Mr. Locke was kind enough to prevent her from killing me, twice. They recovered the files from my iPad."

"Put his gag back on," Cal said.

Tegan peeled off a strip of duct tape and covered Knolls's mouth.

"General Westfield, Commander Knolls will be unable to continue in our discussion. Today, Mr. Grant tried to kill Tegan for the second time, so we have taken steps to go public with the information about the virus. If we cannot come to an agreement, the information will be released through multiple portals that even the NSA will be unable to stop."

Westfield said, "Don't be so sure about that. We have a variety of ways to contain the release of information and many ways to discredit the source."

"You can try to contain the damage, but I would venture to say there are many people in our government, the media, and foreign governments that would be interested to hear how you took a cure and turned it into a bioweapon. I'm also sure Tegan will be able to provide the technical specifications to confirm it."

"You don't threaten me at all."

"I don't make threats. I deal with facts. If we decide to slice and dice Commander Knolls into fish food, you know there isn't a damn thing you can do to stop us."

There was silence on the other end of the line.

Cal continued, "I think you'll agree that it's in our country's best interest, and yours, if our secret never sees the light of day. I think what Tegan has created should remain in the dark. Wouldn't you agree?"

"Yes, I do, Mr. Locke. So what are your terms?"

"My terms are pretty simple. You leave us alone, and we'll leave you and the NSA alone. If you agree, your weapon will remain classified. If any one of us has an unfortunate accident, the world will know everything within minutes. That is, unless you and your friends at the NSA can crash the global network."

"I see. You just want to live in the islands and run charters on the *Whispering Winds*."

"Let me save you some time, just in case you haven't found the classified part of my military service record. I worked in covert operations with some very gifted people, including some that are still at Fort Meade and the Pentagon. I know you're looking for leverage. If you go after my family, I will find you. As you will learn, if you haven't already, I was very good at what I used to do. As for Tegan, well, you eliminated any control you had over her when you killed her family. I'm the one keeping her from going public. Our country doesn't need any more embarrassing incidents."

"I doubt you would ever be able to locate me, Mr. Locke. To put your mind at ease, I have no interest in going after your parents, or your brother, Kevin, or your ex-wife. They are not combatants." Westfield coughed several times and wheezed, sounding as if he was on death's doorstep.

"That sounds nasty," Cal said.

"It's just a cough left over from the flu."

"Hopefully, not from a virus Tegan created. That could be fatal."

"I don't want public disclosure. I'll agree to your terms if you release Commander Knolls."

"Not going to happen. He'll remain our guest until we are able to disappear. Once we're convinced of your sincerity, he'll be released. If we decide you aren't sincere, then he will also disappear."

"Not acceptable. We have no bargain unless Knolls is released unharmed."

"You aren't in a position to make any demands," Cal said.

"Then we are at an impasse, but I believe I have time and resources on my side."

"You may think that to be the case, but you don't. The only way you get Knolls back is to follow my instructions," Cal said.

"I want Mr. Grant's body returned to me. He deserves a proper military burial. How *exactly* did he die?" Westfield asked.

"He died while engaged in close-quarter battle with Tegan. She got the better of him. As to the means of his death, I believe that will be self-evident when you see the body. One of the two pilots you have staying in Marsh Harbour can come and claim him."

"You have been busy, Mr. Locke. I knew the exchange of information in the islands was good, but you surprised me on this one. When and where can I have them retrieve Mr. Grant?"

Tegan couldn't take it anymore. "Grant deserves the same treatment my family and Alessia received. I think I'll burn his body. He wasn't a soldier or a patriot. He was a hired killer. As for Commander Knolls, I think I'll send him back to you a piece at a time."

Tegan wanted to kill Westfield. She was so angry her hands shook.

"Tegan, he was more of a patriot than you will ever know," Westfield shouted. "Osiris was a soldier, and he fought to defend our country."

Tegan said, "Osiris. Even his code name is about death. Did you give him that moniker?"

"Yes. He earned it in the service to his country. He was the best."

"You are a real piece of work," Tegan said.

"I don't know how killing innocent people can be considered patriotic," Cal said. "Does Knolls have a cute code name?"

"No," Westfield replied. "Tegan, you surprised me. You have a warrior's spirit, and I admire that in people. If you hadn't gone rogue, we could have made a good team."

"I'm happy to have disappointed you."

"What exactly do you do for the NSA?" Cal asked.

"You know I can't answer that question. However, as a sign of good faith I will tell you that I represent a facet of our government that you couldn't possibly believe exists. Tegan's work was related, but not in the way you may think."

"I thought you would say something like that," Cal said. "As a sign of our good faith, we will release Mr. Grant's body to one of your pilots. He will rent a boat and come to Man-O-War within the hour. He should approach the dock slowly and tie up by the ice machines next to the dive shop. I'm sure you know where it is. Tell him to bring a body bag. We will be monitoring your people's movements at Marsh Harbor, so make sure he follows instructions."

"He will." Westfield said. "I'm curious how you're going to explain Commander Knolls to Dr. Lee when he joins you."

"That's really none of your concern."

"I believe our conversation is over, for now," Westfield said. "Tegan, I hope to see you in the future."

"Likewise, General," Tegan said, with venom in her voice. The line went dead.

"Your boss sounds like a real charming human being, Bob," Cal said.

"Cal, we need to warn Brian. We need to stop him from getting any deeper into this mess." Tegan was tired. She knew they didn't have the resources to hold Westfield at bay for long.

"I'll take care of that," Cal said.

Tegan sat down in the chair next to Knolls. "I'll watch him for a while. You need to go tell everyone what's happened."

"I'll take the iPad with me," Cal said, then left the office.

Something bothered her about Westfield saying he worked for a facet of the government they didn't know existed. Was he working for a secret section within the NSA? If the NSA intercepted every video telephone call made throughout the day, there had to be criteria in place to determine which calls were of interest. What had triggered him to look at their intercepted calls? What had caught the NSA's attention and motivated them to send the information to Westfield?

Tegan scooted her chair closer to Knolls. "I have a few more questions." She took the tape off him. "Why would your search algorithms key in on an archeological find?"

Knolls just stared back at her.

"What was it General Westfield didn't say?" Tegan suddenly knew the answer to her own question. *The site was not terrestrial in origin.* The NSA had search criteria to look for alien artifacts or sites, and that meant someone was investigating them. Some secret part of the military or the government was involved, and its director had to be Westfield. She smiled at Knolls.

Knolls looked away.

"You found me by mistake, didn't you? You weren't even looking for me. Westfield said he was glad to see I was alive. You're interested in the ancient site we found. I was just a bonus. What else is he involved in?"

Again, Knolls didn't respond.

Tegan leaned closer to him just as Cal and Alex entered the room. By the look on their faces, she could tell they thought they had arrived just in time. Tegan turned back to Knolls. "You're here because Westfield investigates extraterrestrial threats, and the site we found triggered a closer look, didn't it? That's the facet of the government Westfield referred to, isn't it?"

"So much for keeping the alien theory quiet," Alex quipped.

Knolls looked at Alex, then at Cal. "You people are all bat shit crazy. You really think we're interested in aliens?"

Cal smiled and said, "I think he protests too much, but it makes sense as to why they would take an interest in our call to Brian."

Tegan sat back in her chair. "The programmable virus I created could be used as a weapon against an alien species."

Cal looked at Knolls. "Is she right, Bob?"

Knolls turned away from him and snorted. "Like I said, you're all crazy."

Cal said, "I think Tegan is right on target."

"I believe Bob had two missions here," Tegan said. "The first was to determine if I was still alive and kill me. The second was to discover the location of the site and monitor it until they could take control of it."

Knolls looked uncomfortable.

"I think we should head out and find a place to hunker down," Cal said. "I'm quite certain Westfield has the capability to task a satellite or order a drone to spy on us. He knows about the *Whispering Winds*, and if he finds her, he can electronically tag her and get the National Reconnaissance Office to track our movements."

"Which means we can't take the boat to the site," Alex said.

"Correct. Our only ace in the hole is the threat of disseminating the information about the virus. He won't be sure who else has the information or how we plan to release it, so he won't be able to come at us right away."

Cal looked at Tegan. "We'll need to buy burner phones or use the short-range radios we have on the boat."

"You have other radios on the boat?" Alex asked.

"Yes. We provide them to clients when they go exploring. Their effective range is around three miles," Cal replied. "I have an idea."

Tegan said, "Cal, I'm sorry to interrupt you, but I really think we should call Brian before one of Westfield's assassins pays him a visit. He knows Brian's background and his value to us. I'm afraid he'll be the first person he goes after."

"You're right. Alex, call him and let him know he may have visitors. Don't tell him about the virus or the NSA or anything else. His ignorance might just keep Westfield from killing him. Tell him the government is interested in our discovery, but in a bad way. I'm sure he'll understand. If he wants to talk about any new findings, tell him you'll call him back on a secure phone. He's smart enough to figure out that people will be listening. Also, tell him it would be best if he didn't get involved in our field work. That should drive home the seriousness of the situation."

"I'll do it right now," Alex said. She hurried out of the office.

Cal ran his hand through his hair and said, "A few years ago a friend of mine who worked for BIMA, the Biometrics Identity Management Agency, told me about a prototype tracking chip the CIA was field testing. The new chips were small and placed under the skin. They are nearly impossible to detect, even if you knew what to look for. The problem BIMA had with the chip was battery life, especially on longer missions. The interesting thing about the tracking chip was that it not only provided the location of the human asset but also whether or not the asset was still alive."

Tegan nodded. "So you think Bob is chipped, like the animal he is?"

"I'm not sure. Why wouldn't Westfield have known Grant was dead before we told him? You want to weigh in on this, Bob?" Cal asked.

Knolls ignored him.

Cal stepped closer and began examining Knolls's exposed skin. "My guess is the chip would be implanted someplace on the body where most people wouldn't see it. Signal strength would depend on its placement and the power supply. If the power runs low, the satellite will lose the signal. Where do you think they'd put one on old Bob?"

"It could be anywhere," Tegan said, "but one place most people wouldn't spend much time looking at would be near the anus. That would be uncomfortable long-term. The most likely place would be to implant it near the sternum or behind a rib." She pulled up Knolls's shirt.

"Maybe you should start with Grant," Knolls said, looking uneasy.

"You want me to start looking for an incision or conduct a cavity search?" Tegan asked Cal.

"You have got to be kidding me!" Knolls shouted.

Tegan grinned at him, enjoying his alarm.

"Okay, okay. My tracker was removed a few months ago. Medical doesn't recommend prolonged exposure to the device, and we didn't think it would be needed for this mission. There is a small scar behind my right knee. You will find a similar scar on Grant's body. If you examine us closely, you'll see that the surgeon made a small pocket to conceal the device."

Cal smiled at Tegan. "Now we're getting somewhere. Look at Grant's leg and see if he is telling the truth. If Grant's not chipped, it would explain why Westfield didn't know he was dead."

Knolls let out a long sigh and said, "You can slice me, probe and torture me, and remove all my teeth, but you won't find anything. I have no tracking device on, or in, my person. Neither did Grant."

Tegan knelt and found the small scar behind his knee. "There could be any number of reasons for a scar like this one. It looks ordinary to me. You could have another tracker implanted somewhere else, even if they took this one out. Your teeth would make a great hiding place."

"I swear I don't have a second tracker. Tegan, please, just go check out Grant's leg. You'll find an identical scar."

Tegan said, "Cal, if he's telling us the truth, why wouldn't the NSA use trackers for this mission? Seems to me Westfield would *want* to track them, if only to collect geographical data points to give him the exact location of the site once they found it."

"Good point," Cal said. "Well, Bob, what do you have to say about that?"

"We didn't need to be tracked. General Westfield knew where we were. As far as finding the site, we were going to use visual reference and the GPS on the satellite phone."

"That's pretty weak, Bob," Cal said. "The lies just keep on coming. Tegan, check and see if Grant has the same scar. Even if he does, we may still have to conduct a thorough exam of Bob. See if Garth has anything we can use to extract teeth while you're down there."

"There's something you're not telling us," Tegan said. "I know it, and we're going to find out what it is, one way or another. I'll get a pair of pliers while I'm down there. That's all I'll need."

TWENTY-ONE

Alamogordo, New Mexico – July 25

Although there were no bars containing him, Westfield felt like a caged tiger as he paced around his office. His only comfort was in knowing his friend had died the way he would have wanted—in the field engaged with the enemy. He had underestimated Tegan's resourcefulness. Morbidly intrigued, he wondered how she could have bested Grant. He realized his fondness for her had clouded his judgment when he issued the original kill order. If Grant had recorded the kill, would either of them had seen that Tegan wasn't in the vehicle? Maybe then his friend would be alive today. He could not change that now. He would have to live with the consequences of his decision—and the guilt. He would not underestimate his adversary again.

He lit another cigarette. The lack of control over the situation gnawed at him. Westfield inhaled, coughed violently, and then felt a weakness he had not felt before. He exhaled and watched the cloud of cigarette smoke disperse, seeing it as symbolic of his final days with Dark Moon. He was dying. Westfield was used to being in control, but he felt that his cancer and the Strong situation were unresolvable. Tegan was out for revenge, and he didn't blame her. She could have released the information about Deep Sky anytime she wanted over the last few months, but she had never gone public. It wasn't until Grant walked into the lion's den and provoked her that she pounced. He knew now that Tegan had wanted to leave the past behind. Too late to change that now.

Dark Moon was more vulnerable than at any time in the history of the program, and he was responsible for making it that way. He should have retired months ago. However, with all the distractions swirling around his fiefdom, he knew that recruiting and training someone new to take his place was not practical. He needed Knolls, and he needed to figure out a way to get him back.

He already had spent far too much time hiding from prying eyes. *No longer*, he thought. It was time to stop playing defense. His anger swelled at his feebleness. He was angry over the death of his friend, with himself, and with Senator Woodsman's witch-hunt. He needed to make an effective decision, and he knew that when he was pissed off or pushed against a wall, he reacted impulsively. *Rash decisions produce trash results*. He'd learned that the hard way.

He decided that Locke and Tegan weren't going anywhere anytime soon. Tegan's knowledge was their advantage, so Locke would not squander it. He also knew that Locke would watch and wait for him to make the next move. *Let them wonder about my endgame strategy*, he thought.

Woodsman was the immediate threat. If he could get Woodsman off his back, he would have some breathing room. He realized that he should have taken the risk and killed Woodsman long ago. Westfield sat down and ground his cigarette out in the cluttered ashtray. He thought about his sequencing options. First, he would retrieve Grant's body and give his friend a befitting burial. Then he would come up with a plan to neutralize Woodsman. However, before he killed Woodsman, he had to put surveillance assets in place to monitor Tegan. His contact at the National Reconnaissance Office was reliable, but tasking a satellite for a mission over the Bahamas would raise too many questions. Requesting drone overflights would cause even more people to ask questions, and he was sure Woodsman would hear about the activity.

From the classified DoD file on Locke, Westfield knew that he was a worthy opponent. Locke's file said he had four confirmed kills during an extended covert operation. On that mission, he had saved several members of his team from certain death. The rest of his assignments appeared to have been routine. The man had been a good operator and leader, worthy of consideration for Dark Moon if he had stayed in the military. *How had Tegan met him?*

Because of Locke's experience, Westfield was sure he would be on heightened alert. He felt that Locke would plan a defense against a rescue attempt for Knolls and be looking for any sign of unusual activity. He would expect NRO surveillance and alter his movements. He might abandon his boat or use it as a decoy. That didn't matter, because satellite and drone surveillance were not an option. But the threat of the surveillance might force Locke and Tegan to ground.

Westfield decided what he needed was eyes and ears on the island. *Who could blend in and not raise any suspicions on Man-O-War? The one person he was going to send earlier.* Westfield lit a cigarette and inhaled slowly as he pulled up Casey Lane's profile on his computer.

He'd had Casey assigned to the Navy's Atlantic Undersea Test and Evaluation Center, AUTEC, on Andros Island, Bahamas. She periodically provided him with information about Unidentified Submerged Objects and underwater anomalies. She was single, a civilian, and he thought she could go in under their radar. More importantly, she could be in Man-O-War Cay within a few hours.

He'd recruited her years before, following her last deployment in an unfriendly country. The experiences of her final mission had left her unfit for active duty, at least by Navy standards. He knew that Casey had both emotional and physical scars from serving several years embedded with Shadow Watch. She'd been trained as an intelligence infiltration scout, was fluent in five languages, and had often spent months in areas controlled by insurgents. She possessed a gift for blending into almost any environment. Casey had proven to be a very valuable weapon for the Navy, until she disappeared while on a mission.

Casey's mental collapse stemmed from living for nearly three months in a cave in the mountains of northern Pakistan and from the deaths of the local people that had helped in her rescue. She had managed to befriend a woman in a nearby village, and through intermediaries friendly to the United States was able to get word out that she was alive. The woman and her family were tortured before their execution. When Casey returned to her unit, it was obvious her time working in unfriendly territory was over.

The Navy discharged her from active duty, for the good of the service. Her skills were no longer useful to them, but they were exactly what Westfield had needed. He'd pulled some strings and gotten her a research assistant job at AUTEC and the mental help she'd needed to cope with her transition to the civilian world. Westfield had posted Casey to AUTEC for a reason. He needed someone to provide him with information on USOs.

It amused Westfield to know that the Navy actually had personnel assigned to investigate USOs. Those people had no idea Westfield had access to every investigation they conducted. The Navy's secret group was for the most part a very competent investigative organization. Their reports were always thorough and scientifically factual. Casey's work provided another glimpse into the movements of the enemy he monitored. Unlike Dark Moon, the Navy didn't know half of the real story.

The Navy had started their covert investigative team, code-named DS1, following an incident in Shag Harbor, Canada, in October 1967. A strange craft had crashed and sunk into the harbor and had emitted a yellow glow from its hull for days. The Canadian Coast Guard and American military forces stayed on station for over a week investigating the incident. They made many dives examining the craft and had tried to gain entry, but the craft proved impenetrable. A week later, another USO appeared in the harbor. The two ships rendezvoused, and shortly thereafter, both of them disappeared from the sea floor. The incident generated more questions than anyone could answer. Since then, there had been numerous USO sightings, most of which were in the Caribbean, near Tegan's discovery.

Westfield stood and stretched, lit another cigarette, coughed, and called Casey's secure cell phone.

When the phone rang, Casey was eating lunch at her desk, reviewing an interesting seismic readout from a new sensor. She put the sandwich down and answered, "Lane."

"Casey, this is Cecil. I have an assignment I need you to move on immediately," Westfield said.

"Yes, sir."

"I need you on Man-O-War Cay as soon as possible, hopefully within the next few hours. I'm forwarding a file with the mission parameters, specifics on the people involved, and their photos. I cannot overemphasize the importance of this assignment. I have already lost one operator on this mission, and his backup is a captive, so consider it a hot zone. These people have stumbled onto something that I need to locate. Monitoring their activity will lead me to it. You are not to take any direct action. Is that clear?"

"Yes, sir."

"Casey, the site I need to find is underwater. I need you to find where these people are scuba diving. Information about the sailboat they are using is included in the file I'm sending. Be aware that they are expecting my response, so they may change boats in order to continue their exploration of the site. The release of my operator is secondary to your assignment. Do you understand?"

"Yes, sir."

"They will be looking for unfamiliar faces on the island, which is why you'll be on your own. Be careful. They're a resourceful lot."

"I'm a bit confused. If these people are hostile and you've already lost an operator, why am I just going in to be eyes and ears? This seems like a rescue op to me."

"It can't be a rescue, Casey. No one else knows about what they have found or the people involved, and I need to keep it that way. All I need you to do is locate them and monitor their activities so we can pinpoint the location of the site. Can you get to Man-O-War Cay without creating suspicion with the Navy?"

"Yes, sir. I have some vacation time I can take. My boss thinks I'm wound too tight, so he'll be happy to get rid of me."

"Can you locate and monitor these people without asking any more questions?"

"Yes, sir."

"Good," Westfield said, realizing he may have sounded a bit overdramatic. He tried to catch his breath. "Casey, this could be one of your most important assignments. It needs handling quietly and without bloodshed. Taking military action on friendly foreign soil will bring a completely new set of problems to the table. I'm also sure any direct action would result in losing the captive operator. I need you because you are the best at blending into an environment."

"I understand."

"Casey, don't be a hero. If you spot our operator, report it to me and stay on task. Once we have the intelligence we need, I'll initiate a covert prejudicial response and you'll be withdrawn. Do you understand?"

"Yes, sir, I do."

"Good."

Casey said, "General, if I might take another minute of your time."

"Go ahead."

"We're testing a new, highly sensitive acoustical system. It has detected a rather strange intermittent pulsating signal unlike anything I have seen before. I've ruled out system anomalies and have been trying to isolate the source since yesterday. I was going to brief you on it once I understood what I was looking at."

"What kind of signal was detected?"

"That's just it. The signal appears seismic in nature. I almost wrote it off, but then yesterday it recurred at the same intensity and for a longer period. It doesn't seem natural. Could this be related to the site you mentioned?"

"Possibly. Have you passed this information on?"

"No."

"What frequency did you pick it up on, and what's the level of intensity?"

"The frequency bandwidth is very low, at the bottom end of the ULF. The odd thing is that it covers a wide harmonic acoustical spectrum. The signal sounds like it is being generated, and the intensity of the intermittent pulses don't change. There is no degradation of the signal on any of the new underwater sensors. The signal seems just as strong off Cape Canaveral as it does deep off the Mona Rift. It almost sounds like feedback from a low-frequency wave communications system. As far as I know, we aren't testing anything new, so it will become a priority once the Navy is alerted."

"When did you first notice the signal?"

"It started on the twenty-third. I started work on the data yesterday."

"You are sure no one else knows about the signal?"

"Yes, sir, but if I'm gone for several days, someone else will start working on the analysis of the data. The Navy wants a diagnostic report by the end of the month, and this anomaly would have to be explained."

"Any chance you can hide the information to buy us some time?"

"The only way to do that is delete the files. Otherwise, someone will eventually notice what is in the queue. To delete the raw data will require supervisory review."

"Alright. I'll just have to deal with it. The timing could be a coincidence, but I don't believe in coincidences. Forward what you have so far, then leave a copy of the file in your queue, but don't tell anyone it's there. I'll see if I can figure out the source location from my end. Good work, Casey. Once you are on station, I want you to check in every three hours. Now get moving." Westfield disconnected.

Man-O-War Cay – 1230 hours

One of Westfield's pilots arrived by boat and docked next to the dive shop. Cal had Garth make sure no one was around the back of the shop, and then he and Nate carried Grant's partially frozen body to the boat. No one said anything. Once the pilot covered the body, he started the outboard and pulled away. Cal didn't know how Westfield planned to smuggle Grant's body out of the islands, and he really didn't care.

Cal went up to the observation deck above Garth's office and joined Tegan. He scrutinized her for any signs of a delayed reaction as she watched the boat leave the harbor. He knew that every person reacted differently to the experience of killing someone. In this case, Tegan seemed more relieved than upset. He thought Tegan would want to postpone the wedding, but she'd made it very clear that she didn't want to wait, and neither did he.

"Let's get moving," Cal said.

"I'm glad we got that garbage off the island," Tegan said.

"I can tell. We will anchor off Bakers Bay for the remainder of the day and tomorrow for the wedding. I believe we can blend in with the other catamarans sailing around the area, and with *Little Breeze* tied close astern, it will be more difficult for prying eyes to read the name of the boat."

"You don't think they've tagged her already?"

"The more I think about it, the more I feel that Westfield thought this was an easy mission and didn't bother. By the time he gets a satellite or drone tasked, we'll be away from the dock and hard to find. After the wedding, we can move the *Whispering Winds* to a different anchorage every night."

"Sounds simple enough," Tegan said.

"Garth has commandeered the *Deep Current*. It is a new customized fifty-foot Sea Spirit motor yacht. He's taking care of it for a couple who live in Montana. They won't be back until November. He said they'd left instructions for him to run the engines at least once a week."

"So Garth is going to run the engines a little more this week than most," Tegan said.

"He said it would be good for the boat to get some exercise. At least that's his rationalization. Maggie and Jessica will stay aboard the *Deep Current* while they shadow us for the next week. I figure Westfield will be looking for a lone catamaran sailing away from the Abacos. Pairing with another vessel will throw him off."

"Makes sense," Tegan replied. "It will give us a chance to get some answers."

"And since the *Deep Current* isn't linked to any of us, it will provide a good option if we have to abandon the *Whispering Winds*. The *Deep Current* is capable of doing nearly thirty knots, and it has a cruising range of twelve hundred miles."

"That is good. In addition, having two boats and the dinghy will give us the flexibility to continue to work the site. We still need to decide on what to do with Knolls," Tegan said.

"I think he's hiding something, and I don't think it has anything to do with his assignment to find you."

"I agree. What about Garth's businesses while he's away?" Tegan asked.

"Edward is best suited to handle the marina and dive shop operations with the least amount of exposure. He can take care of himself, and he knows to disappear at the first sign of trouble."

"If he can," Tegan said.

"Edward is smart, so don't worry. We will have him check with us periodically and contact us immediately if he sees anyone suspicious arrive on the island. Westfield's men won't be able to sneak up on us. Garth and I are going to meet Edward on his next ferry run. Speaking of which, we need to get going."

$$\infty$$

Alex reached Brian Lee at his home and followed the script she and Cal had discussed. It had taken longer to contact him than she'd hoped. She didn't mention the NSA or explain why she didn't think it was a good idea for him to come to MOW. Unfortunately, she knew her cryptic evasiveness had only piqued his interest more, so she resorted to rudeness.

"Brian, let me be clear. You are no longer welcome here."

"What? That doesn't make sense. Alex, I've found—"

"I don't care, Brian. Another interested party has learned of our discovery. He is unfriendly and has a long reach. Please don't send any information via any open source or come here. In fact, destroy any record of what you have."

"What the hell does that mean?" Brian asked.

She could tell he was growing frustrated with her. "It means don't talk to me via phone, fax, mail, or emails. We won't have any further communication until I contact you again. We're dropping you from the project."

"Why?"

"It's for your own good and for your family's. Is that clear enough for you?"

"I understand, Alex."

"I'll call you later." Alex hung up before he could say anything else. She realized that Brian had information they needed. They'd have to work out a way to communicate with Brian without anyone eavesdropping.

Man-O-War Cay — 1300 hours

The *Whispering Winds* left the dock loaded with enough supplies for them to stay at sea for several weeks. The only thing they would run short of was air for their tanks. Alex had chosen to stay with Cal and Tegan. Cal was surprised when Maggie announced she wanted Jessica to stay with them on the *Whispering Winds*. He thought Mama Aldeberie would have wanted her baby girl nearby, but Maggie explained that she felt they could better protect Jessica. She also wanted Jessica kept away from Knolls as much as possible.

The *Deep Current*, with Garth, Maggie, Nate, and Knolls, left the marina an hour later.

Cal knew that if Westfield sent a team to the island, no one there would know where to find them. He wasn't sure where all this was going to end, but he had faith in everyone, and they had the home field advantage.

Washington D.C. — 1400 hours

The layers of secrecy within the intelligence community astonished TC. He was certain the leaders of the myriad of agencies had designed it that way so they could use their classified knowledge as a means to maintain their power base. Even so, no one had anything of value for him concerning Westfield. Even the new NSA director hadn't discovered anything. Woodsman's investigative efforts hadn't produced any tangible results. He still needed to know if Westfield was going to be a threat to the Antediluvians' incursion. He sensed that Woodsman had something new to relay.

A Secret Service agent led Woodsman into the secure communications room in the West Wing. TC greeted him, and he sat down in one of the plush leather chairs. The agent left.

"I think I've found something, Mr. President," Woodsman began. "Our people have discovered several photographs which were intercepted by an NSA facility. They appear to be pictures of an underwater site in the Bahamas."

"How does this help us?"

"Here, take a look at the photos." Woodsman handed him his MPad.

TC examined the photographs and immediately understood their significance. "Where in the Bahamas is this?"

"The photos were sent from Man-O-War Cay, a small island in the Abacos. I believe that Westfield received copies of these photos."

"How do you know that?"

"The asset you authorized to snoop around CNCI in Utah found something unusual. She stumbled across a very special terminal. At the time of her discovery, a lone technician was operating it and he refused to answer any questions. He was nervous, and he shut the terminal down before she could see what was on the screen."

"So how did we get the pictures, and what does this have to do with Westfield?"

Woodsman smiled. "Our asset managed to hack into a server tied to the terminal and wormed her way into an encrypted file. The file contained these photos and the transcript of a conversation between a professor in the Bahamas and another one in Arizona. The technician had failed to shred the file before he shut it down. It was the only one left on the server linked to the terminal."

"Where's the technician?"

"He disappeared, but she managed to trace the electronic trail from the CNCI terminal to a secret classified system at NSA headquarters. Then the file went to a server located at Wright-Patterson AFB and was forwarded to Groom Lake, Nevada. The server at Groom Lake was equipped with a fail-safe system that electronically terminated the trace once it was detected. We don't know where it went from there. She copied the encrypted file from the CNCI server. We will have access to any information sent through that portal."

"I ask again, how does this lead us to Westfield?"

"With a little digging and some luck, we found a hard copy of the authorization order establishing the Groom Lake server connection. The request was authorized by General Cecil Westfield."

"So Westfield is in Nevada?"

"I don't think so. I believe the Groom Lake Center was another routing point for Westfield. We were able to unlock an algorithm being used to filter all the signal intercepts to the server, but we haven't decoded it completely."

"Where does this leave us?" TC asked, growing impatient.

"I'm betting the information the technician forwarded will force Westfield to investigate. Whoever turns up on Man-O-War Cay will lead us back to Westfield."

"Maybe," TC said. "We know the significance of both Wright-Patterson and Groom Lake. I want teams dispatched to both of those bases on the chance Westfield may be hiding there. Get with Stacy and have her contact Army General Clint Stewart at the Pentagon."

"Who is he?" Woodsman asked.

"He is one of us. I also want him to send a team to Man-O-War Cay. Westfield may be there. Although circumstantial at this point, I think these photos confirm our suspicions about Westfield, and we need to find him before he can do any damage. More importantly, once we find him, we need to determine how much he knows."

"Yes, Mr. President. What do you want us to do when he's in custody?"

"You will bring him to me, and I'll decide what needs to be done. Leave the file with the photographs. Our friends may be able to tell us what it all means."

Man-O-War Cay — July 26 — 0630 hours

Casey Lane approached the dock in the twenty-one-foot Boston Whaler she had rented in Marsh Harbour earlier that morning. She recognized Edward Aldeberie from his picture in the file Westfield had sent. He was standing on the dock, and she gave him a friendly wave. He waved back.

Her journey to Man-O-War had taken longer than expected. The small plane she had chartered experienced mechanical problems, and flying a commercial airliner was out of the question because of the firearms she carried. She had to wait for the aircraft to be repaired. Casey hadn't arrived in Marsh Harbour until after midnight. The ferries had stopped running at sundown, and she was unable to rent a boat until this morning.

"Morning," Edward yelled.

Casey expertly maneuvered the boat alongside the dock, turned off the engine, and tossed Edward a line. "It is a beautiful morning, isn't it?" she said, offering him a sweet smile.

"What can I do for you?" Edward asked.

"I need to find the Hill House. I rented it for the week. I was supposed to be here yesterday, but ran into some problems. I was told to pick up the keys from Garth Aldeberie at the dive shop, so if you'd point me in the right direction, I'd appreciate it."

"You must have been anxious to get here," he said glancing at his watch. "Garth is my father. He's away on holiday, but I can help you."

"That would be great. Thanks."

"The Hill House isn't on the water, so you'll need to rent a boat slip for the week."

"Can you take care of that for me?" She tossed him another smile.

"I can. For a boat this size, a slip will cost you five hundred for the week. Dockside is cheaper, but your boat may not be in the same place every day."

"Dockside will be fine."

"We take the payment up front. It is only two hundred, and that includes a freshwater wash-down daily. If you leave a credit card number, we can have the boat fueled for you every morning."

"I prefer to pay cash. You will accept cash, won't you?"

"Always. My father prefers it, actually."

Casey grabbed the duffle from behind the seat, then threw it to him. The duffle weighed forty pounds, and she had thrown it as if it was an empty cardboard box. For a small woman—at five three and a hundred ten pounds—she was stronger than she looked. Casey had a runner's physique. She was cute, but lacked beauty in the classical sense.

"I can tell by your tan that you're outdoors a lot. Do you play professional sports?" Edward asked. He hefted the duffle onto his shoulder.

She could tell the weight of the duffle had surprised him. "No, I work for a small oceanographic company on Andros. Not much to do there, so I'm at the gym a lot when I'm not working. I swim and run ten miles a day. I'm hoping someday to compete in a triathlon." If anyone was inclined to verify her story, it would pass muster. She jumped up onto the dock. "The company I work for does contract work for the Navy."

"What kind of work do you do?"

"I conduct climate research. It's important work, but it's not very exciting. I look at research data all day." She looked around. "I've never been to the Abacos. I'd like to get in some scuba diving while I'm here. I understand the reefs in the area are spectacular. Perhaps you could chart some good dive spots for me."

"Sure, I'd be happy to. We own the dive shop, and we have plenty of gear in stock for whatever kind of diving you want to do. If you need anything, I'm your guy."

Casey thought Edward was being flirtatious. That would work to her advantage. "So you're my guy, huh?" Casey said. She gave him a slow once-over.

"That didn't come out quite right."

"It came out just fine." Casey replied. She was amused to see Edward's face flush. "So how do I get to the Hill House?"

"It's just a short walk. I'm afraid it doesn't offer much of a view. If you want, I can walk you over."

"That would be very nice," Casey said. "I don't plan on staying at the house much anyway. It's just a place to crash. I plan to explore most of the nearby islands to see what trouble I can get into. By the way, my name is Casey Lane."

"I'm Edward Aldeberie. Trouble may be hard to find around here. Not much to do except fish, scuba dive, and walk on the beach. This is a dry island, so if you were looking for a bar or a party, you should have stayed in Marsh Harbour or gone to Treasure Cay."

"I was hoping you might know some places to have a little fun."

"I would love to show you around, but I can't. My girlfriend, Sara, and I are attending a wedding later today. When I get back, I'll be busy taking care of our businesses while my father is away."

"So you have a girlfriend." Casey said sounding disappointed. "Good-looking guys like you always find a way to break my heart."

Edward smiled. "Check out the dive shop while you're waiting for me. There is breakfast tea on the table by the counter and some homemade pastries. Let me know what dive gear you need, and I'll get you all fixed up."

"Sounds good to me. I could use a spot of tea and a bite to eat. I was in such a hurry to get going this morning I didn't bother to eat breakfast."

"Enjoy it. I won't be long."

That was easy, she thought. Casey instantly liked Edward. She hoped she wouldn't have to put a bullet in his head.

Edward hurried down the dock. He would never guess she was there to spy on his family and friends. She felt confident that he would lead her to where the others were hiding. Westfield would be encouraged by the next report.

Bakers Bay, Great Guana — 0700 hours

Tegan stood naked in front of the mirror, looking for bruises to go with her aching muscles. Finding none, she glimpsed Cal's tanned, muscular shoulders in the mirror. He was facedown on the bed. She could tell he was tired. Every time she had awakened during the night, he was watching her, as if she was going to fall apart at any second. To put his mind at ease, she'd made love to him so he'd understand just how fine she was about everything.

She'd killed a man yesterday, but Grant was really more of an animal that needed to be put down. Tegan felt no remorse, only pure relief after destroying the thing that had taken her family away from her. Her feelings about Knolls had changed. She didn't think he'd been involved in the murder of her family. Still, he had hit Cal, and he was present while Grant had tried to kill her, and for those things she would make his life miserable.

Tegan wished that her family could have known Cal. They would have liked him. Her mom would have been happy for her and would have approved of the nomadic life she was living. Her father would have hated it and would have lectured her about how she was squandering her gifts as a doctor. Maybe he wouldn't have thought that way if he had known what she had done with her degrees.

Cal groaned. He always did when he was trying to wake up.

He opened his eyes and propped himself up on one elbow.

"Good morning," Cal said. "I like the view."

"Don't get any ideas, stud muffin. I think we should wait until after we're married to have carnal knowledge of each other again. You might start thinking I'm easy and try to have your way with me whenever you want."

Cal smiled. "I thought that was why we were getting married."

"You sure you still want to marry me?" she asked, sounding serious.

"I'd marry you anytime and not just for the exceptional sex."

"That's good to know and the answer I wanted to hear." Tegan padded the short distance to the side of the bed, rolling her hips seductively. She bent down and kissed him lightly on the lips.

Cal reached out for her.

"No you don't. Come on, let's get going."

"I thought that was what I was doing."

"Not now," she said, spinning away from him. "We need to check on everyone, then feed and interrogate our hostage."

"Now that's something I never thought I'd hear you say. You certainly know how to put a damper on things." Cal rolled out of bed. "By the way, is Bob invited to the wedding?"

"I thought he was going to be your best man."

"Not after the thumping he gave me yesterday. Look at this bruise." Cal pointed to his side.

"You'll live," Tegan replied, picking up her robe from the floor.

"Are you sure? Maybe I should get a complete physical."

"I gave you an exam last night. You're fine."

The *Deep Current* rocked gently alongside the *Whispering Winds*. The two vessels, with *Little Breeze* tied to the stern of the catamaran, gave the illusion they were traveling vacationers at anchor, enjoying all that the Bahamas had to offer.

Cal dressed while Tegan showered, then he went upstairs to the salon. He poured himself a cup of coffee and started making breakfast.

Garth had come aboard earlier and was sitting at the table.

"Anything new to report?" Cal asked

"Nothing noteworthy," Garth replied, taking a sip of tea. "I'm taking that as a good sign. Edward checked in by radio a little while ago. Everything is good there. I've seen nothing unusual on the radar, just the usual boat traffic."

"Well, that's something anyway."

"How is Miss Tegan this morning?"

"She's surprisingly well. In fact, she seemed rather happy this morning, although she didn't do her morning meditation. She is religious about doing that at sunrise. No sign of emotional trauma, and she has no cuts or bruises from the fight."

"She got some closure yesterday. Just as a precaution, I told Edward to leave the *Alde I* at the dock and to bring the *Blue Angel* over for the wedding."

"Good thinking. How old is that boat?"

"She was built in 1965, but her wooden hull looks as good as the day she first took to the water."

Cal knew that Garth was proud of the classic boat. The original twin 185-horsepower gasoline engines could push the twenty-eight-foot Chris Craft to over thirty knots in calm seas. "It will be good to have another boat nearby," Cal said. "We can use the shallow draft to our advantage, and with her dive platform, we can alternate using her at the site."

Garth nodded and took another sip of tea. "She's anchored in the north inlet off Man-O-War Cay. No one will link her to us."

"It belonged to Maggie's uncle, didn't it?"

"Yes. It's still registered to him. He left it to her when he died last year. I've taken care of it since then. The boat is in better shape now than when it was new."

Tegan walked into the salon, and Cal greeted her with a kiss and said, "You smell good."

"You mean I stank before." She was wearing a pair of white shorts and a red crewneck T-shirt. Her hair was still wet from the shower, and it had soaked the top of the shirt.

"No. That is not what I meant at all. You just smell better."

"Careful, Cal," Garth said. "Women can twist your words in a heartbeat."

Cal looked back at Tegan. "You know what I mean."

She smiled. "Yes. I do. You made me breakfast. Thanks."

"I assumed you'd be hungry."

"Yes. I'm very hungry." Tegan sat down at the table next to Garth and took a sip of orange juice.

"How's our guest doing?" Tegan asked Garth.

"He's just fine. A bit uncomfortable, but otherwise in good health."

"He deserves to be uncomfortable. Did you hear from Edward?" Tegan asked.

"I did. As I just told Cal, he had nothing interesting to report. He did say a young woman arrived from Andros early this morning. She's a scientist doing work for the Navy. He didn't think she posed a threat. The young lady is staying at the Hill House for a week."

Cal gave Garth a quizzical look. "She's a scientist, works for the Navy, and arrived on MOW the day after our encounter with Westfield's men. I'd say that's interesting."

"Not really. We get people from there all the time. Edward said she's a civilian researcher doing climate studies."

"Could be a coincidence, but I doubt it," Cal said.

"If she was here to spy on us, why would she tell Edward where she worked?"

"In case we did any checking."

"You're the expert in the spy game. Anyway, Edward and Sara will meet us at Bakers Bay after lunch," Garth said.

Tegan said, "Garth, the look on your face says there's something bothering you."

"You know me well. I've been thinking about what Bob said about the tracking device that was removed from the dead guy's leg before he came on his mission."

Garth's words hung in the air.

Cal looked at Garth. "Let's not talk about that right now."

"Cal, it's okay. I killed that animal. I get more upset about boiling lobsters. Grant deserved to die. Stop worrying about me or thinking you will say something that will upset me. I appreciate you wanting to protect me, but I think you both are more upset about what happened than I am. Let's just put it to rest. Now, what were you saying, Garth?"

Cal was no stranger to killing. He felt no remorse about taking the lives of enemy combatants. He just didn't want Tegan second-guessing her actions, but based on what he'd seen and heard from her so far, that wasn't going to be a concern. He relaxed.

Garth took a bite of toast. He appeared lost in thought. "Cal, you said standard operating practices dictate that field operators be tagged for operations. In this case, the trackers had been removed, and fairly recently. So I'm thinking that someone didn't want them tracked, and I don't think it was for medical reasons like Bob claimed. So why were the trackers removed?"

"I was wondering that myself. I have an idea, but I want to watch Bob's reaction to the question. So let's pay him a morning social call."

"Can I finish my breakfast before we interrogate the prisoner?" Tegan asked.

"You don't need to be there," Cal said. "You can join us when you're done eating."

"Did it ever occur to you that I may want to be there?" Tegan asked, sounding surly.

The tone of her reply took him by surprise. "Sorry. We'll wait for you."

"Thank you."

Cal remained by the door, watching her as she devoured her breakfast. *She has been moody ever since Alex arrived,* he thought.

Tegan hurriedly finished her breakfast, then said, "I'm ready now."

They boarded the *Deep Current.* Cal greeted Jessica. "Good morning. I didn't hear you leave the boat this morning."

"I came over when my father came aboard the *Whispering Winds.* Mother is watching Mr. Knolls. She fed him his breakfast already. He didn't look happy being fed like a baby, but with his hands and feet tied up, how else could he eat?"

Cal walked down into the galley and approached Maggie. "Can we see you out on deck, please?"

"Certainly. Don't go anywhere, Bob," Maggie said, then followed Cal out. Once on deck she asked, "You aren't going to kill that man, are you?"

"Not today." Cal saw Jessica was listening to them. What kind of an example were they setting for the teenager? She was a party to a kidnapping, had witnessed Tegan's blood lust, and now, was a witness to a veiled threat against Knolls.

"Maggie, you and Jessica may want to go on over to the *Whispering Winds,*" Cal said in a louder voice. "We have some business with Bob, and I don't think you should be present."

Jessica smiled. Cal could tell she knew he was joking. Cal and Tegan went into the galley. Garth stood in the doorway, looking menacing.

Cal sat down at the table across from Knolls. "Morning. Has everyone been treating you well?"

"Knock off the small talk. What do you want to know now?" Knolls asked with a tone of defiance in his voice.

"Let's begin our dialog with what we know, then move on to something that's been bothering us."

"It's your game. Begin wherever you want."

Cal said, "We believe you when you say you had no direct involvement in Tegan's family being killed. Otherwise, you would have been shark bait by now. But you were present when Grant tried to kill her, and you did get a cheap shot in on me."

"You know I had to protect my teammate, right or wrong."

"Yeah, we'll get back to that. I know Westfield will attempt a rescue, but he won't be able to do anything for a while."

"Wouldn't you try to rescue one of your men if he was being held by terrorists?"

Cal leaned back and feigned offense at the remark. "Terrorists! That is an interesting choice of words under the circumstances, but I guess one man's hero could be another's terrorist. I have given some thought as to why both you and your dead associate had your personal tracking devices removed. The only explanation that comes to mind is that Westfield didn't want you to be tracked. Which leads me to ask, why?"

Knolls fidgeted. "I told you they were removed for medical reasons. This op was low-risk, so we didn't need them."

"I think it's more than that. Westfield agreed to our demands far too easily, and from what I know of covert operations and negotiations, he should have put up a stronger show of force. That tells me his response options are limited, and it's not because of our threat to go public."

Cal eyed Knolls, gauging his reaction, then said, "He's interested in what we've found, and I think he has to find a way to locate it without anyone knowing what he's doing. Your mission is a rogue operation, and I'm guessing he doesn't want anyone knowing where his assets are located."

Knolls's pupils dilated slightly just before he looked away. It was a sure sign of deception.

"Think whatever you want," Knolls said.

"So why would Westfield need to run a rogue op? I think your boss has stepped over the line by building biological weapons. I think he's been forced to leave the reservation to do damage control."

Knolls looked back at Cal. "Like I said, think what you want."

By Knolls's response, Cal knew his assessment was partially correct, but was certain there was something else. "That leads me to think your boss needs to stay off the grid until the mess is resolved. I also think he's lost access to the toys he'd normally use to play the game, which is why he sent you and Grant to MOW."

Cal sat back and thought for a moment. "Westfield still has some resources, though. He must have an inner circle of people he can use."

Knolls stared more through Cal than at him.

Cal continued, "Tegan was loyal until she found out Westfield had weaponized her work. Since the NSA is in the business of signal intercept and cyberwarfare, why would he want or need a weapon of mass destruction?

Knolls did not respond.

"Do you know about Tegan's work, Bob?"

"Yes, I'm aware of her work."

"Were you a member of Westfield's team when she was there?"

"No," he replied immediately.

Cal looked at Tegan. She shrugged. Cal turned back to Knolls and said, "What did you do in the Navy?"

"Communications and electronic warfare research."

"Good fit for the NSA. I take it you're on loan, since you retained your military rank."

Knolls did not answer.

"We aren't supposed to be building bioweapons anymore. That gives certain people a strong motive for wanting to keep them concealed, at any cost. But why would he need such a weapon?"

Tegan said, "Cal, maybe General Westfield has to work in the shadows because everything of an extraterrestrial nature would have to be compartmentalized and tightly controlled."

Knolls glared at her.

"That makes sense," Cal said. "I think the site became interesting to Westfield because he's investigating aliens and planning for a real war of the worlds, using your creation."

Knolls clenched his jaw.

"I'm betting General Westfield doesn't really work for NSA. That is only his cover. So whatever he's working on is buried deep, so deep that he's on his own without any official support." He turned to Tegan. "That also explains why postings to his command would be OINO."

"He can't bring the resources of the NSA or the military to bear on us," Tegan said. "Not even our own government leaders know what he does. But he must report to someone in order for his cover at NSA to be sanctioned and to receive funding."

"Maybe he fell under scrutiny when he had your coworker and family killed. Maybe his actions were too much for his superior to justify. He's forced to go underground and thinks all is well, until he finds out you're still alive."

"Could Westfield operate on his own without oversight?" Tegan asked.

"Not likely. However, he could work without the knowledge of the president or the military. Westfield is the guy they'd call if we were attacked by an alien species, but until then, only a select few would know he exists. How are we doing, Bob?"

"I have nothing to say," Knolls stated flatly.

"In the intelligence world, that means we're right on target." Cal stood up and motioned Tegan toward the door. "We have what we need for now. Perhaps you will have more to say after we use you to troll for sharks."

"You want me to chum up the water?" Garth asked.

"No, not yet," Cal replied.

Man-O-War — 0900 hours

The Stoker ferry arrived at the dock on time. There were only seven passengers, six men and Sara Pinder. The men wore an assortment of island casual shirts, khaki cargo-styled slacks, boat shoes, and dark-tinted sunglasses. They all sported a short-cropped, military haircut, and several of the men carried small black suitcases.

Edward was at the dock to meet Sara. He waved at the skipper, John Trowbridge, and handled the lines securing the ferry. As the men disembarked, they did so in a quiet, determined manner. They looked like soldiers. Edward turned his head slightly just in case they were looking for him. When the last man passed, Edward breathed, not realizing he had been holding his breath, and that caught a strange look from John.

"Those guys don't look like tourists," John said.

"No, they don't," Edward replied. They marched down the dock toward the dive shop.

Sara jumped off the ferry and gave him a hug and a kiss. He hadn't told Sara about why his father was away. Edward glanced back at the men. They had stopped at the end of the dock and were talking.

"Who the hell are those guys?" Sara asked. "Not one of them talked to me the whole way over here."

"John, do you know anything about them or how they got to Marsh?"

"Not much. The tall guy in the blue-and-yellow flowered shirt approached me at the dock. He paid for all the fares with cash. I asked him if they were going to stay on Man-O-War long. He told me he wasn't sure. I thought that sounded a bit odd. I tried to find out where they were staying, but the big guy told me I asked too many questions. I was afraid they were going to throw Sara and me over the side if I didn't stay quiet."

"Could you tell where they were from?"

"Nope, but they speak English. American, I would say. No accent. I could ask Steven at customs when I get back if you really want to know. I'm sure he'd remember them."

"I'd appreciate that."

"You're worried about these guys, aren't you?" John asked.

"Yeah, I am. Thanks, John. Have a safe trip back to Marsh."

"You sure you want to stay here with those guys roaming around the island?"

"We have to. We're going to a wedding later today, and my father has decided to go on holiday for a few days afterwards, so I'm minding the business for a while."

"Alright then. I'll check in with you later and tell you what I find out. Is there anyone waiting for a ride to Treasure Cay?"

"No." Edward threw him the lines, and John maneuvered the boat away from the dock. Edward wondered if he should have put Sara back on the ferry. He put his arm around her. "I need to tell you something."

"What's going on? You look nervous," Sara said.

Edward didn't answer immediately. The men split into three two-man teams. One pair headed east, one went north along the docks, and the third pair with the tall guy in the blue-and-yellow flowered shirt seemed to be setting up camp at the entrance to the marina. He needed to radio his father as soon as possible. The radio was in the office at the dive shop. They would have to walk by the two men.

"Come on. I'll explain everything later," Edward said.

They walked down the dock to the dive shop. Edward was surprised to see Casey standing just inside the front door.

"Hi, Edward," she said, greeting him with a big smile.

"Hi, Casey. This is my girlfriend, Sara. I thought you'd be out diving by now," Edward said, feeling guilty. He knew his nervousness wasn't lost on Sara.

"Nice to meet you, Sara." Casey smiled and shook her hand. "Edward was so kind to me this morning. He took care of all my needs. You are one lucky girl."

Sara shot a look at him. "Yes, he's a kind man. How do you two know each other?"

Edward sensed the claws starting to come out.

"I came over from Andros for a break from work. Edward was here when I arrived this morning. He gave me tea and provided breakfast, and then walked me to the house that I rented. He made sure I knew where everything was on the island. He was very helpful."

"That was very nice of him." Sara took Edward's arm.

"Yes, he was very much a gentleman. Well, I need to get a move on. Who were those guys that just arrived?"

"I have no idea," Edward replied. "They don't seem to be here on holiday, though. If you will excuse us, Sara and I have to head off for the wedding. I need to lock up the shop for a while. Do you need anything before we leave?"

"No, thanks. I think I will cruise around the island a bit. You two have fun," Casey said.

"We will," replied Sara.

Hans Bechmeyer entered the shop. Edward's father had told him Hans would take care of the place while he was at the wedding. Hans and his father had been friends for years.

"Hello, Edward," Hans said with a strong German accent.

"Hello, Hans. Thanks for watching the store. This is Casey. She was just leaving."

"If you need anything, I'm your man," Hans said.

"Thanks. It seems this island is full of men wanting to help me," Casey said.

Edward caught Sara's look again.

"See you later, Hans." Edward wondered if he should ask Hans to keep an eye on the men, but decided against it. The less Hans knew, the better. He gave him the keys to the shop, ran upstairs to the office and picked up the portable marine radio, then left.

Edward and Sara walked down the dock. They passed the two men, who took no notice of them. When Edward glanced back, Casey was standing in the doorway of the dive shop. She was watching the men, but the way she was looking at them disturbed him. It looked as if she was sizing them up for a fight.

"Is she what we need to talk about, Edward?" Sara asked.

"No. Well, sort of. I'm not sure. She arrived this morning. She's a real flirt."

"And you flirted back?"

"Maybe a little."

"Are you attracted to her?"

"No! She disturbs me. That's all."

Sara and Edward reached the farthest slip on the dock and boarded the dinghy tied there. Edward rowed them the short distance to the *Blue Angel*. After they climbed aboard the cabin cruiser, Edward opened the engine compartment hatches so any built-up gas fumes could escape. A few minutes later, he started the engines, closed the hatches, and contacted his father on the radio to tell him they were on their way. He also told his father about the six military types who had arrived on the island and how they were acting.

Garth told him to determine if anyone was following them. If so, he was to make a run for Marsh Harbour and stay with friends. Sara gave Edward a quizzical look.

"That is what we need to talk about," Edward said.

Casey watched Sara and Edward walk north along the dock until she lost sight of them. She turned her attention back to the two men at the end of the dock. From her years of experience, she could tell they were military special forces. She knew that the men were searching the island for someone and they weren't Westfield's operators. There were more variables at play here. She needed to contact General Westfield.

Bakers Bay — 0930 hours

Garth relayed Edward's bad news. Cal looked at Great Guana Cay and thought about his options. If Westfield's men were already on MOW, he had underestimated him. They needed to release the information on the virus. The trouble was they were not ready to do that yet. From Edward's description, the men sounded as if they were a special ops team. He decided to call a group meeting.

They all met in the salon, leaving Knolls unattended aboard *Deep Current*, but Cal knew he wasn't going anywhere.

Cal said, "Well, the bad news is General Westfield wasted no time sending his search team. Knolls must not be of much value to him."

"Maybe he doesn't think we'll follow through with our threat," Tegan offered. "Or maybe he's testing the waters to see how determined we are."

"Possibly. The good news is his troops are searching the island, which means he doesn't know where we are. I have a plan for how we can level the playing field."

"We are all ears," Alex said.

"I think the site and Tegan are still Westfield's number-one priority. He needs to contain us, and I think Bob is expendable. If the site represents what we think it does, Westfield needs to locate it as soon as possible."

"Is there a plan here, Cal?" Alex asked.

"I'm getting to it. His men are using the ferry service to get around the islands. Why be so obvious in their deployment? Westfield knows we would find out his men were on MOW. The only reason I can think of is so his team can keep us away from MOW. It buys him time. He could have sent additional teams to the other islands to establish a perimeter to keep us isolated. If he can find a way to shut down all communications to the islands, we won't be able to send anything out."

"But he can't know that we haven't provided the information to someone off the islands," Alex said.

"True. Here's my plan. When Edward arrives, Garth, Nate, Edward, and I will return to MOW on the *Blue Angel*. From what Edward said, there are only six of his men on the island. Two of them are staying near the dive shop. We neutralize that team first. Then we gather some help to take care of the others. They won't be expecting us to take the offensive."

"I'm sorry, Cal, but that's not a plan," Alex stated. "Actually, that's one of the dumbest things I've ever heard you say. Nate is not the commando type, and what do you mean by 'neutralize'? Do you mean kill them or just add them to our hostage collection? Are the people of Man-O-War going to take on Westfield and the United States military?"

Nate said, "Look, as I see it, we don't have many options. Westfield will find us unless we can come to an agreement with him. Based on him sending in the troops, he isn't all that intimidated by our threat. We need to find his weakness and work out a compromise. I'm with Alex, we can't just attack at dawn. Sorry, Cal, but we have to think our way out of this one."

"I've been trained to attack the enemy, not negotiate with them." Cal said. "We need to hit him back hard, and soon, so he knows we're serious."

Nate stood up and paced around the salon. "If Westfield is running a rogue operation, I say we go public now, before he has a chance to shut down our communications. That should neutralize, to use Cal's terminology, any need for us to hide. We can't cause him any more damage, and announcing to the world he has a bioweapon will bring forces to bear on him."

"Who would believe us?" Tegan asked. "We have no evidence. Besides, if we go public, we lose our only advantage. Even going public is no guarantee that he will stop hunting us. I know him. I agree with Cal. We need to take offensive action. I say we eliminate the team he sent a few at a time. Nate, you can stay here. I'll go with Cal."

Alex shook her head. "We have Bob, and with your knowledge of the virus, we can approach the CDC or the World Health Organization, replicate what you developed, and prove we're telling the truth."

"Replicating what I created will take time and a very special facility. I could only provide the theoretical side. Westfield would kill us before I could produce it. Without any hard evidence to present, that won't do us any good."

"That could be why he sent his goons," Cal said. "He knows you can't produce a working copy, and I'm sure he's already moved your work to another facility. No one will find it even if they investigate."

"We still have the site," Alex offered.

Cal nodded in agreement. "Yes, but as soon as we tell anyone where it is, it will be secured and militarized. Even if we know the site was left by an ancient alien civilization, what makes you think the media will believe us and run with the story?"

"We can distribute photographs of it and bring in additional academics to verify our findings," Alex countered.

Cal said, "I'm sure Westfield won't let that happen. The government would debunk the finding, spread false information about us, and clamp a lid on it so tight it would never see the light of day again."

Tegan sighed, then said, "I think we really have only two choices. We release Bob, and I accompany him back to NSA. I'll return to work and help cover up this mess on the condition he doesn't harm any of you."

"That's not an option," Cal said. "Even if he took you back, the rest of us would be held as insurance until you did what he wanted."

Garth said, "Or he may just kill us all no matter what we do."

Tegan looked at Cal. "The second option is to call Westfield and tell him to remove his goons from the island. If he doesn't, I'll kill Bob, and we all disappear. The site stays safe until we pick the time to present our proof and I find a lab that will work with me."

"Doable, but not attractive," Cal said, looking around at everyone. Jessica was staring at Tegan. He'd forgotten she was there. "Jessica, do you want to wait outside while we discuss this?"

"No!" Jessica cried. "I don't think it's right that someone can force a person to do what they wouldn't normally do. I know Tegan doesn't want to kill anyone. Do you?"

Tegan looked conflicted. Cal knew she did want to kill Westfield. She wanted to protect them all from the vortex she had brought to their doorstep.

Tegan didn't answer.

"Jessica," Maggie said, breaking the silence that had descended over the room, "sometimes life throws us challenges we don't want. Tegan would not normally want to kill anyone, but she wants to protect us. Don't you, Tegan?"

"Yes. Jessica, I will do whatever it takes to protect all of you. If Bob is a threat, then I will do what needs doing."

Jessica nodded. "I understand."

"I think I see Edward coming this way," Garth announced, looking out the window. "For whatever it's worth, I'm still with Cal. I have friends that will help us."

"What friends do you want to get involved?" Maggie asked with a look of disbelief.

"We have friends that will come to our aid. We can capture and hold Westfield's men until we can figure out what to do next. In the meantime, Westfield will be down more men and know we are not without resources. He may be more willing to negotiate."

"Edward and Sara should stay close until this is resolved," Tegan said.

"So what are we going to do?" Alex asked.

Cal looked around the room and made his decision. "Perhaps my plan is a bit extreme. As much as I want to take the fight to Westfield, I think it might be best if we hide for a few days. While we are in hiding, we can gather intelligence from sources around the islands. Garth, can you have someone watch over your businesses for a few days?"

"Yes, but I think that's only a short-term solution," Garth said. "We can't hide forever. I think we should contact Westfield and demand he remove his goons."

"We have one problem with that," Cal replied. "The satellite phone is in your office. Remember, we didn't want him to use it to find us. So how do we contact him?"

"I can sneak into my office, snatch the phone, and make the call from a boat just offshore," Garth answered.

"Enough!" Tegan shouted. "You are *not* going to do that. If we can't attack, then we hide like Cal said. I am so sorry for all of this."

"This wasn't your making," Maggie said.

The *Blue Angel* bumped gently against the *Whispering Winds*. Jessica walked out to help secure the lines.

Tegan turned to Cal. "Sara needs to know what's going on, right now, so she has a chance to leave before being sucked into this mess."

Cal nodded. "You want me to tell her?"

"No. This is my doing. I'll tell her."

"You still up to getting married?" Cal asked.

"Yes, the sooner, the better."

New Mexico — 0605 hours MST

General Westfield's secure line buzzed. He knew it was Casey. "Yes," he answered.

"General, did you send another team to the island?" Casey asked.

"No," Westfield replied, feeling a knot grow in his stomach.

"I didn't think so. A six-man special ops element arrived on Man-O-War Cay a little over an hour ago. I've been watching them. They are in search mode. Three teams of two."

"What's the nationality?"

"American, and they aren't the trash mercenary types. I'd say Army, probably Delta."

"Are they armed?"

"Oh, yeah."

"Shit! They could screw everything up. If the primary gets wind of them being there, they will assume I sent them. Did Edward see the team arrive?"

"Yes."

"Goddammit! I'm sure Edward will warn them. Can you stop him?"

"Edward and Sara left the island thirty minutes ago."

"Tell me more about the team." Westfield sat down in his chair and coughed.

Casey filled him in, then asked, "Do you want me to make contact with the team?"

"No. Talk with the locals they speak with and see if anyone knows what they are looking for. You know the drill. This could be a shitty coincidence, but I don't think so. Check in with me if you come up with anything. Otherwise, report in as scheduled."

"Yes, sir."

Westfield breathed in heavily and asked, "Casey, what chance do you think you have of finding our targets in the next twenty-four hours?"

"Chances are slim, unless I get ugly."

"No, don't do that yet. Just continue to monitor." Westfield disconnected.

He sat at his desk, thinking through the possible reasons for the team to be on Man-O-War. The most likely one was that his CNCI communication link had been compromised, which explained the security alert from the fail-safe at Groom Lake. Woodsman, or the president, must have tapped his server and managed to extract enough information to figure they might find him on the island.

He leaned back in his chair and lit a cigarette. He was weary of playing this game. It was time to take the battle to the enemy. He was going to learn what he could from Woodsman before he eliminated him. If need be, his next target would be the president. Knolls would have to wait.

TWENTY-THREE

General Westfield arrived at Reagan National airport, picked up a reserved black Chevy Tahoe, and changed the license plates to the unregistered ones he'd brought with him. He drove to the Capitol and waited for Woodsman to leave the Senate parking garage. Woodsman was a creature of habit, and Westfield knew the route he drove home every evening. He spotted Woodsman's Mercedes as it pulled out of the garage, saw he was alone, and followed him at a safe distance through the congested traffic to the interstate.

Fifteen minutes later, Woodsman left the interstate, turned onto Fairfax Avenue, and pulled into an upscale shopping center parking lot. Westfield stopped on the shoulder of the road across the street and watched as Woodsman parked at the far end of the lot, which suited Westfield's needs perfectly. When Woodsman walked into the grocery store, Westfield pulled into the lot and parked next to Woodsman's Mercedes.

Before long, Woodsman returned, carrying two bags of groceries. He eyeballed the Tahoe, but the window tinting prevented him from seeing inside. As soon as Woodsman opened the trunk, Westfield stepped out with his Glock 36 in hand and waited for Woodsman to close the trunk before making his move.

"Hello, Woody," Westfield said, pointing the gun at him. "I understand you've been looking for me. Well, here I am."

Woodsman's eyes opened wide with shock. He raised his hands.

"No need for that. Put your hands down. We're going to take a little ride and talk things over." Westfield ushered Woodsman to the passenger side of the Tahoe and opened the door. As Woodsman climbed into the SUV, Westfield looped a flex cuff around Woodsman's wrists and yanked it tight. His prey was secure. He could smell Woodsman's fear. He took Woodsman's cell phone and threw it into the grass in front of his car.

"We don't want anyone disturbing our little talk," Westfield said.

Woodsman remained mute, breathing through his mouth like a fish out of water, gulping for air.

Westfield backed out of the parking space. "I have a little place up the road where we can talk in private. You can ask me anything you like, and I will answer your questions truthfully. I expect the same in return."

Woodsman looked at him and said, "You do realize you won't get away with this."

Westfield smiled and headed for a small office complex in the suburbs that the CIA had long ago used for clandestine meetings. Once there, Westfield saw that the rundown building was even more secluded than he remembered. He was sure they wouldn't be disturbed. He had both the electronic key and the access code to the door.

Westfield helped Woodsman out of the car and pushed him toward the office entrance. He coded in and shoved him through the doorway. The reception area was as shabby-looking as the exterior, and it smelled musty. He walked Woodsman down the hallway to an unusually large metal door and unlocked it.

"After you, Woody," Westfield said.

When the door clanged shut behind them, Westfield gestured toward a wooden table and chairs sitting in the middle of the dark-stained, concrete floor. Woodsman took a seat at the table, and Westfield sat down across from him.

"You might have guessed already that this room is soundproof and electronically shielded, so you don't have to worry about anyone hearing us," Westfield said. "We wouldn't want that, now would we?"

Woodsman strained at the flex cuff. "You said you'd answer my questions, so let's start with the most obvious one. Who do you really work for?"

Westfield smirked and said, "A small organization known as Dark Moon. I work with many federal agencies. On paper, Dark Moon is under the Department of Energy."

Woodsman frowned. "What do you do for them?"

"I protect the United States of America from all enemies, foreign and domestic."

"How patriotic of you. So who protects us from you?"

"That is a very good question. Thanks to your efforts, no one really. I reported to Director Bishop. DOE Secretary Stoltz is the only official oversight left, but he isn't interested in what I do. Now it's my turn to ask you a question. Why are you so interested in me and what I do?"

"That's easy. You are a man with too many secrets and obviously too much power and that bothers me. I know you planted the evidence against Talbot. I've never heard of Dark Moon. What is that?"

Westfield knew that Woodsman would never reveal any information he gave him. "Few people know of our existence. We like it that way. President Truman created Dark Moon in 1947. We're a small group of patriots that work covertly on a very special project." Westfield coughed. "Again, why are you so interested in me?"

"The more I investigated, the more intrigued I became as to what you really did. I'm almost certain it has to do with extraterrestrials. That is what we all think, including the president. The name of your group even has that ring to it."

"Why would the president of the United States care about the investigation of extraterrestrials?"

"I think he's curious, as am I. Why would President Truman go to all the trouble of hiding a group of people engaged in looking for life from another world? Surely, he must have had some hard evidence to warrant dedicating resources to the effort. However, I have never heard about any such evidence, nor has the president. Keeping it secret for all these years is quite an accomplishment."

Westfield crossed his arms. "The president is just curious? I think it goes deeper than that. What aren't you telling me?"

"Not much really. You're nothing more than a pet project for us. We found your intercept network attached to CNCI, but you probably already know that. Is the submerged site in the Bahamas something alien?"

"I guess that explains the six-man element you have on Man-O-War Cay. I assumed they were looking for me, but I'm betting you're interested in the site as well. As to it being alien, yes, I believe it has an alien origin."

"Why don't you come back to the White House with me? We can be there in less than an hour. I'm sure the president has questions he'd like answered."

"I'm sure he would find our research enlightening." Westfield had a coughing fit and spit blood on the floor.

"You're not well," Woodsman said. "Should we get you to a doctor?"

"Thanks for your concern, but that isn't necessary." Westfield wiped the bloody sputum from his lips with a handkerchief. "You seem to be the president's go-to guy. I think your sudden rise to power on the Senate Intelligence Committee and the new VP's appointment are intertwined, but I haven't connected all the dots yet. Want to fill me in?"

Woodsman shifted in his chair. "We don't have any secrets. You're the one who has the explaining to do."

Westfield grinned. "You and the VP certainly spend a great deal of time together in the gym with the president. Are you all conspiring on some arcane agenda, or is it some twisted sexual thing?"

Westfield could tell he had struck a nerve.

"You've been spying on the president?" Woodsman asked.

"Not really spying. I was just curious, to use your words, about his hidden agenda. And there are the mysterious circumstances surrounding his wife's death."

"You're a sick bastard."

"I've heard that before. I believe it is time to make the president my next priority. Once I'm done with you, I'll be meeting with him, but you won't be in attendance."

Woodsman looked worried. "You plan on killing me?"

"That all depends on your continued honesty." Westfield stood, rounded the tabled, and sat beside Woodsman. "What's your real interest in aliens, Woody?"

"The same as most people, I suppose."

"Well, they exist, and I know they have gray skin, and they've been exploring Earth for some time. I'm just not sure why, which is what troubles me. Let me give you a little history lesson."

Westfield told him about the Kawich crash, the alien specimen, and the strange metal fragment found there. He wasn't aware that Woodsman and the president already knew about the crash. He gave Woodsman the highlights of the more pertinent sightings and watched for Woodsman's reaction. There was none.

"You don't seem shocked by what I've told you."

Woodsman sat quietly and didn't respond.

"Do the marker and the symbols mean something to you?" Although he didn't answer, Westfield knew by Woodsman's twitch they did. "Why are you and the president so intrigued by the site, Woody? You aren't somehow involved in an alien conspiracy, are you?"

There was the twitch again. From experience, he knew the closer to the truth he got, the quieter the subject would be and the more physical a response they would exhibit.

"I thought we were bonding, Woody." Westfield smiled. "If I cut you, are you going to bleed human or alien blood?"

Woodsman glared at him, but still said nothing. Westfield punched Woodsman in the face breaking several of his teeth and splitting his lip. "Sorry, Woody, but I need a sample of your blood. You know, so I can determine what you are."

Woodsman looked up with blood streaming from his mouth. "I won't tell you anything."

Westfield nodded. "You just did. Now let's get down to business."

Several hours later, Woodsman lay dying on the concrete floor. Westfield's methods were effective, but to Woodsman's credit, he had held out longer than he thought he would. In order to break him, Westfield had used some special pharmaceuticals. Unfortunately, the side effects left Woodsman's lungs mostly paralyzed.

Westfield had learned everything Woodsman knew about the Antediluvians and their plans, including the president's involvement and his altered DNA. He knew why the president had killed his wife and the identity of the other Awakened, at least the ones that Woodsman knew about, which included Vice President Preston. Westfield was astounded by the length of time it had taken the creatures to position themselves for an assault, although Woodsman had never called it an invasion. Armed with the information he now possessed, he could begin taking the necessary steps to protect humanity.

Westfield looked down at Woodsman's battered body. He was glad the traitor was going to die painfully, even if he did believe they were saving the planet. Westfield knew if the Antediluvians were successful, humanity would relinquish all freedoms to an alien invader. President Collingsworth and the other Awakened were a far greater threat than he could ever have imagined.

Woodsman hadn't known the strength of the alien force, their weaponry, or any information beyond what TC had told him. The only real actionable intelligence Woodsman had provided was that the Antediluvians needed the president and the other Awakened in order to establish their foothold on the planet and that their arrival was imminent. Westfield was intrigued to learn that the small partial arm found in the Kawich crash had been from an Antediluvian.

Westfield was tired of Dark Moon hiding in the shadows. Woodsman's disclosures gave him the information he needed to strike. *Grant had died too soon*, he thought. Having Grant by his side for the coming battle would have been glorious and a more fitting end to Grant's career than what had befallen him.

One thing was certain. Westfield now understood how an obscure college professor had managed to worm his way into becoming president. At least he knew the type of man, or half-man, half-something else he was dealing with now. TC was a ruthless adversary and a devoted conspirator, and he was controlled by an alien species. With the enemy embedded in society, Dark Moon would have to deal not only with the Antediluvians but with the Awakened as well.

Westfield lit a cigarette. He needed to devise a strategy to eliminate the Awakened and keep an alien occupation from becoming a reality. He looked down at Woodsman's glazed eyes. He wasn't breathing anymore. Westfield spit on him. *These little aliens' inability to wage war directly would be their undoing*, he thought. They required human conspirators to help them engage in asymmetric warfare, which indicated they didn't have enough firepower to attack on a planetary scale, at least not directly.

A plan started to take shape in his mind. It would require getting Tegan back into the lab. He needed Deep Sky modified so it could isolate and attack the Awakened. If he could infect and eliminate the Awakened, the war might be over before it began. Even if the Antediluvians were able to establish bases of operation, Deep Sky was still a viable weapon against them. Time was of the essence. His best hope for success was going to directly her and persuading her to help. *Perhaps it was fate that Grant had missed his target.*

His first stop needed to be Los Alamos. He wanted the MBRG team to start work on isolating the Awakened gene. He would take a sample of Woodsman's blood; he had plenty of it for them to work with. Next, he would travel to the Bahamas and link up with Casey, then find Tegan. He would have to convince her of the Antediluvian threat and get her to put her need for revenge on hold.

Woodsman claimed that the alien marker they had found wasn't an Antediluvian artifact. If he could get the symbols deciphered and share the translation with Tegan, it would prove his willingness to cooperate. He needed to establish common ground with her, but so far the supercomputer had not provided any results.

Westfield dropped the still burning stub of his cigarette onto Woodsman's bare chest and watched it sear his pale white skin. The head of the snake had to be cut off, but with the president and vice president at Camp David, he couldn't get close to them for a few days. First, he needed to find Tegan, and then he would kill the president and vice president.

He coughed several times and wheezed. He could tell by the frequency and amount of blood he was coughing up that he didn't have long to live. Westfield needed to fulfill what was sure to be his final mission. He left Woodsman's body behind. Someone else would have to take out the garbage.

Camp David, Catoctin Mountains, Maryland

TC was alone and deep in thought in the rustic Aspen Cabin. The cabin was a treasured retreat for him, a place he visited to clear his mind of mundane tasks and decisions. Almost everyone assumed he'd gone to Camp David following Sandra's funeral because he wanted to be alone to grieve. The real reason he was at the two-hundred-acre facility was to enjoy the amenities, especially the woods around the complex. He found a sense of escape when he walked along the trails that snaked through the property. Lately, he found he required more time alone in order to digest all the information provided by the Antediluvians. He assumed his mind was like an athlete's body. It required periods of rest in order to function optimally. The walks and the swims in the heated pool helped him with absorbing the never-ending flood of information.

A sudden jolt of pain radiated through his head. His connection to Woodsman was gone. Over the last few weeks, his powers had increased exponentially. He could sense the essence of those closest to him, even at great distances, but he couldn't always communicate with them. The sudden loss of the connection to Woodsman felt as if he had ceased to exist. TC reached out to find him, to make sure, but there was only emptiness. Woodsman was dead. He reached out to Stacy.

Vice President Stacy Preston was eating dinner in the Laurel Dining Hall a quarter of a mile away when she felt the urgency of TC's summons. She received the news of Woodsman's demise. She ran to the Aspen Cabin, drawing the attention of the Secret Service detail. When she arrived, she was out of breath. An agent escorted her into the study, where TC stood.

"How can this be?" she asked immediately.

TC motioned for the agent to leave. He didn't care if the agent wondered what Stacy meant by her question. He just needed him to follow orders. The agent left them alone.

"I believe General Westfield found a way to retaliate for our actions in the Bahamas. We must be close to finding something if he feels threatened enough to attack." TC looked out the window. "I fear that Westfield has more resources than we gave him credit for. He got to Woody because he was the weakest link and the easiest to eliminate."

"Do you think Westfield knows about us?"

"Possibly. I'm quite certain General Westfield and his people are skilled at extracting information. If he knows what we are and what we are doing, he will come after us."

"Do we need to increase our security?"

"What reason would I give? I can't tell the Secret Service I felt Woody die or send agents to conduct a search where I last felt his essence. I want you to return to Washington today. You must find General Westfield."

"I will."

"Westfield may be nearby, so you should have our assets start in Washington. We may be wasting our time looking for him in the Bahamas."

Stacy said, "We don't know that Westfield is anywhere around here. One of his men could have killed Woody. The team in the Bahamas still needs to find the alien site. Let's give them time to search the surrounding islands and see what they turn up."

"It's your call, but I want him and that site found."

"I understand." Stacy walked out of the study.

TC looked into the fireplace, focusing on the carbon that stained the opening. A memory punched into his thoughts. He pictured Sandra lying naked in front of their fireplace at their old home in Indiana. He remembered the warmth of her skin against his as they made love, and for a moment he felt as if he were someone else. He tried to hold on to the feeling, but it faded.

TC sat back down in his chair, connected to the Antediluvians, and told them about Woodsman and General Westfield and the possible threat of discovery. They instructed him to eliminate the threat, which he'd planned to do anyway. A peaceful arrival and gradual assimilation of the population required that the Awakened remain hidden. If compromised, he would be of no value to them. Stacy had to find Westfield at any cost.

Bakers Bay, Great Guana — July 26 — 1630 hours

Cal stood in the shade under a white canvas canopy. The sun burned brightly in the blue Bahamian sky. Puffy cumulus clouds drifted peacefully westward on the late-afternoon breeze, dragging their shadows across the island. The bay sparkled as if millions of crystals were scattered across the calm surface. Along the shoreline, the transparent water was dotted with patches of floating seaweed. If it wasn't for the breeze blowing through the Australian pines, the heat would have made the beach unbearable for those attending the wedding ceremony.

Cal wore khaki-colored slacks and a green floral-print shirt. Cal knew that people are usually nervous as they waited to take their vows, but he didn't feel that way. He was sweating because of the heat, but even the temperature couldn't distract him from the joy he felt in his heart.

A welcome gust of wind filled the canopy as if it were a sail. Edward checked the tie-down rods. Cal got the thumbs-up from him, letting him know the canopy was secure. The canopy had been a last-minute purchase. It hid them from any potential spying eyes from above, and it provided relief from the sun.

Tegan appeared at the tree line as if she had materialized from the ether. Cal tensed at the sight of her. She looked beautiful in her simple white cotton dress. Tight at the waist and knee-length, it fluttered in the breeze. Her blond hair cascaded over her sun-browned shoulders. She carried a small clutch of white roses with two red roses nestled in the center, symbolizing their hearts.

Garth looked like a proud father with Tegan on his arm. She was indeed a member of the Aldeberie clan now. When she took her place next to him, she gave his arm a gentle squeeze. Nate stood slightly behind Alex, while Maggie, Edward, and Sara stood together. Tegan had told Sara what was happening, and she had decided to stay.

Tegan smiled at Cal. The glow about her confirmed for him that the day was perfect. She handed Jessica, her bridesmaid, the bridal bouquet. Tegan's hand felt warm in his. They faced each other. For a moment time stood still as they looked deeply into each other's eyes.

Cal said, "You're beautiful."

Tegan replied. "I love you."

"We haven't started yet," Garth said. "Let's hold those comments until I pronounce you husband and wife."

Everyone laughed.

Garth stepped in front of them and cleared his throat. "We are gathered here today to bear witness to the joining of these two loving people. As a designated officer of the Register General's Office and the officiator of this joining, I must make sure we abide by the laws of the government of the Bahamas to make this legal. I need both of you, before these witnesses, to repeat after me."

Garth looked at Tegan. "I do solemnly declare that I know not of any lawful impediment why I, Tegan Leigh Strong, may not be joined in matrimony to Calvin Alexander Locke."

Tegan repeated the words slowly and clearly.

"I call upon these persons here present to witness that I, Tegan Leigh Strong, do take Calvin Alexander Locke to be my lawful husband."

Tegan repeated the oath.

Garth had Cal recite the same pledge.

"The official part of the ceremony is now complete," Garth said, "but before I declare them to be husband and wife, they want to express their love for each other in their own words. Cal, you may begin."

Cal squeezed Tegan's hands and said, "Tegan Leigh Strong, I take you as my shipmate, my wife, and my soul mate for the rest of time. You have showed me the meaning of true love. I will do my best to comfort you when you need it. I promise to do my best to never give you cause to be angry with me. Although I'm certain I won't be successful."

Everyone laughed.

"I commit to you my life and promise to provide for you, protect you, and love you always."

"Place the ring on her finger," Garth said.

"Oh, right," said Cal. He turned to Alex. She was holding the gold and platinum wedding band. He took the ring from her and slid it onto Tegan's finger. "You are my wife."

"Now Tegan, your vows to Cal," Garth said.

"Calvin Alexander Locke, I vow to be faithful to you and to love you more than life itself. You are my one true love. I don't know what the future has in store for us, but I promise to be by your side for whatever awaits us. I will love you always and forever."

Jessica handed Tegan the matching wedding band. Tegan kissed the ring and placed it on Cal's finger. "I take you as my husband."

They kissed softly.

"We haven't gotten to the kissing part yet," Garth said, drawing another chuckle from everyone. "It is my great honor to proclaim you to be husband

and wife under the laws of the Commonwealth of the Bahamas. Cal and Tegan, you are officially married, and now you may kiss one another."

Cal and Tegan embraced and kissed with more passion. When they came up for air, Cal shook Garth's hand and thanked him. Tegan gave Garth a big hug and a peck on the cheek.

"Well, now, Tegan Locke. I guess you are officially spoken for, so I can't flirt with you anymore."

Maggie shook her finger at Garth. "He only flirts with women he knows won't take him seriously." Maggie hugged Tegan and winked at her husband.

Alex congratulated Cal and gave him a kiss, then said, "You've done well for yourself. Don't screw it up."

Cal drew back. "I won't, I promise."

They laughed.

Cal looked at Tegan and smiled. He could tell she was happy, and he wanted her to savor the moment. Their future was uncertain, but whatever was to come, he knew they would face it together.

TWENTY-FOUR

Somewhere over Western Texas – July 27

General Westfield's Gulfstream jet flew toward the Bahamas. He had left Woodsman's blood sample at the lab in New Mexico, then flown on to Alamogordo. Not knowing how long he'd be gone, he wanted to make sure the bunker was secured before he left. He knew that the president would intensify his efforts to find him once he realized Woodsman was dead.

He listened to the drone of the jet engines and contemplated his next move. He lit a cigarette, inhaled deeply, and opened his laptop. He pulled up the Kawich crash file and stared at the picture of the metal plaque found in the wreckage. It was the basis for the Dark Moon emblem. His command existed to identify the nature of an alien presence and determine if it was a threat. He had answered those questions.

Westfield took a long drag from his cigarette and blew out a series of perfect smoke rings, watching them dissipate as they rose toward the cabin ceiling. Lack of sleep had left him feeling exhausted. He knew he would soon succumb to the cancer and rest for eternity. He needed Knolls free to fight the battles that were on the horizon, which meant that he had to find a way to get him released.

The Antediluvian DNA from the Kawich crash had been mapped long before, but it wasn't until Woodsman told him it was an Antediluvian ship that had crashed that he knew for sure he could use it against them. The MBRG team would complete the analysis of Woodsman's blood within a few days, so he had until then to find Tegan. She was the only person who could adapt Deep Sky and neutralize the threat from the Awakened. If there was any chance of a future for humankind, he had to have her back.

After running through his options, Westfield knew that even if he eliminated President Collingsworth, someone else would take his place. He also knew that no one would believe an alien invasion was imminent without proof. The alien artifact Tegan had discovered would provide evidence of an alien presence, and that would force his contacts at the Pentagon to listen.

He'd decided to brief Casey on Dark Moon's mission. If she hadn't located Tegan by the time he landed, he'd have to find a way to get Tegan to come to him. The more pressing issue was to ensure the president's commandos did not interfere in their attempt to make contact. Casey said the president's team operated in pairs, so they would be on equal footing if they attacked each team separately. Finding the right time and location and killing them quickly and quietly was the challenge.

Westfield looked out the window of the airplane and saw the faint outline of the Texas coastline. He opened his email and found situational reports awaiting his review. He knew that anything forwarded from CNCI would find its way to Collingsworth. He had bypassed the compromised server, but he still could not rely on the information to be secure. He downloaded the files and began to read.

Bakers Bay – July 27 – 0830 hours

Tegan Locke awoke later than usual. When she sat up in bed, her head throbbed. In the midst of all the drama that was her life, she had managed to drink too much celebratory champagne after the wedding.

She looked at her sleeping husband. Tegan wanted to savor the moment, but her head and bladder reminded her she needed to get moving. A few minutes later, Tegan found Alex sitting in the salon, drinking her coffee and looking at something on the tablet.

Alex looked up. "Good morning, sleepyhead. You ready to take on the day's challenges?"

"I need water to start rehydrating, a Tylenol, and a cup of tea, in that order." Tegan took a bottle of water from the counter. She opened a drawer by the sink and found the Tylenol bottle, took out two extra-strength tablets, and gave Alex a halfhearted smile as she opened the water bottle. Tegan raised the bottle in salute, took the pills, and drank the entire bottle of water without stopping for air.

"Thirsty?" Alex asked.

"Yes," Tegan said. She took another bottle of water from the counter, opened it, and looked out the window when she heard the sound of the *Blue Angel's* engines starting. Garth was waving to Edward and Sara as they motored away. "Alex, I need a word with Garth."

"I'll be here."

Tegan walked from the salon to the stern. "Morning, Garth. Edward and Sara are leaving already?"

"Good morning, Mrs. Locke. I thought it best they get an early start. How did you sleep last night?" There was a suggestive twinkle in his eyes.

"Like a proper married woman should, Mr. Aldeberie. How's our hostage this morning?"

"He's fine and behaving himself. He knows if the boat sinks, he goes down with it."

"Cal's still in the rack. Are Sara and Edward going directly back to MOW?"

"Yes. I wanted Edward to check and see if those men are still nosing around the island. He's going to check with friends on Treasure Cay and Marsh Harbour to see if there are any more of Westfield's men there."

Tegan didn't like the idea of Edward and Sara going back to MOW alone, even though the men had seen Edward and Sara the day before and had shown no interest. Maybe it was okay. She felt a hand on her shoulder.

"Good morning, wife." Cal kissed the top of her head.

"Good morning, husband."

"So Edward and Sara are off to gather intelligence for us," Cal said.

"I thought it best to find out if anything new had developed," Garth said.

"Hopefully everything is nominal."

"Is that geek-speak?" Garth asked.

"Yup. We have some diving to do today, but I think we will wait until this afternoon. I think someone had too much to drink last night and isn't fit to dive just yet."

"That would be correct," Tegan replied.

Man-O-War Cay — 0850 hours

Edward tied the *Blue Angel* to the anchor buoy in the north harbor and rowed the dinghy back to the dock. There was no sign of the men along the waterfront.

"Looks like we're home free," Edward said.

"This is exciting," Sara said. She seemed to be enjoying the adventure.

Edward saw Casey Lane standing on the seawall in front of them at the same time he felt Sara tense. He knew it wasn't a chance meeting.

"Hi, there," Casey said.

"Hello," Edward replied.

"How was the wedding?"

"It was very nice."

"Did the happy couple leave on their honeymoon?"

"Yes. You will have to excuse us, Casey. We have a lot to get done today and lots of calls to make."

Casey turned as they walked past her. "Edward, the guys that got off the ferry with Sara left the island at sunset yesterday. I thought you might want to know. You seemed concerned about them."

Edward stopped, turned, and said, "Why would you think that?"

"I was watching you when they got off the ferry. I could tell you were nervous."

Edward's muscles clenched as Casey took a step forward. "Casey, why were you watching me?"

"Because I was standing there and had nothing else to do. Don't make a big deal out of it. What's got you so paranoid?"

"I'm not paranoid. I just don't like being spied on."

"Message received. I won't watch either of you anymore. I'm going over to Marsh Harbour in a little bit anyway."

"I need to check in with Hans at the dive shop," Edward told her.

"I'll let you get to work then." Casey fell in behind them on the narrow walkway.

$$\infty$$

When Sara and Edward went into the dive shop, Casey untied her boat from the dock, jumped aboard, and started the engine. As she cleared the inlet and headed for open water, she pulled out her satellite phone and called Westfield.

"Yes," Westfield answered.

"I'm headed to the airport. Sara and Edward are on MOW. I have nothing new to report."

"I think the other team screwed up our plans. Casey, we need to discuss some important things. Your mission parameters are going to expand far beyond anything you can imagine. I hope you're ready for it."

"I'll do my best, sir."

"I know you will. I'll be on the ground in Marsh Harbour at 1100 hours. Call me if anyone is waiting for me. I don't want to end up in someone's crosshairs."

"Are you expecting trouble?"

"I'm not sure. Just keep an eye out."

"Will do. How's my mission being modified?"

"I'll tell you everything when I see you. Once you are fully up to speed, I will want Tegan to know I am in the Bahamas. We will have to be more direct in our search for her. I may have to act as bait to get her to come out of hiding. Hopefully, that will save us time trying to find her."

"Understood, sir. I will await your arrival."

Marsh Harbour — 1130 hours

Casey rented a car and drove to the airport. When she spotted two team members watching the terminal, she called Westfield just as his plane touched down.

"Yes," Westfield answered.

"Two members of the team are at the airport."

"They're probably looking for me. Do we have transportation?"

"Yes, I have a small, white four-door Nissan. There's a boat at the dock."

"When I clear customs, I'll meet you at the front door. Be ready." Westfield hung up.

Casey checked to see if there was a round chambered in the Glock concealed in the backpack on the seat next to her. If the team spotted Westfield, she hoped they would only follow them to the docks, but if they tried to take him here, she was prepared to deal with them.

Twenty minutes later, Casey saw Westfield exit the terminal. She drove up to him, cutting in front of another car. He threw his gear into the backseat, but kept his briefcase with him. She turned the little Nissan around just in time to see that the team had spotted them. She hit the accelerator and blew by them. She watched as they jumped into their car from her rearview mirror. One of the men was already on his phone. "It looks like we'll have to do this the hard way."

Westfield opened his briefcase, removed his laptop, and opened the false bottom of the case. A custom-made Beretta and a suppressor were inside. He attached the suppressor and chambered a round. "How are we doing?"

"They're stuck in some traffic. We'll beat them to the dock. I don't know if we'll have a reception committee waiting there or how much time we'll have to get out of the harbor before they catch up. I think we're only facing the one six-man team."

Westfield glanced back. "We'll need to do whatever it takes to escape. I must find Tegan."

Casey pulled up to the dock, parked, and grabbed her backpack. "I'll get the engine started and cast off while you grab your duffle."

Westfield got out and went to the back door. He pulled out his duffle and slung it over his shoulder. He coughed as he labored to the boat. She took his duffle and helped him aboard.

Tires screeched on the road just as Casey gunned the outboard and cleared the dock. Not wanting to lead the team back to MOW, she headed east toward Hope Town.

She looked back in time to see a second car pull up. Four men got out. "It looks like the whole gang has arrived. Are you going to tell me why they're looking for you?"

"Just get us someplace safe. Then I will fill you in."

"Yes, sir."

Scotland Cay – July 27 – 1140 hours

Garth watched from the deck of the *Deep Current* as the *Whispering Winds* motored up and tied alongside. The shallow water between the southern tip of Great Guana Cay and Scotland Cay was a perfect rendezvous point. The marker was only three miles to the north of them, close enough for them to reach it quickly and yet far enough away to keep it concealed if they were located.

"How was the trip?" Garth asked.

"We circled the island and passed over the site," Cal replied. "No other boats were there. Did you find us a base of operations?"

"I think Scotland Cay will work best for us. As you know it's a private island and it's close to the site and to MOW. The marina has deep-water slips and an airfield with a three-thousand-foot-long runway. I'm sure we can find someone to fly the women off the island if necessary."

"That sounds good, but I don't think Tegan will leave."

"Let's hope it won't come to that. All I need to do is find my friend Geoffrey Crane and rent one of his properties. He will let us know if any strangers arrive on the island."

"Don't tell him too much," Cal warned.

"I won't, but he wouldn't say anything anyway. Mind if I borrow *Little Breeze* for the run to Josef's Marina?"

"It's all yours."

"Thanks."

Garth jumped into *Little Breeze*, started the engine, and headed for the marina. He figured he would find Geoffrey on his huge yacht, sipping his martini, which was exactly where he found him.

Geoffrey was an older man who sported a thick gray beard and short-cropped hair. He looked more like a homeless person than a multi-millionaire. After sharing a drink with his friend, Garth was able to rent a house for a month. He bid farewell to Geoffrey and motored back to the *Whispering Winds* to give everyone the good news.

Garth wanted Knolls away from his family. Keeping him at the house would give them more room on the boats and would prevent Knolls from learning the location of the marker. When he got back to the anchorage, Garth gave Maggie the keys to the house and assured everyone that Geoffrey wouldn't ask questions or intrude on their privacy. He told them that Geoffrey had a Piper Saratoga at the airport and he'd agreed to fly five of them off the island at a minute's notice. Garth knew that Westfield would be hard-pressed to find them on the island, and trapping all of them there would be nearly impossible.

Hope Town – 1215 hours

Casey and Westfield sat inside the Frog's Tail Bar and Grill in Hope Town. The Frog's Tail was located near enough to the docks for them to keep an eye on the arriving boat traffic. They could keep watch through large panoramic windows. Their table was in the back of the restaurant near the exit by the kitchen. Westfield ordered a Scotch and a hamburger. He was hungry. Casey chose the mahi sandwich and a beer.

"They'll eventually find my boat," Casey said.

"I know. We need to make it to MOW. I don't want a public confrontation with them, but if that happens, we won't be concerned with collateral damage. Is that clear?"

"I understand."

"I will be as direct as I can be with anyone who knows how to get in touch with Tegan. If Edward and Sara are still on MOW, we'll be forceful in our request."

"If Tegan and Cal come for you, what are my orders?"

"The world needs Tegan alive. Cal is expendable, as are any others with him." Westfield coughed.

Casey said, "I'm not worried about Tegan. Cal concerns me. He's well trained and motivated."

"Don't underestimate Tegan. She killed my best friend in CQB, and he was an exceptionally skilled operator. Do not make the same mistake. As for Mr. Locke, you are correct. He is an adversary worth respecting.

He has combat experience with confirmed kills. He won't hesitate to drop the hammer on you."

Westfield stopped talking when the server delivered their drinks. "Time is not on our side." He considered the compact soldier he was depending on so heavily. She was now one of his most important assets. If anything happened to him, it would be catastrophic. Westfield coughed again.

"Are you alright?" Casey asked.

"Yes, I'm fine." Westfield felt a burning sensation in his chest as he wiped the blood from his lips with a napkin.

"You're coughing up blood."

"I said I'm okay," he snapped.

"You want to read me in on what's really going on?"

"I guess now is as good a time as any. There is a good possibility you will have to complete this mission without me. I command a unit known as Dark Moon. Our primary mission is to investigate, react to, and defend the United States against any alien threat."

"By 'alien' you aren't referring to illegal immigrants?"

Westfield chuckled. "In a manner of speaking, yes, I am. But the border we're responsible for protecting is our planet."

Westfield briefed Casey on everything that had happened over the last few months, along with some of Dark Moon's history. He talked for nearly half an hour about what was germane to the mission at hand. The more he talked, the more he coughed.

He realized that Casey found it hard to comprehend that the president of the United States was working to pave the way for an alien invasion and was himself the product of alien genetic intervention.

"We have company," Casey said.

Westfield saw them. The two men walked into the courtyard of a small hotel across the street.

"We can go out the back, get the boat, and head for MOW," Casey said.

Westfield coughed. "Eventually, the president's team will find us. It'll be better if we select the battleground."

Casey looked through the window. "Perhaps a straight-up fight would be best. We can take out those two over there quietly." She pointed at the inn across the street. "The area around the courtyard is concealed."

"Not a bad idea. Go out the back and work around behind them. I'll go out the front. I'll give you two minutes to get in position."

Casey got up and walked toward the kitchen.

A waiter said, "Hey, you can't go in there."

"I don't feel well. I don't think you want me being sick in the restaurant."

The waiter moved aside.

Westfield paid the bill, picked up his briefcase, and left through the front door. He paused to look around and caught a glimpse of Casey crossing the street. When he looked back at the courtyard, one of the operators stepped out from behind a planter and nodded at him. They stared at each other. Westfield couldn't see the other man, but he was sure his partner would be calling for reinforcements. *Casey had better hurry*, he thought.

Westfield pulled a pack of cigarettes from his pocket, took one out, lit it, and took a deep drag. He flicked the cigarette into the street and walked straight toward the man.

The operator pressed two fingers against his ear. *He was saying something to someone*, Westfield thought. A few seconds later, his partner joined him. Westfield could tell that both men were tense and eager for a fight. They had all the markings of good warriors. He wasn't going to enjoy killing them. They were just following orders given to them by an enemy they didn't even know existed.

When Westfield reached the other side of the street, he said casually, "I bet you're looking for me."

"Yes, we are," one replied.

Two muffled pops announced Casey's gunfire, each round true. Both operators dropped where they stood.

Westfield moved into the courtyard. He dropped his briefcase, grabbed one of the men by his ankles, and dragged him into the tropical plantings. Casey did the same thing with the other body. She snatched a beach towel from a chair and wiped the blood from the sidewalk.

Westfield searched the dead men, taking one of their earwig radios. "Two down, four to go."

The radio broke squelch without any chatter. Westfield knew that meant the team leader wanted an update. He also knew the leader would interpret silence as one of two things—either they were busy or had been compromised.

The radio crackled again, but this time an insistent voice came through. "Sit rep!"

Westfield tapped his earwig twice, hoping the team leader would think they had acknowledged but needed radio silence. Maybe this would buy them some time, but he doubted it. The second team advised they would secure the dock.

Westfield looked back at the bar. "Casey, we have to make a run for the boat. The people at the restaurant saw what happened."

A moment later, they were running across the courtyard. Westfield coughed repeatedly, then pulled his weapon from his briefcase. He didn't care if anyone saw him. A panicked crowd could aid their escape. When they reached the dock, the area looked clear. A siren wailed in the distance.

"Casey, get the engine started. I'll cover you."

Casey bolted to the dock and jumped down into the boat. He heard the outboard start at the same time he saw the Ford coming at them. As he ran he yelled, "Casey, we have hostiles at your eleven o'clock." Rounds fired from the hurtling car whined over his head. He dropped flat onto the dock as he reached it, then coughed violently from the exertion.

Casey sprang from the boat, scrambled to the edge of the floating dock, grabbed Westfield, and pulled him onto the lower dock. "You hit?"

"Negative, but I'm really pissed off." He coughed up blood, then threw his briefcase into the boat.

The screech of tires announced that the Ford had slid to a stop.

"I don't think we have time to get out of range," Casey said.

"I agree. We'll have to face them here."

Westfield saw two operators jump down at the end of the floating dock. A second later, a silenced automatic MP-5 spat death from the passenger window of the Ford. Westfield returned fire.

"Casey, take the two on the dock," Westfield shouted.

Casey screamed, feigning a frightened cry, and dropped behind an equipment locker. The distraction worked. She popped back up just as the two men pointed their weapons at Westfield. She took down both men with two shots each. One fell into the water, the other into an occupied boat. Screams came from the people sitting in the boat.

Westfield looked around. They had no place to run for cover. The automatic fire kept him pinned down below the upper dock. When he heard the slide on a weapon lock back, its magazine empty, he came up firing. Running a magazine dry was not what he expected from a trained operator. It was a fatal mistake. His rounds hit the operator standing just above him in the head. The man toppled backward and landed with a thud. A second later, a searing pain exploded in his chest as the last remaining team member fired two rounds into him. The pain was unlike anything he had felt before, and then he found himself lying on the dock, confused about how he had gotten there.

He caught sight of Casey running toward him and heard her warrior's scream. It was music to his ears. Above him, the man who had shot him turned to point his gun at Casey. *Action is always faster than reaction*, he thought. Casey fired at him, and the operator fired several times in return. Then the last team member fell off the upper dock and landed next to him.

He stared at the dead man's eyes, which were staring back at him.

Casey knelt beside Westfield. A large pool of blood spread from under his body. Blood dripped between the boards into the water. She put her gun down and rolled him over. His wounds were fatal, but he was still alive. The pain in her thigh intensified as her own blood cascaded down her leg. It wasn't the first time she'd been shot.

Westfield coughed up blood, opened his eyes, looked up at her, and said, "It's up to you now. Find Tegan and Knolls." He coughed again. "And find a way to stop the president. You report to Knolls now."

"You're going to be alright. I'll get you help. Just hang on."

Casey stared down at his glazed eyes. He managed a weak smile. "You're a lousy liar. Now complete the mission." He wheezed one last time.

Casey sat there for a moment looking into his world-weary, deeply lined face. She closed his eyes. He had helped her come back from a dark place. He had trusted her when no one else would. She knew he couldn't hear her, but she said softly, "I will complete the mission as ordered, General Westfield."

The sound of people screaming and the wail of more sirens converging on the dock forced her to think about her next move. She laid Westfield's head down and stood up. The pain in her thigh was excruciating. She checked the wound. The bullet had cut a furrow across the muscle tissue. *A lucky shot*, she thought. She glanced around. The voices were growing louder, and a group of people crept toward the dock to see what was going on.

She searched Westfield's body and took his money and keys. She left his fake passport. Casey picked up his gun and tucked it in her waistband. She needed to leave, but she'd been trained never leave a comrade behind. His last orders echoed in her mind. She had to leave him to fulfill his last command.

Casey did something she'd done too many times. She snapped to attention and saluted the men who had died here today. They were all soldiers doing their duty.

She hobbled toward the boat as fast as she could, cast off, and rammed the throttle forward. She glanced back at Westfield's body as she roared out of the harbor. Once in open water, Casey found a first-aid kit under the seat. It contained what she needed—large gauze bandages, antiseptic wipes, and tape. There was a bottle of Advil in the case as well. She swallowed two pills without water and bandaged the wound while steering the boat with one knee. Edward or Sara would certainly hear about the firefight and about a woman matching her description being involved. If Westfield wanted Tegan to know he was here, he had gotten his final wish.

Casey threw her weapon over the side just before she reached MOW and secured Westfield's gun in his briefcase with the laptop. She navigated into the Man-O-War harbor, motored to the dock, and stopped behind a ferry. Edward trotted down the dock, with Sara right behind him.

"You're hurt," said Edward.

"We need to talk, right now!" Casey said, climbing from the boat. She followed Edward and Sara to the office above the dive shop. She plopped down on the couch, feeling emotionally drained and in pain. Westfield was dead, and her new boss was a hostage. All she could do now was hope Edward or Sara would listen to her objectively. She had no doubt they knew where Knolls and Tegan were. Casey spent the next hour telling Edward and Sara her story.

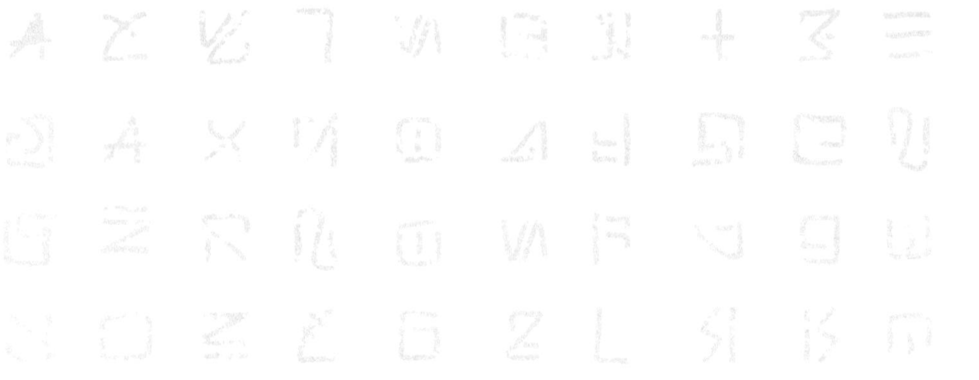

TWENTY-FIVE

Great Guana Cay — 1330 hours

Tegan stood on the flybridge, her hair blowing in the wind. Jessica secured the *Whispering Winds* to the mooring buoy, and Tegan shut down the engines. Cal and Nate had the gear ready for them when they walked into the cockpit.

Cal said, "I threw the transducer over the side. Like before, three of us will wear the full-face masks. Who's it going to be?"

"I'll take the regular mask and regulator," Tegan said. "I agree with Jessica. The FFM is great for communicating, but it is hard for me to use."

"Okay. Jessica, you will stay aboard and be responsible for safety and communications. Remember, the system is ultrasonic, not radio, so the range is limited. If you need to move the boat for any reason, you won't be able to hear us."

"Got it."

Tegan and Alex were the first over the side. They floated away from the stern in the current. Cal and Nate followed. Their telltale bubbles moved toward the marker.

"Com check," Jessica said.

"We hear you just fine," replied Cal, his voice distorted.

"Roger that. Keep in touch."

It had been two days since they were on site, and thankfully, nothing appeared disturbed. They explored the area for a while, then Tegan swam over to the marker and placed her hand on it. The marker glowed under her touch. When she placed both hands over the center symbol, the light intensified and pulsed as it had the last time she touched it. She felt a sense of euphoria and became acutely aware of everything around her. The burble of the air bubbles and the crackling sound of the coral seemed louder. Tegan sensed that the marker was reaching out to her. The glow of the light beneath her hands followed her hand movements. When she pulled them farther away, the light disappeared, as did her sense of peace.

When she placed her head against the center symbol, a blue-white aura appeared. As she backed away, the light disappeared.

She pulled off her mask and handed it to Cal. She opened her eyes and felt only minimal discomfort from the saltwater. Cal appeared blurry, as did almost everything else around her. Tegan turned back to the marker, placed her forehead against the center symbol again, and focused her mind.

Suddenly a blue energy field enveloped her. After a few seconds, a narrow ray of neon teal light shot from the center symbol into her eyes. Tegan thought she could actually feel it follow her optical nerves into her brain. Then her vision cleared.

She remained motionless and allowed the energy to flow through and around her. She had the oddest feeling that the marker was welcoming her home after a long journey. Tegan backed away from the marker, but this time the light maintained contact. She gazed in awe at the face of the marker. It was as bright as she had ever seen it, illuminated like a beacon for all to see.

Cal watched with trepidation as the sphere of light captured her. He felt intense power emanating from the marker. It was like standing next to high-voltage power lines, but he could see that Tegan looked perfectly normal, almost blissful. In fact, she looked like an angel. He reached into the field to touch her arm. On first contact with the energy field, the hairs all over his body stood up. When he touched her skin, the electrical sensation faded, as if he had grounded himself.

He looked back at Nate and Alex. They were transfixed. "Everything is okay, guys." Cal found himself drawn to the light. He didn't want to leave, but somehow he knew they must. He pulled Tegan away from the marker.

Tegan felt as if she was awakening from a dream, but she couldn't remember what the dream was about. She knew that the marker was trying to communicate with her and that she was close to understanding what it all meant. Tegan turned toward Cal, and he handed back her mask. She cleared it and looked at him. She could tell by the look on his face something wasn't right.

Cal pointed to her eyes. "Hey, guys. Tegan's eyes are glowing."

"What do you mean they are glowing?" Alex asked.

"Just what I said," Cal answered.

"I have to see this," Nate said.

She could tell she was the topic of conversation. Nate was in front of her, shaking his head, and then Alex looked at her.

Tegan's emerald eyes were shimmering brilliantly, as if a part of the energy field had stayed within her. She touched Cal's arm and took the regulator out of her mouth, giving him a big smile, and then pointed toward the surface. They all started up.

∞

As he ascended, Cal felt an odd sensation come over him. Something was beckoning him to return to the light. When they broke the surface, he looked at his beautiful wife. Her eyes were normal.

"What's the problem?" Tegan asked.

"Your eyes were glowing," Cal said. "How do you feel?"

"I'm fine. So that's why you all were looking at me?"

"Yes. I felt the marker reach out to me when I was holding on to you," Cal said. "It seemed like it wanted me to stay in the light."

Tegan nodded. "I felt the same thing. It's unworldly, isn't it?"

"Yes, it is." He looked toward the *Whispering Winds*. "I think we should head back."

"That is a very good idea," Nate said. "I also felt myself being drawn toward the light."

"Me, too," Alex said. "Unbelievable."

Nate and Alex started for the boat, but Tegan took his hand, keeping him from following.

"Cal, I wanted you to see what I saw and felt. I think whatever is down there understood my wishes."

"I believe it did. I think we need to get going. The less time over the site, the harder it will be for Westfield to find it."

They swam back to the boat, boarded, and briefed Jessica about what had happened.

"I wish I could have felt it," Jessica said.

Cal shook his head. "No, you don't. Now let's get under way."

Scotland Cay — July 27 — 1530 hours

Tegan was at the helm of the *Whispering Winds* when they rendezvoused with the *Deep Current* a mile off the western tip of the island. As they tied up alongside, Garth and Maggie met them. They both looked stressed out. Her first thought was about Edward and Sara.

"What's happened?" Tegan asked.

Garth said, "I heard from Edward. There was a gun battle in Hope Town. I didn't want to tell you anything over the radio. Seven confirmed dead. Edward says your General Westfield was one of the casualties."

Tegan gasped. "Westfield is dead? How would Edward know that? Are they okay?"

"They're both fine. We'll come aboard and tell you the rest."

Maggie and Garth boarded, and everyone gathered in the salon.

Garth said, "Casey Lane is with Edward and Sara at the dive shop. She claims that she and Westfield killed the team Edward saw on MOW. Casey wants one of us to call her. It seems she needs our help."

"Casey is the scientist visiting from Andros you told us about?" Cal asked.

"That's the one. Cal, you were right. Casey is more than a scientist. She told Edward she worked as an infiltrator for the military, and for Westfield. Edward said she's been wounded."

Tegan felt perplexed. "I don't know what to think. Did it sound like Edward was under duress?"

Garth shook his head. "No, and I've confirmed the firefight took place. Nothing of this magnitude has ever happened in the islands before. I wouldn't be surprised if the authorities lock down all of the Abacos while they investigate."

"That would put a big kink in our plan to move around," Nate said.

"I imagine since those involved are Americans, your government will be swarming the area very soon," Garth said. "It's going to be difficult to tell the good guys from the bad guys."

Tegan felt ill. Eight people killed since Westfield learned she was still alive, and the people she cared the most about were having their lives turned upside down. She softly said, "I'm sorry."

"Tegan Locke, this is not your fault," Garth said. "Stop saying you're sorry."

"How can you say that? Even if I'm not pulling the trigger, people are dying, and I'm forcing everyone I care about to live in fear."

"You're not the one dealing the cards," Garth said softly. "You must understand that we want to help you. No matter what happens, we're all here for you."

Tegan looked at Garth, then at Maggie. She could see neither of them held ill feelings. Somehow, she thought it would be better if they did blame her.

Garth cleared his throat and said, "Edward told me there is more to the story. He said it was very important we call Miss Lane."

"It still doesn't explain what's going on," Cal said, sounding concerned. "Westfield was an enemy we knew something about. We have no idea who killed him or why."

"I know. It might be best to contact Miss Lane and see what she wants. Maybe she can tell us what the bloody hell is happening," Garth said.

"We need to make contact," Tegan said. "But no one is meeting her on MOW, and I think Edward and Sara should leave immediately."

Cal said, "Garth, how long did you say we had the house on Scotland Cay?"

"We have it for a month. The house is perfect for our needs. It sits on a low bluff with westerly views of the Sea of Abaco. It's fairly well concealed and isolated from the cart paths to the east, and it's only a short walk to the marina."

"Is there room for all the boats in the marina?"

"I've already secured two adjacent slips at the end of the dock where the water is plenty deep enough for both the *Whispering Winds* and the *Deep Current*," Garth replied. "We can tie the *Blue Angel* and *Little Breeze* alongside. The locals know me, so no one will bother us. The only problem is if the police extend their search grid. It would be hard for us to explain having a hostage."

Cal snickered. "That's a very good point, but the least of our worries. We will deal with that problem if it becomes an issue."

Maggie stepped over to Garth, took his arm, and looked at Tegan. "I think Scotland Cay will be the last place any investigating will be done. We'll be fine there."

"I'll be glad to have Bob away from the boats," Cal said. "We can rotate babysitting shifts while we continue our research. We will alternate the boats going to the site and limit our time there. Garth, let's call Casey and see what kind of game she's playing and make sure Edward and Sara aren't pawns in Westfield's endgame. He may have staged this to bring Tegan out of hiding."

Garth retrieved one of the burner phones that Edward had bought for them while on Great Guana. He dialed the dive shop and put the phone on speaker.

Casey answered on the third ring.

"Is this Casey?" Garth asked.

"Yes. Is this Garth?"

"Yes. I heard you wanted me to call."

"It's vital that I establish contact with the recently married couple." Casey sounded as if she was selecting her words carefully.

Cal and Tegan moved closer to the phone.

"I'm not sure who you're talking about," Garth replied.

"Garth, we don't have time to play games. I need to speak with them ASAP, preferably in person. In fact, if my guess is right, I need to speak with all of you, but not over the phone. Can we meet someplace?"

"I'm not anywhere near Man-O-War Cay. Why can't we talk on the phone?"

"I know you're closer than you want me to think you are. What I have to say requires the utmost privacy. You never know who might be listening. Edward already said too much on the unsecured line. I have information that's vital to your friend's, um, work."

Garth didn't reply. Finally, Casey said, "Garth, are you still there? Please, I'm on your side. You can pick the time and place for us to meet, but it needs to be soon. I know you have someone in your … care. I very much need to make contact with him."

"Put Edward on the phone," Garth said.

"Edward and Sara are downstairs. He said he had some things to do. I'm not going to harm them. You need to trust me." Casey sounded desperate. "The person in your care is the key to saving our future. You must keep him safe. Do you understand?"

Cal interrupted her. "Casey, you're on speaker. My wife and I are the newlyweds. Your friend is well. What are you selling?"

"I'm selling a path to a long and happy life for both of you and everyone you know. The sooner we meet, the better it will be for all of us."

"How do we know you're not baiting us? Did your friends have a bit of trouble recently?" Cal asked.

"I had only one friend, and he was killed."

"Can you tell us what happened?"

"Yes, but I'd prefer to tell you in person. I told Edward and Sara some of it, but there is more to the story—much more."

"Were you directly involved?" Cal asked.

"I was a party to the festivities."

Tegan had Garth call Edward while Cal kept Casey on the phone. A minute later, Garth whispered, "Edward says they're out on the dock, fueling a boat. They're fine."

"Do you have access to a boat?" Tegan asked.

"Yes."

"Get in your boat and head north out of the anchorage. Stop a mile out and come alone. Do you understand?"

"Yes. I'll leave right away. It may take me a few minutes to get to the marina. I'm not at my best."

"So we've been told," Cal said.

"See you soon." Casey disconnected.

Cal said, "That wasn't smart, Tegan."

"I need confirmation from the source that Westfield is dead. I will go and meet her."

"Not a chance," Cal said. "I'll go. If I don't return in an hour, you all need to disappear."

Tegan said flatly, "I'm going with you."

"No, you are not."

"I said, I'm going with you, and that's final." Tegan faced the others. "If we aren't back in an hour, do as Cal said."

"Edward said Casey is alone, but I'm not sure I trust her," Garth said.

"We need answers," Cal said. "Move the boats to the Gap after we leave and anchor there. Jessica, you will handle the *Whispering Winds*. Nate and Alex will help you."

Alex said, "You both know this is really dumb, don't you?"

Tegan nodded and said, "Garth, call Edward every five minutes until we return."

Garth smiled. "Aye. I'll keep in touch with him."

When Cal joined Tegan in the *Little Breeze*, the grip of a Glock 21 semi-automatic was visible in his waistband. "No sense taking any chances," he said. Then he turned around so everyone could see the dive knife nestled in the small of his back. "And a little something to give my wife comfort."

Garth said, "Be careful now."

"We will," Tegan replied.

Cal started the outboard and handed Tegan the dive knife.

North of Man-O-War – 1605 hours

The trip took only fifteen minutes. A few boats lay at anchor near the entrance to the harbor, but nothing looked out of the ordinary. Cal cut the throttle and let *Little Breeze* drift to a stop. Tegan scanned the harbor and the sky with the binoculars.

"Nothing above us but a few birds," Tegan said.

"A small boat is headed this way. It's moving fast," Cal said, pointing to the boat.

Tegan swung the binoculars toward it. "That must be her. I see no other boats following, and I don't see anyone else with her."

Cal pulled the Glock from his waistband, took the binoculars from Tegan, and scanned the area. "She seems to be alone."

As the boat neared, the engine throttled back. The small boat closed to within a few yards.

Tegan said, "Cal, I don't see anyone below the gunwale. She's alone."

Cal raised his weapon, but didn't point it at Casey. "Come alongside."

Casey expertly maneuvered the small boat. The boats bumped gently, and Casey grabbed hold of *Little Breeze.*

"I'm Casey Lane."

Tegan asked, "Do you think she's chipped? Could be they're using her to pinpoint us?"

"Keep your eyes peeled." Cal said.

"I've come alone. I'm not being tracked." Casey held her hands up and turned slowly in a circle.

Tegan said, "Westfield is really dead?"

"Yes. He wanted to meet with you to explain everything. He was truly sorry for his decision to kill your family."

"How do we know he's really dead? Why should we believe you aren't being tracked?"

Casey sighed. "Please, just trust me."

"You didn't come out here to make small talk. What do you want?" Cal asked.

"I know it's hard to take anything I tell you at face value. I understand your skepticism, but the truth is General Westfield died in a firefight in an effort to meet you. He died in my arms. We have many things to discuss. I assume Commander Knolls is alive and well."

"He is," Cal said.

"Cal, you know how the game is played, but I'm being sincere. The team we ran into was looking for General Westfield and what you discovered."

Cal and Tegan glanced at each other.

"How many more of Westfield's people are on the island?" Cal asked.

"I'm it. Westfield sent me here after you captured Knolls. I was to locate you and report."

"That has a familiar ring," Tegan said.

"So you and Westfield killed a six-man element with only one casualty," Cal said. "That's impressive."

"It's true. I was wounded." Casey pointed at the bandage. "I managed to escape before the police arrived. Westfield gave me one last assignment, and I intend to carry it out."

Tegan slid the knife from its sheath. Cal pointed the Glock at her.

Casey raised her hands higher. "It's not what you think. I'm not here to kill you. He told me to find Tegan and Commander Knolls. The president sent the team we killed. He is the enemy. I have General Westfield's laptop to prove it."

Cal said, "The POTUS ordered a team to find Westfield and us?"

"Not you exactly. The president wants to find the site you discovered and use it for his own purposes. My assignment is to protect Tegan and Commander Knolls and make sure the president doesn't find the marker."

"Why in the hell would the president care about an underwater archeology discovery, and why would Westfield assign you to protect me?" Tegan asked, not knowing what to make of the news.

"It will take some time to explain."

"That's something we don't have," Tegan said, putting the knife away. "This is all a bunch of crap. Cal, shoot her, and let's be done with this. The longer we sit here, the closer the bad guys are getting to us."

Casey stared at her and said, "Tegan, I know how this must sound, especially in light of what has occurred. However, the president is actually the enemy. Can we go somewhere to talk, please?"

Tegan replied, "I don't believe you."

"Tegan, I mean you no harm, honestly," Casey pleaded. "The president is working with an alien race. You and the site you found may be our only hope for survival."

Cal relaxed his stance, then said, "I think we should let her board."

Tegan nodded knowing there was a hint of truth in what she was saying.

"Throw out your anchor, Casey, and come aboard," Cal said. "Tegan, you search her. After all, you're the doctor."

After Casey had anchored and turned on the anchor light, Tegan said coldly, "Take your clothes off and throw them to me. The laptop goes over the side."

"Wait a second," Cal said. "The laptop may have good info in it."

"Maybe so, but it may also be a means to track us. For all I know, Casey could have swallowed a tracker, but I'm not going to wait for her to take a shit to confirm it."

"Point taken," Cal said. "Casey, give me the laptop."

She complied without hesitation.

"What's the password?" Cal asked.

"I don't know, but Commander Knolls might."

"Great. This is probably useless then," Cal said.

"Your clothes," Tegan demanded.

Casey stripped, and Tegan searched her clothing thoroughly. "Alright, come aboard so I can examine you."

As Casey boarded, Cal covered her with his gun. Tegan examined her body for any signs of a subcutaneous tracking device. Finding none, she ripped off Casey's bandage.

Casey winced. "Shit! That hurt!"

"That's too bad." Tegan eyed the groove in the muscle tissue where the bullet had passed through the flesh. She examined the wound. "It's fresh."

Cal said, "You don't embarrass easily."

"I've grown accustomed to being naked in mixed company. I spent time in the field with a military unit."

"Sit down, Casey," Tegan said in a softer tone. "The round only grazed the muscle, but I imagine it bled profusely. Your leg will be stiff for a while, but you won't die, at least not from that wound. It will seep for awhile, and you'll have a nasty scar after it heals."

Tegan reapplied the bandage and tossed Casey her clothes. "We'll take you to your friend. If you don't answer our questions, we may have to kill both of you."

Cal handed Tegan the firearm and said, "If she moves, kill her. If anyone approaches us, kill her."

"I get the picture," Casey said. "You have nothing to fear from me."

Tegan leaned back to keep a safe distance between them. She had one hand on the gun and the other on the knife. It would be difficult for Casey to take both from her. The *Little Breeze* came up on plane as they headed for the *Whispering Winds*.

Cal nudged *Little Breeze* up against the *Whispering Winds*, and Garth tied it off by the bow. Then he helped Casey aboard. "I didn't know you were going to bring her back here," Garth said.

"It may be a short visit," Tegan replied, keeping the gun pointed at Casey. "Take her into the salon."

"Where is Commander Knolls?" Casey asked as she walked into the salon.

"He's resting comfortably next door," Cal replied, following behind her.

"When may I see him?"

"After you've explained what's going on."

"It's important he hears what I'm about to say so he understands his mission has been scrubbed and the urgency of his new assignment."

"You tell us first," Tegan said. "Then we'll decide if he needs to know."

"We're wasting precious time!" Casey shouted. "Let me brief all of you at the same time. If you don't believe what I say, shoot us both."

Tegan placed the firearm on the chart table in front of her, still pointed at Casey. "I may do that anyway."

"Garth, Nate, would you please go tell Bob he has a visitor," Cal said, taking the gun from the table and tucking it in his waistband.

"You sure you want to put that away?" Garth asked.

"She's not a threat," Cal replied. "Besides, we outnumber her, and she's not armed."

A few minutes later, Garth pushed Knolls into the salon. He was unshaven, greasy-haired, and odiferous. Seeing Casey, he said, "So the group keeps getting bigger. Who's she?"

"Put a sock in it, Bob," Garth said. "God, you stink."

Cal said, "It appears you two don't know each other."

Casey answered, "No, we don't. Commander Knolls, I am Casey Lane."

Knolls smirked. "What's going on?"

"I think we'd all like to know that," Alex said.

"I worked for General Westfield. He recruited me after my last tour in Afghanistan and got me posted on Andros as a researcher. For the last several years I've fed him bits of information without the Navy's knowledge."

"We appreciate your service to our country, but is this what you came here to tell us?" Cal asked.

"No." She took a breath and said, "General Westfield called me and told me Commander Knolls had been taken hostage and that Tegan had killed Master Guns John Grant. My orders were to go to Man-O-War Cay and become friendly with anyone who could lead me to Tegan. Once I located her, I was to inform General Westfield of her location. I wasn't to take any action to rescue Commander Knolls."

"Hear that, Bob?" Cal said. "I guess Westfield didn't care about you."

"He did care about Commander Knolls, but finding Tegan was a priority."

Knolls said, "I don't believe any of this shit. Is this some kind of new game you're playing?"

Casey stepped closer to Knolls and said, "Your mission has changed. General Westfield was killed today, and I was wounded, as you can see." Casey pointed to the bandage on her leg. "As General Westfield was dying, he told me to tell you that you are now in command of Dark Moon."

Knolls paled, then flushed red with anger. "What did you say? I don't know anything about Dark Moon."

"Yes, you do. It's the most secret organization in the world, and you are now in command of it," Casey said. "I cozied up to Edward and Sara, hoping they'd lead me to Tegan. At our meeting today, General Westfield told me why he needed Tegan back at Dark Moon." She looked at Tegan. "Your work is the key to stopping an imminent invasion by an alien species known as the Antediluvians. I'm not privy to all of the specifics of your work, but from what I understand you developed a biological weapon which could be used against them."

"Shut your hole!" Knolls shouted.

Knolls appeared livid. What Casey was telling them, or at least part of it, was true. "Let her speak, Bob," Cal said.

"I know this sounds incredible," Casey said, "so I understand your reluctance to believe what I'm telling you, but General Westfield was certain the alien threat of invasion was imminent. The president of the United States is involved with the invasion."

"These people are not cleared for any of this!" Knolls cried.

"We have no time for secrecy," Casey snapped. "The general was very clear about that. He told me Dark Moon needed to accomplish its mission. I don't know everything about Dark Moon or its operations. Like I said, I just learned of it this afternoon. What I do know is that General Westfield believed Tegan was critical to the success of defeating what's headed our way."

"This is nuts," Knolls said.

"Surely you can see that I've been read-in. You have no choice but to listen to what I have to say. Commander, he told me Tegan needed all the time you could buy her in the lab in New Mexico. He said you are the only one left that knows everything about Dark Moon's operations." She paused. "When Westfield briefed me, he had a fatalistic tone, almost as if he had a premonition he wasn't going to survive."

Tears welled in Casey's eyes. Cal believed what she was telling them was the truth.

"Damn it!" Casey said. She turned and wiped the tears away. "His last words to me were, 'Carry out the mission.'"

Cal could see by the look on Knolls's face that Westfield *was* dead.

Casey continued, "Westfield told me that some of Dark Moon's operations had been compromised. A Senator Woodsman was spearheading the hunt for General Westfield and the site. Westfield captured and interrogated Woodsman and learned of the impending invasion and the information I've just disclosed to you. He also learned that the president killed his own wife to protect the Antediluvians from discovery. He and the vice president are genetically altered humans known as Awakened. Woodsman was one of them. The Awakened are loyal to the Antediluvians.

Woodsman's DNA is at the lab in New Mexico, and Tegan needs to report to a group called MBRG. I'm not sure who they are."

"My God!" Garth exclaimed.

"This is too detailed to be made up," Cal said.

"I'm telling you the truth. The president is the leader of the Awakened, and his genetic modifications allow him to communicate with the aliens through an orb he keeps with him. He will prevent any nation from launching a military strike against the Antediluvians when they arrive."

Cal looked around the room. Everyone appeared stunned. He pointed at Westfield's laptop and said, "Is there anything in here we can use?"

Casey said, "Commander, do you know his access code?"

Knolls looked at the computer. "No. He never shared that with me."

"Then keeping the computer is useless," said Cal. "I'm going to get rid of it in case someone figures out how to track it." He walked out of the salon and threw the computer over the side.

Tegan waited for Cal to return and then asked Casey, "Did Westfield give you any idea as to how long this *awakening* has been happening?"

"According to Woodsman, the president was awakened sometime last year. Westfield didn't mention the others."

"What happened to Senator Woodsman?" Tegan asked.

"General Westfield killed him."

"Any other Awakened we need to know about besides Vice President Preston?" Cal asked.

"General Westfield said that former President Jackson was involved. There are others, but he didn't tell me who they were. We didn't have much time together."

"This just keeps getting better and better," Alex said, shaking her head. "What in the hell have we stumbled into?"

Casey said, "The president supposedly has special abilities that are growing stronger every day. I know this all sounds strange, like science fiction, but it is the truth.

"Tegan, General Westfield said he hoped there was a common trait in the Awakened DNA that you could program Deep Sky to attack. He thought they would all have a common genetic marker."

"Deep Sky is the virus you created, right?" Nate asked Tegan.

"Yes." Tegan now knew why her recruitment, training, and work had been so secret. It explained why Westfield wanted to stop her from sharing Deep Sky with the world. "So we're supposed to be the saviors of Earth," she muttered. "We have to do battle with an alien race we know nothing about and without any support from any government. It's crazy."

"Let's not forget dealing with the president and the military who want to find the site," Alex added.

"Why haven't we heard anything about Senator Woodsman being killed on the news?" Nate asked.

"I don't think his body has been found yet," Casey said. "The general said he'd left it at a remote facility."

"What exactly do you know about all of this, Bob?" Tegan asked.

Knolls looked at everyone. "Honestly, I'm in the dark as much as you are. I have never heard of an Antediluvian, and I was not aware of anyone called an Awakened. I know that General Westfield had his suspicions about the president's wife's death, and I can tell you that Senator Woodsman and the president were trying to find us."

"I believe what Casey's telling us," Tegan said. "Does anyone not believe her?"

No one spoke.

Tegan stepped up to Knolls and unsheathed her dive knife. "Are you going to behave, Bob?"

Knolls looked at Casey, then back at Tegan. "Yes. Haven't I been a good hostage? And by the way, my name is Rob, not Bob."

"Being a good hostage and working together as allies are two different things, especially since you came here to kill me. But it appears circumstances have changed." Tegan cut him loose.

Cal said, "Do you think that's wise?"

"Yes. As I see it, Knolls is the only person with the resources to help us face the Antediluvians and the Awakened."

Tegan looked at Casey. "I'm not going back to New Mexico. I can program Deep Sky in a few hours once I have the mapped DNA. I think it best we stay here for now and figure out what the symbols mean. It may give us an insight into how to stop the invasion."

"I have to agree," Cal said. "If the president wants to find the site, then it has significance."

"We've secured a house on the island, which will act as our base of operations," Tegan said. "I think there's been enough killing. Don't you, Casey?"

Casey nodded. "I most certainly do."

"Garth, how big is the house?" Tegan asked.

"It has five bedrooms, three bathrooms, and a large common area. It will suit our needs."

"Are we going to stand out?" Cal asked.

"Probably. A large group of new faces on the island will make people inquisitive, especially with what happened in Hope Town. The authorities are going to be looking for someone matching Casey's description." Garth pointed at her bandage. "And that will be hard to explain. Everyone trusts Maggie and me, so if we tell anyone who asks that the others are clients from one of your charters, they should leave us alone."

Tegan glanced at Casey's leg. The bandage was bloody. "I'll help you clean that up in a few minutes. We'll have to find you something to wear and a way to alter your appearance."

Cal asked Knolls, "Does the president know about Dark Moon?"

"No. If Senator Woodsman was one of them, it explains why he was so interested in our operation, especially after the NSA director and Woodsman got into it. Woodsman has always been the president's lackey."

"Are you referring to Director Bishop?" Cal asked.

"Yes. Do you know him?"

"I do," Cal replied.

Tegan said, "Cal, is he the person you told me wanted to recruit you for a OINO assignment?"

"That's the man. Who else knows about Dark Moon?"

"Director Bishop and the Secretary of Energy are the only people that know about our mandate," Knolls replied. "I don't think Secretary Stoltz is aware Deep Sky exists. It's buried within another classified group known as S-3."

"Why is the Secretary of Energy involved?" Cal asked.

"Dark Moon has been hidden under the DOE since President Truman created it."

"I see why no one would look for you there. It's odd that President Collingsworth doesn't know about Dark Moon."

"Not really. The last president to know was Kennedy. Dark Moon has operated just fine without presidential oversight. It seems President Kennedy was going to reveal Dark Moon's mission, but he was assassinated before he had the chance."

"What are you saying?" Alex asked.

"Nothing," Knolls said defensively. "I'm only stating a fact."

"If you are a secret organization that the president doesn't know about, how did he find out about the site?" Alex asked.

"Like I said, Dark Moon's communications are compromised," Casey answered.

Alex said, "Interesting choice of name for the aliens."

"What's so significant about their name?" Tegan asked.

"Antediluvian is a biblical reference. It refers to people who lived before the great flood. Why would an advanced species capable of interstellar flight, with technology tens of thousands of years ahead of ours, need genetically altered humans to help them?"

"That's a very good question, Alex," Tegan replied, "and one I think we need to find an answer to. Casey, when did Westfield say they were altered?"

"No specific timeframe was given. But it sounded like it had been many hundreds of years."

"A hundred years ago we didn't have nuclear or biological weapons," Cal said. "Why wait?"

"Westfield said the NIBs are traveling a long distance, and that takes time," Casey said.

"What's a NIB, and what do these Antediluvian creatures look like?" Nate asked.

"NIB is an acronym we use for an alien," Knolls answered. "It means Nonterrestrial Intelligent Being. Very few people are aware of what I'm about to disclose, but in the interest of building trust, I will tell you we possess a biological specimen. It was found in a crash no one but a select few has ever heard of."

"Where was the crash and when?" Tegan asked.

"It occurred June 26, 1947, near the summit of Kawich Peak."

"Where the hell is Kawich Peak?" Nate asked.

"It's about thirty-five miles east of Tonopah, Nevada, about halfway between Las Vegas and Reno. Before anyone asks, that's not where Area 51 is located, and it's not related to Roswell."

"Same year, isn't it?" Nate asked.

"Yes. In this case, two geologists working in the area witnessed the crash. Because of the shape of the ship, the geologists thought they had seen a military aircraft go down. Their description of the explosion after the crash was similar to the detonation of a nuclear bomb. They were never told anything different."

"No one else saw the explosion?" Cal asked.

"No. The area back then was desolate, and the crash took place during a severe electrical storm. They recovered biological material two miles from the epicenter of the blast. It survived the heat because it was sandwiched between two pieces of metal. It's the only remains of an alien we've ever found."

"Exactly what kind of specimen was found?" Tegan asked.

"Part of what we think was an arm. The epidermis was gray and thick by human standards, but soft to the touch, almost velvety. The bone structure was hollow, devoid of the marrow. Over the years there have been other reported alien sightings where the description of the alien corresponds to the color of the skin found in the wreckage."

"If these creatures spend a great deal of time in a weightless environment, their bone structure would be less dense," Tegan said. She saw the look on Alex's face. "You're thinking these are the Ancient Ones described in Native American folklore, aren't you?" Tegan asked.

"Possibly," Alex replied. "You know the history well enough. The word *Antediluvian* is also used to refer to the Ancient Ones."

"The Apache and Navajo legends may be based on factual events after all," Tegan said.

"What are you talking about?" Knolls asked.

"Sorry, you weren't here for our Native American folklore lecture," Alex said. "A few days ago we discussed Native American myths and legends as a way to brainstorm possible reasons for the origin of the marker and an alien connection. Apache legend describes 'Gray Ones' coming from the sky."

Knolls looked stunned. "I've never heard of that legend. However, we do believe the occupants of the crashed ship were the NIB's known as Grays. Their mapped DNA is on file in New Mexico. They must be the Antediluvians."

"What do the Grays look like? I mean besides their skin color," Nate asked.

"I thought everyone knew what they looked like," Knolls replied. "The Grays are short and thin, which matches the structure of the arm. They have an oversized skull with distinctive deep, dark eyes. They're also called Zetas. Why, I have no idea. They appear to be the most predominant species involved in alien encounters and abductions. We intercept reports of NIB encounters almost daily from around the world."

"Some of the Grays are already here?" Jessica asked.

"The vast majority of the reports aren't real. If they're here, there aren't many of them," Knolls answered. "But it makes sense that they could have been abducting humans to modify their DNA. When were these Native American sightings?"

"They go back thousands of years," Alex replied.

"So the marker was left by the Antediluvians?" Jessica asked, sounding more interested.

"Well, who else would have left it?" Alex answered. "It's probably a homing beacon."

Knolls said, "If what you found down there is related to the Antediluvians, why would the president need to send a team to find it? Wouldn't the Antediluvians simply tell him where it is so he could deploy assets to protect it?"

"That's what I was wondering," Casey said.

"Maybe it isn't Antediluvian," Knolls said.

"If the site isn't Antediluvian, then whose marker is it?" Alex asked.

"Another very good question," Knolls replied.

A very scary thought crossed Tegan's mind. "The Antediluvians have mapped our DNA and are able to manipulate our genetic sequencing. It makes sense they have catalogued all known viruses and bacteria that could harm them and the Awakened." Tegan shivered as she realized

Deep Sky might be useless. "They'd know about our diseases and how they are transmitted. The Antediluvians and the Awakened may very well be immune to all known infectious pathogens."

"True," Knolls said, "but General Westfield believed Deep Sky could change the battlefield. You can create a virus no one has seen yet. Even if what you create doesn't kill them, with the ability to continually alter Deep Sky, the Antediluvians would have to dedicate resources to find ways to counter it, and that would buy us time. That has to be another reason why Westfield felt it was so important for you to come back."

"Can you create a new virus?" Cal asked.

Tegan said, "Yes, but that doesn't mean it will work. They may have an immune system or another means that can protect them. I need to see the information about the specimen from the Kawich crash. Before we release something new into the environment, we'll also need to immunize everyone against it."

"But how do you immunize billions of people and then do it again every time you release a new virus?" Alex asked.

"I don't know. Let's go ashore and get settled in the house."

Garth said, "I'm going call Edward and Sara and make a run to MOW to get them. I want them with us in light of what we've learned."

Maggie nodded her agreement.

"I'll pick up extra supplies while I'm there, check in with Hans, and tell him we're going to extend our holiday with the whole family. I'm sure Hans won't mind taking care of everything for a while longer. Any objections?"

"Wouldn't they be safer if they stayed away from us?" Cal asked.

"I want everyone together where I can keep an eye on them. Besides, the shooting will have the authorities looking under every rock. I am sure the FBI or some other government investigative body from America will join in. If your president is looking for the site, he knows about us, and with Westfield dead, they will get around to looking for Edward and Sara. Better they join us now."

Cal smiled. "You've given this some thought, haven't you?"

"I'm always thinking, contrary to what people say about me."

"I could use that shower now," Knolls said.

"That sounds good to us," Tegan replied. "Nate, show Rob the shower. Casey, let me take a better look at that leg."

TWENTY-SIX

Washington D.C. — July 27 — 2200 hours

Vice President Stacy Preston had just received a report from General Stewart informing her about the action in the Bahamas. She reviewed the report and the photographs of the scene. It was a gruesome sight, but she recognized Westfield instantly. There was no doubt he was dead, but so was the entire team. *How could that have happened?* Stacy wondered. Westfield must have had help. How many others were involved? Why wouldn't they have taken Westfield's body with them? Too many unanswered questions. *TC won't be pleased,* she thought.

She continued reading the witness testimony and noted that Westfield was with a petite, redheaded woman. The description of the woman was of no value. Stacy didn't believe the woman could have killed six trained operators. She guessed there were others involved. The question was whether Westfield's organization was still a threat to the Antediluvians' plan. She needed to know what had happened.

Knowing that President Collingsworth had returned from Camp David a few hours earlier, Stacy reached out to him in her thoughts. He responded to her immediately. Their bond was growing stronger by the day. She related the events of the action in the Bahamas and could feel both TC's relief when he learned of Westfield's death and his concern that a threat still loomed.

TC needed some time to reflect on the news. He blocked Stacy from his thoughts. As he contemplated the possible hazards they faced now that Westfield was dead, he gazed coldly at the picture of Sandra and his two sons sitting on the desk. The picture was there more for appearance than for any sentimental reason. He felt nothing for them any longer and shook the memories away.

Whatever unit Westfield commanded, it was now without a leader, which meant the likelihood of its discovery was minimal. He decided that finding the other alien site could wait. There would be no further distractions as they prepared for the arrival of the Antediluvian ships.

He reached out to Stacey and instructed her to retrieve Westfield's body and the bodies of the team. He wanted it done quickly. The Bahamas was no longer a factor. He pushed her from his mind.

His powers had grown stronger as the invasion neared, but he was starting to feel as though his thoughts and decisions weren't his own. A moment of doubt crept into his psyche. Was he only being used as a pawn? *That couldn't be, could it?* The thought gave him a moment of alarm. TC reached out to ask the question, without using the Orb, testing the limits of his new gifts.

He felt an odd sensation as he projected his desire to communicate into the dark abyss of space. The longer he waited for the connection, the more panicked he became. Finally, he felt the familiar Antediluvian essence. Their minds locked, and his fear abated. He was safe.

Trakar sat in a chamber designed especially for her aboard the Antediluvian expeditionary ship. The bulbous gray skin flaps covering her large, black, almond-shaped eyes remained closed as she solidified her connection with TC. She held her small slit of a mouth tightly shut and breathed slowly through the tiny openings of her nostrils. This was the first time a human and an Antediluvian had interacted without an Orb.

Trakar was unique. Genetically engineered and trained for one purpose, she interfaced and controlled the human puppets her kind had created.

She had spent years learning to adapt her mind and senses to communicate with the Awakened, her thoughts amplified and filtered for translation by the communication system surrounding her. However, today she was communicating with a human without the use of the system. This new experience of connecting directly with an Awakened was unsettling.

Antediluvians communicated with one another in two ways, through chemical excretions in close proximity and by enhanced telepathy over distances. Sometimes their communications were a combination of both. The Awakened were supposed to be devoid of the finer chemical receptors and inherent mental acuity needed to communicate this way. Somehow, her mind was accepting the electrical brainwave impulses from the human. She wasn't sure if it was the human that had pushed through the barrier or if it was her highly advanced ability to capture his thoughts without translation. A more disturbing thought was that she was becoming more human.

She'd been selected from the others that were developed to perform the same function in which she was now engaged. Trakar was one of the few that could tolerate contact with the primitive human mind without suffering lasting negative effects. During her training, she demonstrated a distinct talent for being able to control multiple Awakened. Her natural ability proved critical to the Antediluvian plan, thrusting her to a higher station. She ultimately found that understanding human emotions was not something any other Antediluvian could do.

She felt TC's anxiety as he inquired about the meaning of his sudden increase in ability. Trakar sensed he felt conflicted. She forced the thought from his mind and replaced it with the impression that the world would be a better place soon. She could tell he understood. She felt his contentment once again. Trakar provided all that he needed to know. After receiving the information about Westfield's death, she terminated the connection. All was as it should be.

Trakar opened her eyes and moved with precision and some urgency as she manipulated a series of small lights with her thin, elongated fingers on a large holographic screen in front of her. She knew that the fate of their species rested on her being able to control TC. She sensed that he was having independent thoughts. She understood that being inquisitive was a trait hardwired into human beings. This human trait found a way to resurface on occasions even after thousands of years of reprogramming. Still, TC was one of the finest specimens of their genetic reengineering project. She was determined to keep him under her control.

She connected to her director and conveyed not only the newest developments, but also the fact that TC was adapting faster than expected. If he continued to evolve at this rate, he would be more useful to them when the time came to invade. The director reminded her that TC could also become more dangerous. Subterfuge was paramount to their success. Trakar was provided a glimpse of their past. She found the information enlightening and understood why her role was so important. The Monan and the Collective could depend on her.

Palmer Land, Antarctica — along the 77th West Meridian

Beneath the Bellingshausen Sea, southwest of Alexander I Island, where Palmer Land joins the Antarctic continent, The Watcher received another urgent message from the remote outpost in the Bahamas, this time with more intensity.

He noted the unique genetic signature relayed to him. He had deemed the previous inquiries to be anomalies, but this time the sentry provided more detail. It had been over twelve thousand years since the Bahamian outpost was sealed. None of their kind had been there since. The signal provided him with but a glimpse of the being's essence. Its signature was from an Igigi line long vanquished from this place. Regardless of the risk, a closer examination must be undertaken. They had to know the truth. From deep beneath the ice, he dispatched a drone.

Scotland Cay — Midnight

Tegan had waited anxiously for Garth to return with Edward and Sara from MOW. They had secured a month's worth of provisions and additional gear for Basecamp Alpha, which was what they were calling their new home. The *Blue Angel* lay alongside the *Deep Current*, stuffed with addition scuba gear, canned goods, and fishing equipment. Garth had been very thorough in his provisioning.

She thought the house was ideal for their purposes. Nate, Alex, Sara, and Edward would stay ashore with Casey and Knolls, which left two bedrooms for storage of supplies and equipment. She planned to sleep aboard the *Whispering Winds* with Cal, while Garth, Maggie, and Jessica would bunk aboard the *Deep Current.*

The group gathered in the large living room, and for the first time in a long while, they had elbow room. Everyone looked tired. Cal and Tegan finally explained what had occurred on their last dive, bringing Casey and Knolls up to speed about how the marker reacted to Tegan's touch.

Knolls told them about alien incidents and went into more detail about Dark Moon.

"I guess we were lucky Westfield was forced into hiding," Tegan said.

"Yes, you were," Knolls replied. "Things may have turned out differently. Tegan, you may not believe me, but I'm glad Grant didn't kill you. I'm truly sorry for the loss of your family."

"I appreciate that."

"We're going to have to trust each other over the coming months. It is important that we start fresh. Cal, Grant told me never to apologize because it shows weakness. However, I apologize for hitting you."

"I accept your apology. But I'm not going to tell you that I'm sorry for putting you down."

"I wouldn't expect you to," Knolls replied. "I initiated contact."

"Why don't we all just join in one big group hug," Nate joked.

Everyone laughed.

Alex set up her computer on a driftwood coffee table by the sofa. "I've decided to wait to contact Brian until tomorrow."

"I think that's a good decision," Tegan said. "I'm exhausted. I'm going to bed." She excused herself and headed for the door.

"I'll walk back with you," Maggie said. "I think we could all use some rest."

"I'll join you in a few minutes," Cal said. "I want to speak with Casey and Bob about something."

"My name is Rob. Romeo. Oscar. Bravo. Got it?" Knolls asked.

Cal smiled.

Tegan and Maggie walked out into the night air. After the din of conversations, the quiet was a relief to Tegan's ears. They walked the short distance to the dock together without saying a word.

"Good night, Maggie," Tegan said. She boarded the *Whispering Winds*.

"Get some rest," Maggie replied, boarding the *Deep Current*.

Instead of going into the salon, Tegan walked to the bow and sat down on the trampoline. She breathed in slow, methodical breaths while taking in the sounds of the night. The gentle breeze felt cool against her warm skin. She was finding it difficult to maintain her focus. So much had happened today, but she felt relief knowing that Westfield couldn't hurt her or anyone else ever again.

The breeze moved the rigging gently, causing it to strike the aluminum mast with a soft clang. Waves splashed against the breakwater at the entrance to the marina. Tegan picked her focal point on the horizon, focused her mind, and finally found her peaceful center.

After a few minutes, she felt refreshed. She looked out across the dark expanse of water to the west, where the lights of Treasure Cay glowed. People were oblivious of what lay ahead. Her calm faded as reality took hold again. There was going to be mass panic and destruction all over the world, and she didn't know if they could stop it from happening. She closed her eyes.

The thought of an alien invasion frightened her, but she still had faith that if they could decipher the symbols and prepare Deep Sky that they could stop them. So much had changed since January. Her old life had been so simple, even though it didn't seem so at the time.

After a few minutes, Tegan opened her eyes again. In the distance, she saw the red port light of a boat several miles away. It was traveling fast. People didn't normally operate boats in these waters at night, especially at high speed. Judging by the distance of the light above the water, she guessed that it was a small powerboat, but there was no engine sound.

Tegan stood to get a better view. The light suddenly pulsed several times, then changed colors that spanned the visible spectrum, and finally returned to red. The sequence of light pulses was different for each color displayed. The light was intense enough to illuminate the water beneath it. It wasn't a boat. A chill went up her spine.

The red glow moved south, stopped without having slowed down, and disappeared. The red light blinked on a second later. It moved back to the north, altering its speed as it went, stopping, starting, and changing colors until it disappeared again. A few moments later, the red glow reappeared, but now it was closer to Scotland Cay. Tegan suddenly realized the path the light had taken followed the same route they had taken to meet Casey. She likened the movement of the light to that of a bloodhound following a scent. The light stopped and hovered where they had anchored earlier in the Gap. It pulsed once and went out.

When the light reappeared, it was moving toward her at an incredible speed. Still there was no sound. As the light neared the breakwater to the marina, it dove beneath the surface. It was close enough for her to see the glow underwater as it continued toward the boat.

"Maggie!" Tegan screamed, hoping she could warn her to get away before it arrived.

Maggie came out on deck. "What is it, Tegan?"

"Get back to the house and warn everyone," Tegan said, pointing at the light. The bubble of light rose from the water and hovered in front of the *Whispering Winds.* Maggie screamed. Then there was complete silence. She never heard Maggie begging her to run. The sounds of the night that had been there a moment ago were gone. She only saw the light hovering in front of her.

The light was about five feet in diameter. A small, translucent craft was suspended within it, reflecting lights across its surface. A few seconds later, a blue glow materialized in the center of the object. Tegan had no doubt it was here for her, and she wasn't going to lead it back to her family.

She remained motionless as the craft flashed another series of lights. The object glowed more intensely, and the lights pulsed, changing colors more rapidly. Tegan sensed no heat or electrical discharge coming from the craft. She was about to take a step backward when the object rose slightly above her.

She froze as a small, spherical object about the size of a softball shot from the center of the craft. A moment later, two narrow beams of blue light burst out of the small sphere. She was lifted off the trampoline and slowly rotated. It was scanning her body.

Tegan couldn't stop what was happening. She could tell she was floating. Flashes of ghostly images appeared before her. When the lights lowered her back to the trampoline, she assumed a lotus position. Then the beams narrowed, joined, and focused on her eyes. She tried to close them, but she couldn't.

Strange images flooded her mind, crashing over her as if she was caught in a heavy surf. Tegan sensed they were probing her thoughts and asking her questions. She didn't know if she was answering them. The feeling was similar to what she had experienced with the marker, but more intense. She focused her thoughts on the lights, trying to understand.

The light beams disengaged and retracted into the probe, and then the probe entered the translucent craft. Tegan's senses returned. The craft emitted a soft, orange glow. It blinked twice, then shot straight up into the sky at an unimaginable speed and disappeared.

A moment later, Tegan felt a soft touch on her shoulder. She knew it was Cal. Had Cal seen what had happened? She turned and his face came into focus. He looked worried.

"Tegan, are you alright?" Cal asked. "Talk to me."

She tried to speak, but all she heard was a strange clicking noise. It sounded like a dolphin echolocating. She felt disoriented. She took a deep breath, possibly the first one in a while. As she gazed at Cal's face, she grew more lucid. A moment later, she found her voice. "*That* was different."

Cal laughed and hugged her tightly. The others gathered nearer.

"She's okay," Cal said. He helped Tegan stand.

Tegan felt weak. Flashes of the images still bounced around in her head, as did the strange clicking sounds. One recurring image was of the marker affixed to a rock above the ocean. Beside it was a shimmering portal that extended down to the water's edge. A primordial instinct told her to return to the marker. The feeling was similar to the one that had brought her to the islands, but much stronger. She winced and squeezed her eyes shut as another image exploded in her mind. She understood.

She faced the group and said, "The marker wasn't put here by the Antediluvians, but I know who did put it here. They are very much like us. Cal, there's a large entrance next to the marker, just like you thought."

"How do you know that?" Cal asked.

"I saw it."

"You saw it? You never left the boat."

"I need to go to the marker at sunrise," Tegan said.

"You mean *we* need to go there," Cal said, pulling her closer and stroking her hair.

"You aren't invited." She pushed Cal away and looked at the others. "None of you are."

"What do you mean we aren't invited?" Cal said. "You aren't going there by yourself. Either we all go or no one does."

Her feeling of disorientation faded. *Why had she told them they weren't invited?* She jumped off the boat onto the dock and strode toward the house.

"Where's she going?" Jessica asked.

"I think to the house," Garth replied. "Let's follow her."

Once in the house, Tegan went to the table, opened the photo file on the pad, and enlarged the photographs of the marker. She was still examining them when the group filed into the living room.

Cal said, "The craft left just before we got to the boat. Tegan, are you sure you're alright?"

"Yes."

Maggie said, "Tegan, as we approached you the lights appeared to be scanning you from head to toe, like a medical scanner."

"I think that's exactly what it did," she said without looking up. "I watched the craft follow the path Cal and I took when we went to meet Casey. It took the same route back to the anchorage in the Gap. Then it followed us to the marina, just like a hunter tracks its prey." Tegan bit her lower lip.

"I remember telling Maggie to run, and then it ... invaded my mind. It seemed to be trying to figure out who I was." That was the only way she could think of to describe the sensation. She scrolled through the pictures of the marker again, thinking she should know what the symbols meant.

Tegan rubbed her forehead, which had begun to throb. "Every physical contact I've had with the marker produces a bluish-colored light. The craft, or whatever it was, emitted a myriad of colored lights, even though its body appeared translucent. The probe and the interior of the craft radiated the same bluish light as the marker. Could the symbols represent a method of communication involving light waves? Maybe the symbols are designed to respond to light."

"Interesting idea," Alex said.

"You mean you want to flash lights at the symbols to get it to react?" Nate asked.

"It wouldn't be that easy. It may react to a specific light-wave frequency. Finding the right light-wave pattern and sequence, in conjunction with my biometric signature, would take far more time than we have."

"Nothing has been easy since all this started," Cal said. He looked at Knolls. "Rob, in all the research you guys have done, is there anything you can add?"

"There's nothing in the files like what we saw tonight."

Casey said, "Before I left Andros to come here, we were testing some new acoustical sensors. I mentioned to General Westfield that I'd picked up a broad-spectrum ULF wave that was emanating from this area. I believe he thought they may be related to your discovery, but we didn't talk any more about it."

"When did you detect the signal?" Knolls asked.

"The first time was on July 23. There were multiple, short pulses, and I thought there might be a glitch in the system. The next day it recorded harmonic pulses across multiple bands. I'm not sure how else to describe it. I didn't have an opportunity to investigate it any further. Westfield sent me here."

"The timing coincides with when Tegan began interacting with the marker," Cal said. "After Tegan's first encounter with the marker, we experienced a magnetic or electronic anomaly as we left the site. Whatever it was, it made the compass spin around and point at the marker until we were a good distance away. The compass never reacted like that again. Were you able to pinpoint the source of the ULF waves?"

"No. I wish I could offer more. They have to be related."

"And you just now decided to share this tidbit of information?" Tegan asked, sounding accusing.

"I didn't think it was important until you started talking about light waves," Casey replied.

"Could light also produce an acoustical wave in the bandwidth you were monitoring?" Cal asked.

Casey nodded. "We've been experimenting with sound lasers, SASERs, for a while now. They have an obvious military application in an underwater environment. The next generation of a SASER incorporates a blended approach, but most of the tests have been in the higher frequency bandwidths."

"I wonder if the symbols could represent a language communicated by sound and light," Cal said.

"Maybe," Alex said. "Rob, I'm sure you have access to a supercomputer."

"I do."

"Does it utilize algorithms designed to look for abnormal linguistic patterns tied to sound waves or light transmissions?"

"I'm sure it utilizes a number of creative search algorithms. I wish I could be of more help, but that end of the process was left to the programmers."

Cal looked skeptical.

"I'm serious. I don't know what specific algorithms are used."

Tegan went back to looking at the pictures of the marker. When she felt someone touch her shoulder, she turned to see Jessica standing beside her.

"You know, the shape of the marker reminds me of something," Jessica said. "I thought of it earlier, but I didn't want to sound stupid."

Jessica looked so young and hopeful. "What does it remind you of?" Tegan asked.

"Okay, don't laugh. I took a class in astronomy, and we studied the different planets, stars, galaxies, and nebula."

"We don't need to hear about your schoolwork," Knolls said. "Just tell us what it reminds you of."

"That's enough, Rob," Tegan said. "She's trying to help."

Knolls shook his head and said, "I'm sorry, Jessica. I'm keyed up, and so far all we have done is make wild guesses. Get to the point."

Jessica faced him. "You ever heard of the CMBR?"

Knolls said, "No, what's that?"

"Of course," Cal said. "Why didn't I think of that? Jessica, you're a genius." He kissed the top of her head.

Tegan asked, "What are you talking about, Jessica?"

"It reminds me of the Cosmic Microwave Background Radiation image of the universe," she replied, looking pleased. "If you take off the symbols, the marker looks like the picture of the CMBR in my textbook. It is the same shape, and the dark patches on the marker look like hot or cold spots, depending on whether the marker is a positive or a negative image. I don't know what the smaller lines are, though. We never studied anything that looked like them. Maybe they represent dark matter, gamma rays, or pulsars. The center circular symbol with the narrowing edges looks like it could represent the Milky Way."

Tegan looked at the picture again.

"Out of the mouth of babes," Alex said, putting an arm around Jessica. "It makes sense that they'd shape the marker the way they did. If you were from another world, leaving a marker depicting the universe would be logical. The symbols could be reference points to help us understand where they are from. Jessica, you are one smart cookie."

Garth and Maggie grinned, looking like proud parents.

"What do you think, Rob?" Cal asked.

"I don't know."

As Tegan looked at each symbol, she allowed her mind to wander. A flash of an image hit her. A tall man stood on a beach, but she couldn't make out any facial features. She could tell he was looking out toward the sea. He had long, white hair that hung down over his shoulders. Then the image faded.

Tegan closed her eyes. The man reminded her of the wizard Merlin. She opened her eyes, then said, "Rob, did you guys ever document or hear of an alien being that's tall, human-looking, with long white hair?"

Knolls looked at the ceiling and let out a breath. "Yes, I read about encounters with a creature known as a Nordic. They're also known as Pleiadians or Norsemen. By all accounts, they appear to be Scandinavian. They're reportedly seven feet tall with a thin build and have pasty white or translucent skin. They're supposed to have brilliantly colored eyes."

Tegan looked at Cal. He wore a serious expression. She knew he was thinking about how her eyes had looked after her last contact with the marker. "Anything else you can tell us?" Tegan asked, feeling there was more that Knolls was not saying.

Knolls nodded and said, "Legend has it they possess great magical powers. Most reports claim these creatures are omniscient and friendly."

Tegan went back to looking at the photographs. The room remained silent. After a minute, she looked up. "This is going to sound strange, but I keep seeing a vision of a tall man with long, white hair. He is wearing a dark green robe, and he's standing on a beach, looking out over the ocean as if waiting."

"Waiting for what?" Cal asked.

"For me to arrive," Tegan said. "The marker is a beacon guiding me to him."

"You think the craft and the marker are Nordic related?" Knolls asked.

"It's crazy, I know. I read a neurological report years ago that was written by a neuroscientist who claimed that memories can be passed down from generation to generation. It's supposed to be an evolutionary quirk found only in a select group of people living in a small town in Wales."

"I read that report," Alex said. "The study claimed their brains excrete a chemical that when exposed to a strong external stimulus produces latent memories of things only their ancestors could have experienced."

"That's the one," Tegan said. "The research findings were never taken seriously because the group declined to continue in the study, so the results couldn't be duplicated."

"Why wouldn't the people do the study again?" Knolls asked.

"Many of them experienced troubling visions following the experiment, and they feared their symptoms would grow worse if they went through another study."

Cal said, "You mean an ancestor's experience is passed down to future offspring through their DNA? The person's descendants can actually remember the original experience?"

"Exactly," Tegan said. "The memory gets hardwired into the offspring at a molecular level. When I read the article, I thought it was hokum, but I wonder now if there isn't some merit to it. That could explain why I felt a calling to come here."

"So you think you have this latent gene, which when stimulated produces a vision your ancestors experienced?" Knolls asked.

"I can't say that for certain."

"Couldn't it be an image planted in your mind by the encounter with the alien craft?" Cal asked.

"It feels more like I've *experienced* what I'm seeing. For lack of a better explanation, the vision feels like it has depth."

"Why do you think you may possess this gene?" Knolls asked, sounding disbelieving.

Tegan looked at Knolls. "All of my ancestors came from Great Britain. My father traced his family lineage back to the twelfth century, and my mother traced hers back to the seventh century. She came from Norse and Scottish roots. My father's bloodline is pure Welsh, or as pure as it can be. Both of their families lived in the area where they did the study. We also know the marker only reacts to my touch."

Alex asked, "It's responding to your genetic signature and causing you to have latent memories?"

"Maybe, and the alien craft tracked me down like a bloodhound following my scent to figure out who or what I am."

"I knew there was a reason I liked her," Garth said with a big grin. "She's one of us. Do you know what your name means in Welsh?"

"Yes, it means 'pretty one.'"

"Well, that certainly fits," said Garth.

Tegan caught Maggie's look and added, "Maggie, my twin sister's name was Megan. In Welsh, her name means 'pearl,' just like yours."

Maggie gave Tegan a warm smile. "Yes, I know."

"Can we please get back to the relevant subject?" Knolls requested.

"I'm sorry, Rob," Tegan said, "but I thought the article and my family tree may be relevant to the subject. Especially since you asked."

Cal said, "Do you think that's why you were so frightened when you first encountered the marker? Is it possible your latent genes received a jolt from an ancestor's experience and you didn't know how to interpret it?"

"That could be, I guess. Maybe the image of the Nordic is a memory, or maybe it is something that they planted during the scan. I just don't know."

Knolls said, "You said you felt as if you were being welcomed home. So the Nordic posed no threat?"

"No. In fact, I felt at ease in his presence. It was as if I knew him. I feel I'm close to figuring this out. Maybe my DNA is slightly different from what the marker recognizes, but it's a close enough match to illicit a reaction. Maybe that is why the craft came looking for me. The marker could be sending out signals in an attempt to find me. Perhaps that's the signal Casey intercepted."

"You know for certain the marker and what scanned you wasn't sent here by the Antediluvians?" Knolls asked.

"Yes. I'm positive. It belongs to a different alien race."

"The craft had to be close," Alex said. "It's only been a few days since your first contact with the marker. They have to be nearby."

A chill went up Tegan's spine. They were indeed close.

Cal said, "I think we should try to get some rest and discuss this situation in the morning when we're fresh. I don't think the aliens will return tonight."

"No, they won't be back tonight," Tegan said matter-of-factly, then started toward the door. She stopped and turned to look at everyone.

"I know how strange this is for all of us, and I don't know where all of this is going or how it will end. But I'm glad you all were here with me tonight." Tegan looked at Cal. "I think we should take Commander Knolls with us to the site tomorrow. Maybe he'll see something we've missed."

"Okay," Cal said. "We need answers, and we need them fast. Rob and Casey will ride over with us. Garth, you take Alex, Nate, and Jessica with you on the *Deep Current*. Maggie, Edward, and Sara will stay here at the house. I need the three of you to socialize with the neighbors and see if they saw the light show."

"We'll scout the island for you," Maggie said.

"I think we have a plan then," Nate said. He bowed his head and whispered, "*Ad Astra per Aspera.*"

"What did you just say?" Cal asked.

Nate looked up and said, "It's Latin. It means 'A rough path leads to the stars.' Those words are on a plaque next to launch pad 34 at Cape Canaveral. When I was a kid I visited the Kennedy Space Center, and I wondered what it would be like to go into space and meet an alien. I guess I should have been more careful about what I wished for, huh?"

"I think the words are appropriate for what we're facing," Garth said.

"I believe they are," Tegan said. "Our world faces an uncertain future from a species that won't be easy to stop. I'm certain the site holds the answers for our salvation. But no matter what happens, I'm happy we're making the journey together."

Palmer Land, Antarctica

Intermittent pulses of light danced across Manatu's pale face as he stood facing a holographic image displaying streams of symbols. He was on the command bridge of their largest interstellar vessel buried deep beneath the Antarctic ice. It had been there for over eight thousand years. Its flat black outer hull matched the darkness of space, but it stood in stark contrast to the vast ice fields above its current resting place.

He was the leader of the Igigi, a Watcher. Their kind had been on Earth for over thirteen thousand years. Their purpose was to watch over the human race. By some quirk of nature, human beings resembled them in both appearance and DNA. Perhaps it was for this reason the Igigi felt compelled to do what they could to help humankind survive.

The results of the scan were conclusive. Tegan was a descendent of the first daughter of Ninurtu, an Igigi exiled for actively defending the human species against an alien race they called the Etu Inu Idimmu.

After being disavowed for his actions, Ninurtu had taken a human mate over seven thousand years ago. This one called Tegan was a warrior's child. Her genetic makeup was more Igigi than that of any other human ever encountered since the first of their kind came to exist. In light of what the scan had revealed, Manatu thought she might offer hope for human survival against the Etu Inu Idimmus' return. He reached out to the others like him. They agreed with his course of action. He would grant Tegan Locke access to the outpost the next time she touched the marker.

Deep space

The planet was not yet visible, at least not to the naked eye. The leader of the Antediluvians, the Monan, looked at the forward-view screen. The command deck of the ship where she stood was aglow in a pink hue, as was the rest of the interior of the ship. Long-range optics displayed the point of light that was to be their new home. It appeared unremarkable at this distance, but the Monan knew what awaited them.

She sought out Trakar and learned their human puppets were ready. The Monan understood the threat the Igigi posed, but that was no longer important. The invasion plan would remain unaltered. The Awakened would guarantee their success.

The Monan submitted an accolade of record for Trakar's commitment to the revolting task she undertook every day. She did not issue her acknowledgement as a form of individual recognition but rather as a message of support to the collective whole of the colony. Trakar's status would be elevated. She could now take a mate and breed. It was something very few of their kind were permitted to do. The Monan knew that she would need more like Trakar in the future, and she would select her breeding partner for her.

The Antediluvians were bipedal, with black eyes that displayed no discernable pupil. This would change as they adjusted to the sunlight on the new world.

The Monan stood six feet tall, with bluish-gray skin. She was a foot taller than the others of her kind. Thin lines of royal violet adorned her two arms and legs. The same markings angled upward from the corners of her eyes and encircled her massive, smooth skull. The lines came together to form the royal crest at the crown of her head. She had been born to reign, had ruled for over four hundred years, and would continue to lead them for at least another six hundred years before she joined her ancestors.

Billions of Antediluvians occupying tens of thousands of spacecraft followed the Monan's command ship. They would reach their new world soon. Their first expedition to Earth eight thousand years ago had ended in a staggering defeat. The expeditionary force had encountered hostile resistance, something not expected. They'd been forced to withdraw. Only one starship and dozens of scout ships stayed behind to continue their work until the fleet could reach Earth.

The Monan sniffed the air through the two nasal slits on her face and transmitted her displeasure. The strong odor of the two bioengineered Xunta flanking her was repugnant. She commanded they move away. The Monan knew she needed to grow accustomed to their presence and their smell, because once they landed the Xunta would be by her side at all times to protect her. For now, they could keep their distance.

The Xunta would protect all of them after they landed. After thousands of years of research and testing of the human species, the Antediluvians understood well what would strike fear into a human soul. The Xuntas' physical appearance was repulsive. Their genetically designed pheromones could paralyze their human prey until they chose the time to kill them.

The Monan anticipated a smooth transition to the planet's surface and an easy establishment of the Protectorate, which would be her home while they reengineered Earth's climate to resemble what had attracted them to the planet so long ago. She planned to build the Protectorate in Antarctica, the coldest and most remote place on the planet. If the Igigi challenged them, they were prepared this time.

Earth would be their new home.

Acknowledgements

First, thank you for reading the first novel in the ARKLIGHT series. Also, I want to thank those who took time out of their lives to read the drafts, make suggestions, provide editing, and offer encouragement in the writing of this novel. As in any great endeavor, it takes a team to make it to the finish line.

To my wife, Terry, thank you for your honest analysis, critique, guidance, and patience in countless rereads of this novel. Your ideas and organizational skills were invaluable. I could not have done this without you.

I am indebted to a great group of beta readers. All of you have my heartfelt gratitude for your assistance, your friendship, and all your hard work. A special acknowledgement to Jeff Weber and Ellen Picardi for their painstaking work, attention to detail, and detailed notes on the unedited first version of Revelations. You both went above and beyond the call of duty. My sincere appreciation to Abby High, Don McLaughlin, Tina and Brian Egnatuk, and Laurie Allen Klein for your generous feedback.

To my editor, Mr. Paul Thayer of Thayer Literary Services, a big thank you for taking the time to provide numerous mini-lessons in the art of writing and for your editing services.

Thank you to Nathan Van Coops for offering advice and assistance in navigating the publishing industry.

Finally, I want to thank Kimberly Martin and her team, Stephanie Anderson and Jason Orr, at Jera Publishing for all of their assistance in walking me through the publishing process.

A Note About the Author

G. B. Holley is the author of the ARKLIGHT Ancient Alien Adventure series. He is a native Floridian and a retired law enforcement commander who spent more than three decades serving with a Florida Sheriff's Office. He's a former leadership and high liability trainer and was an adjunct instructor at St. Petersburg College for many years. He earned his MPA and BA degrees from the University of South Florida, Tampa, Florida. He's a pilot and loves reading science fiction and adventure novels. He enjoys flying when he's not writing.

Connect with Gary:

www.gbholley.com
facebook.com/gbholley1
twitter.com/gbholley1

Author's Note

I hope you enjoyed the first book in the ARKLIGHT series. Please leave a review on Amazon and let me know what you thought of the story.

Read on for an excerpt from the second book:
ARKLIGHT Recondite. Available now!

The third book, ARKLIGHT Regulus, will be coming soon.

Do you want to be notified when the next book is released? Subscribe to my email list at www.gbholley.com.

ARKLIGHT
Recondite

Great Guana – July 28 – 0730 hours

The *Whispering Winds* and the *Deep Current* were heading to the site of the alien marker. Tegan had chosen to keep to herself after her encounter with the drone. She sat with her legs dangling off the leading edge of the trampoline, the saltwater spray splashed up as the twin hulls of the catamaran plowed through the shallow swells of the Atlantic. Images of a wizard standing on a beach talking to her in high-pitched clicking sounds ran through her thoughts. They were the same sounds she had heard for a brief time after the alien craft had scanned her last night. She couldn't shake the flashes of the strange places she kept seeing. Were the images and sounds memories, or were they something else? Regardless, they seemed familiar to her.

After the *Whispering Winds* was secured to the mooring buoy over the marker, she walked back to the cockpit and prepared her dive gear. She glanced up as the *Deep Current* tied up alongside them. A few minutes later, everyone was aboard the *Whispering Winds*.

"On this dive I'll buddy with Tegan and Alex," Cal said. "Rob, you're with Garth. Nate, Jessica, and Casey, you will be responsible for surface communications and safety. Are there any questions?"

No one asked any.

Tegan dropped her BCD into the water and stepped off the dive platform. The warm Bahamian water caressed her as she watched the others enter the water behind her. She put her mask on, cleared it, took a drag of air through the regulator, and dove.

The marker looked the same as when they'd discovered it. It was embedded in the coral and shimmered in the light from above. This was the first time Garth and Knolls were seeing the marker and she was interested in their reaction. They ran their hands over the uneven coloring of the metal and appeared mesmerized as they traced the lines of the intricate symbols.

Tegan removed her mask, handed it to Cal, and gently nudged Garth and Knolls aside. She placed her forehead on the center symbol and the light bloomed and penetrated her eyes. She opened her mind. A tidal wave of new images overwhelmed her. The clicking sounds grew in intensity, but she knew that she was the only one that could hear them. She was close to a breakthrough. She could feel it. Then suddenly, the intensity of the energy flow subsided, the blue light pulsed, and the clicking sounds stopped.

What are you? She felt a response. A chill ran through her, the marker had understood her inquiry. She sensed it was welcoming her home.

Cal touched her arm. She wanted to continue but Cal's tugs were becoming more insistent. He was interfering and she wished he would stop.

Suddenly, he did. The energy field she had experienced days earlier returned. Cal was pushed away from her. The marker had understood her and took action. She could hardly believe it. She exhaled a bubble stream and slowed her breathing. She wanted to know. She had to know.

Tegan visualized the stars and asked where the people who had left the marker had come from. Symbols invaded her mind. She didn't understand any of them, but the blue-white light blazing into her eyes slowly faded, then the energy field disappeared. Tegan floated free feeling a sense of disappointment. When she turned to face Cal, she caught the reflection of her enlarged emerald eyes in his faceplate.

A vibration rippled through the water. Something was happening. The intensity of the vibration increased and turned to a low rumble. She swam away from the marker with Cal close beside her. Then the coral and rock shook violently creating a large silt cloud, followed by a strange sound. Suddenly, pieces of coral, sponges, and sea fans were adrift in the current. The silt cloud blossomed. Hundreds of fish bolted into clearer water. Then all went quiet.

The sound of her air bubbles and the crackling of the coral were gone. It was as if she had stepped into the vacuum of space. She looked at Cal. He was staring back at her. A moment later, her hearing returned, and the large silt cloud dispersed. Tegan could hardly believe what she was seeing. In front of her was a vertical, blue shimmering wall of light that covered what they had thought was an entryway beneath the island. The large illuminated barrier was outlined by a three-foot-wide, black border made of the same material that held the marker.

As Tegan gazed at the portal, a six-foot-square platform materialized beneath the marker next to a switchback staircase that hadn't been there a second earlier. The staircase extended down to the ledge fifty feet below her. The surface of the shimmering wall that now lay across the opening reminded her of the surface of a pool on a sunny day. She swam closer to the energy field and stopped when she saw what lay beyond.